Praise for Lily

"Another triumph of deliciously sensual romance played against the fascinating world of Restoration England."
—*Booklist*

"Readers will enjoy a warm historical romance starring charming protagonists."   —*Midwest Book Review*

Praise for Violet

"This delectable romp is sure to be just the confection readers need for a sweet night's read. . . . Utterly adorable characters and the addition of real historical personages as well as a sweet love story are guaranteed to charm."
—*Romantic Times*

"Lauren Royal treats readers to another winning novel, filled with laughter and humor, precocious children, sensual scenes that sizzle, and another eccentric family fans will fall in love with."   —*Romance Reviews Today*

"Fascinating period details . . . engaging. . . . The delightfully unconventional cast of characters gives [Royal] the chance to display her gift for understated humor."
—*Booklist*

continued . . .

Emerald

"Fast-paced. . . . The well-drawn backdrop adds depth to the characterization and enhances the plot line. Lauren Royal will certainly garner more readers with this glittering gem of a novel." —*Romantic Times*

"A passionate tale that brings late seventeenth-century England vividly alive . . . fast-paced and filled with action from the very first page to the climax."
—*Midwest Book Review*

"With strong characters and an action-filled plot, *Emerald* is a royal flush." —*Affaire de Coeur*

"Warm and wonderful . . . the story is one that will enthrall. Exhilarating." —*Heart Rate Reviews*

"Brimming with action, adventure [and] love. Ms. Royal brings Restoration England to life right before the reader's eyes. I highly recommend *Emerald*."
—*Romance Reviews Today*

Amethyst

"An accomplished debut." —Patricia Gaffney

"Enchanting . . . fascinating . . . delightful."
—*Old Book Barn Gazette*

"Brimming over with passion and excitement."
—*Romantic Times*

"All of these characters are so well drawn and developed . . . a promising debut." —*The Romance Reader*

ALSO BY LAUREN ROYAL

Lily

Violet

Amber

Emerald

Amethyst

"Forevermore" in
In Praise of Younger Men

ROSE

Lauren Royal

A SIGNET BOOK

SIGNET
Published by New American Library, a division of
Penguin Group (USA) Inc., 375 Hudson Street,
New York, New York 10014, U.S.A.
Penguin Books Ltd, 80 Strand,
London WC2R 0RL, England
Penguin Books Australia Ltd, 250 Camberwell Road,
Camberwell, Victoria 3124, Australia
Penguin Books Canada Ltd, 10 Alcorn Avenue,
Toronto, Ontario, Canada M4V 3B2
Penguin Books (N.Z.) Ltd, Cnr Rosedale and Airborne Roads,
Albany, Auckland 1310, New Zealand

Penguin Books Ltd, Registered Offices:
80 Strand, London WC2R 0RL, England

First published by Signet, an imprint of New American Library,
a division of Penguin Group (USA) Inc.

First Printing, October 2003
10 9 8 7 6 5 4 3 2 1

For Taire Martyn,
Karen Nesbitt,
and Alison Bellach,
three crazy North Americans who share my love of
music, the UK, and good books

Acknowledgments

I wish to thank:

Audrey LaFehr, my editor, for her wonderful ideas that helped make this book the best it could be; Elaine Koster, my agent, for her amazing, unstinting support; my critique partner, Terri Castoro, for putting up with me through seven books (she truly deserves a medal); Brent Royal-Gordon, for designing and maintaining my award-winning Web site; Jack, Brent, Blake, and Devonie, for supporting me through writing another complete trilogy (without threatening to leave on grounds of neglect); fellow romance authors Glynnis Campbell and Cherie Claire, for being the two best friends a writer could have; Ian Franklin and Michelle Griffiths, State Apartment Warders at Hampton Court Palace, for directing me to the right places, and, in Ian's case, giving me incredible information; Philip Sidebotham, Adrian Moles, and Tiffany Green at Sir Christopher Wren's House Hotel in Windsor, for graciously allowing and assisting a crazy author to poke around and take photos of Wren's house; Amy and Rick Tanaka, for their expert advice on matters architectural; Brent, Blake, and Devonie Royal-Gordon and their friends Darci Dipo, Dan Mehefko, and Anna Pione, for helping me explore Hampton Court Palace through many different perceptive eyes; Andrew Metz, for the videotape on Hampton Court's history; Barry Waller, for converting the videotape on Hampton Court's history so that I could actually watch it; Alison Bellach, for sharing a laugh with me over the yipping sex in the hotel room next to ours and then challenging me to put it in a book; my parents, Joan and Herb Royal, as always, for everything; my official First Readers, Ken and Dawn Royal, Taire Martyn, Karen Nesbitt, Jane Armstrong, and Alison Bellach, for telling it like it is; my Awesome Publicity Team—Rita Adair-Robison, Debbie Alexander, Dick Alexander, Joyce Basch, Alison Bellach, Diana Brandmeyer, Carol Carter, Terri Castoro, Elaine Ecuyer, Dale Gordon, Darren Holmquist, Catherine Hope, Taire Martyn, Sandy Mills, Karen Nesbitt, Jack Poole, Caroline Quick, Joan Royal, Wendi Royal, Diena Simmons, and Julie Walker—for all their hard work and support . . . and all my readers, whose wonderful e-mails and letters inspire me to write more books.

Thanks, everyone!

Chapter One

Trentingham Manor, the South of England
September 1677

Standing in her family's small, crowded chapel, Rose Ashcroft shifted on her high-heeled shoes, wishing she were in a cathedral so there would be somewhere to sit.

Wishing she were *anywhere* but here watching her sister get married.

"Lord Randal Nesbitt, wilt thou have this woman to thy wedded wife, to live together after God's ordinance in the holy estate of Matrimony? Wilt thou love her, comfort her, honor, and keep her in sickness and in health; and, forsaking all others, keep thee only unto her, so long as ye both shall live?"

"I will." The confident words boomed through the magnificent oak-paneled chamber, binding Rand Nesbitt to Rose's sister Lily.

But Rose wasn't listening to the ceremony. Instead she heard *twenty-one, twenty-one, twenty-one* running through her head. Twenty-one and a lonely spinster . . . while both her sisters had found love.

Happy tears brightened their mother's brown eyes. She leaned closer until she bumped against Rose's left side, her voice made breathy by emotion. "They're perfect together, are they not?"

Rose could only nod dumbly, staring at her sister's petite

form laced into a gorgeous pale blue satin wedding dress embroidered with gleaming silver thread. Lily's hair, the same rich sable as Rose's, cascaded to her shoulders in glossy ringlets. Beside her, Rand beamed a smile, looking tall and utterly handsome in dark blue velvet, his gray gaze steady and adoring.

The two were so clearly in love, Rose knew they belonged together—and truly, she was happy for her sister.

If only Lily weren't her *younger* sister.

The priest cleared his throat and looked back down at his *Book of Common Prayer*. "Lady Lily Ashcroft, wilt thou have this man to thy wedded husband . . ."

Standing on Rose's right, her older sister Violet shifted one of her twin babies on her hip and gazed up at her husband of four years, Ford Chase. Sun streamed through the stained-glass windows, glinting off her spectacles. "Oh, is this not romantic?" she sighed.

Holding their other infant, Ford squeezed his wife around the shoulders. Seated cross-legged at their feet, their three-year-old son Nicky traced a finger over the patterns in the colorful glazed tile floor, obliviously happy.

Rose gritted her teeth.

Her friend Judith Carrington poked her from behind. "I cannot believe Lily is getting married before I," she whispered in a tone laced with disbelief. "*I* was betrothed first!"

Rose couldn't believe Lily and Judith would *both* be married before she even received a proposal.

". . . so long as ye both shall live?" the priest concluded expectantly.

In the hush that followed, even knowing it wasn't kind of her, Rose half wished Lily would fail to reply.

But Lily didn't, of course. "I will," she pledged, her voice as sweet as she was, ringing clear and true.

A few more words, a family heirloom ring slid onto her finger, and Lily was clearly and truly wed now, the Countess of Newcliffe.

And Rose was clearly and truly miserable.

When Rand lowered his lips to meet Lily's, Rose turned away. Behind her, Judith was grinning up at her own betrothed—although only a little way up, since his stature was less than impressive. Lord Grenville was five-and-thirty to Judith's twenty, and his pale brown hair was thinning on top . . . but Rose imagined that the way Judith looked at him made him feel like a king. And he looked down on her in a way that surely made pretty, plump Judith feel like a queen.

Rose wanted someone who could make her feel like a queen. Good God, a duchess or countess would do. Or even a lowly baroness . . .

As the years crawled by without a husband on the horizon, Rose was getting less picky. So long as the man was titled, handsome, rich, and powerful, most anyone was acceptable.

The guests parted as Lily and Rand made their way from the chapel, followed by a cat, a squirrel, and a chirping sparrow.

Rose moved to hug her sister. "'Twas beautiful," she murmured. "I'm so happy for you."

She was. Truly she was.

Lily leaned down to pick up the cat, straightening with a brilliant smile. "Your turn next."

A hurt retort came to Rose's mind, but she wouldn't snap at her sister on her wedding day. "I'm happy for you, too, Rand," she said instead, rising on her toes to give her sister's new husband a kiss on the cheek. But not too far up on her toes, because Rose was a tall woman. Too tall, perhaps, or too slim, or too quick-tongued . . . or too something.

There had to be some reason she had yet to find love.

Too intelligent, most likely. At one point, she'd thought Rand might be the man for her. Handsome, titled, and a professor of linguistics at Oxford—surely a good match for Rose, given her own exceptional command of foreign languages.

But he'd chosen her little sister. "I'm the luckiest man in

the world," he said now, making Rose feel the unluckiest woman.

· She'd had better days.

Lily must have noticed her dejected expression, because her fingers stopped stroking the cat's striped fur. Concern clouded her lovely blue eyes. "You *will* be next," she said quietly.

"Undoubtedly so, since I'm the only one left," Rose quipped. "Unless, that is, Rowan manages to find himself a bride before I nab a groom."

They both swung to look at their eleven-year-old brother where he stood with Violet's young niece, Jewel, their dark heads close together as they whispered animatedly. "He may have found himself a bride already," Rose added dryly.

Lily's laughter rang through the chapel, echoing off the molded dome ceiling. "Surely someone will claim you long before Rowan gets it in his head to wed. Why, you're the most beautiful of all of us, Rose!"

Rose had always thought Lily the *most* beautiful, but she knew she was beautiful, too. Yet beauty, she had learned, was not enough to hook a husband.

Well-wishers pressed closer. Rose started moving toward the drawing room and found Judith by her side. Forsaking her betrothed, Judith clutched Rose's arm. "Who is *that* handsome fellow?" she whispered conspiratorially.

Rose slid a glance to the man in question, a friend of Rand's whose gaze suddenly met hers, then skimmed her body in a way that might have made her heart pound . . . if she were at all interested. "Mr. Christopher Martyn—Rand calls him Kit. He's an architect," she added dismissively.

"Christopher Martyn, the architect?" Awe hushed Judith's voice. "Has King Charles not recently awarded him a contract to renovate Whitehall Palace?"

"Along with Windsor Castle and Hampton Court."

"Ah, a man of intelligence to complement yours." Clearly Judith considered the man's lack of a title no im-

pediment. "No need for you to play the featherbrained co-
quette for him."

"I've no interest in him. And I've never acted featherbrained." But perhaps now was the time to start. On her sister's advice, Rose had tried to win Rand by appealing to his
intellect, but that hadn't worked at all. Never again would
she attempt to attract a man by flaunting her brains. No
matter what her family or Judith said, she knew there were
better ways to entice men.

Unfortunately, where Rand was concerned, she'd come
to that conclusion too late. To her intense embarrassment,
she'd stooped to propositioning him in her family's summerhouse, and when that hadn't worked, desperation had
driven her to attempt bribery and trickery of the worst kind.

She couldn't imagine what had come over her that day
and had half-feared she'd never be able to look Rand in the
face again. But to her utter relief he seemed at ease with
her, as though he'd graciously forgotten that humiliating
episode.

"You cannot tell me," Judith whispered, dragging Rose
back to the present, "that you don't find Mr. Martyn attractive."

Rose slanted Kit another covert look. Dressed in forest-
toned velvet, he was tall and lean, his hair dark as jet, his
eyes a startling mix of brown and green. She dredged up a
wry smile. "I'd have to be blind to claim that."

"And he looks ever so nice. Is he not nice?"

"He's nice enough." Except for those unusual eyes,
which were decidedly *not* nice. *Wicked* would be a better
description.

"And good Lord, he's building things for the King! I'm
certain he has money—"

"Money," Rose interrupted pointedly, "does not make up
for lack of a title."

Her sister Violet walked up, sans children for once.
"Who needs a title?"

Judith crossed her arms. "Rose, apparently."

"Oh, well." Violet sent Rose an indulgent smile. "That is only because she has yet to fall in love."

Rose smiled in return. "And given 'tis as easy to fall in love with a titled man as one without, I've decided to concentrate on the former."

Violet and Judith exchanged a glance that set Rose's teeth on edge, then left her, to return to their respective men.

The wedding party was small, since Lily had given their mother only two weeks to plan the event. Still, there were more than enough guests to fill the drawing room and spill out onto the Palladian portico and into the exquisite gardens.

Trentingham Manor was known for its gardens, thanks to Rose's father and his passion for flowers and plants. But it was a warm, sunny day, and Rose feared for her creamy complexion, so she opted to stay indoors. She wandered the crowded drawing room, sipping from a goblet of the new and frightfully expensive champagne that her parents favored for celebrations. Although she enjoyed sharing a word or two with various relatives and neighbors, she was generally feeling at loose ends.

Until, that was, she caught a snatch of her father's conversation and turned to see him talking to Kit Martyn.

". . . one of those newfangled greenhouses," Lord Trentingham was saying. "On the east side of the house, I'm thinking, to catch the morning sun. Since autumn is almost upon us, I'd be much obliged if you could start immediately."

Rose hurried to join them, unable to believe her ears. She was half tempted to ball up the lacy handkerchief that was tucked in her sleeve and stuff it into her father's mouth instead. "Mr. Martyn builds things for the *King,* Father! Palaces, for God's sake. He hasn't—"

"Well, not quite palaces," Kit corrected her. "Renovations to palaces, additions to palaces, but I've yet to build an entire—"

"See?" Rose met her father's deep green eyes, speaking slowly and loudly to make sure he could hear her over the hubbub of the celebration. "Palaces. He hasn't the time to build you a greenhouse."

Kit sipped from his own goblet of champagne, then grinned at Rose's father. "Oh, I think I might find the time," he disagreed, his words infused with a hint of laughter. "In exchange for a dance with your beautiful daughter."

He shifted to look at Rose, making it clear which daughter he meant. His green-brown gaze swept her slowly, almost as though he were mentally undressing her . . . and if his expression was any indication, he plainly liked the results.

Lord Trentingham frowned. "My bountiful bother?"

Kit looked confused, and Rose knew she should remind him that her father was hard of hearing at the best of times—and in a crowded room, he was all but deaf.

But she couldn't seem to speak. The audacity of the man, thinking he could trade a building for her company. Surely her father would never—

"I will be most pleased to build your greenhouse," Kit reiterated, "if your lovely daughter will oblige me with a dance."

"Oblige you with advance?"

Understanding dawned in Kit's eyes, and he raised his voice. "A dance. May I have the honor of a dance with Lady Rose?"

"Yes. Of course," her father said. "Now, about that greenhouse—"

"I'll do a preliminary design before I leave," Kit practically bellowed.

"Excellent." Lord Trentingham turned a vague smile in Rose's direction. "Run along, dear. Enjoy yourself."

Her mouth dropped open, then shut again when she found herself propelled from the drawing room by a warm hand at her back. Then she was stepping out onto the covered portico, which had been pressed into service as a dance floor.

Three musicians in one corner were playing a minuet, a graceful dance that facilitated conversation. The wedding guests chatted and flirted, their shoes brushing the brick paving in unison. Though the dance was already in progress, Kit handed both their champagne goblets to a passing maid, then took Rose's hands and swept her into the throng.

She'd never touched him—certainly not skin to skin— and the contact reminded her just how attractive she'd thought him the first time they met. The mere sight of him had set her blood to singing inside her. But that, of course, had been before she'd discovered he was a plain mister. Since then, seeing him had had no effect on her at all.

So it was disconcerting to find that touching him now seemed to make the champagne bubbles dance in her stomach.

"Lovely Corinthian capitals on the columns and pilasters," Kit noted, ever the architect. "Do you know who carved them?"

She pliéd and stepped forward with her right foot at the same time she finally found her tongue. "Edward Marshall, who also carved the Ashcroft family arms in the pediment. And in future, please keep in mind that there is no need to ask my father's permission for a dance. Ashcroft women make their own decisions."

Kit breezed over the implication that she might have refused him. "So Rand has told me." They rose on their toes, and when he pulled her closer, she caught a whiff of his scent, a woodsy fragrance with a base of frankincense and myrrh. She wondered if she could duplicate it in her mother's perfumery.

"Your family is an odd one," he said. "I do not allow my sister to make her own decisions. Not the important ones, in any case."

She felt sorry for his sister. "Our family motto is *Interroga Conformationem*."

He looked at her blankly.

"Question Convention," she translated. What sort of educated man didn't know Latin? Certainly not one she'd ever consider husband material.

'Twas a good thing he wasn't in the running.

They dropped hands to turn in place, then he grasped her fingers again. "Is it true, as Rand said, that your father allows his daughters to choose their own husbands as well?"

She noticed Lily and Rand dancing together—much closer than the dance required. Surprisingly, envy didn't clutch at her heart this time. She only smiled. "Yes."

"In future, I'll keep *that* in mind," Kit responded with a disarming grin.

Ignoring his impertinence, Rose gazed across the wide daisy-strewn lawn toward the Thames. Suddenly Rowan raced onto the portico, looking like a miniature version of their father in a burgundy suit, his long midnight hair streaming behind him.

A quite ordinary-looking man followed more sedately, but as he wore red and white—the King's livery—he attracted more attention.

The musicians stopped playing, and the dancers ground to a halt.

"There he is," Rowan said, pointing to Kit in the sudden silence. "Mr. Christopher Martyn, the man you seek."

Chapter Two

"If I may speak to you in private, sir," the messenger said. "I bring word from His Majesty."

Kit nodded and stepped off the portico, silently leading the way to the summerhouse he'd spotted earlier. He felt the eyes of the other wedding guests following him and heard their speculative murmurs, but the sudden appearance of the King's man didn't intrigue him as it did them. After all, he was completing several royal projects. Likely Charles simply wanted a change.

As Kit crossed Lord Trentingham's celebrated gardens, he thought instead of Rose, vaguely wondering where he'd found the nerve to imply he might be interested in marriage. He'd been attracted to her when they first met, but dismissed it when she failed to respond to any of his advances. He was, after all, a man—feelings of attraction toward a woman were no novelty.

But today she'd sipped champagne, and he'd noticed her lips were made for kissing. And he'd taken her hands and felt something like a punch to his gut. And she'd challenged him verbally, and those words had jumped out of his mouth.

Ludicrous words. As a man who had never wanted for female attention, he was frustrated by Lady Rose's obvious disinterest, but pursuing her was an absurd waste of time. It didn't matter that she was everything he wanted someday in a wife. Although he thought her lovely and intelligent—he'd watched her decipher a coded diary weeks earlier and been nothing short of astonished—he had no illusions of winning Lady Rose. Or, for that matter, any lady at all. He knew his place in the world.

Untitled.

He was determined to change that. He knew that, social perceptions aside, he was damn well as good as anyone else. But in the meantime, he was well aware that he wasn't considered good enough for an earl's daughter.

And wishing things were different would never make them so.

The circular redbrick summerhouse was a small building with classic Palladian lines. He ushered the King's man inside. Owing to the admirable design—large arched windows over each of the four doors—it was bright beneath the cool, shaded dome.

Bright enough to make out the seriousness in the messenger's eyes.

Apprehension suddenly soured the champagne in Kit's stomach. "Yes?" he asked.

The man's words were anything but reassuring. "This concerns one of your projects. I've been sent to advise you that the ceiling at Windsor Castle is falling—"

"Falling? Has anyone been hurt?"

"I should say chunks of plaster have fallen—not the ceiling itself. But it is sagging, and there are many cracks. There have been no injuries, but His Majesty wanted you to know—"

"I understand." Kit understood Charles's underlying message all too well. If he failed to complete this project on time and satisfactorily, his dream of being appointed Deputy Surveyor—a step toward someday becoming Surveyor General of the King's Works, the official royal architect—would be as good as dead.

And without that, the rest of his dreams—his plans to obtain a title for himself and marry his sister Ellen to a nobleman—would die along with it.

He yanked the door back open. "I will depart for Windsor posthaste."

"Sir." The man bowed and preceded him outside.

Back at the house, Kit looked around for Rand, but his friend was nowhere to be found. He went instead to give his apologies to his hostess. "Forgive me, Lady Trentingham, but I must take my leave. There is a problem at Windsor Castle. I cannot seem to locate Rand—"

"He and Lily have a habit of disappearing," she told him with a suggestive twinkle in her eye that took him by surprise. She was, after all, the girl's mother. Then her brown eyes turned sympathetic. "I'll explain," she added. "He'll understand."

In no time at all, Kit was settled in his carriage, rubbing the back of his neck as the vehicle lumbered its way toward Windsor.

Could he possibly have made an error in designing Windsor's new dining room? Had a flaw in the plans gone unnoticed? He unrolled the extra set he always carried, spreading the linen they were drawn on over his lap. But he couldn't seem to concentrate. Especially when his carriage jostled past the village of Hawkridge, where he'd been raised.

Toying with the small, worn chunk of brick he carried in his pocket—a chip off his first building—he found himself staring out the window as memories assaulted him. Nights whiled away in his family's snug cottage, he and Ellen playing on the floor while their mother read by the fire. Days spent with his father, learning carpentry and building. Afternoons fishing with the local nobleman's son, Lord Randal Nesbitt, both of them starved for companionship of their own age.

That felt like a lifetime ago. Rand was married now, a man who declared himself in love. As for Kit, love was not high on his list of priorities.

A luxury, love was, and one Kit felt quite capable of living without. After all, love had done his parents no favors. They'd been happy together, content with their simple lot in life—and both ended up in early graves.

That wasn't going to happen to Kit or his sister.

For twelve years—through school, university, and a quickly rising reputation—he had dedicated himself to one goal. The Deputy Surveyor post was almost within his grasp.

He couldn't fail now.

"You look melancholy," Chrystabel Ashcroft said. Standing with Rose in her perfumery, she picked over the many flower arrangements on her large wooden worktable, plucking out the marigolds. "Why the long face, dear? Are you sad to see your creations destroyed?"

"Of course not." Rose added a purple aster to a pile of flowers and some ivy to a bunch of greens. She looked up and forced what she hoped sounded like a romantic sigh. "The wedding was beautiful, wasn't it?"

"Made more so by your lovely flowers." Rose had filled the house with towering creations made of posies cut from her father's gardens. "Which is why," her mother added, "I thought—"

"I do not care what becomes of my flower arrangements. Honestly, Mum, it makes no sense to let the blooms wither and die when we can turn them into essential oils for your perfumes. I don't mind in the least." With a bit more force than was necessary, Rose tugged two lilies from the vases and tossed them onto the table. "Whatever happened to Kit Martyn, do you know?" she asked in an attempt to change the subject.

"That messenger brought news of a problem with one of his projects. He had to leave."

"Which project?" Rose asked.

"He didn't say. Or perhaps I just don't remember."

Chrystabel fixed her with a piercing gaze. A motherly gaze. "Does it matter?"

"Of course not. 'Twas only idle curiosity." A headache threatened, pulsing in Rose's temples. "Why should I care what happens to the man's projects?"

"You danced with him—"

"Father traded that dance for a greenhouse. It meant nothing."

Her mother nodded thoughtfully, beginning to pluck petals from a bunch of striped snapdragons. "You just look melancholy."

If Rose weren't already suffering from a headache, that swift change back to the original subject might have prompted one. She lifted the lid off the gleaming glass-and-metal distillery that Ford had made for her mother while he was courting Violet. "'Tis nothing, Mum."

"It doesn't bother you that your younger sister is wed?"

"Why shouldn't I wish her happy?" She was chagrined to hear her voice crack. "I do, Mum, I vow and swear it."

"'Tis no failing of yours, dear, that Lily found love first."

"Stuck as we are in the countryside, 'tis a wonder she found a man at all, love or not." 'Twas an ancient complaint, but in her present mood Rose had no compunctions against dragging it out again. "We hardly ever get to London, or anywhere else we might meet eligible—"

"You have a point," Mum interrupted.

"Pardon?" Rose blinked.

"You heard me. You haven't much opportunity here to meet men." Chrystabel tossed the pink petals into the distillery's large glass bulb. "I am thinking that we—you and I—should attend Court."

"Court?" Rose decided she couldn't be hearing right. One of them had clearly drunk too much champagne. "As in King Charles's court?"

"I believe they're at Windsor now—they do move around, as you may know."

"What I *know* is that you and Father have always claimed Court is no place for proper young ladies."

"Well, you're not so young anymore," Chrystabel said, then came to wrap an arm around Rose when she winced. "I didn't mean it that way, dear. But you're one-and-twenty now, a woman grown. And I *will* be there to chaperone. 'Tis perfectly acceptable."

'Twas more than acceptable, Rose knew—girls as young as fifteen went to Court, many of them *un*chaperoned. And she also knew the licentious men there treated them like full-grown women. Violet had been to Court with Ford, and she'd come back with stories that had made Rose's eyes widen.

A little part of her wondered if this was really such a good idea.

But she wasn't going to argue when faced with such surprising good fortune. "Gemini, I'd best go talk to Harriet. She'll no doubt need to alter some of my gowns, and 'twill take me hours to decide what to bring before she can even begin."

"There is no time for alterations, dear." In opposition to Rose, whose stomach was churning with excitement, Chrystabel calmly plucked petals. "I mean to leave tomorrow."

"Tomorrow!" Rose dropped the stem in her hand. "Tomorrow?"

"There's no time like the present," her mother said with an enigmatic smile.

At another time, Rose might have been vexed at the implication that she was getting only more spinsterish as the days sped by. But this was no time to be touchy. No, 'twas time to prepare.

She was going to Court! Leaving her flowers on the table, she rushed to her chamber to pack.

"What a day." Chrystabel slipped beneath the counterpane to join her husband in bed, sinking into the mattress as she relaxed for the first time in what seemed like weeks. "Thank God they're married at last."

"Are you not really thanking God they can no longer create a child out of wedlock?" Joseph teased, leaning up to kiss her lightly on the lips. He lowered himself onto an elbow, smiling into her eyes, his own a deep, sparkling green.

She pushed a lock of dark hair off his forehead. "Well, there is that," she admitted. When Lily and Rand's marriage plans had been threatened by Rand's father, she'd been mortified to realize she'd allowed them to share a bed before her daughter was safely wed. It had seemed a fine idea at the time, but it wouldn't be happening again with Rose— or Rowan, for that matter.

Chrystabel reckoned she could learn from her mistakes.

"But mostly," she added, "I'm just gladdened to see them happy at last. Everything worked out."

"It usually does," said her ever-practical husband.

She released a contented sigh. "Another wedding."

"Another wedding night," he responded with a lustful grin.

A tradition, their wedding nights. 'Twas one of the reasons she so loved arranging other people's marriages. Not that either of them needed an excuse to make love, but there was something thrilling about watching a wedding while anticipating the night to come.

She smiled as he kissed her again, sighed when he slipped a hand beneath her night rail's neckline to caress a sensitive breast. For long minutes they said nothing, their breathing growing louder and more ragged in the stillness of their thick-walled room.

Here, in their quiet, private chamber, her Joseph could hear whatever she said. Every word, those spoken as well as the silent ones that passed between two as attuned as they.

But they didn't need words now. Actions would do. A

brush of lips, warm skimming hands. Bodies coming together, creating a thrill that the years had done nothing to
dim. Soft cries filled the chamber, matched by a low groan
of pleasure that echoed into the night.

When their hearts had calmed, when Joseph leaned away
to blow out the one remaining candle, Chrystabel sighed.
"I'll miss you."

"Where are you going?" The words vibrated against her
throat where he'd settled back into her arms.

"I'm thinking to take Rose to Court at Windsor. With
your permission, of course," she rushed to add, knowing he
would never deny her.

"Court? Do you expect that is wise? The men there—"

"I will watch her like a hawk. And 'tis only one man I'm
interested in for her: Kit Martyn. He's there as we sleep,
checking on a project—"

"Kit Martyn? Chrysanthemum my love, I know you fancy
yourself a matchmaker, but Rose has shown no interest—"

"Which is exactly why he's the perfect man for her."

Joseph lifted his head and searched her eyes in the dim,
flickering light from the fire. "Come again?"

"You know how she is. As soon as she sets her sights on
a man, the act begins. The flirting. The flattering. Don't you
see? She has a much better chance of winning a man for
whom she has no interest. With Kit she'll be herself.
Charming, intelligent, sharp-witted . . . why, he cannot fail
but fall in love with her."

"I suspect he's taken with her already," Joseph said dryly.
"But what good will that do if she doesn't fall for him?
We've promised her she can choose her own husband."

"Making her fall," Chrystabel said, "will be Kit's problem, and I've no doubt he's up to the task. I've only to pro-
vide the opportunity."

"You cannot push, Chrysanthemum."

Her laugh tinkled through the darkness. "I would never. I

know full well our daughters pledged not to let me arrange their marriages. Yet I managed to match both Violet and Lily without either being the wiser, did I not? Have no fear, darling—Rose's romance will follow suit . . . and she'll have no idea I was behind it."

Chapter Three

Kit stood in a corner of Windsor Castle's soon-to-be new dining room, watching two carpenters affix carvings of fruit to the paneled wall. The piece, exquisitely worked by Grinling Gibbons, was made of the finest wood.

He wished he could say the same for the rest of his project.

His gaze went to the sagging ceiling on the side of the room that had recently been part of a brick courtyard. Jagged cracks ran this way and that, and bits of broken plaster littered the floor underneath. On his orders, men were hastily erecting scaffolding to support the damaged ceiling until it could be repaired from above.

All day, Kit had measured and figured, tearing out parts of the ceiling to search for causes, to find where his planning had gone wrong. It hadn't, he'd finally discovered—the plans had been perfect. That was, if they'd been executed with the fine materials he'd used in his calculations.

But Harold Washburn, his project's foreman, had apparently not seen fit to order those materials, no matter that he'd been supplied with the funds. Instead, the new portion of the room had been built with inferior goods that weren't strong enough to support the ceiling. Kit had found beams made of wormy wood that had obviously been hit by lightning, weakening it; and cheap, substandard plaster that might look fine on first inspection, but wouldn't hold up over the years, sagging ceiling or not. And Washburn, no doubt, had pocketed the savings.

Making Kit look the fool.

Seething, calculations in hand, he stalked toward the bald, dark-eyed man. "Washburn!"

The man swung around, his beady gaze hooded. "Aye, Martyn? Have you a plan to repair the faulty addition?"

"Faulty?" Kit struggled to keep his temper in check. "The only thing faulty is the material you ordered to build it—which isn't anywhere near the quality in my specifications."

Washburn had the gall to pretend shock. "Sir! I would never—"

"Never again for me, at any rate." Kit gestured with his rolled-up sketches. "Be gone."

The man's breath huffed in and out through a large nose crisscrossed with tiny red veins. "You cannot just dismiss me," he snapped.

"Lord Almighty, you're a nithing half-wit. The damn ceiling could have fallen on your good-for-nothing head. You're lucky I'm only dismissing you."

To Kit's astonishment, Washburn simply shouldered past him and walked away, looking almost smug.

Kit consciously unclenched his jaw, reaching for the scrap of brick he usually carried in his surcoat pocket. His fist clenched around it; he'd been itching for a fight.

After a moment, though, the anger faded and relief settled in its place. The problem, after all, had been resolved more quickly than he'd any right to expect.

He took a deep breath, promoted a grateful man to take Washburn's place, then headed to the small chamber he'd been given to use as an office, already revamping the schedule in his head.

This project would still finish on time. That there were greedy men in the world was not news to Kit. But this particular man would not cost him the Deputy Surveyor post.

'Twould take a much bigger problem to destroy Kit Martyn's plans.

"Hurry," Rose said. "Or by the time we walk over to Court, the presentations will be finished."

"Worry not, dear." Seated together with Rose at the single dressing table in the rooms they'd been assigned at Windsor Castle, Mum held very still while her maid, Anne, used hot curling tongs to put the final touches on her hair. "We will still be allowed inside, even if we're late."

With all the last-minute preparations, they'd left home today much later than they'd planned. Chrystabel had needed to leave instructions for the running of the entire household, and Harriet, Rose's maid, had taken forever to pack. It had been dark by the time they'd reached Windsor, and Rose, dying of curiosity, had hardly been able to see anything of the huge castle as a warden showed them by torchlight to the small apartment they'd been assigned.

"I don't *want* to be late," she complained. Beneath burgundy satin sleeves fastened at intervals with jeweled clasps, her skin prickled with suppressed excitement. "I want to meet the King and Queen."

"You will, dear." Chrystabel met her gaze in the dressing table's mirror. "You look very pretty."

"Yes, you certainly do," Harriet added as she wove matching burgundy ribbons through the bun on the back of Rose's head. "And just think of all the new men you're going to meet! I can hardly believe I'm here, so far from Trentingham."

Actually, 'twas not far at all—little more than a couple of hours downriver. Though Rose had never been inside the castle before, she and her sisters often came to Windsor to visit the shops. But Harriet had been born at Trentingham Manor and, at age nineteen, had yet to leave the estate until today.

Rose suspected that was half the reason for their late

start. Harriet had been so flustered, she'd been unable to keep her mind on the preparations.

"You might meet a new man, too," Mum told Harriet, a familiar light coming into her brown eyes. Always happiest when matchmaking, Chrystabel cared not if the couples were royalty or servants. So long as two people, thanks to her, were finding their lifelong mates.

"Do you think so?" Harriet's fingers fumbled with the ribbons as she breathed a romantic sigh. Rose had never thought of Harriet as pining for marriage. Harriet was just Harriet, a sturdy girl with frizzy red hair and pale green eyes in a wide face full of freckles. But now those eyes went dreamy. "I would so love to fall in love."

"I shall keep that in mind," Chrystabel promised her.

"There, Lady Trentingham, you're finished," her own maid Anne said. "And you look pretty, too. As for you," she added to Harriet, "she will find you someone to love."

Four years earlier, Chrystabel had successfully matched Anne with a coachman from the Liddington estate. Today, they both lived happily at Trentingham, and so far they had produced one little future chambermaid and a tiny stable-boy-to-be.

Chrystabel stood and smoothed her peach silk skirts, looking to Rose. "Come along, dear. What is taking you so long?"

A retort hung on the tip of Rose's tongue, but she kept her mouth shut and followed her mother from the apartment. As they crossed the Upper Ward, excitement churned in the pit of her stomach. She was about to meet the King and Queen of England.

When they reached the open courtyard called Horn Court, where two red-and-white-liveried footmen stood guard at the door, she paused and pulled a curl forward to rest artfully on one bare shoulder. Her breath was coming short, and it had little to do with the rigid, pointed stomacher that stiffened the front of her bodice.

"Shall we?" Chrystabel asked, gesturing toward the door.

One of the footmen pulled it open. To Rose's disappointment, the monarchs weren't waiting right inside. Instead, she followed her mother into a tall, wide hall that held nothing but a staircase.

But what a staircase. "Oooh," she breathed. "'Tis beautiful!"

"It looks French," Chrystabel whispered back. "While exiled on the Continent, King Charles was much taken with Versailles."

French or English, Rose thought the staircase lovely. Twin flights of steps rose to their right and left, meeting at a central landing above. The rooms they had been given here were rather ancient, with plain plastered walls, but these walls were covered in colorful painted murals depicting Greeks and Trojans. Giants battled on the deeply coved ceiling that towered over her head.

As Rose climbed the steps, carefully holding her skirts, she felt very small and insignificant. She supposed that was the desired effect. Even here, outside his chambers, the King would want to project strength and power.

At the top of the stairs, she held her breath while another liveried footman opened another door.

But she was disappointed again. The enormous rectangular room beyond held no furniture and just a few lords and ladies absorbed in softly murmured conversations.

Rose's and Chrystabel's high-heeled shoes made clicking sounds on the planked floor as they crossed the chamber. Rose huffed out a sigh. "Where are the King and Queen?"

"We're getting there, dear. This is the Guard Chamber."

As though she couldn't have guessed. Military trophies covered every inch of the walls: helmets and drums, shields and armor, guns and lancets, swords and knives.

"Are there any weapons left for the army?" she whispered.

Mum's laugh broke the hush of the chamber. "I certainly hope so!" She met Rose's gaze, her brown eyes glittering. "'Tis an impressive display, but all the same, I expect we are still well defended."

The painted ceiling featured Jupiter and Juno seated on thrones at either end. In the center, a glassed octagonal opening provided a view of the stars and, Rose imagined, a great splash of natural light in the daytime.

Before the door at the far end, Chrystabel paused. "Lady Trentingham and Lady Rose Ashcroft," she announced, her voice laced with quiet dignity.

Finally. Rose lifted her burgundy satin skirts as one of the six guards bowed and opened the door.

But the room beyond was deserted, save for an usher at the other end.

"What is this?" Rose demanded.

"The King's Presence Chamber." Chrystabel curtsied in front of the magnificent red velvet throne, taking Rose's hand to make certain she did the same.

Thinking it the most ridiculous thing she'd ever done, Rose frowned as she straightened. "Despite the name of the chamber, the King," she said pointedly, staring at the empty throne, "does not seem to be present."

"Come along," her mother said with a half concealed smile.

Rose looked to the heavens for patience, seeing instead a painted ceiling where Mercury was presenting a portrait of the King to the four corners of the world. She was beginning to think all this decoration might be a bit overdone.

A red-and-white-garbed usher grandly opened the next door. By now, Rose wasn't expecting to see Their Majesties on the other side. In fact, she figured that at this rate she'd be a wrinkled old crone by the time she met them.

"The Audience Chamber," Chrystabel intoned softly. "You'll curtsy to this empty throne as well." She glided toward the canopied seat. "Charles does actually sit here to receive visitors in the daytime."

"Does he never sit in the other throne?"

"'Tis naught but symbolism, dear. Ceremony."

Rose had been sure she'd find the Court's pageantry intriguing and exciting, but in truth, it all seemed a little silly!

The next chamber made her jaw drop open, and it had nothing to do with the gaudy decorations—or even the spectacular clothing and jewels that adorned all the people milling about.

Staring, she drifted slowly through ·the room by her mother's side. There, in that dark corner, a woman sat sprawled on a man's lap, her head thrown back in laughter. Across the chamber, a fluttering curtain left the distinct impression that there was action of some sort going on behind it.

Nearby, another couple were kissing. No, more than kissing. Rose squinted, wishing there were more chandeliers overhead, or that the yeomen holding flaming torches would move closer to . . . her eyes widened. The woman's stomacher was unhooked down one side, hanging drunkenly, and the laces beneath were undone, and the man had his hand—

He turned a bit, and his gaze met Rose's for a moment. Or at least she thought it had—she couldn't be sure, given how quickly she shifted to focus on the ceiling above. But the monarch painted there in his golden chariot did nothing to erase the shocking-but-intriguing mental picture. There, the painted Charles was surrounded by naked angels, just as the real Charles was apparently surrounded by naked—

"Come along, dear. We're about to be announced."

"Announced?" She'd been so shocked, she hadn't even realized she'd finally made it to the chamber where Their Majesties waited.

Rose had always considered herself unshockable, but suddenly she felt like an innocent country mouse. Father had been right all along, she thought. Court was no place for a well-bred young lady.

Good thing she wasn't so young anymore.

The couple in front of her bowed and curtsied and moved out of the way, and she found herself approaching a red-canopied dais.

"Lady Trentingham!" the stuffy usher called. "Lady Rose

Ashcroft!" Rose held out her satin skirts—so plain compared to the jewel-encrusted gowns of the other ladies—and dropped into a deep curtsy. When she came up, she aimed a smile at King Charles, a bit startled to find that he was, after all, just an ordinary person.

She'd seen paintings, of course, but of a younger man, and somehow not such a real one. The King was forty-seven now, and a bit of gray-streaked hair peeked out from beneath his long, curled black periwig. His dark eyes were as sharp as ever, though—or at least as sharp as Rose had always heard. They swept her from head to toe, a gaze both approving and more than a bit lascivious.

Well, he was known for that.

In contrast, Queen Catharine's eyes were a warm, liquid brown. She wasn't a beauty, but her looks weren't displeasing, either—she looked sad, and a little world-weary.

After fifteen years of marriage, she had yet to present her husband with a child.

Since Rose stood before Catharine, she mimicked what her mother was doing with Charles, lifting the Queen's hand to press a kiss to the back.

She was rewarded with a smile. " 'Tis a pleasure to make your acquaintance," Catharine told her in flowing, Portuguese-accented English.

"The pleasure is mine," Rose returned. Really, she couldn't imagine why her sisters had gone all fluttery over the prospect of meeting the monarchs. They were, after all, just people.

She switched sides with her mother and bent her lips to the King's hand.

He gripped her fingers. "You're as lovely as your mother."

Beside her, Chrystabel blushed. Rose grinned at Charles. "Your reputation is well deserved, Your Majesty."

Still holding her fingers, he grinned back. "My reputation, my dear?"

"As a ladies' man."

Chrystabel gasped, but Charles just threw back his head and laughed. Rose shot her mother a triumphant smile.

Charles looked around them. "It seems you are the last to be presented," he said, not looking at all displeased about that. "Would you honor me with a dance?"

Now it was Rose's turn to gasp. She knew the protocol was for ladies to ask His Majesty to dance, not the opposite. Feeling light-headed, she curtsied again, then grinned. "'Twould be my honor, Sire."

"The second dance, then," he said, rising from his throne. He held out a hand to Catharine, and she rose as well and let him guide her to the dance floor, the jewels on her gorgeous lavender gown twinkling as she moved.

The incessant chatter in the room went quiet for a moment as everyone turned to watch the King and Queen dance the first dance.

Rose drifted to join the small crowd that surrounded the dance floor, hugging herself with excitement. After the King danced with her, surely other men would want to do the same.

Maybe one of them would end up her husband.

In fact, before the first dance even ended, she felt a light tap on her shoulder and turned to see a handsome specimen. The man was tall and fair, his clothing dripping with lace, his manner oozing aristocracy.

He struck a pose, one hand resting lightly on the jeweled hilt of his court sword, the other on the head of his high, beribboned walking stick. "Lady Trentingham, may I have the honor of an introduction?"

Rose wasn't surprised that he knew her mother's name. Lady Trentingham was known far and wide as an amateur matchmaker—and a very successful one, at that. For him to ask for an introduction must mean . . .

"Lord Rosslyn, may I present Lady Rose Ashcroft. *My daughter*," she added meaningfully before turning to Rose. "Rose, this is Gaylord Craig, the Earl of Rosslyn." Chrystabel turned back to the earl. "And how is your wife, my lord?" she asked in pointed tone.

"She is well," the man replied blithely. His gaze wandered to the left, where Rose saw a woman half entwined with a man who looked a decade her junior. "Like most here at Court, we have an understanding."

Rose was half tempted to bash him over the head with his own walking stick, but before she could react, Charles appeared by her side. He bowed, then held out a hand. "My lady?"

Rosslyn's eyes widened, and Rose felt rather triumphant as she joined the King on the dance floor.

'Twas a country dance, performed in two lines, one of women, one of men. When it was her turn to parade down the center with Charles, their joined hands held high, Rose felt the eyes of the entire chamber on her.

And the King's eyes as well. Dark and glinting, they captured hers quite effectively. The fabled Stuart charm. "'Tis a pleasure to have a new face at Court, my lady. Especially one as lovely as yours." He danced superbly, graceful for so tall a man, his voice just as smooth. "Why have you never graced us with your presence before now?"

She blushed—becomingly, she hoped. "My father thought me too young."

"Young?" he echoed.

And then they had to return to their respective lines.

As she executed the simple steps, she furtively glanced around. There were ladies of her mother's age, certainly, but there were also girls of fifteen and sixteen. Or perhaps she should think of them as women, since they hung on the arms of grown men, flirting madly.

Clearly, she was not too young.

The next time she met up with the King to parade down the center, she had a more plausible answer. "I have come to Court to find a husband."

"Ahh." His dark eyes glittered speculatively. "Interesting choice of word, my lady. Husbands we have, although many are already wed." He smiled at his own jest. "Take me, for example—"

"I won't be," she interrupted archly.

She worried for a moment that he might be offended, but he only laughed. "You *are* your mother's daughter," he conceded good-naturedly.

In a world filled with promiscuous spouses, her parents were known as uncommonly devoted.

The dance came to an end, and the King raised her hand to his mouth, pressing warm lips to the back. " 'Twas a pleasure, my lady. I wish you every success here at Court."

For a moment, while he still held her hand, Rose found herself suffused with wonder. Here she was, in the King's Drawing Room at Windsor Castle, with none other than Charles himself. An experience like this could go to a woman's head, she thought giddily.

Then he led her from the dance floor, and she watched him go straight to a girl of no more than seventeen and kiss her soundly on the lips. Rose couldn't help but notice his queen studiously gazing elsewhere, resignation etched clearly on her small, foreign-looking face.

Apparently all was not lightness and fun here at the castle.

But this was Rose's first evening at Court, not a night for sad contemplation. She looked away, enjoying the spectacle that was Charles's Court. Gentlemen walked with swaggering, elegant movements, and ladies fluttered exquisitely painted fans.

"May I claim the pleasure of a dance?"

Startled, she turned to see a heartbreakingly handsome man. "Absolutely, my lord . . . ?"

"Bridgewater. The Duke of Bridgewater," he clarified with a warm smile and a smart bow. Rose was pleased to see he wasn't carrying one of those foppish ribbon-topped walking sticks.

And he was a duke! Not only that, a youngish duke—of

an age, Rose guessed, not above thirty. Most dukes, in her experience, were doddering old men of forty or more.

As he swept her into the dance, her heart skittered with excitement. Already she was dancing with exactly the sort of man she'd come here hoping to meet.

"My given name is Gabriel Fox," he told her quite pleasantly. "You're Trentingham's daughter, are you not?"

"Yes. Rose Ashcroft," she said, gazing up at him—for he was tall. Tall enough to make her feel almost as petite as her sister Lily. Her gaze skimmed him from the top of his very-English blond head, past blue eyes, and down a patrician nose to his smiling mouth, each detail making her even happier.

He was perfect!

She was certain she was falling in love already.

"My lady Rose—may I call you Rose?" he asked, and then continued without waiting for confirmation. "I hope your mother will approve of our dancing without a proper introduction."

Not only a duke, a gentleman as well.

She gave a well-practiced flutter of her lashes. "To be sure, Your Grace." Imagine being called *Your Grace*—her stomach fluttered at the mere possibility. "My mother brought me here to meet men such as you." *Men exactly like you,* she revised silently, thrilled to have the attention of such a great catch.

And she *did* have his attention. His hands gripped hers a little tighter than was necessary, as though he were loath to let her escape. Not that she minded. To the contrary.

Court was *wonderful.* Even while dancing with Gabriel—for already, she thought of him as such—she couldn't help but be aware of her surroundings. The entire room glittered with the light of hundreds of candles in the chandeliers above and tall torches held by liveried yeomen, not to mention all the flashing precious metal and gemstones that adorned everyone in attendance.

That observation prompted her to check out Gabriel's

jewels. A heavy gold chain draped flat across the peacock blue velvet of his surcoat. Beneath that, a strand of fat pearls gleamed in the firelight, swinging a bit as he moved with the dance. His lacy white cravat was secured with a large diamond pin, and the buttons on his suit boasted sapphires and diamonds set in glittering gold. Froths of lace spilled from his sleeves onto hands adorned with various rings set with rubies, emeralds, and jet. His high-heeled shoes sported gold and sapphire buckles.

Not only was he a duke, he was a rich duke!

Rose felt deflated when the dance came to an end. One never danced with the same man two tunes in a row. But when Gabriel bowed over her hand and kissed it, she knew he would ask her again.

No sooner had he straightened than another man rushed over and begged the honor of a dance. And after that, another. And another and another until the evening grew late and the men all blended in her head. They were marquesses and earls and barons, but, quite frankly, none of them was as perfect for her as the Duke of Bridgewater.

Chapter Four

Kit walked briskly through the dark castle grounds toward Christopher Wren's apartments—the official apartments of the Surveyor General, apartments he hoped to own for himself someday. Not that he'd actually live there. He'd just put the finishing touches on a brand-new house here in Windsor, situated on an enviable plot of land on the banks of the River Thames.

In fact, his sister, Ellen, was waiting for him there now. At least, he hoped she was waiting for him. She had declared herself in love with a completely unsuitable man—a pawnbroker, for God's sake—and he feared she might be off at his damned pawnshop.

Ellen had never been the type to pay heed to his brotherly concerns.

Arriving at his destination, he knocked twice on the old oak door and waited for Wren to admit him, slightly startled when the man himself answered, dressed in shirtsleeves. He'd obviously been working. He wore no periwig, and his long, dark hair was a mite disheveled, as though he'd been raking his hands through it.

Wren didn't reside in the official Surveyor General's apartments, either, using the rooms as office space instead. The Dean of Windsor's son, he'd been raised right here in the castle deanery, a playmate of the young Prince of Wales—now King Charles. Wren had recently built an impressive house for himself in town, but he and his monarch were still intimates—and Kit was hoping that long-standing relationship would help Wren convince the King that he was the right man for the Deputy Surveyor post.

But the look on Wren's face was not reassuring. "This new development does not bode well," he said without preamble, motioning Kit inside. He waved him toward a chair but didn't sit himself, instead perching one hip on a large drafting table strewn with copious drawings.

Like Charles, Wren was two decades Kit's senior, but they'd been acquainted for years, ever since Kit had found himself Wren's student at Oxford. Professor and pupil had grown close, and although Kit knew Wren was also acquainted with his rival for the position, he knew as well that Wren had never held the man in high esteem. Gaylord Craig, now the Earl of Rosslyn, had never been a stellar student, and Wren was a man who valued intelligence augmented by hard work.

Unfortunately, however, the decision was not Wren's alone. Charles owed many Royalist families for their support in the Civil War—and government appointments were less costly than most methods of repayment.

"Until this inopportune occurrence," Wren continued, "you were the front-runner for the appointment. But Charles hasn't the patience for costly errors—the monarchy, I'm afraid, is as cash-strapped as ever."

Kit rubbed the chunk of brick in his pocket. "The 'error' wasn't strictly mine—my foreman chose to use substandard materials. Not," he rushed to add, "that I don't take responsibility. Quite clearly I erred in hiring the man in the first place. I will cover the losses."

Wren nodded thoughtfully, his brown eyes sympathetic. "Regardless, I am now under pressure to award the post to Rosslyn. Last I saw, the dining room was coming along beautifully, though—your design and eye to detail are impeccable. Charles plans to inspect it tomorrow, so if you can make certain the site is safe and any debris is cleared—"

"Of course."

"—perhaps we can divert his attention to the impressive decoration."

"I have everything under control," Kit assured him. If necessary, he would comb the town for extra hands and have the men work overnight. Sufficient scaffolding would be erected to assure no safety concerns, and the site would look pristine, whatever it took to make it that way. "What time have you scheduled the visit?"

"Noon."

"I'll be ready by ten."

"Make sure you are." Wren's words were serious, but he tempered them with a small smile. "With any luck, we can pull this off."

"I've never put much stock in luck. Hard work and perseverance have done well by me so far." Kit returned the smile with a wry one of his own. "But I suppose a little luck wouldn't come amiss."

Wren rose and opened the door, giving Kit a companionable slap on the back as he ushered him through it. "I'll do what I can."

"I'm counting on it," Kit said. Hard work and perseverance. He'd always believed that with both, anything could be his.

He headed back to his site. The castle grounds were quiet this time of night, the Round Tower on its huge mound of earth looming tall and imposing between the Lower and Upper Wards. His footfalls echoed off the cobblestones as he skirted the circular structure and made his way to Horn Court.

Nodding a familiar greeting, the usher there opened the door to admit him to the King's Staircase. Kit hurried up the steps and through the progression of chambers—rooms he didn't belong in, if one went strictly by rank, but as one of the King's architects, he had free access.

Someday, he would have the rank, too.

His mind on his project and what he would have to accomplish tonight to assure its successful completion, he fairly ran through the Audience Chamber and into the King's Drawing Room, where Court was in full swing this evening. There, he stopped short.

Rose Ashcroft was on the dance floor.

His breath caught at the sight of her, a vision in wine-colored satin. The wide neckline bared her creamy shoulders. Her long sleeves were caught at intervals with jeweled clasps that left gaps, revealing tempting glances of a diaphanous chemise underneath.

He had no idea how she'd come to be here, but she was dancing with some lucky bastard who was tall, blond, and exceedingly aristocratic.

As she spun in the other man's arms, he felt that punch in his gut again—and a ridiculous surge of wanting. Jealousy spurted through his veins. Absurd jealousy, both aggravating and unproductive.

Mr. Kit Martyn was still years away from gaining the title that could give him access to Lady Rose Ashcroft. Wren hadn't been knighted until well after he'd become Surveyor General. Deputy Surveyor was only the first step.

Unless . . . what if he truly impressed King Charles with his abilities as a master architect? Windsor's new dining room would prove to be spectacular, of that he was certain. The renovations at Whitehall Palace and the new building at Hampton Court—apartments for Charles's long-time mistress Barbara, whom he'd created the Duchess of Cleveland, and his five children by her—could prove to be Kit's making. Charles might be pleased enough to award him a knighthood along with the Deputy Surveyor post . . . speeding along Kit's plans, and perhaps allowing him to win the stunning woman now gliding on the dance floor in the arms of another man.

His jaw set with determination, he tore his gaze from Rose and strode through the glittering assembly, exiting the drawing room into the small, as-yet-unrenovated vestibule that led to his project.

"Martyn."

Kit turned to see the Earl of Rosslyn follow and close the door behind him. The vestibule seemed quiet after the hubbub of Court, the music and voices muffled to a dull hum.

"Yes, Rosslyn?"

Slim, fair, and elegant in an almost effeminate way, Rosslyn shook his head sympathetically. "I was sorry to hear of your misfortune."

Given that they were competing for the same post, Kit wondered if the man was sincere—but after all, they went back a long way. Oxford, of course, and before that, they'd both attended Westminster School. They'd never run in the same circles, Kit being a King's Scholar with his tuition paid by the Crown, while Rosslyn stuck to his wealthy crowd. But Kit had always got on well with everyone, and as it had become clear in the last few weeks that he and Rosslyn were the final candidates for Deputy Surveyor, he'd found himself a bit disconcerted to be competing for the post with a friend.

Not that that dimmed his determination to win. He felt like he'd been working toward this appointment all his life. Now he was so close.

He tried for a blithe smile. "What misfortune is that?"

"Your project here has suffered a setback, has it not?"

Kit managed an unconcerned shrug. "Minor, I can assure you. I will finish within deadline as planned."

"Excellent." Rosslyn toyed with the ribbons that crowned his walking stick, his pale blue eyes speculative. "Do you know, I have mixed feelings about winning the Deputy Surveyor post over you. The last thing I need is more projects—I'm overwhelmed with commissions as it is." One square-toed high-heeled shoe tapping, the earl eyed Kit's plain suit with ill-concealed disdain. "And I certainly don't need a knighthood."

Kit was glad to hear it. Apparently Rosslyn wasn't feeling competitive. Kit grinned and held out a hand. "Well, then, for the sake of the kingdom, may the best man win."

Rosslyn's grip had always been of the limp variety, and this occasion was no exception. Kit knew he was the best man. He just had to prove it.

Chapter Five

As the evening wore on, Gabriel sought out Rose for a second dance, and then a third. "People will talk," she told him as he guided her toward the dance floor once again.

"Do you care?" he asked.

"Of course not." Rose's attention was drawn by a spectacle that was already becoming familiar: King Charles crossing the chamber followed by a bevy of yipping spaniels. Amused, she smiled as she saw him stop before a short woman and slide an arm around her possessively. "Who is that?" Rose asked.

The duke barely spared the couple a glance. "Have you never met Nell Gwyn?"

"Is that Nell Gwyn? Gemini!" Rose knew of the woman, of course; she doubted there was a soul in England who hadn't heard of the brothel-born actress who'd stolen His Majesty's heart. But she'd expected Nell to be exquisite. Although the woman enthusiastically kissing Charles was pretty, Rose wouldn't call her beautiful. Her small body was lushly curvy, her hair a riot of red-brown curls. Rose's eyes widened as Charles worked his mistress toward a chair and tumbled her onto his lap. Over the music, Nell's delighted laughter mixed with the ever-present yaps of the King's dogs.

"I had no idea she was allowed at Court," Rose mused. "Has Charles granted her a title?"

"Of course not." Gabriel maneuvered her around to where she couldn't stare. "But Charles made their young son the Earl of Burford, and Nell herself was appointed Lady of the Queen's Bedchamber these two years past."

Rose blinked. "And what does our dear Queen think of that?"

"I don't expect our dear Queen was given a say in the matter." The duke raised a brow as he looked down at her. "Wives usually aren't."

"Not all wives," she said archly. "I'll have you know my family's motto is *Interroga Conformationem*."

"Question Convention?" he translated, looking amused.

Rose smiled, pleased. On top of everything else wonderful about him, the man knew Latin.

After a couple more dances with men who failed to measure up to the duke, Rose sneaked off toward the ladies' attiring room, hoping for a rest. As she approached the small chamber, Nell Gwyn's distinctive laughter drifted out. "Aye, my ladies, the tale is true."

"Tell us," a feminine voice demanded.

"Yes, do tell!" came a veritable chorus.

Wondering just how many ladies were crowded into the attiring room, Rose stopped outside the door and listened.

"I took His Majesty to a bawdy house," Nell confided, "and encouraged him to run up a bill treating everyone to drink. Incognito, of course—'tweren't the type of place his cronies frequent, you understand." That was met with titters of laughter. "By and by, I took him up to a room and got him undressed, and then ran away with his clothes."

"You're a bold one, Nelly Gwyn," someone chortled out. "What happened after that?"

"Well, the brothel owner wasn't disposed to believe this man wrapped in a sheet to be her sovereign—you cannot blame the poor fool, can you? He carried no money, so to pay his debt and for something to wear, he offered an emerald ring as security. 'Twas all he had on him, you see."

"And fair enough," a lady pointed out.

"Well, the proprietor refused, claiming 'twere paste for certain. Our dear King almost burst a vessel, he did, when fortunately someone recognized him and convinced the owner as to his identity. So all was well."

"He must have been furious," someone breathed.

"You know not my Charles," Nell declared. "Once it were all over, he thought it a fine jest indeed!"

Hoots of laughter greeted Rose when she stepped into the room. "Good evening, ladies."

Her smile faded as the chamber fell silent and, one by one, the women shouldered their way past her and out the door. Finally only Nell was left.

She shrugged and made her way to Rose. "Don't pay them no mind, milady." Like a man, she held out a hand. "I'm Eleanor Gwyn, Nell to my friends."

"I know." Nell's hand felt small and warm for the moment Rose held it. "I'm Rose Ashcroft."

"*Lady* Rose Ashcroft, I've been told." Nell's twinkling eyes almost closed when she smiled. "They're only jealous of your beauty. And afraid you'll steal their men."

"Gemini!" Rose exclaimed. "Most of them are married!"

"Ah, a babe in the woods." Nell gave a kindly sigh. "Here at Court, that makes no difference. No difference at all. The women consider all male courtiers fair game, and the men hunt amongst the women just as freely. Fidelity went out with Cromwell," she concluded, then wiped her tongue and spit, having uttered the hated name.

Rose slanted her an assessing glance. "*You* don't seem to worry that I'll help myself to a courtier or two."

Nell's infectious laughter poured forth. "Bloody hell, sweetheart, what do I need with the pompous fools? I bed with the King. It doesn't get any better than that!"

Rose wondered if by "better" Nell referred to Charles's exalted status or meant that he was a great lover. 'Twas on the tip of her tongue to ask when another lady barged in, her milk white complexion mottled with angry red. She gave Nell a glare that said she wished her dead, then plopped onto a green baize bench with her back to them both, her dark ringlets shaking with barely controlled fury.

Nell snorted, then sailed out the door with Rose in tow. "Don't pay no mind to her, either," she said, none too quietly.

Rose waited until they were out of earshot to ask, "Who is she?"

"The high and mighty Louise de Kéroualle."

"The Duchess of Portsmouth?" Another of Charles's mistresses—this one, Rose knew, not nearly as popular with the people. Of course, that was due to her Catholicism rather than any fault of her personality, which, after all, they could hardly be acquainted with. Nell, on the other hand, had been known to proudly proclaim herself "the Protestant whore."

"Squintabella is in a snit," Nell said now, "because she arrived today after a long journey from Bath, but although Charles took dinner with her, he didn't invite her to stay the night, preferring *my* bed instead."

"Squintabella?" Rose echoed weakly, her head spinning with all this delicious Court gossip.

"Did you not notice the slight cast in the duchess's eye? I was here at Court before her, and I'll be here long after she's gone. She's managed to send Barbara running across the Channel, but she won't do away with me so easily."

"Barbara has left England?" The news was a shock. Barbara was Charles's longest-standing mistress, having accompanied him home for his Restoration.

"She's on the outs now, thanks to Louise. Living in Paris. But she'll return—she always does. And no matter what she's done, Charles always forgives her."

"You must find that maddening," Rose observed.

"Hell, no. She's had him wrapped round her finger for seventeen years. I know better than to expect that to change now." Nell laughed as she bussed Rose on both cheeks, sang "Good luck, dearie!" and flitted back into the drawing room.

No sooner had she left than Louise came out the door. "Enjoying Court, Lady Rose?"

Still reeling, Rose turned to her in surprise. "Very much," she told the gorgeous woman. Baby-faced with almond-shaped eyes, full red lips, and enough jewelry hanging all over her to stock a small shop, Louise made Rose feel plain in comparison.

But the duchess's demeanor was not so beautiful. "You'd do best," she advised haughtily, "not to fraternize with such as she."

"Could you mean Nell?" Bristling, Rose couldn't help but notice that small squint Nell had mentioned. "Whyever not? Charles seems to think her good enough."

"I cannot credit that he's taken with such a coarse, common orange wench." As a young girl, before she'd stepped on stage at the King's Theatre, Nell had been employed there selling oranges. "She calls him her Charles the Third, you know."

Rose could feel jealous venom spewing from this bitter woman. "Charles the Third?"

"Her earlier lovers included Charles Hart—a common actor—who then passed her to Charles Sackville, Lord Buckhurst. She called *him* her Charles the Second, and now the King has become Charles the Third."

Rose's lips twitched.

"'Tis not amusing," Louise sniffed. "His Majesty deserves respect—not least from one such as she."

Louise de Kéroualle, daughter of a Breton family of ancient and distinguished lineage, quite obviously considered herself much above Nell Gwyn. But Rose couldn't help liking the "coarse orange wench" better. Louise was rumored to be a French spy, which Rose suddenly had little difficulty believing.

Pretty is as pretty does, her mother had always told her three girls. Rose was imagining Louise's lovely face transforming into that of a hag when Gabriel appeared and laid a hand on her arm.

"Did you not promise me the next dance?" he asked, although she hadn't. Before Rose could answer, he nodded toward Louise. "Your Grace."

"Your Grace." The pale beauty nodded back, a smile curving those bloodred lips, her voice suddenly as sweet and smooth as honey.

The woman, Rose realized, was a natural-born predator. Although she knew tongues would wag when the duke led her off toward the dance floor yet again, she went more than willingly.

Her heart pounded with the thrill of it all. She'd always said 'twas as easy to fall in love with a titled man as one without, and the Duke of Bridgewater certainly had a title worth falling for.

The dance was a branle, and all the running, gliding, and skipping rendered her breathless. Or maybe it was the duke . . . she couldn't be sure. She only knew that when he took her by the arm and drew her toward a door, her heart gave a little lurch.

"We shouldn't—" she started.

"Whyever not?" His smile looked innocent enough. "Are you not heated after that dance? I certainly feel overwarm . . ." One pale, arched brow rose, and his tone implied that the heat resulted from more than just exertion.

Well, she shouldn't refuse him, should she? After all, 'twas naught but a walk outside. She glanced toward her mother, but Chrystabel was engaged in conversation across the room. The men at Court had wicked reputations, but surely if Mum were concerned, she'd be watching more closely.

In any case, it hardly mattered, since while Rose was dithering, the duke had managed to steer her from the room.

She'd never liked the dark, so she was relieved to see a few torches. 'Twas a mild evening, but no one else seemed to be outdoors enjoying the favorable weather. "Should we be out here?" she asked nervously.

"'Tis open to the public. Charles expanded this terrace recently, and he's invited the townspeople to enjoy the views. 'Tis crowded as hell in the daytime."

She'd bet it was—and for some reason, she found herself wishing all those people were here now. But when he took her hand and started walking, her fleeting unease was replaced by a sense of wonder. Her first time at Court—how amazing that she should find such a perfect man so quickly! She should have come to Court years before.

"How long have you been here at Windsor?" he asked.

"We arrived only today."

"I guessed as much—or I would surely have spotted you before now."

They fell quiet as Gabriel guided her toward the edge of the terrace and stopped by the rail. This castle, like most, was built on high land, and the terrace afforded magnificent views. Beneath the castle wall, parkland gave way to a few twinkling lights and the moon reflecting off the Thames in the distance. Stars winked in the heavens above.

"'Tis a lovely night," Rose said to fill the silence.

"Yes, it is." He smiled down at her, his face lit by the moon. "Made more so with such lovely company."

Rose liked what she was hearing. Surely there was no reason to feel uneasy.

No reason at all.

Chapter Six

Kit had six men erecting scaffolding, two chipping off the ruined plaster, and another two hauling away the debris. At the same time, he had a team on the way to London to fetch the quality materials that had been figured into his original specifications. Hopefully, they would return on the morrow, or at worst, the day after that.

Construction work generally halted at dusk. There were no chandeliers in the room as yet, so the men worked by the light of torches and candelabra. If he could convince the rest of his crew to remain on the job twenty-four hours a day, he would. But they, of course, were snug in their beds while he fretted. Artists, especially, were temperamental creatures.

"Careful!" he warned, one eye on the crew while he reworked the schedule again in his head, trying to plan contingencies in case the new materials arrived late. "We're strapped for time, but I won't have injuries. Or a fire."

"Pardon me!" a musical voice exclaimed. He turned to see the swish of peach-colored skirts as Lady Trentingham swiveled away, narrowly missing being whacked in the head by three men rushing out with a beam. "I've apparently stumbled into the wrong room."

Emerging from the shadows, Kit strode toward her, his footfalls muffled by the protective tarpaulins on the new oak flooring. "'Tis perfectly all right, Lady Trentingham." Taking her arm, he drew her over to a safe corner.

"Mr. Martyn!" she said warmly. "I was searching for my daughter—"

"Lady Rose? I thought I glimpsed her earlier. What a surprise to find you both here."

She turned slowly, inspecting the chamber. "I've brought her to Court to find a husband."

He should have guessed. A woman as beautiful and bright as Rose would be snapped up here within days—if she wasn't debauched first. Absurdly, disappointment tightened his chest as he watched Lady Trentingham scan the room and saw her pretty brown eyes—so like Rose's— widen with appreciation.

"This ceiling is going to be exquisite," she commented, gazing up at the half-painted details on the older portion of the room—the part that wasn't ruined. "A banquet of the gods, is it not? Fish and fowl . . . look, a lobster! How very charming."

"I'm pleased you think so. I envisioned it both exquisite and somewhat amusing." He hoped the King would be even half as impressed as she. "I've got Antonio Verrio painting it. You may have heard of him?"

"Heavens, yes. The Duke of Montagu brought him from Paris, did he not? I arranged his marriage. The duke's, not the artist's." She ran a hand down the intricate oak carving on the wall beside her, a melange of fruit and vegetables. "And who is responsible for this?"

"Grinling Gibbons, assisted by Henry Phillips."

She nodded approvingly, still looking around. "The cornice is his work as well, if I'm not mistaken. Are you interested in my daughter, Mr. Martyn?"

He blinked at the rapid change of subject. Not to mention the subject itself. "Lady Rose is quite interesting," he replied cautiously. "And please, call me Kit."

"Kit." She dropped her gaze to meet his. "That is not the sort of interest I was enquiring about, and"—a small smile curved her lips—"I suspect you know it. Do you want Rose?"

He wished there were furniture in the room so he could sit down. "Do I want . . ."

"I do not mean in a carnal sense," she said, then her eyes twinkled. "Well, of course that is part of it, but do you want her as a wife?"

"A *wife*?" Furniture or no, if this line of questioning continued, he was going to have to sit. The floor was looking mighty tempting. His knees felt weaker than the plaster that had recently crumbled. And he hadn't the slightest idea what sort of reply Lady Trentingham was seeking.

He rubbed the back of his neck. *Do you want her as a wife?* Only in his most ludicrous dreams. If he answered yes, would Lady Trentingham berate him for aspiring far above his station? If he answered no, would she take offense on her daughter's behalf?

She saved him from answering at all. "You would make me a fine son-in-law, but if you wish for that to happen, you'd do best to hide my approval from my daughter."

Kit could hardly believe his ears. Elation sang through his veins, tempered by a rush of confusion. "I . . . does it not bother you that I'm not of noble birth?"

"I know a good man when I see one, and a title rarely has much to do with it. In my opinion, that is. I wish I could say my Rose felt the same way." Her voice was laden with warning. "I'm afraid you'll have your work cut out for you."

He wondered if he was up to the task. But with the approval of Rose's mother, he was damn well willing to try. "She told me she is allowed to choose her own husband."

"Yes, she is. And furthermore, she is determined not to wed anyone of *my* choosing. I'm rather known as a matchmaker," she added, but 'twas not a boast, just an honest bit of information. "Like my other daughters, she wants no part of any marriage I arrange."

"I see."

She cracked a smile. "Nevertheless—and unbeknownst to my children—I chose both Violet's and Lily's husbands. I aim to make it three for three. How's that for an impressive accounting?"

"My lady, I wish you every success in attaining that goal." He'd never spoken more earnest words, since her success would mean his as well.

"I'm pleased to hear you agree. One more thing." Her hand on his arm, she commanded his gaze. "My daughter is an innocent . . . and I expect her to remain one until the day she is wed. I'm well aware of the goings-on here at Court—"

"I'm no courtier," he rushed to assure her. He waved an arm, encompassing the half-finished chamber. "I am only the hired help."

"I'm glad to hear it." She smoothed down her skirt. "Now I must leave your glamorous room and seek out my daughter, before another man—who *is* a courtier—gets his claws into her. Can I convince you to accompany me in my search?"

As Rose and Gabriel walked, she found herself mentally bouncing back and forth between trying to be her most charming and marveling that the Duke of Bridgewater was choosing to spend so much time with her. As a result, she feared their conversation had been a bit stilted.

But that was only to be expected, was it not? After all, they hardly knew each other. Still, her family had always been rather vocal, discussing anything and everything with great enthusiasm, so the awkward silences made her uncomfortable.

"What do you think," she asked after a particularly long gap in their dialogue, "of the maritime agreement we have just signed with France?"

"Maritime agreement?" The duke's perfect brow creased in puzzlement.

Did people not discuss these matters at Court? Did he

not read *The London Gazette*? She plucked a yellow bloom off a hollyhock plant. "English ships will now be permitted to carry Dutch cargoes without fear of French interference."

A little chuckle burst from his lips. "What would a woman know about that?"

"Oh, just something I heard." She forced a laugh in return, cursing herself silently.

Though she wasn't a student of history or prone to philosophical musings, she'd always been interested in what currently went on in the world. But how could she have forgotten her own rule to dazzle men without revealing her intelligence?

She sniffed the flower daintily. "I was just wondering if you could tell me what the agreement might mean to us here in England." When he gave her a blank stare, she worried that he no longer liked her. "The significance of such an action escapes me," she lied in a desperate effort to redeem herself.

"'Tis quite all right." Walking her closer to the building, he squeezed her hand. "Don't worry your pretty little head, my dear."

Could he still like her, then? she wondered. But suddenly he drew her between a turret and a stand of trees, and she knew.

He still liked her. In fact, he was going to kiss her.

She could tell when a man was aiming to kiss her. After all, it had happened before. She'd lost count of the number of men who had contrived to press their lips to hers. She supposed it wasn't surprising, given that she was a comely woman and not nearly as proper as her sisters. And they were only kisses, for God's sake—'twas not as though she allowed men to take further liberties.

So she'd been kissed before, and she knew what to expect. But she had a sad secret.

She didn't much care for kissing.

"Gabriel," she whispered when he turned her to face him. "May I call you Gabriel?"

"But of course, sweet Rose." His voice had deepened, and he raised a hand and skimmed her cheek. Then it curled around the back of her neck as he drew her closer, and before she could say anything further—before she could attempt to slow him down, to possibly suggest they get to know each other better before sharing this intimacy—he lowered his head.

His other arm went around her, and his hand pressed into the small of her back, drawing her against his body. As the flower dropped from her fingers, his mouth crushed down on hers.

She stiffened, but he didn't seem to notice. His lips coaxed hers open, and his tongue pushed into her mouth, wet and frantic. Just as she'd expected, she thought with a mental groan. Most men seemed to prefer this kind of kiss, and the duke was apparently no exception.

Gabriel let out an amorous little moan and shifted her in his arms, slanting his lips across hers. Faced with such honest passion, she tried to relax and participate, tried to learn to enjoy this kiss. But try as she might, it didn't feel as wondrous as it was supposed to. In fact, it didn't feel like much at all beyond a messy mashing of mouths.

She was relieved when he pulled away—even more relieved when her mother's distinctive soft laughter floated to her on the night. She turned and stepped back onto the terrace.

"Mum! And . . . you," she added rather ungraciously as her gaze shifted to her mother's right. There stood Kit Martyn, looking impossibly handsome.

A commoner had no right to look so good. She felt those champagne bubbles again, and she hadn't even been drinking spirits.

"What are you doing here?" she asked him.

"Building a new dining room for the King. What have

you been doing here?" he asked in a way that made it clear he thought he knew.

Rose felt herself turning red.

"She's with me," the duke said, sounding rather possessive. "Though what business is it of yours, I wonder?"

Picturing these two in a fistfight, she feared Kit might win. "Your Grace," she said quickly, "may I present Mr. Christopher Martyn. Kit, the Duke of Bridgewater." She looked up at Gabriel. "He's a friend of the family," she added, feeling it necessary to explain.

"And I asked Kit to help me search for you," her mother put in. "I felt it unsafe, as a woman, to be out in the dark alone."

"Yes, 'twould not have been wise." Kit held Gabriel's gaze until the man looked away. "I'm glad to have been of service, but I must be off. I've much to accomplish before tomorrow. Lady Trentingham, Lady Rose." He nodded toward them both, then addressed the duke with an elegant bow. "Your Grace."

Slightly disconcerted, Rose watched him walk away.

"We should return as well," her mother told her. "I am grateful to have found you in such safe hands."

If Chrystabel's voice held a bit of warning, Rose chose to ignore it. On their way back to the drawing room, she smiled up at Gabriel. She'd liked the way he'd made it clear she was there with him.

He truly was perfect, and it wasn't his fault that she didn't enjoy his kisses.

She'd listened, jealous beyond belief, while her sisters rhapsodized about the sensual kisses they enjoyed with the men who were now their husbands. But kisses had never been like that for her. In all honesty, she found them more than a mite disgusting.

Of course, she'd never told her sisters that, so she sometimes wondered if they, too, were hiding their distaste. But she thought not. Both her sisters were honest to a fault.

How they could enjoy men mauling their mouths was beyond her, but apparently they did.

She wished it could be the same for her, but experience had convinced her otherwise. She could only hope that the rest of what happened between men and women wasn't nearly as repugnant.

Chapter Seven

"I am pleased." King Charles nodded thoughtfully, his dark eyes skimming the dining room again with approval. "And I'm satisfied with your explanation, Mr. Martyn. Do be certain, however, to complete this project per schedule."

"I can assure Your Majesty that will not prove a problem." Kit walked with Charles toward the double doors and threw them wide. "I thank you for taking the time to visit."

Kit smiled as he watched the King make his way through the vestibule, several of the man's ever-present spaniels yipping after him. After pulling the doors shut, he unfolded some tarpaulins and laid them near the side of the chamber that was supported by scaffolding. Then he strode through a door at the other end, along a corridor, and into Brick Court. "Come along, now! Beams, lumber—move!"

Dazed, he stepped aside to let the workmen through with the first of the new materials he'd ordered. If it wouldn't be such a bad example, he'd slump against the wall.

He'd passed.

He wandered back along the corridor and into the dining room, keeping out of his crew's way. He'd been up all night supervising, reevaluating, working with his own hands while his men secured the damaged area and hauled away all evidence of the mishap. He'd attached countless strips of decorative molding, polished all the oak paneling,

stripped off the tarpaulins and polished the new floor, too.
All in hopes of charming the King's eye.

He'd passed.

Dropping onto a fresh stack of wood and using it as a
chair, he flipped blindly through a book of architectural
renderings. He should go home; he was exhausted and
needed to check in with his sister. Ellen had a habit of finding trouble when he wasn't around.

The drawings before him blurred. He'd passed. All was
not lost.

When the double doors reopened, his heart seized as he
wondered wildly whether the King had some complaint,
after all. He sagged with relief when two women entered
instead. Then sat straight when he recognized them.

Rose and her mother, both dressed in bright, cheerful
colors. Surely a sight for tired eyes.

"Oh!" Lady Trentingham exclaimed, meeting his gaze. "I
didn't expect to find you here."

He wouldn't wager on that.

"I just wanted to show Rose this beautiful chamber," she
added.

Kit shut his book. "I was about to leave anyway. 'Tis
time I went home."

"Home? Surely you're not finished here. It looks wonderful, but—"

"'Tis stunning, Mum! Even better than you described."
Rose gazed up at the ceiling. "Beauty and whimsy all rolled
into one. I am not overly fond of the decoration here at
Windsor. Overdone, if you ask me. But this room does not
take itself as seriously as the others."

"Thank you," Kit said. Relishing the admiration in her
voice, he watched her wander the chamber, touching a
carved panel, the white marble mantel, a bit of grooved
wainscoting. Smiling, he turned to her mother. "The project
is well in hand for the moment; I'm not abandoning it, I assure you. I live right here in Windsor. Not a ten-minute
walk."

"Is that so? I imagine your home must be lovely."

He knew a hint when he heard one. "Would you like to see it?"

"Mum, I don't think—"

"We'd love to," Lady Trentingham cut in. "Were you not just saying, dear, how tedious it is here in the daytime?"

Kit led them on an easy walk from the castle down the hill to the Thames. Rose decided it felt good to be out in the fresh air. And there truly was nothing to do at Windsor Castle in the daytime . . . with the exception of the palace staff, it seemed everyone was still abed, sleeping off the excesses of the night before.

When Rose had hit her pillow after midnight, Court had still been in full swing. She would have to adjust her country hours, perhaps take a nap early this evening before Court got under way. They had just been setting up gaming tables when she left, and although she'd never gambled, she imagined it was much fun. Perhaps she could win enough money for a new gown.

The curved, steep street followed the castle wall. Across the road, townspeople went about their business, entering and exiting rows of gabled shops with living accommodations above. Women carried baskets over their arms, gathering purchases as children and dogs played tag in the cobbled street.

No dirt road here, in this bustling town where the King kept a household.

"Look," she said as they reached the bottom of the hill. "A bookshop."

"John Young, Bookseller," Mum read off the old, cracked wooden sign.

Rose was always looking for new books to help practice her skills. "I wonder if they might have any books written in foreign languages."

"Oh, yes," Kit put in. "I found this there." He raised the book tucked under his arm. "'Tis Latin."

"You read Latin?"

"Hell, no," he said, not surprising her. He hadn't understood her family's Latin motto, after all. "I bought it to study the drawings." He flipped open the book and held it up as they walked. "See? Classical architecture."

"But there are words," Mum pointed out. "Explanations."

"True." He sighed and closed the cover. "I believe, actually, that this book is meant to instruct one in how to accurately draw buildings. But even though I cannot learn what it sets out to teach, I enjoy studying the pictures."

"Rose can read Latin," Mum said.

Rose avoided her mother's gaze, instead looking longingly inside the bookshop as they passed. "May we stop here on the way back, Mum?"

"Perhaps."

"We can stop now, if you wish," Kit offered, pleasantly surprising Rose. She thought fleetingly that were it the Duke of Bridgewater walking beside her, she wouldn't have dared show an interest in books.

'Twas freeing to be with a man she didn't care about.

"Later," Mum said. "I am anxious to see the house."

Finally they came to the end of the street. On the bucolic River Thames, swans glided majestically. Rose gazed across the Windsor Bridge toward the charming town of Eton. "Where do you live?" she asked Kit.

"Right here," he said, gesturing toward an imposing red-brick house that sat beside the river.

No, not a house. A *mansion.*

She consciously closed her gaping jaw. "It looks like Rand's house."

Her mother smiled. "Rand's house is white, not brick."

"But the style in which it is built . . ." Rose looked toward Kit, knowing he would understand what she meant. "It looks nothing like Windsor's dining room."

"The dining room reflects Charles's preferences, not my own."

"I like yours much better," she murmured as he led them under a small columned portico and into the house.

She paused on the threshold, admiring the clean, modern lines of the entry hall. The black marble floor was studded with small white marble diamonds. Smooth, pale stone walls were set off by classic dark oak molding. A high ceiling led to a corridor beyond, where Rose glimpsed a series of archways that vaguely reminded her of a vaulted cathedral.

As she'd said, it reminded her of the house Kit had built for Rand in Oxford. But better. Not to mention at least twice the size.

Kit Martyn was quite obviously a wealthy man.

"Mr. Martyn." A butler dressed in dark blue hurried to meet him. "Welcome home. Shall I have Mrs. Potts prepare dinner for three?" His inquisitive pale blue gaze swept Rose and her mother.

"Thank you, Graves, but I don't believe the ladies are staying long."

"As you say, sir." The butler took himself off.

"You wanted to see the house?" Kit asked, directing the question to Chrystabel.

"We'd love to," she assured him.

He led them through to a drawing room, all white paneled walls and a gray marble fireplace. The furniture was upholstered but not fussy, the windows large and tall, allowing sunshine to flood the room.

"I prefer natural light to candlelight," he told them. "Would you care to sit?"

"No," Rose breathed. "Show us the rest, please."

He shared a smile with her mother.

Rose's favorite room on the ground floor was the dining room, a complete contrast to King Charles's in its simplicity. Other than wide crown molding, the ceiling was smooth and white—at night it would reflect the light of the single carved oak chandelier that hovered over the round table. The walls were covered with dark oak paneling, rich and simple except for a few ornately carved sections above the fireplace.

"Sixteenth century, all of it." Kit waved the book he still held, indicating the wood that graced the walls. "I rescued it from a house I renovated—the owner wanted something more extravagant."

Rose turned in a slow circle. "Something more like Windsor Castle's decorations?"

"Very much."

"That owner has no taste," she declared.

Kit grinned. "Would you like to see upstairs?"

A small, exquisite stained-glass window threw colored light onto the curving staircase. "Another item I rescued," Kit said, waving the book at it, too. The bedchambers upstairs were not simply sleeping rooms, but suites—and there were many of them.

His sister's was peacock blue with a lovely canopied bed, a sitting room with a settle, a desk, and a marble fireplace, and a mirrored dressing room that made Rose fairly seethe with jealousy. They were also the only cluttered rooms in the house, with pretty little items decorating every flat surface. She wondered what his sister was like.

Kit's chamber boasted more classic oak paneling, a red-draped half-tester bed, and a beautiful sitting room surpassed only by the luxurious dressing room. It had the biggest bathtub Rose had ever seen—not a tub that the servants had dragged upstairs, but a permanent one positioned before a fireplace.

Rose could imagine herself in that bathtub, not to mention that bed. She hoped the Duke of Bridgewater lived half as nicely. Many of the estates she had visited were much too old and drafty, and she'd met quite a few men who seemed more than happy living with their grandmothers' choices in decor.

When the Ashcrofts had seen and admired everything,

Kit led them downstairs. "Ellen isn't here," he muttered darkly as though to himself. "Anywhere."

"Ellen?" Rose asked.

"My sister," he explained, rubbing the back of his neck. "Graves!" he called. The butler reappeared. "Will you send someone to the pawnshop to seek out Ellen? Should she be there, I wish to see her directly."

"Of course, sir." The butler went off, presumably to fetch and instruct a footman.

"Well." Kit set the book on a small marble-topped table in the entry. "I hope you enjoyed the grand tour."

"I did." In truth, Rose was overwhelmed. She'd never imagined a commoner would own such a lovely home. And Kit not only owned it, he'd designed it. He was responsible for the pleasing proportions of each room, the tasteful wall and window treatments, the spare but perfect accessories.

All it needed, she thought absurdly, was flowers. Yes, beautiful arrangements of flowers would be the crowning touch. Her fingers itched to design them. She'd use silver vases in simple classic shapes to match the house.

Chrystabel lifted the book. " 'Tis a shame you cannot read this."

"Languages." Kit flashed a self-deprecating smile. "The one subject I failed in school."

"Rose could read it to you. Could you not, dear?"

Rose was still planning her flower arrangements. Red, she thought, would suit this entry perfectly. The black-and-white floor called for something bold.

"I desperately need to lie down, but why don't you stay here and translate this book for Kit? I'm certain he can find someone to escort me home."

"Stay here?" Rose echoed, wrested from her vision of the multicolored arrangement she would create for the lovely dining room.

" 'Tis early still, and you have nothing else to do until Court this evening. 'Twould be a kindness."

She collected her thoughts and considered. Not only was

Mum right, she was known for being hospitable. While Rose herself was known, she knew, for being selfish. Inside, she'd never felt like the woman others seemed to perceive her, and if she wished to alter those perceptions, 'twould not be a bad thing to follow in her mother's hospitable footsteps.

And truth be told, she'd enjoy the challenge of translating a book on architecture. Although she generally hid her linguistic talents from men, Kit was just her brother-in-law's friend and—now that he was building the greenhouse—her father's hireling. She certainly didn't care if he thought she was too intelligent, since she wasn't interested in him as a husband.

"Rose?" her mother queried.

"Very well."

Kit's eyes lit, suddenly looking more green than brown. "Graves! It seems we'll be requiring dinner, after all."

Chapter Eight

Before Rose could change her mind, her mother had departed, and she and Kit were in the beautiful paneled dining room, a lovely dinner of beef in claret and carrot pudding set before them. To her surprise, she found Kit very good company.

" 'Tis odd," she realized in the middle of their meal. "You're quite easy to talk to."

A forkful of carrot pudding halfway to his mouth, he laughed. "Do you always say exactly what is on your mind?"

"Usually." Unless she was with a man she thought of as husband material; then she had to watch her words. Thankfully that wasn't the case here. "Do you not find it odd at all? After all, we hardly know each other."

"Perhaps we should get to know each other, then." He sipped thoughtfully from a goblet of Madeira. "What is your favorite color?"

"Red. Why?"

He met her eyes. "Color can say a lot about a person."

"Oh, yes?" She took a swallow of the sweet wine. "What do you suppose red says about me?"

"I imagine that you're decisive . . . and perhaps a bit daring."

She liked that description. "What is *your* favorite color?"

"The clear blue of a summer sky."

"But your bedchamber is red," she remembered.

"Red is also a color of power," he said, leaving her to ponder the significance of that.

Was he powerful in the bedchamber? What exactly did that mean? She felt her pulse flutter a little as she contemplated—

"Do you prefer sweet or savory?" he asked, interrupting her musings.

"Pardon?" She blinked and swallowed.

"To eat. Sweetmeats or real meats, which is it?"

"Oh, sweets, most definitely," she told him, a bit relieved to be on a different subject. Enjoying this game, she eyed a cherry tart one of his serving maids had placed on the table. "But I'm not passionate about it."

"Passionate?" He raised a brow.

Rose felt herself blush, certain he'd taken her statement the wrong way. "Violet's sister-in-law, Kendra—she'd have a wedge of that tart on her plate already. She always eats dessert first. In case she wouldn't have room for it later."

"Hmm. I like a passionate woman."

Her cheeks grew even hotter. "And you? Sweet or savory?"

"Give me a hunk of beef any day." He speared a piece of meat and popped it into his mouth. "Which do you enjoy more, Christmas or your birthday?"

"My birthday. 'Tis mine alone."

He sipped, looking amused. "But Christmas is a time for sharing."

"Exactly." Two could play this game. "What is your favorite book?"

His eyes narrowed as he considered. "*The Odyssey.*"

"Homer's *Odyssey*? In Greek?"

"Hell, no. George Chapman's version."

"Homer's is more poetic." She swallowed the last bite of the buttery carrot pudding. "Why do you like it?"

He set down his fork. "Odysseus faced terrible obstacles, but he persevered and triumphed in the end. I admire that sort of man, that sort of success."

He sounded very serious. "He did it for love," she reminded him.

"For his wife, Penelope, yes. She waited for him twenty years."

Rose dreamed of such enduring love, but she couldn't imagine waiting twenty years for anything. "Penelope was more patient than I."

He smiled. "What is *your* favorite book?"

"Aristotle's Master-piece," she said without hesitation, even though it was a scandalous marriage manual. It seemed she could tell him anything. "I learned much from that book."

"Did you?" That brow went up again, and she wondered if he knew what the book was about or was assuming it was Aristotelian philosophy. But his thoughtful expression didn't give him away. "Musically," he asked, "do you prefer instrumentals or songs?"

"Songs. I love to sing." To demonstrate, she trilled a few notes, then grinned when he smiled. "Do you sing?"

"Not where anyone can hear me." Still smiling, he sat back, twirling his goblet between his palms.

"My turn," she said, focusing on the pewter cup. "Red wine or white?"

"Red. Most definitely red. 'Tis richer, deeper, more complicated." He fixed that wicked gaze on her. "And you? Red or white?"

"Champagne," she said, feeling like she'd just sipped some.

"Rare and expensive. It fits."

Her face heated again. "The bubbles tickle my senses."

There was a definite pause, during which he looked as if he was going to respond but then thought better of it. "Are you early to bed or late to rise?" he asked instead.

"Both," she admitted with a chuckle. "But that is about to change. Last night I was so early to bed, I have no idea what time the Court festivities ended. Do you know, or did you seek your bed beforetime, too?"

"I never sought my bed at all. I had work that kept me there throughout the night."

Her jaw dropped. "You haven't slept?" She began to rise. "I must leave you to get some sleep, then. Although my mother's heart was in the right place when she suggested I read to you, she was clearly unaware of the circumstances."

He rose and helped her to stand, his hand warm on her arm through the thin silk of her purple gown. Her skin seemed to prickle underneath.

"No, I would have you stay and read," he said. "If you're finished with your dinner, we'll adjourn to the drawing room."

"But you must be exhausted—"

"Think of it as a bedtime story, then."

She laughed, and his eyes glittered green in response. "Honestly," he added, "tonight will be soon enough for me to rest. I'm accustomed to keeping long hours when a project demands it."

And that was just the point, wasn't it? she thought as she let him guide her back through the entry and into the light-flooded drawing room. The people in her life had no demands that would keep them up all the night—or at least none they hadn't put on themselves. She had nothing in common with this man.

But despite that—despite *herself*—she liked him. His ease, his self-confidence, his quick sense of humor. In fact, she liked him a little too much. When he fetched the book and sat beside her on the pale moss green settle, she briefly considered moving to a chair. But considering they needed to work from the same book, that would be silly—not to mention insulting.

She took the book from him. "'*Perspectiva Pictorum et Architectorum,*'" she read aloud, "which means, 'Perspective in Architecture and Painting,' by Andrea Pozzo."

"Just as I thought." He reached to open the cover and flip pages, and she caught a whiff of his scent again—the same mix of frankincense and myrrh that she remembered him wearing at Lily's wedding. 'Twas woodsy and masculine and made the champagne bubbles dance in her stomach, no matter that she'd been drinking Madeira instead.

She would have to try to duplicate it. Perhaps the Duke of Bridgewater would like some.

"See here," Kit said. "There's a sketch of how to properly mount paper on a board for drawing. I've done it, but I couldn't tell what to do after that." He rose and strode across the room to a desk, lifted a piece of wood with sheets of parchment tacked to it. "What does that page say?"

"To the lovers of perspective. The art of perspective does, with wonderful pleasure, deceive the eye, the most subtle of all our outward senses . . ."

While she read, Kit grabbed an inkwell and quill and wandered back to sit beside her.

She turned the page. "This section is called 'Explanation of the lines of the plan and horizon, and of the points of the eye and of the distance.'" She read on, turning the Latin into English as she went. "That you may better understand the principles of perspective, here is presented to your view a temple, on the inner wall of which . . ."

With quick, precise motions, he sketched the lines of the classic Greek temple pictured beside the Latin words. He nodded as he followed her translated instructions, adding a man—tiny, as fit the proportions—standing before the structure with its high, arched windows.

"Let me see," she said when she'd finished reading the page.

He set down the quill and turned the sketch board to face her. "What do you think?"

"'Tis lovely."

"Just lovely?"

"Well, you've drawn it skillfully, of course."

He smiled. "'Tis a perfectly proportioned structure. Can you see the way the arched windows echo the arches in the rest of the building? A true thing of beauty."

If she couldn't quite appreciate the structure itself, she couldn't help but notice his enthusiasm. "You find buildings beautiful."

"Not all buildings, but the well-designed ones." He cocked his head, piercing her with those all-seeing eyes. "What do you find beautiful?"

A little flutter skittered through her, but she ignored it. "Are we back to playing the getting-to-know-each-other game?"

"Tell me. Beauty is . . ."

"Oh, flowers, jewelry, rainbows—"

"No. Not what others find beautiful; what *you* find beautiful. For example, this curve of cheek to chin"—he reached a long finger to trace along her face—"is a thing of beauty."

She shivered.

"Tell me," he said softly.

Your eyes, she thought. *Your voice, when you talk like that. Your ideas . . .*

"Flowers," she repeated aloud. But then she added, "When they've just been kissed by the rain."

He nodded solemnly. "What else?"

"Children's laughter."

"And?"

"The sun reflecting off the Thames at dusk."

He seemed to be staring at her mouth. "Yes."

Her lips tingling, she licked them. "And my sister, playing the harpsichord. Even more beautiful when her husband sings with her."

Kit nodded again. "Rand has an incredible voice."

"Yes, he does." And it didn't hurt anymore to think of him as Lily's husband.

"How about," Kit suggested, "the first blade of grass that pushes through the ground in the springtime?"

"Oh, yes." Yes, she'd never thought of it before, but a blade of grass could be a thing of beauty.

"Church bells ringing through the fog."

"Fog," she repeated. "Tendrils of fog creeping over the rooftops of London."

"The fog in London?" Laughing, he picked up his sketch board and ripped off the top sheet of paper. "Perhaps we are getting carried away. Read on, please."

She hesitated a moment, wishing the game could continue. "'*Figura Tertia*—The Third Figure. The delineation of an oblong square in perspective . . .'"

Rose read while Kit sketched all that pleasant long afternoon. And the longer he spent with her, the more he wanted her. She was much more than just a pretty face. He'd known that, somehow—known it in his gut before he'd even really known her. But now he knew for sure.

"You've never seen these buildings," she commented after translating the text accompanying several more figures. Eleven, or maybe twelve—he'd lost count. "In person, I mean. Have you?"

"No." He placed the sketch board facedown on the table and stuck the quill into the inkwell. "I've always dreamed of traveling to Italy to study the classical buildings, but"—he couldn't help but laugh at himself—"I fear to do so, since my one failing in school was languages."

"I've never been out of Britain." Her dark eyes grew even darker, hazy. "I'd dearly love to go to Italy, too—to travel anywhere, really, where I could see the world and make use of all my languages."

"How many?" he asked.

"I don't know." She lifted one shoulder in an elegant shrug. "I've never counted. Ten, eleven . . . maybe more. You get to a point where new languages become easier, where the words and grammar parallel ones you've already learned."

"*You* get to that point," he said, then smiled when she laughed.

She was charming in that easy dismissal of her abilities. And she shared his dream, to travel. Although it was clear she wasn't talking about traveling with *him,* Kit couldn't help but remember her mother's matchmaking hopes and think that such a talented wife could assist him not only in the study of architecture, but to go far in other ways.

And Rose was kind, too—willing to sit with him all the day and patiently translate his book. He enjoyed her quick laughter, her ready wit.

She returned his smile, displaying dimples that made his own smile widen more. He wanted to kiss those little indentations, one on each side, then settle warm on her mouth.

"You must have done well in school overall, though," she said, startling him back to reality, "in order to get where you are today."

He shook his head to clear it. "I did fine in my other subjects. I had to."

"What do you mean?"

"My parents both perished in 'sixty-five—"

"The Great Plague."

"Yes." That year of horror. "Did it not affect your family?" he asked.

"We went off to Tremayne, a castle my grandfather owned near Wales. 'Tis Rowan's now. We were safe there. Isolated."

"We weren't," Kit said succinctly. "My father was a carpenter, my mother a secretary and housekeeper for a local widowed noblewoman. They owned no land; we had no place to go."

"I'm sorry," she said. "Do you miss them terribly?"

"I did, but 'tis been twelve years. My sister, Ellen, was but six when they died. She only remembers snatches of that life."

"But you remember your parents well."

"My mother was the daughter of a cleric, and she taught us how to read. My father taught me how to build. They were good people." Not that that had saved their lives. The few titled families in the area had escaped before falling ill, but common folk like the Martyns hadn't any choice but to stay behind. Kit and Ellen had survived, but their parents had not.

The Martyns, Kit had resolved—what remained of them—would not be left behind ever again.

Rose leaned closer and laid a hand over his. "What happened after they passed on?"

"I was sixteen and determined to care for my sister, but we had no income, after all. Alone in our tiny cottage, we almost starved."

Her fingers tightened on his, and she leaned closer still, swamping him with her rich, floral scent. "Oh, Kit . . ."

He waved off the sympathy. 'Twould do him no good. He'd long ago learned to face life's problems and work toward solutions. Wallowing in self-pity got one nowhere.

"When my mother's employer, Lady St. Vincent, returned to Hawkridge after the danger had passed, she felt great remorse for having left our family behind. Accordingly, she took in Ellen and sent me to Westminster School. She saw to it that I was made a King's Scholar and promised to send me on to university if I did well. So I did," he concluded simply.

He'd been given a chance in life, and he hadn't been about to waste it.

"Did she follow through with her promise?"

"Absolutely. She sent me to Oxford, and not on charity, either. She paid my expenses and made sure I was treated as well as the best." He waited a beat, hoping Rose would say he *was* the best, as good as all the titled lads at school.

But she didn't, of course. She hadn't been raised in a world that believed that.

She glanced down to their connected hands, looked startled and pulled hers back. "You enjoyed your years at Oxford," she said. "I can hear it in your voice."

"I was anxious to finish and get on with life, but the years were hardly a trial. Rand was there, a Fellow already—we'd been friends since childhood. And a few stu-

dents from Westminster School ended up there, too. Gaylord Craig—"

"The Earl of Rosslyn?"

From the tone of her voice, he gathered she didn't like
the man. "You know him?"

"I met him last night. He's your friend?"

"Of a sort. We were never close, but I always got on with
everyone."

"I'm not surprised," she said, sounding as though she
meant it.

Perhaps he was making inroads, he thought with an in-
ward smile.

She licked her lips, and he wanted to kiss off that delicious sheen. "Someone's here," she said.

He heard footsteps on the marble in the entry, the low
murmur of Graves's voice followed by one with a higher
pitch.

"That will be my sister, Ellen," he told her, rising. "Will
you excuse me?"

Chapter Nine

As Rose watched Kit leave the room, a clock somewhere in the house struck the hour, chiming six times. Where had the afternoon gone? The bookshop would have closed by now, and she'd wanted some reading material to pass the long, empty days at the castle. Court would be commencing soon, and she'd wanted time to rest. And she needed time to choose a gown and ready herself.

Mum must have been very tired, because surely she'd have come to fetch her if she wasn't still napping.

Voices sifted through the drawing room's closed door. Rose couldn't tell what Kit was saying, but he didn't sound happy. She couldn't understand his sister's replies, either, but Ellen was clearly giving as good as she got.

Rose hadn't even met Ellen, and she liked her already. Smiling to herself, she idly reached for Kit's sketch board and turned it faceup.

Her heart skipped a beat. Stunned, she could only stare. He hadn't been drawing Greek temples or Roman theaters.

He'd been sketching *her.*

And he'd captured her perfectly. She still stared, mesmerized. The woman staring back was not the flirting Rose, the one with the big smile. Instead her lips curved as though she shared a secret, her eyes glittered not with forced gaiety, but with simple pleasure in what she was doing.

Translating a book. Sharing a quiet afternoon.

'Twas not a painting, nor a work of careful artistry. The black ink on white gave no hint that her gown was a rich purple, her cheeks were pink with carefully applied cosmetics, her lips were dyed red and ripe. The drawing was plain and stark. True.

'Twas the Rose not many people ever saw.

How had he seen the real Rose? she wondered. And what had made him sketch her while she was describing how to draw classical buildings?

She blew out a shaky breath as Kit and Ellen barged in.

"I am entitled to live my own life," Ellen said, continuing their argument as though Rose were not there. "And you had no right having me fetched from the pawnshop as though I were your property."

"You *are* my property," Kit ground out. "Until you're wed—"

"Let me wed, then, and we'll both be happier."

"Not if you wed *him.*"

"Him?" Rose asked.

They both turned to look at her, fire and surprise in their matching eyes.

"Thomas Whittingham." Ellen tossed her head of long jet hair.

"A pawnbroker," Kit spat.

Rose set down Kit's sketch and stood. "I'm Rose Ashcroft," she said to Ellen. "Tell me about this pawnbroker."

"My apologies for not introducing you." Kit's gaze nervously snapped between Rose's face and the drawing he'd done of her. He took a deep breath. "Lady Rose, this is my sister, Ellen. Ellen—"

"*Lady* Rose," Ellen drawled before her brother could complete the belated introduction. "Do you not think, Kit, that you're aiming a bit out of your range?"

"We're just friends," Rose rushed to clarify.

Surprisingly, she really *did* feel Kit was a friend. The pleasant afternoon had changed her view of him entirely.

But she wanted to be Ellen's friend, too. With her sisters

both married and moved away, and the women at Court giving her the cold shoulder, she desperately needed a female friend. And she sensed Ellen could be one. She liked this forthright woman.

She sat again and patted the seat beside her. "Tell me about this pawnbroker," she repeated.

Ellen slid onto the settle and folded her hands in her lap, a female version of Kit dressed in an innocent tone of yellow. "He's kind and generous and handsome, and I love him."

"She wants to marry him," Kit said derisively. He swept the sketch board off the table and crossed the room to place it facedown on the desk. "I'll not see her wed to a pawnbroker. To go from this"—he waved a hand, indicating the house, the life he'd built for the two of them—"to live above a pawnshop, is—"

"—what I want," Ellen finished for him. Then she met Rose's eyes, her own pleading.

Apparently they were friends already.

"How old are you?" Rose asked.

"Eighteen."

Rose had fancied herself in love at eighteen, too. But she knew now, having seen her sisters find love, that she'd been wrong. She knew now she'd never been in love at all.

Even once.

"You're young yet," she said gently. "Can you not wait a while? Perhaps you'll find—"

"I *love* him. Kit has no right to dictate my life."

Ellen was wrong; legally, Kit had every right. But Rose was torn between that truth and the fact that she believed, truly believed, that women should be allowed to make these decisions for themselves. She knew her own parents were considered odd for permitting it, but she'd also listened to hours upon hours of her sister Violet spouting all her radical philosophy.

Violet thought she never paid attention, but that simply wasn't true.

And yet . . . she looked to Kit, who only spread his hands and shrugged an exasperated shoulder. And back to Ellen, who looked so much like her brother. Just as hot-tempered too, from all indications. They probably butted heads precisely because they were so much alike.

But Ellen was young yet. And Rose had never before felt so old.

"Do you know, Ellen," she said carefully, " 'tis as easy to fall in love with a titled man as one without."

"Oh!" Ellen cried. "You don't understand!" Tears sprang to her eyes as she jumped up and ran from the room.

Rose and Kit listened to his sister's footsteps until they faded up the stairs. "She likes you," he finally said.

"And our navy will conquer the Dutch tomorrow." Rose sighed. "I think I'd best return home."

"Home" right now for Rose was Windsor Castle. That was what Kit wanted for Ellen—the rank that would give her the security of feeling at home in a castle. Or anywhere. The rank that would assure that she would never be left behind.

And yet, when Rose had supported his position, he'd found himself not grateful, but vexed. Her voice still echoed in his ears, so measured and reasonable.

'Tis as easy to fall in love with a titled man as one without.

Never mind that it was exactly what Ellen needed to hear, Rose's attitude didn't bode well for his own suit.

The sun was setting as he walked her back to the apartment she was sharing with her mother, the two of them chatting amiably. All the way past the Round Tower, into an Upper Ward building, and up a staircase, he listened to her amusing banter and watched her mobile lips.

Lips that begged for a kiss.

When she reached for the door latch, he stopped her with a hand over hers, and she turned and looked up at him, her dark eyes questioning.

"Thank you for a pleasant day," he said quietly, watching the light dance over her face from the single torch that illuminated the deserted corridor. "And for the translation. 'Twas much appreciated."

"You're very welcome," she said, looking relieved. "I enjoyed myself."

He felt her trying to draw back her hand, but held it tight in his. There was something between them, whether she knew it—or wanted it—or not. "I'm happy to hear that," he told her.

She gifted him with a tentative smile. "No, I mean I *truly* enjoyed myself. I can see why Rand is happy to count you as a friend. You're the best—like a brother, but better."

Kit didn't want to be Rose's brother. Her mother had given him hope, but she'd warned that the decision was Rose's—apparently for good reason.

Like a brother. He had to respect that, didn't he? Respect her. His heart heavy, he released her hand, then leaned to give her an innocent, brotherly thank-you kiss, a brush of lips against cheek.

She smelled of roses, pure and heady. He felt something—an involuntary sway of her body toward his, an indefinable spark—and all his resolve simply melted away.

His mouth slid across her satin skin, past a hidden dimple he'd wanted to kiss earlier, and met her lips in a sudden rush of heat. A consuming heat. His arms wound around her to draw her close. Locked against him, she was everything he'd dreamed of and more.

And Rose's world turned over.

She didn't like kisses, hadn't wanted one, but his mouth seemed made to fit hers. Tender and urgent all at once, his kiss was a delicious sensation. Wantonly, she pressed herself closer, reveling in the feel of his hard body against her softness. An odd ripple shuddered through her, and her knees weakened.

This dreamy intimacy felt nothing like the other kisses she'd experienced.

She inhaled his woodsy scent, drawing his essence inside her. He nipped at her lips, then traced the line between them, inciting shivers, making heat pool in her middle.

Then his tongue delved inside to touch hers, but it didn't feel intrusive. Her senses skidded and whirled. She returned the caress, and it turned into an exciting, tangled dance.

All too soon, he drew away, leaving her shaking. And stunned. A sigh eased out between her still-parted lips.

Kit's kiss had been every bit as wondrous as those her sisters had described. A thing of beauty, she thought dizzily. But she didn't say it aloud, because she feared he would take it the wrong way. Not to mention she felt incapable of saying anything just at the moment.

His eyes glittered green in the torchlight, his gaze piercing right into her as though he could divine her scrambled thoughts. As she watched, his mouth curved into a faint smile that might have been smug.

"Good night," he said and walked away.

Chapter Ten

Rose closed the lodging's door and leaned back against it, then released a long, long sigh. A sigh of relief.

She didn't dislike kissing after all!

Kit, of course, had no business kissing her, but she couldn't find it in herself to be sorry he'd done so. She'd watched him walk away, knowing she should call after him, berate him for having the nerve to take such a liberty, inform him that he was never to do so again.

But she hadn't found the strength to do that. She'd felt weak, boneless. And happy—so happy to find that nothing was wrong with her. She enjoyed kissing! And somehow, after experiencing Kit's kiss, she knew that she would enjoy the other things that happened between a man and a woman. All the things that the marriage manual *Aristotle's Master-piece* had described . . . those things she'd been so eager to try until she'd tried kissing and decided it wasn't to her taste.

Now she knew differently. How silly she'd been to jump to such a conclusion. Obviously a woman's enjoyment of kissing depended on the skill of the man. How unlucky she'd been to kiss so many men and never find a talented one until now.

"Dear? Are you out there?"

"Yes, Mum." Rose took a deep, calming breath and crossed the small sitting room toward the even smaller bed-chamber she and her mother were sharing.

Chrystabel was seated at the heavy carved wood dressing table. While her maid Anne twisted the back section of her hair up into a bun, she tore a small sheet of Spanish paper from a tiny booklet and rubbed it lightly on her cheeks. "Did you have a nice time, dear?"

Feeling heat flare in her face, Rose was glad her mother was busy looking in the mirror. " 'Twas a fine day," she said carefully, not wanting to sound too enthusiastic.

She certainly didn't want her mother finding out she'd allowed Kit—a commoner!—to kiss her.

Mum set down the Spanish paper and lifted a kohl pencil. "What did you do?" she asked, carefully rimming an eye.

"Oh, we had dinner and then I translated part of the book." The sound of an ungraceful snore drew Rose's gaze to Harriet, dead to the world on a pallet laid out on the floor. Shaking her head, she crossed to her trunk and rummaged through it herself. "I met Kit's sister, Ellen."

"Was she nice?"

Rose held up a frosty pink gown and then rejected it; she was feeling much bolder than that. "I liked her. But she is eighteen and fancies herself in love. With a *pawnbroker*."

"Perhaps she *is* in love. And in a bustling town like this, a pawnshop is likely to be a thriving business."

"She can do much better than to live life above a pawnshop. Look at the house she's living in now!"

Chrystabel turned to her, raising one kohl-darkened brow. "You liked it."

"Kit's house?" Rose shook out a bright red gown. Perfect. She laid it on the old canopied bed. " 'Twas very impressive. It must be lovely to live right on the river like that. And the house is beautifully designed."

Another thing of beauty, she thought, standing over her sleeping maid. "Harriet!" she called softly.

The girl bolted upright. "Yes, milady." She scrambled to her feet. "Forgive me, milady."

Rose waved a dismissive hand, thinking she was a mite tired herself.

"You like the house's designer, too," her mother said.

"Kit? He's a pleasant man." Memories flashed—his smile, his laughter, his eyes . . . his kiss. Rose shivered, then made a show of rubbing her arms, moving closer to the fire in the grate. Curling tongs sat in the embers, heating. " 'Tis cold in this stone building, do you not think?"

"Not particularly."

Her mother's gaze was making her uncomfortable, so she turned to let Harriet unlace her gown. "I've been thinking, Mum . . ."

Shifting back to the mirror, Chrystabel opened a little jar of pomade. "Yes?"

"You've always cautioned us to kiss a man before we agree to marry him. I think that is *excellent* advice. I believe that if I see Ellen again, I will tell her. Perhaps she will find she doesn't love the pawnbroker, after all."

Chrystabel slicked the pomade on her lips, then stood and waved Rose toward the stool in her stead. "Love has to do with more than kisses, dear."

"Well, of course it does!" Rose settled herself, watching in the mirror as Harriet slid the pins from her hair. "But since a woman is expected to kiss her husband, she should at least make sure she likes it."

She leaned forward, darkening her lashes with the end of a burnt cork while Harriet used the hot tongs to fashion perfect ringlets. It was really too bad the Duke of Bridgewater was such an abysmal kisser. He'd seemed so perfect.

Well, there were other suitable, handsome men at Court. With any luck, she wouldn't have to kiss them all before she found one as talented as Kit.

"Kisses," Harriet murmured with a sigh.

Chrystabel stepped into high Louis-heeled shoes fashioned of golden brocade to match her gown. "Have you met any men here at Windsor yet, Harriet?"

The girl's freckles went three shades darker. "No."

"Harriet is shy," Anne put in.

"Well." Chrystabel straightened and gave her skirts a shake. "We shall have to see about an introduction."

Rose barely resisted an impulse to snort. Whoever heard of "introductions" for servants? Only her hopelessly romantic mother would even think of such a thing. "Mum," she started.

"Yes, dear?"

On the other hand . . . at least Mum didn't seem to be foisting any men upon *her*.

"Never mind," she said lightly, thanking her lucky stars her mother had found someone else to bedevil. The last thing she needed was interference in her love life.

Better Chrystabel busy herself matching Harriet.

Kit looked down the hill toward Ellen dragging along behind. "Come along, will you?" Walking backward, he squinted at her in the darkness. "What is that you're carrying?"

"A book."

"A book?" He stopped to wait for her to catch up. "Since when do you spend your time reading?"

"Since you went stark raving mad and decided I had to spend half the night watching you work. Since then." 'Twas dark as hell, too dim to see her expression, but he could hear the pout in her voice. "Why will you not let me stay home?"

"I would let you stay home if you *would* stay home. But I know you, and you won't. I'd return to find you're at the pawnshop again."

"I love him," she said for the hundredth time. Or maybe the millionth.

"I want better for you."

As they passed through the gate at Windsor, the drowsy old scarlet-uniformed guard snapped to attention. "Evening, Mr. Martyn."

"Evening, Richards."

The man narrowed his rheumy eyes. "Who goes with you?"

"My sister."

"Pretty thing." He smiled, displaying half a mouth of teeth. "Go on through."

"My thanks." In the torchlight of the gateway, Kit glanced again at the book clutched to Ellen's chest. "Where'd you get that? 'Tis not even English."

She clutched the book tighter, as though she were afraid he might snatch it from her hands. "You don't want to know."

"Whittingham?"

"Maybe."

"He's a pawnbroker. Can he even read? Why would he give you a foreign book?"

He thought perhaps she blushed, but they were still walking and had left the circle of torchlight, so he couldn't be sure. "I am hoping your friend Rose can translate it for me," she said, neatly evading his question.

"She's not my friend." He didn't want to be Rose's friend. He didn't want to be her brother, either. He hoped he'd made that clear earlier this evening.

"You drew a picture of her."

"You weren't supposed to see that."

"'Twas good," she grudgingly said. "You should draw pictures more often. Of things besides buildings, I mean."

"I'm too busy trying to make you a good life."

Her answer to that was a sullen silence.

He sighed as they skirted the Round Tower. "You cannot see Rose tonight. You'll be at my construction site. She'll be at Court." He wouldn't walk Ellen through the King's chambers—they would take the long way around. "Ellen Martyn does not belong at Court. Until, that is, she marries a title."

"I'm marrying a pawnbroker," she said.

*   *   *

Rose had kissed three men already—one behind the heavy velvet curtains in the huge bay window, one in the little unfinished vestibule, and one out on the terrace . . . and she'd loathed all three experiences.

But at least her quest was getting easier. The first two men had been pleasantly shocked when she'd asked them for a kiss, but the third had come to *her.*

And here came another, swaggering her way. Trying to appear casual, she leaned a hand on the solid silver table by the wall where she stood. It felt cold—and very expensive—under her fingers.

"Lovely, isn't it?" the man asked, coming to a stop before her. She looked him up and down. Although he wasn't any taller than she, he wasn't shorter either, and he had a pleasing face.

"The engraved top is nice," she said, unable to summon yet another charming and flirtatious reply.

Her face hurt from smiling so much.

He tried again. "Louis the Fourteenth has silver furniture like this all over Versailles."

"Does he? Gemini, that palace must be even more overblown than this one."

He appeared nonplussed. "I don't believe I've had the pleasure of an introduction."

She lazily waved her fan while she considered him. His hair was covered by a long, curled periwig, but she guessed from his fair complexion that it was blond. That was, if he wasn't bald underneath—but she could hope not. His periwinkle suit wasn't too ostentatious, adorned with just enough jewels to make known his wealth.

He would do.

"Lady Rose Ashcroft," she replied with a calculated smile.

He took her free hand and raised it to his lips, pressing a kiss to the back. A bit wet, but not totally disgusting. "Lord Cravenhurst at your service."

His voice wasn't too grating, and, unlike the last man,

she guessed he'd bathed within the week. His perfume was light and not too cloying. Perhaps he'd ask her to dance before claiming a kiss. That would be nice.

But she was not to be so lucky. He leaned close, sneaking a peek at himself in the silver-framed mirror above the table. "I hear you enjoy kissing," he uttered in a confidential tone.

Rose fluttered her lashes. "Why, yes, actually, I do." If it was with the right man.

Maybe he would be the one.

Although she would prefer a dance—or sitting somewhere alone where she could put her feet up—she allowed him to guide her behind the curtain again. There was a good view over Eton, but apparently he didn't feel like looking. One arm came around to clamp her tight, and his mouth descended on hers, parting her lips immediately.

She dropped her fan. He tasted funny, and his tongue felt slimy. When he snaked a hand down her bodice, she gasped and shoved him away. "I never gave you leave to do that!"

He didn't look at all fazed. "I was told you were a wild one."

"By whom?"

He shrugged. " 'Tis all the buzz."

"Well, the buzz is wrong. A kiss is not an invitation to be mauled." One hand went to cover her probably bruised breast while she tossed open the curtain with the other. "Now go out there and tell everyone they were mistaken."

"And let them all know you refused my advances? I think not," he huffed and stalked away.

She barely had time to catch her breath before another man hurried over.

The Earl of Rosslyn, Kit's friend. Since they'd already been introduced, he wasted no time on preliminaries. "My lady," he said with a bow, "I have it on good faith that you particularly enjoy kissing."

The cur. "You're married!"

He grinned. "Then you know I have much experience."

"What I *know* is that you're an adulterer."

"Why should that matter?"

Indeed. Looking around the chamber, she spotted couples in all sorts of embraces, doing everything, it seemed, short of actual coupling—and she had grave doubts that most of them were married. To each other, at least.

And where was her mother? She might as well have come here by herself for all the chaperoning she was receiving.

She scooped her folded fan off the floor, half tempted to bash Rosslyn on the nose with it. "Go away," she told him instead.

To her vast relief, he did. She aimed a shaky smile at two passing women, but they both pointedly avoided her gaze, whispering behind their fans. And yet another man was headed in her direction.

The Duke of Bridgewater, she realized, her tension easing. At least he was a real gentleman. He was wearing russet tonight and looked even more aristocratic than she'd remembered. She composed herself as he drew nearer, opening her fan and curving her mouth in welcome.

"Gabriel," she greeted softly with a sigh. "Where have you been all this evening?"

"I was detained until now," he apologized smoothly, "and I've dearly missed your company. Was Rosslyn bothering you?"

In truth she could take care of herself—had she not just proven it? But she sidled up to him, waving the fan coquettishly. "I'm glad you arrived to protect me."

"You're in good hands, my dear." Looking pleased, he linked an arm through hers and started guiding her toward the terrace.

Good God, the blasted terrace again.

"Would you not rather dance?" she asked, then whirled at hearing the meaty sound of a fist connecting with someone's skull.

Nell Gwyn's voice carried across the chamber. "Don't

make me sorry I talked Charles into releasing you from the Tower!" she spat as she stalked off.

The Duke of Buckingham stood watching her go, his mouth hanging open, one hand held to the spot above his ear where petite Nell's punch had apparently landed.

What a woman. Rose wanted to applaud.

Gabriel reclaimed her arm. "Come along."

"What happened?" she asked.

"The idiot tried to kiss her." The duke managed to har-rumph in a genteel manner. "Everyone knows that unlike Louise and Barbara, Nell is totally devoted to Charles."

"Is she?" Rose wondered, gratified to discover that this was possible even at Court.

"Oh, yes. She has never slept with another man since Charles made her his mistress. Nine years, almost."

Gabriel's apparent amazement at that feat gave Rose pause, but she consoled herself that at least he sounded ad-miring. She glanced back at the Duke of Buckingham, who still stood rooted in place. Even with his long black peri-wig all mussed, he looked entirely too dignified to have re-cently been a prisoner. "Why on earth was he in the Tower of London?"

"He's not the first man Charles has clapped in there, and he certainly won't be the last. 'Tis political, my dear. You wouldn't understand."

Certain she *would* understand, Rose was about to ask for an explanation when he added, "Are you and your lovely mother coming along to Hampton Court tomorrow?"

Rose blinked, effectively diverted. "Hampton Court?"

"Have you not heard? The Court is moving—getting ever closer to London as it were. The household will spend a few weeks at Hampton Court and then move to Whitehall for the winter, in time for the Queen's birthday celebration on the fourteenth of November." He guided her toward the door. "Will you be coming along?"

"I know not. I suppose I will have to ask my mother."

"Well, I certainly hope she'll agree. I would feel bereft without your company."

He sounded sincere, and she couldn't help but respond to his flattery. He really was the most handsome of all the courtiers. And the tallest—only King Charles was taller—not to mention the highest ranked.

There was the kissing problem, of course, but having experienced an excellent kiss herself, maybe she could teach him how to perform one.

'Twas worth a try, she decided as he drew her out to the blasted terrace. She was getting nowhere in her search.

Chapter Eleven

"**B**urning the midnight oil, eh, Martyn?"

Working in the blaze of torches and candelabra for the second night in a row, Kit looked up from his plans to see the Earl of Rosslyn. He offered his old friend a wry smile. "Oil lamps are a bit dim for my purpose, but you've got the gist of it, yes."

Rosslyn paced the chamber with an elegant swagger, his tall walking stick clicking as he progressed. He paused, watching men and supplies go in and out of the two sizable holes cut in the ceiling that gave access to the area above, where Kit's crew was busy reinforcing the structure. "'Tis coming along nicely."

"Thank you." While unsurprised that his rival should check on his progress, Kit was pleased with the man's pleasant tone. "And your own projects?"

"Oh, fine, fine." Rosslyn pulled a tortoiseshell snuffbox from his pocket. "You've done an excellent job recovering here, Martyn. But then, you always were up to the task, weren't you?"

Kit could remember a few occasions, back in their school days, when Rosslyn *hadn't* been up to the task. But then, he'd had no compelling reason to excel, as Kit had. The secure life of a nobleman had been awaiting him.

"What made you become an architect?" Kit asked.

Having partaken of a pinch of snuff, Rosslyn sneezed. "Monuments."

"Monuments?"

"I wish to leave something behind. Something so men will say there went Gaylord Craig, the Earl of Rosslyn."

The man wasn't as shallow as Kit had thought. "Your theater in London is a masterpiece," he conceded.

"I rather prefer my last church. But I thank you." Rosslyn tucked the snuffbox back into his pocket. "Well, the ladies are waiting. I shall leave you to it." He turned on a high heel and swaggered toward the door, letting loose another sneeze followed by an "Oof!"

"Pardon me!" Lady Trentingham exclaimed.

"My apologies, my lady." Holding his walking stick in a wide stance, Rosslyn swept her a deep bow. "I was just leaving."

She turned and watched the man mince away.

"Lady Trentingham," Kit called over the bangs and scrapes of construction.

Rose's mother looked over and smiled. "Good evening," she greeted him, her own voice carrying well. He supposed that came of dealing with her half-deaf husband. She walked farther into the dining room, lifting the hem of her gown to step over a few boards and skirt her way around a sawhorse. "My, that scaffolding went up quickly."

"That's why I'm here," he told her, shooting a glance to his crew. "I long ago learned that my presence makes all the difference." He rolled up the plans. "Can I help you with something?"

She met his gaze, her own forthright. "I am wondering what happened this afternoon with my daughter."

Kit slanted a look at Ellen. She'd stopped sulking and had her nose buried in her book. He would have to take a look and see what she was finding so fascinating.

In the meantime, though, he'd rather not have her hear his answer to Lady Trentingham's question. In fact, he was damned uncomfortable at the thought of answering the question at all. No matter that she'd encouraged his suit, the Countess of Trentingham was unlikely to approve of Mr.

Christopher Martyn kissing her high-born daughter before there was a formal commitment.

He supposed there was nothing for it, but he wouldn't humiliate himself in front of his sister. "Would you mind stepping out onto the terrace?" he asked Rose's mother. "I feel the need for some fresh air."

The pounding of hammers and scraping of saws receded as they exited the room, leaving a pleasant quietness in their wake. The terrace was deserted, and for a minute or so, Kit procrastinated, listening to the tandem sounds of their footsteps, the thud of his heavy boots and the click of her feminine heels.

"I know you told me Rose is innocent," he finally began. "But—"

Her sudden laughter was startling. "So you kissed her, hmm? Good for you. I suspected as much when she came in babbling about what an excellent idea it is for a woman to kiss a man before she marries him."

"Before she marries him?" he echoed. His heart suddenly threatened to beat its way out of his chest. He and Rose had enjoyed a nice afternoon, and an incredible kiss, but surely she wouldn't be swayed that easily. "She cannot be thinking to marry me," he said, hoping against hope he was wrong.

"No. Not yet, anyway. At the moment, she seems to be looking for another man with your skill. Interviewing them, you might say."

Now his heart threatened to stop. "She's kissing other men?"

"Not very successfully, from what I can tell. And unfortunately, she seems to be acquiring quite a reputation. As a mother, I'm a mite concerned about that. I am considering leaving tomorrow; I believe Rose could benefit from a short break from Court."

Kit's head was spinning. He knew full well he had no right to be vexed at Rose for kissing other men, but he couldn't control his gut reaction.

His gut didn't like it.

And if Lady Trentingham wasn't angry because he'd kissed her daughter, what did she want with him?

He slid a hand into his pocket. "Charles is leaving Windsor anyway, and everyone else will follow him, of course. To Hampton Court."

"A perfect excuse, then, should I decide to take our leave." She walked to the edge of the terrace and gazed over the wall at the darkened Thames Valley. "As for Rose being innocent . . ."

He came up beside her. "Yes?"

"Well, for the record, my daughter may tell you that I heartily approve of kissing."

He blinked. "You heartily approve?"

"Yes, of kissing and—in your case—most anything else it takes to convince Rose you're the only man for her." She paused—for effect, he suspected. "Do you understand?"

His fingers gripped the top of the wall so tightly that stone scraped flesh. Thank God she was still looking at the landscape. "You cannot mean . . ." He couldn't say more.

"Nothing that would get her with child—and that's an absolute."

"Of course," he choked out. Lord Almighty. Could she be telling him to make love to her daughter? Not to culmination, but—

Her laughter pierced the night again, and he turned his head to find her looking straight at him. "You've gone white; I can tell even by this dismal torchlight. Surely that is not such a daunting task? Or an unpleasant one?"

Words stuck in his throat. She was Rose's mother. He couldn't bring himself to tell her that seducing her daughter would certainly be pleasant, indeed.

When she laid a hand on his arm, the gesture eased some of the shock. "As my husband is fond of reminding me," she said softly, "I was not a nun before we wed. I don't expect my daughter to remain one, either. But I'll not have her risking a child out of wedlock, and the decision of whom she will marry will absolutely remain hers."

He would never—*never*—have considered telling a man to make love to his sister—even up to only a certain safe point. Even were it a fine nobleman he hoped she would marry. In fact, short of marriage, he would tell any man to keep his hands the hell to himself.

But Rose's mother must know her very well.

"She'll be in good hands," he promised her.

She squeezed his arm before releasing it. "I'm counting on it."

Even the King had tried to steal a kiss! As he and Rose had ended a minuet, he'd murmured his intentions in a low, velvet-edged voice and then leaned close, apparently unconcerned that anyone might be watching. Luckily, Gabriel had walked up right then to claim she had promised him the next dance, because Rose had no idea how to gracefully turn down the King—but she had no intention of kissing even one more man that night.

A good loser, Charles had gone away happily enough, smiling when he spotted Nell Gwyn sashay into the chamber. And now, as Rose and Gabriel performed the complicated steps of the galliard, she was aware of all the gazes on the two of them.

Jealous gazes. The women were jealous because she had captivated the most coveted bachelor at Court. The men were jealous because he'd made his intentions crystal clear, and one didn't elbow aside a duke.

All the attention was positively heady, and part of her was thrilled beyond belief. A duke, and such a handsome one as well!

The only catch was his kisses. She'd allowed four more, trying vainly to coax him to change his style. When that hadn't worked, she'd tried—really tried—to learn to enjoy his technique. Because truth be told, she couldn't imagine why she didn't. Upon close examination, it seemed to her that his kiss was not all that different from Kit's.

Some of the men had been positively boorish in their approach, but Gabriel didn't fit in that category. His kisses weren't too terribly slobbery, his breath was fresh, and he had the manner of a gentleman, if an impassioned one. She couldn't put her finger on what Kit had done specifically that made his kiss magic while Gabriel's had no effect on her at all.

Or at least not the *desired* effect.

Perhaps she would have to allow Kit another kiss, in order to discern the difference. Once she figured that out, it should be a simple matter to explain to the duke what she wanted. Practice, after all, should make perfect.

If only the practice weren't so tedious.

"Thank you, Your Grace," she said kindly when the dance came to an end. She loved calling him *Your Grace,* not to mention imagining being called *Your Grace* herself. She noticed the musicians setting down their instruments. "Is the dancing over so early?" she asked with a frown.

"Only temporarily." Gabriel gestured to another corner of the room. "I believe Nell is about to grace us with an entertainment."

Chairs had been arranged to leave the corner open for the presentation. Rose and the duke drifted closer as the performance began, a clever comedy mocking Court life and filled with bits of song and dance. Nell had apparently brought friends, for other actors and actresses took the makeshift stage along with her. When the brief play ended, the chamber burst into applause, the King's the loudest of all.

"Extraordinary!" he exclaimed, the remnants of laughter still on his face. "Extraordinary!"

Half laughing herself, Nell swept him a bow. "Then, sir, to show you don't speak like a courtier, I hope that you will make the performers a handsome present."

Charles made a great show of patting his velvet clothing.

"I have no money about me." He turned to his brother, the Duke of York. "Have you any coin, my dear James?"

His eyes dancing, the duke shrugged. "I believe, sir, not above a guinea or two."

Laughing harder, Nell turned in a circle, her arms outstretched. "Od's fish," she cried, borrowing the King's favorite oath, "what company have I got into?"

Rose laughed along with everyone else. With her robust sense of humor, Nell truly was delightful.

Gabriel tucked a hand beneath her elbow. "Shall we adjourn to the North Terrace?" he asked politely.

Not again. Her high spirits quickly faded. "I think not. I feel, um, a bit peaked. I should like to find my mother and see if she's ready to leave."

"Already? The gaming has not even started."

And she'd wanted to try that. But not as much as she wanted to escape now. Somewhere—anywhere—where she could find some peace and think about all that had happened this day. "I believe I saw my mother head in that direction," she said, indicating the portion of the castle that was under construction—an area she suspected the fastidious duke would have no wish to enter. "Thank you for the dances."

She hurried away without looking back, hoping he wouldn't follow and heaving a sigh of relief when she made it into the unfinished vestibule without hearing any footsteps behind her. Thinking to hide herself even better, she slipped into the half-built dining room and sagged against an exquisitely carved wall.

This late at night, she'd expected it to be deserted, but it wasn't. Across the chamber, Kit and Ellen were having words again.

Did the man never sleep?

"Let me see it," he said, reaching toward his sister. "Why should it be a secret?"

"'Tis mine," Ellen shot back, clutching a book to her

chest. "Why do you have to stick your nose into everything that's mine?"

Dazed, Rose stared in their direction. It struck her suddenly that in his fine but plain suit, with his gleaming black hair free instead of tucked beneath a wig, Kit looked anything but aristocratic. His skin was browned from working outdoors, and he carried his lean, rangy body with easy authority, not the controlled movements necessary to carry off the weight of layers of heavy fabric and ribbons.

In an odd way, she found the lack of fussiness appealing. But she wanted an aristocratic husband.

'Twas a good thing he was just a friend.

"Rose!" Ellen exclaimed, spotting her and abandoning Kit to hurry over. "I was hoping to see you tonight."

"Were you?" Rose asked.

"Yes. I brought a book I'd like you to translate."

"Did you?" Her gaze still fastened on Kit, Rose seemed to be reduced to two-word responses.

"Will you try?" Ellen grabbed her by the arm and pulled her down the length of the chamber. "I am dying to find some fresh air—this place is filled with sawdust."

Before Rose could protest, Ellen had propelled her out a door at the end of the chamber. As it shut behind them, Rose sneaked one more glance at Kit. The last she saw of him was those wicked green-brown eyes.

It should be a crime for a commoner to be so attractive.

Chapter Twelve

Ellen led Rose down a long back corridor, around a corner, and out into a small brick courtyard. Unlike Horn Court with its uniformed guards and staircase to the King's chambers, this homely area was lit by a single torch and held naught but stacks of building supplies and a weathered wooden table with two chairs. Rose gratefully dropped onto one of them, amused to hear assorted bangs, scrapes, and curses coming from high in the building to her right.

"We're almost back where we started, aren't we?"

Ellen took the second chair. " 'Tis the dining room on the other side of that new wall, yes."

Despite the sounds of construction, the courtyard seemed private enough. "Why wouldn't you show Kit the book?"

"He'd make certain I never saw Thomas again."

"Oh?" Rose felt drained, but her curiosity was stronger. "May I see it?"

"In a minute." Ellen laid it on the table and ran a finger over the gold lettering that gleamed in the torchlight. "Kit drew a picture of you."

"I know. I saw it. 'Twas very well done. I had no idea he was an artist."

"He's not. Or not anymore. He used to draw all the time, and paint, too." Ellen's voice was so melancholy, Rose's throat tightened just hearing it. "Da used to bring extra wood home from his work—he'd spend hours sanding it smooth and cutting it to size so Kit could paint on it. And Mama would bring home leftover paints. The lady she worked for painted landscapes as a hobby."

"They sound like they were very devoted parents."

Ellen nodded, still absently tracing the gilt title. "They were. But Kit hasn't painted since they died. Not anything. He says he's too busy, but I'm not sure I believe him."

"He *does* seem very busy," Rose said gently.

Ellen's eyes, so like Kit's, went from sad to furious in a heartbeat. Brown to green. "All he wants to do," she said between gritted teeth, "is make money and add it to my dowry. He thinks he can buy me a titled husband. I don't *want* a titled husband. I want Thomas."

Rose had never been afraid to ask questions when she wanted answers. "How much is your dowry?"

"He adds to it constantly. Half of every penny that comes his way. Last I heard, 'twas up to eleven thousand."

"Pounds?"

"Pounds."

"Gemini," Rose breathed, stunned. "Mine is only three thousand." Hardly a pittance—three thousand pounds was ten years' income for a gentleman. "I have another ten from my grandfather, but that money is mine to control."

Ellen pushed back her unruly dark hair. "Kit doesn't let me control anything."

"He just wants what's best for you." Rose was sure of it. She was also sure Kit was going about it in a typical male, pigheaded way, but she wouldn't say that, not now. "He took responsibility for you so young," she said instead. "Only sixteen, wasn't he?"

"And I was six."

"Well, then, of course he couldn't let you make your own decisions."

"But I'm older now. Why can he not see that I've grown up? I *hate* being at odds with him. I hate the harsh words. I love him—but I love Thomas, too." Ellen fought to hold back tears. "Will you help me convince him?"

Rose blinked. "Me? Why should Kit listen to me?"

"He *drew* you," Ellen reminded her. "He hasn't drawn anything but buildings in twelve long years."

And he'd kissed her, too, but Rose wouldn't be telling Ellen that. "I suppose I can try," she promised her. "But I'm not at all sure I can make any difference."

Pigheaded. That was Kit.

But Rose also thought he was right—at least where Thomas was concerned. A pawnbroker, for God's sake!

"Do you know, Ellen," she ventured carefully, "it might be a good idea for you to kiss Thomas before you decide you want to marry him."

"Kiss him?" Dashing away the tears, Ellen burst out laughing. "Mercy me, that is precious."

For a moment Rose was confused, but then she just felt a fool. Of course Ellen had kissed her love. The girl was eighteen, and Rose had contrived to be kissed long before that.

She just hadn't enjoyed it.

"Show me the book," she said.

Sobering, Ellen pushed it slowly across the table. "I would like to read it together with Thomas," she said, for the first time sounding a bit shy. "But 'tis not English."

"Yes, you said so." Rose looked at the title. "'*I Sonetti Lussuriosi* di Pietro Aretino,'" she read aloud. "'Tis Italian.'"

"Ah. I was wondering." Ellen scooted closer. "What does it mean?"

"'Tis authored by a man named Pietro Aretino, and 'tis called *The Licentious Sonnets,*" Rose translated with some relish. This sounded good, maybe even as good as *Aristotle's Master-piece.* She flipped open the book—and stared.

There, above the first sonnet, was an engraving of two people.

Naked people. On a bed.

She leaned forward to study it closer, wishing for more than the flickering torchlight. The man and woman were embracing, both lying on their sides, their legs entwined. Most of the woman's body was artfully hidden behind the man, but the man's bare bottom was there for the world to see in all its well-muscled glory.

So *this* was how people made love! Gemini. This was definitely better than the *Master-piece*. Much more instructive—the pictures made all the difference.

A small smile flirted on Ellen's mouth as she gazed at the picture, too. "He's a fine specimen of a man, is he not?" she asked conspiratorially.

Rose wouldn't know—she didn't have anything to compare him with. But Ellen obviously did . . .

Suddenly instead of feeling like the older, wiser woman to Ellen's eighteen, Rose felt about five years old.

Ellen wanted this book translated. Ellen wanted to share it with her love. No, her *lover.*

"No wonder you laughed when I counseled you to kiss Thomas!"

Ellen didn't even blush. "We're in *love,*" she said in an impassioned tone, as though that explained everything.

And maybe it did.

"What does the sonnet say?" Ellen asked.

"'*Fottiamci anima mia, fottiamci presto; Poi che tutti per fotter nati siamo.* Let us make love, my beloved, quickly, for we were made to make love.'" She looked up. "That is nice, no?"

Ellen looked disappointed. "I thought it would be . . . you know, more *racy,* to match the pictures."

"The picture is not all that racy." Now that she'd recovered from the shock of seeing naked people on the page, Rose decided the engraving was rather nice. "'Tis tasteful enough, all considered." She turned the page. "Oh . . ."

Not quite so tasteful, the woman was now on her back, half reclined against the headboard, while the man knelt between her spread knees, his body meeting hers in exactly the right place.

"Oh," she said again.

"Look at the next one." Ellen reached to flip the page.

"Oh!" Rose tilted her head, then turned the book sideways. There seemed to be so many arms and legs, she really couldn't tell *what* was going on.

Could people really do that? She'd never imagined—

"And the one after that."

In *Posizione Quattro,* Position Four, the woman and man were both seated, facing each other, she on the edge of a bed and he on a chair pulled close. Staring at the picture, Rose felt a wave of heat ripple through her. The woman's legs were spread wide. The man was touching her *there.* And the woman was touching his . . . yard, *Aristotle's Masterpiece* had called it.

Rose hadn't heard the term *yard* before reading the *Masterpiece,* but she guessed Ellen would already know that word—and probably more.

Although Rose considered herself educated, she now realized the *Master-piece* had only explained how everything worked in clinical terms. The whole process of making love had remained somewhat of a mystery.

Until now. A strange ache spread low in her middle as she tried to imagine herself as the woman in the engravings. The only problem was she couldn't envision doing any of those things with anyone she'd ever met . . . except Kit.

That odd ache intensified, and she shut the book.

After taking a moment to collect herself, she drew a shaky breath. "Where did you get this?" she asked Ellen.

"I found it in Thomas's shop."

"Someone *pawned* this book?"

"People pawn everything. Jewels and pottery and pistols and swords . . . 'tis like a treasure trove, I'm telling you. My favorite place in the world. You should pay a visit, Rose. The shop is right on the High Street."

Rose had never thought she'd like a pawnshop—they were seedy places, from what she'd heard. Disreputable, along with their owners. "Does Thomas have other foreign books?"

"Not like this." Ellen laughed. "But yes, I've noticed other books that aren't in English. This book was part of a whole library someone pawned; I don't think Thomas ever looked through the titles to see what he had. He seemed surprised when I showed him this one."

"I'll bet he did." Rose couldn't imagine sharing this book with a man. Or rather, she could, but only one certain man—and she didn't *want* to think about that.

"Can you translate the rest of the first poem?" Ellen asked.

Rose slowly reopened the book, grateful that the words, at least, didn't seem disturbing. She would just read those and try not to look at the pictures.

"Let us make love, my beloved, quickly, for we were made to make love. And if you adore my . . . yard . . ."

Ellen nodded. She *did* know that word.

". . . then I will love your . . . your . . . seat of womanly pleasure. Good God." Rose felt her cheeks heat; in fact, she could not remember blushing so much in her whole life as she'd done since coming to Court. "This is not sounding at all sonnetlike, is it? I have never before attempted to translate a sonnet."

"'Tis fine," Ellen assured her. "I am *sure* Thomas will enjoy hearing this." Her eyes glittered with anticipation. "I will never remember it, though. Let me try to find quill and paper so I can write it all down."

Rose wasn't at all certain she felt up to translating these sonnets aloud in a courtyard in the middle of Windsor Castle. Especially with Kit somewhere on the other side of that wall. For all she knew, he could be heading here to fetch nails or a beam any minute.

She'd never considered herself a prude, but a lady had her limits.

"Never mind," she said when Ellen stood. "I shall take the book back to my apartments and write down the transla-

tions myself. That way I'll be able to think about the wording. Perhaps I can make it more sonnetlike."

"Oh, that is a very kind offer. But do not trouble yourself
to work on the wording overmuch. Thomas is no devotee of
sonnets."

Rose was looking forward to meeting this Thomas. She
couldn't imagine that he was a very refined man, but Ellen
certainly didn't seem to mind.

"When will you bring me the words?" Ellen asked. "Tomorrow morning, at the pawnshop?"

"'Tis past midnight already." Rose stood with a yawn.
"How many sonnets are there?"

"Sixteen."

All those engravings to study. She had a lot to learn . . .
and that odd heat was starting already, just thinking about
it. "I could translate one by the morning." 'Twas late, not to
mention she'd like to keep this book for a while. "Will Kit
allow you to go to the pawnshop?"

"He has to sleep sometime," Ellen said with a mischie-
vous smile. "I imagine once he allows himself to succumb,
he will sleep like the dead. I should be able to sneak out
early easily enough. When he wakes, though, he will surely
come for me and drag me back here while he works all the
day."

"And half the night," Rose agreed. Kit was the hardest-
working man she'd ever met.

"Probably." Ellen sighed. "Will you visit the pawnshop
tomorrow, then? In the morning?"

"I'll come," Rose promised. She grabbed the book, and
the two of them returned to the dining room.

Kit was up on a ladder inspecting something or other.
He'd taken off his surcoat and wore only shirtsleeves rolled
up almost to his elbows. His forearms were muscular and
sprinkled with crisp black hair.

The blasted man looked better than ever.

"Did you two have a nice visit?" he asked. As he climbed
down the ladder, Rose saw muscles rippling under his thin

white cambric shirt, too. She hadn't sipped any champagne tonight, but her stomach seemed to think she had, anyway.

"Very," Ellen said, but Rose couldn't remember what that was in response to. She was thinking about how she'd decided to let Kit kiss her again, to find out what he did differently from Gabriel.

And she was thinking about the pictures in the book.

Oh, this wasn't good at all!

"How did the translation go, then?" he wondered, his gaze on the book in Rose's hands.

She knew he was hoping to get *his* hands on it. "'Twas more difficult than Ellen had anticipated, so I'm going to take it home to work on it. Please excuse me. I must go find my mother."

She felt very relieved to escape. At least until she walked back into the drawing room and two men immediately headed toward her.

Gabriel and someone she had yet to meet. Though the stranger wasn't as handsome as Kit, he might be a good kisser. But she didn't have the will left to find out. Not to mention she was holding a lewd book clutched to her chest.

She had to get rid of it.

When Gabriel got to her first, the other man turned away dejectedly. "Pardon me, Your Grace," she said quickly. "I was just heading to the ladies' attiring room."

"Are you quite all right?" Gabriel asked, his blue eyes radiating concern.

He really was terribly nice. "Oh, yes. I'm just feeling a bit, um, peaked."

"Still?"

"'Tis all the excitement, I'm certain," she told him with a practiced, romantic sigh.

He smiled, and she knew she'd succeeded in convincing him he was responsible for her excitement. He leaned close and lowered his voice to an intimate murmur. "I do hope you'll be feeling better soon."

She didn't care for his perfume. 'Twas too flowery. "Oh,

I'm certain I will," she said blithely and sailed out of the chamber.

Blessedly, the attiring room was empty. She stuffed the book under her cloak and then dropped onto one of the green baize benches.

She really *was* feeling a little bit peaked.

Chapter Thirteen

"Kit," his sister said a few minutes later, "I need to talk to you."

"One moment, Ellen." He turned back to inspecting the latest materials that had arrived.

She yelled across the courtyard, "I need to talk to you *now*."

"'Twill do nicely," he told his new foreman, then took a deep breath and strode over to his sister, thinking, not for the first time, that it had been a bad idea to bring her along while he worked. "What in your little selfish world is so important you had to interrupt me?"

Instead of bristling, she looked smug. "Lady Trentingham wishes to see you."

He slanted her a suspicious look. "Lady Trentingham doesn't even know who you are."

"Could that be because you weren't polite enough to introduce me?" She straightened her slim eighteen-year-old shoulders. "Well, she noticed me, anyway. Came right up and introduced herself, then asked where she might find you. I gather she looked in the dining room, but of course you were out here."

"Where did she find *you*?"

"On the terrace. She's waiting for you there."

He headed in that direction, wondering just what Ellen had been doing out on the terrace now that she no longer had her book to occupy her. He admitted to himself that it probably hadn't been fair to expect her to entertain herself all evening long.

But he hadn't felt as though he'd had a choice. If he'd left her at home, she'd surely have run off to spend the evening in the company of that damned pawn dealer. Doing God knew what.

He certainly didn't want to know.

Life had been much simpler when he was off at school and Lady St. Vincent was still alive and caring for Ellen. He and his sister had spent glorious times together during the weeks he'd been able to visit. They'd never argued.

Well, rarely. Only when she'd begged him to take her with him back to school.

He stopped in the dining room long enough to shrug back into his surcoat before stepping out to the terrace.

Lady Trentingham turned in a swish of golden brocade skirts. "Kit. Ellen found you."

"I apologize for not introducing you earlier."

She waved that off. "I knew at first glance you were related. She looks just like you. A little prettier," she added with a smile.

He grinned back. "I should hope so."

"I wanted to let you know that Rose is in the ladies' attiring room. I thought, considering our earlier conversation, you might want to be there when she comes out."

He'd almost convinced himself he'd dreamed that conversation. This whole day seemed naught but a dream born of wishful thinking . . . everything going right with King Charles, the wonderful afternoon with Rose, the kiss, his materials showing up in a timely fashion, Lady Trentingham encouraging him to seduce her daughter . . .

No, he was still fighting with Ellen. *That* was no dream.

And neither, apparently, was this. Lady Trentingham leaned closer to straighten his cravat. "Shall I show you where Rose will be coming out?"

"She's looking for you," he said. "She mentioned that the last time I saw her."

"Well, she is going to find *you* instead."

Rose had almost steeled herself to venture forth from the attiring room when two young women walked in.

"Oh," the blond one said when she spotted her. "*You're* here."

Rose didn't care for her tone. She wanted to slap her across her pinched face. But she also wanted to be liked here at Court, so she plastered on a smile. "I'm Rose Ashcroft. And you are . . . ?"

"Lady Wyncherly." The woman fetched her drawstring purse and pulled out a tiny silver box.

"And I'm Lady Wembley." The other woman joined her friend at the large gilt-framed mirror. Her hair was so black Rose imagined she dyed it *and* used a lead comb.

"I am pleased to make your acquaintance, Lady . . ." *Willoughby? Wemperley?* "Ladies. You're both married, then?"

"Yes," they said in unison, and then the dark-haired one added, "and you're not."

Rose could think of worse things than not being married. Like being one of these shrews.

The blond Lady W touched a pimple on the other's face. "Right there," she said.

The woman glared at herself in the mirror. "Hell and furies, another one."

"Here, choose a patch."

While the pimply Lady W rummaged through the little oval box with a fingertip, the blond one turned to Rose. "Why are you not busy kissing someone?"

Rose was rapidly concluding 'twas just as well none of the women here seemed to like her, because she certainly didn't like them. But she decided to ignore the slur. "I am resting until the gaming."

"There will be no gaming tonight," pimply Lady W said, choosing a crescent-shaped patch.

"No gaming?" Rose echoed, crestfallen.

Blond Lady W pulled some adhesive from her purse and dotted it on the back. "Have you not heard?" She stuck the black velvet on her friend's face. "This will be an early evening, because we're all leaving tomorrow for Hampton Court. Will you be coming along?"

She sounded as though she hoped not.

"I'm not sure," Rose told her. She'd found no opportunity to discuss it with Mum yet. Half of her wanted to go to Hampton Court just to spite these women, but the other half thought the peace of Trentingham Manor would be heaven in comparison.

Unfortunately, there were no potential husbands at home.

The blonde chose a patch for herself—a cupid—even though she was wearing nine already and had no pimple to cover. Patches were quite in fashion, and Rose wore one herself—a small heart at the outside edge of her right eyebrow—but she thought the woman's face looked diseased with all those black shapes all over it.

Maybe she *was* diseased. Maybe most of the patches were hiding hideous smallpox scars. Although Rose knew it wasn't nice of her, the thought of that made her smile.

"What?" the Lady Ws barked together.

Rose just shrugged and walked out of the little chamber. She was certain they started talking about her the moment she cleared the door—and she doubted they had anything good to say.

She stepped into the drawing room and stopped short when she saw Kit, who was standing there gazing into space and looking uncomfortable. Well, he didn't belong here at Court, so that wasn't such a surprise. Perhaps the King wanted the drawing room renovated too, and he was studying it.

She noticed he was taller than she, but not terribly much taller. Maybe half a head, while she only came up to

Gabriel's chin. Kit didn't make her feel petite like the duke did.

He finally took note of her. "Rose," he greeted with a smile.

No *Lady.* Did that mean he considered her a friend now?

"Kit." She nodded, then suddenly remembered her plans. "Will you kiss me?" she asked.

"Here? Now?" His eyes widened, becoming more green than brown.

"I didn't mean it like that," she rushed out, cursing herself silently for her habit of speaking before she thought. "I just . . . well, I just want to see how you do it."

His smile turned amused. "Like anyone else does it, I imagine."

He was wrong, *so wrong,* about that. As he moved closer, the little bubbles began dancing in her stomach. He was very, very wrong.

His gaze locked on hers, now purest green with just flecks of brown. Flecks she was close enough to see. His scent wasn't heavy but it still overwhelmed her, that woodsy perfume mixed with the clean sweat of hard, honest work. "Are you certain you want a kiss now?" he teased. "Right here, in front of the entire Court?"

"Have you not heard?" another man cut in. "Our Lady Rose quite enjoys kissing."

Startled, Rose turned to find Lord Davenport standing behind her. She'd kissed him earlier and been disappointed, but at least he hadn't been rude. "Greetings, my sweet Lady Rose," he said and kissed her again, right there—as Kit had said—in front of the entire Court.

'Twas a chaste kiss, but it snapped Rose out of her trance. What had she been thinking, asking Kit Martyn—a common architect—for a kiss before England's finest?

"Thank you," she told Lord Davenport, meaning it. If only she liked kissing him, she would give him another for saving her from humiliation.

"My pleasure," the man said, reaching for her again.

Hearing a throat clear, she turned back to Kit, but he was gone.

The Duke of Bridgewater was there instead. "Ah, Lady Rose. You promised me this dance, did you not?"

She hadn't, but before she could say so he'd started leading her away. Lord Davenport just shrugged. Apparently he didn't feel up to challenging the duke.

"I don't like seeing other men kiss you," Gabriel said.

"Then don't look," she suggested, laughing when he started to protest. "I didn't encourage him."

"Shall I call him out, then?"

"Gemini, no!" She laughed again, furtively searching for Kit. He was nowhere to be found. "Lord Davenport isn't worth your time, Your Grace."

The duke's pretty blue eyes sparkled, telling her he liked hearing that.

They danced an almain and once again received jealous glances from men and ladies alike. Gabriel was a perfect gentleman. But after the dance, when he contrived to draw her behind the curtains, she sighed. If only she enjoyed his kisses instead of dreading them, life would be so much better.

They weren't the only couple in the big bay window. In one corner, a man had his hand down the front of a lady's bodice, and if Rose could judge from the woman's moans, she was enjoying that very much.

As she watched, Rose felt her own breasts begin to tingle, and a strange, lazy warmth stole through her body, weakening her knees. She licked her lips, imagining a man doing that to her.

But the man wasn't Gabriel.

"Don't look," he whispered, turning her to face the other corner.

There, a man had his hand up a lady's skirts! The lady had raised one of her legs and wrapped it around his. Rose suddenly pictured one of the engravings in Ellen's book.

She needed air.

"I wish to go outdoors," she told him.

"Excellent idea. There is a distinct lack of privacy in this area."

She hadn't meant with him; she'd submitted to four of his kisses tonight, and she didn't intend to allow a fifth. Not until she'd kissed Kit again and figured out how to teach the duke to kiss her better.

As they emerged from behind the curtains, Rose looked around for rescue, relieved to meet the gaze of Viscount Hathersham. She'd kissed him, too, and from what she could remember, it hadn't been *that* bad.

Not bad enough that she couldn't risk encouraging him a little if it might save her from another private outing with the duke. "Lord Hathersham!" she called, waving him closer. "I completely forgot that I'd promised you the next dance."

She hadn't, of course, but thankfully he wasn't dim enough to say so. Instead he bowed and took her by the hand, raising it to his lips. His kiss was a bit more blubbery than she'd remembered, but at least it was to her hand, not her mouth. " 'Twill be my pleasure, Lady Rose. Well worth the wait."

As they moved toward the dance floor, Rose sent Gabriel what she hoped he would take as an apologetic glance.

"I never asked you to dance," the viscount said in a low tone that she imagined he thought was seductive.

"Well, you should have," she told him with a smile.

"You feel we are suited, then?"

"For a dance."

A vigorous country dance would have been more to her liking, but the musicians had chosen a minuet. As the dancers went to their toes, the viscount pulled Rose near. "I am hoping I can persuade you we are suited for more than a dance." One of his hands slipped around her and rested on the small of her back. "You move nicely," he said.

"Thank you, my lord."

"I have nice moves as well." She tried to gain some distance, but he pressed her even closer. "Especially," he added, "in bed."

She forced a girlish giggle. "Oh, my lord! There is no bed here."

He raised a brow. "We can find one," he murmured as his hand slid down to her bottom. And pinched.

"My lord!" She twisted subtly out of his embrace, not wanting to make a scene. "That is not appropriate," she told him in a voice colder than the ice sculpture that decorated the refreshment table.

"But, my lady—"

"Hush up and dance!"

She held herself in check, though she wanted to rant and rave—and perhaps bash him over the head with something good and heavy. The Chinese vase on that silver table would do nicely. The nerve of him, touching her bottom!

When the dance ended, she muttered a stiff "Thank you, my lord," and took off for the solitude of the terrace.

•

Chapter Fourteen

"She's distressed," Lady Trentingham said, standing with Kit in a dark corner of the drawing room. "And alone. Go to her."

"I'd wager she'll not be alone for long," Kit predicted. A safe bet, given the Duke of Bridgewater was meandering toward the door already.

"Take her away from here for a while. She'll appreciate it."

"Away?" Rose's mother never failed to surprise him.

A short laugh escaped her lips—or maybe it was a snort. "Not for the night—just for an hour. You can find solitude, yes? You know this castle better than anyone." She gave him a little push. "Now, go. I'll keep an eye on Ellen."

He went, quickly, feeling like a poltroon as he elbowed his way past the more sedate duke and handily beat him outdoors. This entire courtship was beyond humiliating. Lady Trentingham had made it clear she approved of him pursuing her daughter, and he shouldn't be needing her encouragement—or worse, her nagging—to make every move. He'd always gone after what he wanted with no holds barred, and from now on, he'd do the same with Rose.

Silhouetted in the moonlight, she stood at the edge of the terrace, gazing over the darkened Thames Valley.

"Rose," he called softly as he approached.

She started, then turned, looking amused. "Kit? You always turn up."

A glance back told him the duke had made it out to the terrace. "Would you fancy a stroll?" Without waiting for a reply, he started walking.

She followed without hesitation. "Where would you take me?"

"Around the courtyards, or—"

"Lady Rose!"

"'Tis Bridgewater," she whispered, quickening her steps. "Ignore him."

"Do you not like him?"

"Of course I like him! He's a duke!" She walked even faster, amazingly fast considering her high heels. "I just need to leave Court for a while, that is all."

Her mother really was quite perceptive. "And why is that?" he asked, steering her around a corner.

"I am making a fool of myself here," she said with a sigh, never one to mince words. "I wish to break the cycle."

He laughed, then glanced back, but thankfully they'd lost the duke. "A fool? I think not. 'Tis quite obvious all the men like you." He hadn't enjoyed watching that popinjay kiss her.

"And all the ladies hate me."

"They're only jealous."

"I know that."

As he led her through a small courtyard, he laughed again, enjoying her candor.

"They're vulgar bores, anyway," she declared. "But a woman needs friends. I miss my sisters. I enjoyed talking with Ellen," she added.

"She enjoyed you. She's in a much better mood than when we arrived. Thank you for that."

She waved a hand. "I cannot think what I did, besides possibly offer friendship."

"She needs friends, too. Of late, she spends all her time with *that* man." He steered her around the Round Tower. "What was the title of the book she brought along?"

"I'll not know until I translate it," Rose said glibly.

So glibly he suspected it was a fib. That book was making him more and more curious.

She stopped before the castle gate, turning her face up to him. Torchlight danced over her fine features, highlighting her puzzled smile and the charming little indents it made in her cheeks. "Where are we going?"

He hadn't known, but suddenly he did. "To the river, if it pleases you."

Although Lady Trentingham had suggested he take her daughter to a secluded part of the castle, surely the river would do as well.

Rose knew she shouldn't have left the castle, especially with a man. But she'd wanted so much to escape. And Kit was a friend.

She'd never had a male friend before.

"'Tis quiet out here," she said. Other than the nobility, most folk rose with the dawn and went to bed shortly after the sun did. The hill was steep, the uneven cobblestones treacherous. "And 'tis dark, too," she added, a little wobble in her voice matching a sudden lurch in her gait.

He reached to steady her. "You're not afraid of the dark, are you?"

"No," she snapped, then added, "Well, maybe. A little," when she caught him looking at her sideways. What was it about this man that made her spill her most embarrassing secrets?

She waited for him to laugh, but he didn't. "I'd know the way with my eyes closed," he said. "Here, take my hand."

She did, though she knew she shouldn't be doing that either. But Kit's fingers felt good linked with hers, comforting instead of intimidating. Warm skin, his palm rougher than those of the other men who'd touched her tonight. Work-worn, she supposed. And while she was holding his hand, the night didn't seem so dark.

At the bottom of the hill, rowdy laughter drifted from a

tavern called Bel and the Dragon. The sound of common men thick with drink. Kit was common, too. But for now, she didn't care. 'Twas peaceful here away from Court, and no one was threatening to kiss her.

Not even the man she wished would.

When they reached Kit's house and he turned and started up the steps, Rose pulled her hand from his. "You said we were going to the river."

"We're only stopping here a minute." He fished a key from his pocket and unlocked the door; 'twas late enough that Graves wasn't there to open it. "Wait here," Kit whispered, ushering her into the entry. He reclaimed her hand, raising it to his mouth, pressing warm lips to the back. She knew she shouldn't allow it. But his kiss on her hand felt different from Lord Hathersham's, so different it made her shiver. "I'll be back," he added before leaving her.

She rubbed her hand while she watched him walk deeper into the house, then hugged herself while she waited. Through an open window, more laughter floated from the river, faint and joyous. People celebrating on a barge, she imagined, watching a dark shape move slowly in the distance.

She didn't have to wait long. A minute later Kit was back, a cloth sack in one hand and a cloak in the other. "Ellen's," he explained. "I thought you might be cold."

He moved close and settled it over her shoulders, wrapping her in its warmth. Fine gray wool with black and silver braid, it was much heavier than her own velvet one and smelled faintly of Ellen, a light, carefree fragrance compared to her own heavier perfume. But Kit being so near, his own scent seemed stronger—woodsy, masculine, and heady enough to overwhelm her. She was on the verge of asking for a kiss again when he stepped away.

"Thank you," she said quietly as he guided her back outdoors. " 'Twas very kind of you to take me for a walk. Away from . . . all that."

"I needed a break from my work. And now that I've taken it, I'm realizing I'll be needing sleep soon, too."

Ellen was counting on that, Rose thought, wondering why she suddenly felt disloyal. Whose side was she on in this brother-sister tug of war? She wasn't sure. She only knew that right here, right now, she was in the right place.

The streets were deserted this time of night, the river slow and dark, the moon illuminating its ripples. Kit guided her past the bridge that led to Eton, its shops dark and shuttered. They came to a wooden gate with white lettering that gleamed in the moonlight. "Romney Walk," Rose read.

It creaked when Kit opened it. "There's a place near Trentingham named Romney as well, is there not?"

"There are many such places, I believe." Beyond the gate, the path angled closer to the river. She allowed Kit to keep a steadying hand on her elbow although the moon provided enough light that she could tread on the packed dirt without tripping. "The name derives from a Saxon word, *rumnea,* meaning water."

He looked at her admiringly. "You know ancient languages, too?"

She smiled, liking that look. She couldn't remember a man ever admiring her for more than her appearance. 'Twas the difference between a suitor and a friend.

"No, Rand told me about that. I'm not so much interested in old tongues—I'd rather learn languages I can use someday when I travel. What is in the sack?"

"Bread. For the swans." Several had been following them as they walked, gliding soundlessly on the water. One of them honked now, as though he'd heard Kit and knew food was in the offing. "I thought you might like to feed them."

" 'Twould never occur to me to bring bread. Lily would think like that."

"She loves animals, doesn't she?"

"Almost as much as she loves Rand." She wondered, briefly, what her sister was doing now. In the middle of the night, so soon after her wedding . . . Rose was afraid she knew. She'd lay odds Lily was doing those things that were still a mystery to her, those things that she feared would be distasteful . . . except when she thought about doing them with the man here with her now.

She released a long sigh. "Lily is nice to everyone and everything, human and animal alike. I could never live up to her perfection."

"No one is perfect, Rose. Not Lily or anyone else." He reached into the sack and handed her a few cubes of stale bread. "Shall we sit?"

The bank rose here, forming a little grassy hill that overlooked the river. Rose lowered herself to the springy ground, tucking Ellen's cloak beneath her. She tossed a bread cube out on the water and watched the swans rush to gobble it. "I wonder what it is about you that makes me so glib," she mused.

He sat beside her. "You don't seem tongue-tied with anyone else."

She blushed, thankful for the cover of darkness. "I don't generally admit to people that I'm imperfect."

"Oh," he said. "I imagine they could figure that out without you informing them."

Laughing, she shoved at his shoulder, then tossed more bread. Swans honked, demanding still more. Across the river, a tiny bridge was barely visible over small rapids gleaming white in the moonlight. The sounds of running water were soothing.

"Will you kiss me?" she asked.

"Shy as usual," Kit teased, sounding pleased as he reached for her.

Her heart suddenly started pounding. "I don't mean . . ."

Agitated, she scrambled to her feet. "Good God, I just want to see how you do it."

He stood and moved closer. "Like any other man, as I told you." He leaned down, his face next to hers, his warm breath brushing her lips. "A kiss is a kiss."

"Oh, no," she breathed. "It isn't."

Then she couldn't say more, because his mouth had met hers.

She tried to concentrate on his technique, truly she did. But as his work-roughened hands cupped her face, as his gentle pressure turned into more, as the kiss deepened and his tongue tangled with hers, she couldn't seem to think straight.

Was he more tender? Not really—not at all when the caress turned more demanding. Was he more skilled? She had to think so, but she couldn't discern how. Did he taste different? Well, certainly. He tasted like Kit, only Kit . . . the most divine flavor ever to grace her lips.

She heard a moan and realized it was hers, and then she couldn't think at all. She could only feel. A wonderful heat began spreading, claiming her. She wound her arms around Kit's neck and threaded her fingers into his hair, pressing her body against his. It seemed she could feel his pulse, his lifeblood, beating in tandem with hers. A perfect moment.

A thing of beauty.

When he broke the kiss, she tugged him back for another. After obliging her a moment, he drew away with a low laugh. "So I'm different, am I?"

"Oh, yes," she sighed. "I just cannot figure out how. I . . . I don't *like* deep kisses."

"Oh," he said, "I think you do."

"Only yours." He was kissing her neck now, little wet kisses that should disgust her, but they didn't. Instead, they made her shiver. "How do you do that to me?"

"Maybe," he said, his tongue teasingly warm on one earlobe, "I do that to you because we belong together."

"No." That couldn't be it. She couldn't *belong* with a commoner. Kit was her friend, that was all. "No."

"No?" He nibbled lightly along her jaw. She should hate this, but she didn't. His lips inched closer to her mouth, making her own lips tingle with anticipation. "Shall I kiss you again to prove it?" Closer, but not quite there.

Frustrated, she took his head in both hands and turned his mouth to meet hers. With another low laugh, he set to proving his words right.

'Twas a kiss to sink into. This time his arms went around her. His hands spread on her back, pressing her close. She molded her curves to his body as the fluttery bubbles in her stomach became a hot, insistent ache.

Then his hands moved lower and cupped her bottom. She would swear she felt their warmth through her gown and Ellen's cloak, along with an odd, exciting tingling. The viscount had touched her there, and she'd hated it. But Kit's hands pulled her closer, and the tingling increased. She felt a hardness where their bodies met, a hardness that made her think of the engravings in *I Sonetti*.

"Rose." He tore his mouth from hers to open the cloak and press kisses to her throat, her chest, the tops of her breasts where they were displayed in her low decolletage. Lord Cravenhurst had touched her there, and she'd felt nothing but revulsion. But now her skin prickled, and beneath her chemise and the long, triangular stomacher that covered her laces, her nipples tightened.

'Twas all she could do to keep from tearing her own clothes off. This would never, ever do.

"Kit," she sighed.

He lifted his head and kissed her mouth, a warm clinging of lips. "Hmm?"

"I think we should go back." She didn't want to go back, but she had to. This wasn't where she belonged. "Please, take me back. I . . . this is not right."

He paused a long, heart-stopping moment before stepping away. Then he took her hand and started down the path.

"I think, dear Rose, it is very right," he said after a while. "And I think in time you will agree."

'Twas a good thing he was just a friend, because she was afraid she might agree already.

Chapter Fifteen

"Lady Trentingham?"

Chrystabel turned to the Duke of Bridgewater and took note of his troubled expression. "Yes?"

"Your daughter is missing."

"Oh?" Poor man, he really seemed to care. "Whatever makes you think that?"

"She went off over an hour ago. I . . . I was hoping she'd return within a reasonable time so I'd have no need to alarm you—"

Feeling sorry for him, she laid a hand on his arm. "Kit Martyn is a friend of the family. I asked him to escort her."

"Back to your apartments?" When she didn't answer, he apparently took that for an affirmative. "She did say she felt peaked. Will she be returning later this evening?"

"I'm not certain," Chrystabel said slowly, feeling a twinge of guilt for misleading him. But she hadn't really lied, had she? She'd only allowed him to jump to a conclusion. He truly did seem concerned. A pity he was all wrong for Rose—too dull and unchallenging.

Although her daughter would make her own decision, Chrystabel had no doubt that, with her subtle help, in the end she would choose the right man.

Bridgewater suddenly frowned. "Besides Lady Rose, it seems a number of other ladies have gone missing."

Chrystabel looked around, surprised to find he was right. There were noticeably fewer women than there had been earlier. The abandoned men shifted restlessly, standing in little groups and talking about God knew what.

"Do you expect they are all feeling peaked?" Bridgewater asked. "Perhaps the prawns were bad."

"You men ate prawns, too, did you not?" Dull, just as she'd thought. But his heart was in the right place. "Oh, here comes Rose now."

Her daughter's step was lighter, her cheeks pinkened from the fresh night air—and perhaps an encounter with Kit.

Chrystabel could only hope.

Bridgewater swept Rose a bow. "We missed you, my lady."

"Did you?" she murmured distractedly.

Chrystabel took that as a good sign. If Rose was failing to flirt with a *duke,* she must have another man on her mind.

"Are you feeling better?" he asked politely.

"I . . . um . . . not really, I'm afraid. I . . . I just returned for my cloak."

"You're wearing a cloak," he pointed out.

"Oh." She blinked. "I borrowed this one." She unfastened the gray wool garment and shrugged it off, handing it to Chrystabel. "Will you both excuse me?"

The attiring room was so crowded, Rose had to edge her way inside.

"Marry come up!" a lady was saying. "Will you look at this? How do you expect it works?"

"Very well, I can assure you," another courtier said smugly.

"But this"—there was a pause during which Rose heard pages flipping—"*this* looks bloody uncomfortable."

As a mass, the women all leaned closer. "Uncomfortable

for the man," a high-pitched voice put in. "But I'd like to
be that lady!"

Amid laughter, Rose worked herself toward the center.
And then froze. Eleven—no, twelve—courtiers were huddled over Ellen's book.

She was starting to back away when one of them glanced
up. "Lady Rose! Could this book be yours?"

"Mine?"

The pimply, black-haired Lady W held up Rose's purple
cloak. "We found it under this. 'Tis yours, is it not?"

"The cloak, yes. But the book . . ." She couldn't leave it
here, so there was no sense in lying. "It belongs to a
friend," she said, holding her head high. After all, given the
behavior she'd witnessed here at Court, these women had
no call to think her a wanton—not for simply having a
book.

"A friend? Wherever did he find it?"

"She," Rose corrected. "And why? Have you heard of
this book?"

"Heard of it?" A plump brunette sighed. "Why, *I Sonetti
Lussuriosi* is known far and wide." She pronounced the
Italian words with a horrible English accent. " 'Twas suppressed by the Vatican in the last century; did you not
know? There are few copies surviving, and many men
searching for them."

"And women," someone added, prompting giggles.

"Lord Chauncey has a set of the engravings on his bedchamber walls," one lady slyly informed them. "I've seen
them."

"A crude set," a second lady put in. "Copies. Nothing
like the fine artistry of these originals."

"You've seen them, too?" a third lady asked.

"You haven't?" a fourth replied with an arched brow.

From the laughter that ensued, Rose concluded that Lady
Number Three—and she—were the only women at Court
who hadn't found their way into Lord Chauncey's
bedchamber.

Odds were *he* might be a good kisser. Unfortunately, he also sounded like a terrible rake.

A wistful sigh came from one of the ladies. "I do so wish I could read Italian. These sonnets must be fascinating indeed."

"That they are," Rose said.

As one, the assembled group stopped staring at the book and swung to her instead. A few of them sidled closer. "Can *you* read Italian?" one of them asked. Or rather, slurred. She was wearing the newly fashionable plumpers—cork balls inside her cheeks to round out her face.

Rose nodded. "Yes, I can read it." Perhaps it wasn't considered ladylike to study languages, but she was far past trying to impress these women.

And oddly enough, they didn't seem disapproving at all. Quite the contrary. "Will you read this book to us?" one asked.

Rose's face flamed at the thought. "I . . . I don't read Italian that well," she fibbed. "Not well enough to read aloud."

They all sighed together rather theatrically.

"But I am translating the sonnets for a friend," she found herself telling them. "One at a time. I could bring the written translations to Court, too, if you'd like."

The brunette's overly made-up eyes widened at this offer. "Would you?"

The pimply Lady W smiled. "We would be most grateful."

"Mosht grateful," slurred the woman with the plumpers.

The blond Lady W stepped forward. "I must say, dear Lady Rose, that is very kind of you indeed. I am so pleased to have made your acquaintance here at Court."

'Twas a good ten more minutes before Rose managed to make her way out of the attiring room, *I Sonetti* hidden under her cloak. 'Twas another hour before her mother had fallen asleep and she could sneak from their bedchamber into the tiny attached sitting room. She closed the door between the two rooms quietly, then lit a candle, fetched paper and ink, and set to work.

In the old days, she would have feasted her eyes on the engravings first thing, but she was determined to become a new, better Rose. She would not allow herself to look at the pictures until she'd translated the first sonnet for Ellen.

It proved an exercise in frustration. She worked until the candle guttered and she had to light another. But try as she might, she couldn't seem to make the English sound like a sonnet.

Let us make love, my beloved,
quickly, for we were made to make love.
And if you adore my yard,
then I will love your seat of womanly pleasure.
The world would be worthless without this.

And if it were possible to make love after death,
let us make love until we die of it,
and then make love to Eve and Adam,
who found death so distasteful.

Truly and verily,
if the scoundrels had not eaten forbidden fruit,
I know not whether the lovers would have been contented.

But let us stop speculating, and drive your yard into my core,
until my spirit comes alive and then dies.
And if it be possible, push even more of you inside me,
So we should witness every pleasure of making love.

'Twould have to do, she finally decided—Ellen had said that Thomas didn't care for sonnets, anyway. A clock on the mantel was striking three when at last she allowed her gaze to stray to the drawing.

'Twas nice, as she'd remembered. Bare skin notwithstanding, the couple looked relaxed, the pose romantic. Their arms were wrapped around each other, their lips meeting above while their bodies met below. As Rose studied the picture, that slow heat started building again in her middle.

She imagined herself with one special man, and the heat built to an ache. This, she realized suddenly, could be beautiful.

Releasing a shuddering sigh, she turned to the second engraving, and then the third and the fourth—the one where the man and woman were reaching out to touch each other. Her cheeks burned, no matter that she was there alone. Unable to resist, she flipped to Position Five, an engraving she had yet to see.

The man sat on the edge of a bed, the woman on his lap, facing away. She was reaching between her own legs and back to grab his . . . yard and guide it into herself. . . .

Rose swallowed hard and forced her gaze to the words.

Such pleasure I feel with my yard in your hand,
I shall explode . . .

On the next page, the woman had settled on the man's lap.

You are filling me, thrilling me,
and I could stay seated here for a year.

And then she was lying on the floor, the man standing over her, holding her raised legs.

Spread your thighs, let me see your lovely bottom
and your seat of womanly pleasure.
The sight makes me pulse with passion,
and I've a sudden urge to kiss you . . .

Ah, she remembered the kisses. Kit's kisses. And the thought of her on the floor, a man standing above . . . a certain man . . .

That ache was intensifying. A yearning ache, all but unbearable. Right where the man in the drawing was looking. *Spread your thighs . . .*

Quickly she flipped another page and froze, staring.

Will you look at this? she remembered a high-pitched voice saying. *How do you expect it works? This looks bloody uncomfortable.*

Uncomfortable, indeed. Why, the lady was practically folded in half, and . . . Good God. Rose's hand fluttered up to her throat. Would her husband expect her to *do* this?

Position Nine was even worse, and Position Ten—did bodies twist like that? In Eleven the woman arched on one elbow and foot, her other leg raised in the air, while the man—

Gemini. If this was what awaited her in her marriage bed, she'd as soon remain a spinster. She flipped hurriedly through the rest of the engravings, sixteen in all, and finally slammed the book shut.

Shaking, she hid it carefully, then folded the translation and tucked it into her embroidered drawstring purse. As the clock struck four, she tiptoed back into the bedchamber and slid beneath the covers, leaving a lamp burning low as always.

But sleep eluded her as the pictures played over and over in her head.

Did her sisters do these things? Were Lily and Rand doing them even now? *Aristotle's Master-piece* had warned there would be "some little pain" the first time, and Rose had never worried about that. But from what she could see, there must be pain *every* time. And not a little, either. She ached just *thinking* about those positions.

The fire in the grate sputtered and died, leaving naught but glowing embers—and still Rose lay sleepless. At long last, she forced herself to remember the first engraving.

The beautiful one.

Her skin tingled where the sheets seemed to caress her . . . and she wished they were male hands instead. The man in the engraving hadn't had a clear face. She shut her eyes tight and tried to picture the duke.

But the face she saw was Kit's.

Chapter Sixteen

"Did you not sleep well, dear?" Chrystabel frowned as Rose yawned for the dozenth time. "Perhaps you should go back to bed."

"I slept fine, Mum." And she had—for the three hours she'd actually slept. "I overslept, in fact. 'Tis after ten already, and I promised Ellen I'd visit her at the pawnshop this morning."

"The pawnshop?"

She crossed to the window to check the weather. "I never made it back to the bookshop yesterday, and Ellen said the pawnshop has books. Foreign books. And I need to return her cloak." It looked sunny, so she decided against wearing her own. "'Tis amazing how quickly we've become friends."

"Sometimes friendships are meant to be. Just like some men and women belong together."

"Like the ones you introduce to be married?" With an indulgent laugh, Rose turned from the window. She grabbed her little purse, slid the cord over her wrist, and draped Ellen's cloak over one arm. "The Court leaves today for Hampton; did you know that?"

"Of course."

"Will we go with them?"

"Do you wish to?"

"I'm not sure." Rose didn't want to make this decision. She watched her mother pick up her own drawstring purse. "Where are you going?"

"You didn't think I'd let you go to the pawnshop alone, did you? A young lady does not parade around town on her own."

Plenty of young ladies did, but Rose didn't feel like arguing. She only hoped she would be able to slip Ellen the translated sonnet without Chrystabel noticing. Not that anything was wrong with what she was doing . . . but it wasn't something she felt like sharing with her mother.

Outdoors, the courtyards were abuzz with servants hauling luggage. There was no sign of any courtiers, however. "Have they left already?" Rose wondered, half hoping they had. Maybe she'd arisen too late to leave for Hampton Court, and the decision would be out of her hands, at least for today.

But as they skirted the Round Tower, Chrystabel only laughed. "I am certain few have arisen from their beds."

"I thought everyone was planning to leave early."

"That," came a male voice, "depends on your definition of *early*."

Rose turned to see the Duke of Bridgewater fall into step along with them. He looked very dapper this morning with a broad-brimmed, ostrich-plumed hat shielding his golden head from the sun. "And what is your definition of early, Your Grace?"

"Oh, before noon, I suppose. I'm certainly proud of myself for being up and about before the sun reaches its zenith." He grinned, his blue eyes twinkling. "But most everyone else wakes as the sun sets. I'm afraid they will find it tedious today to have to rise and travel in broad daylight."

She laughed, enjoying the company of so pleasant and impressive a man. Even for traveling, he was dressed to the height of fashion. His bright burgundy suit sported rows of gold buttons along the front edges of both the long waistcoat and the embroidered surcoat that went over it. The breeches beneath were secured at the knee with gold buttons, too. His lace cravat was tied at his neck in a wide bow, and, unlike Kit, he wore shoes instead of boots—heeled, with a double sole and small gold spurs.

She smoothed her red silk day gown, wishing it were adorned with pearls or something else extravagant. She'd always considered her clothes fashionable, but the ladies here made her feel like a country frump.

"I'm so glad to see you are feeling better this morning." The duke took her arm. "Please tell me you're coming along to Hampton Court."

She exchanged a glance with her mother, who shrugged, apparently leaving the decision up to her. "We're just on our way to the pawnshop," she said, evading an answer.

"The pawnshop?"

If Rose could judge by the duke's tone, he and Kit held the same opinion regarding pawnshops. "We're not pawning anything," she assured him with a laugh. "Just visiting a friend there."

"A friend?" Sounding slightly disturbed, he gripped her arm tighter. "I shall accompany you, then, at least as far as the door."

"'Tis not necessary," Rose protested.

"I was planning to take a walk in the Great Park, anyway. A brisk morning stroll does wonders for a man's constitution. I usually leave from the castle, but I can enter off Park Street, no harm done."

There was no arguing with him, it seemed. They walked through the Lower Ward, Rose wishing some of the ladies were around to see her on the arm of the tall, handsome duke. Perhaps she should go to Hampton Court, because she sensed she was on the verge of snagging him.

Beyond the gateway, 'twas a short stroll down Castle Hill and a left onto the High Street. The pawnshop was right there, as Ellen had said. Three golden balls—the pawn trade's age-old symbol—dangled from a bracket that projected from the building. As they approached, Rose couldn't help but notice that the business looked prosperous. A wooden sign overhead said WHITTINGHAM'S PAWN SHOP in fresh gold paint.

Then she lowered her gaze from the sign to find a gorgeous pair of earrings in the window. Set in delicate gold filigree dangles, rubies sparkled and pearls gleamed. "Oooh," she breathed, fingering her few coins through the thin fabric of her drawstring purse.

Dozens of items crammed the window, but the earrings stood alone as dainty works of art. She fairly itched to own them.

"Are these earrings not beautiful?" She stared at them on their bed of black velvet. "If we go to Hampton Court and there is gaming tonight, maybe I will be lucky enough to win them."

"They match your gown superbly," Gabriel observed. "I think this *is* your lucky day."

"Pardon?"

He grinned. "I've never patronized a pawnshop before, but wait here, ladies, if you will." He bowed and then entered the shop, a bell jingling as he pushed open the door.

Rose pressed back against the building to avoid a careening carriage. "Mum, do you expect he is going to buy those earrings for me?"

Chrystabel shrugged and smiled. "It seems so."

A masculine hand went into the window, square with pale hair sprinkling the back. Rose watched the earrings and the hand disappear. "I hope he won't think I belong to him afterward."

"Do you not want to?" Chrystabel raised a brow but didn't wait for an answer. "In any case, they are only earrings. A trifling item for a man like the duke."

Rose breathed a sigh of relief, for the truth was, she wanted the earrings. She could hardly wait to see them on her ears. She hoped someone had pawned a mirror.

A moment later, the duke stepped back outside and presented the jewelry to her with a flourish. "Enjoy, my lady."

The rubies sparkled even more in the sunshine; the pearls

shone like they held secrets; the gold was intricate, fashioned by a talented hand. Chrystabel slipped into the shop as Rose fumbled to put one on.

"Here, let me help." Gabriel took it from her and stepped close to fasten it on her lobe.

He still smelled of too much perfume, but Rose didn't care. "Thank you, Your Grace."

" 'Tis nothing." He reached for the other earring. "Beautiful women deserve beautiful things."

She turned her head to allow him greater access. "I love them."

"I am glad. I want to see you happy, Lady Rose."

She smiled. He truly was very nice, and generous and handsome and a duke, too. When he was finished, she tucked her long ringlet curls behind her ears, the better to display her new treasures.

"Stunning," he pronounced. Then he leaned close and pressed his lips to hers.

She tried to act enthusiastic, because truly, a kiss was a small price to pay for such beautiful earrings. But she was glad that Ellen's cloak over her arm gave her an excuse not to embrace him. Thankfully, the kiss was short. Gabriel was too polite to attempt a seduction in broad daylight on Windsor's High Street.

But short as it was, all Rose could think was that his kiss was nothing like Kit's.

When Gabriel pulled away, he reached into one of the deep pockets in his breeches and pulled out a handful of coins. A small, secret smile curved his lips as he counted them, dropping each into a little leather pouch. " 'Tis just as I thought."

Rose touched her new earrings, assuring herself they were still there. "What is that?"

"The fool gave me too much change. A crown more than I was due."

" 'Twas good of you to notice. I'm sure he'll appreciate its return."

He blinked his nice blue eyes. "Return? Why the devil should I return it?"

" 'Tis dishonest not to. Besides, I imagine he needs it much more than you do."

"A pawnbroker? I think not." He tucked the pouch into his pocket. "The knaves prey on the most unfortunate, paying pence on the pound for their goods, then charging exorbitant fees for their return. Ten percent a month—and when the poor clodpolls cannot pay, the brokers sell their goods at an enormous profit."

Rose reached up to finger the ruby earrings. She didn't like to think of them as belonging to a "poor clodpoll." Surely they hadn't. "So you'll just keep the money?"

"His loss, my gain. A wise man is more careful when doing business." The duke patted the leather pouch where it was hidden inside his pocket. "Now I must be off for my walk. I'll need to get back to the castle in time to see all my luggage is safely transported." He executed a small, formal bow. "Your servant, my lady. I hope to see you at Hampton Court late this afternoon."

"Thank you for the earrings," Rose called as he walked away. Then she went into the shop. The bell on the door was still jingling as she headed toward a pockmarked blond man who was polishing a glass counter. He was younger than she had pictured Ellen's Thomas, but looked very industrious indeed. And certainly not like a knave who preyed on the unfortunate.

"Lady Rose!" Ellen came running over. "Thomas and I were just having the most lovely conversation with your mother. And the duke bought you earrings, did he?" She waggled her dark brows. "Mercy me, imagine that."

"Kit loaned me this last night," Rose said, handing over her cloak.

Ellen looked at her sharply. "When?"

"Later, when it grew cold." Rose dug in her drawstring purse and pulled out a silver crown. "Mr. Whittingham gave Bridgewater too much change. He asked me to return it."

Ellen set the cloak aside, effectively distracted from wondering how she'd come by it. "That was not Thomas's doing, but the new apprentice he is training." Her disapproving gaze went to the young man behind the counter. "Thomas will have a word with him for certain."

Rose felt sorry for the boy. "I'm sure it was an honest mistake."

"Fear not, Thomas doesn't beat the lad. But he must learn to be more careful." Ellen took the coin gratefully. "Please thank His Grace for returning this, next time you should see him. Thomas needs every penny, because he dreams of moving the shop to London—to the Strand, no less!" She laughed as she walked over to add the crown to the till.

Noticing a fine gilt-framed mirror perched on the wall, Rose went over to admire her new earrings. She turned her head this way and that, watching the rubies catch the light. "Where is your Thomas?"

"In the back, talking to your mother. Come, I cannot wait for you to meet him."

The shop was deceiving, because although it looked large enough on the inside, even more space was hidden behind. Here, apparently, was where Thomas kept the goods that he was holding for customers to return and claim—and he had more in that category than goods for sale. Things were piled up on shelves and stacked in trays and spilling out of trunks—a treasure trove, as Ellen had said.

"Mr. Whittingham has been telling me all about the history of pawning," Chrystabel said after the introductions.

Rose traced the silver embroidery on a deep green velvet surcoat. "It has a history?"

"Most certainly." Thomas had brown hair, blue eyes, and a strong chin that lent him a mature air although he looked no older than five-and-twenty. "Pawnbroking can be traced back over three thousand years to ancient China, and there are also records of it in early Greek and Roman history."

Thomas seemed intelligent, too. More learned than she'd supposed a pawnbroker would be—certainly more learned than Kit seemed to give him credit for. "And the three gold balls?" she asked. "From where did that symbol come?"

"In times past, the Medici family in Italy were well-known moneylenders. Legend tells that one of the Medicis battled a giant and slew him with three sacks of rocks. The three balls became part of their family crest, and eventually, the sign of pawnbroking."

"'Tis an honorable business," Ellen put in. "Where else can the common people find money should they need it? 'Tis not as though they can approach noblemen for loans. Pawnbroking has saved many families' homes and farms—they consider themselves lucky to have a broker to turn to."

Rose remembered Gabriel's opinions about preying on "poor clodpolls." "Even when they cannot afford to redeem their pawned goods?"

"Sometimes they just choose not to." Ellen lifted her chin. "'Tis a business, after all. Thomas is entitled to make a living."

"Of course he is," Chrystabel said.

Rose turned to Ellen's love. "However did you get into this trade?"

"My father was a pawnbroker, and his father before him."

She hadn't thought of a pawnshop as something a man could inherit. In fact, she'd never thought about pawnbroking at all. 'Twas unlikely she would ever require such a service. But she had to admit, standing here amongst neatly tagged jewels and guns, tools, household goods, swords, and clothing . . . the business was not nearly as seedy as she'd assumed.

She wondered if Kit had ever really looked at Whittingham's shop with an open mind. Not to mention listened to the man's plans. She smiled at Thomas. "Ellen was telling me you wish to move to London."

"I do, as did my father before me. He saved for twenty years toward that goal. Trade in London would be much brisker—there are so many more people."

"So many more *destitute* people," Rose put in.

"We can help them," Ellen said. "This trade is not about taking advantage, no matter its reputation."

Rose hadn't missed the *we*. "Why the Strand?" she asked.

Thomas waved an arm at the trays and trays of jewelry—clearly the most often pawned item. "The Strand is home to many of London's goldsmiths. Whittingham's could compete favorably, drawing customers—paying customers, not pawning ones—from the patrons that frequent the area. The real estate there, however, can be prohibitively expensive. My father never did manage to save enough to make the move. And prices are still rising—the Great Fire made London's remaining developed land even more precious."

"But after we're wed . . ." Ellen murmured, then left it at that.

Rose knew she was thinking about her dowry. Eleven thousand pounds—surely more than enough to open the fanciest shop on the Strand.

But she also knew that Kit was not going to be happy turning that money over to this man.

The bell tinkled in the outer room, signaling another customer. "Pray excuse me," Thomas said.

As he left, Chrystabel turned to examine a sword with a jewel-encrusted hilt. "Is this not beautiful?"

"It is, Mum."

She hefted its shining weight, watching sapphires and emeralds twinkle in the light from the small, barred windows. "If this is not claimed, I'll be tempted to buy it for your father."

Rose couldn't imagine he'd be too impressed—the sword wasn't a flower or plant, after all—but she knew

Chrystabel liked for him to look nice when they went out in public. "I'm certain he'd love it, Mum." She sidled closer to Ellen and pulled the paper out of her purse. "Here," she whispered, passing it to her surreptitiously.

"The sonnets?"

"One of them. It took me half the night." She didn't mention that was because she'd spent the majority of the time goggling at the engravings.

And thinking about Kit.

"Thank you." Ellen tucked the paper into her skirt. "Thomas will enjoy reading this."

From the glint in Ellen's eyes, Rose suspected the two of them would enjoy it together.

Chrystabel turned from the sword. "You've a fine young man, Ellen."

"Thank you. I think so. I just wish I could convince Kit." She sighed, then took Rose's arm. "Come out front. Thomas has so many wonderful things for you to see."

"I want to see the books. Especially foreign ones."

But as they stepped back into the main room, they spotted Kit through the window, striding purposefully toward the door. Ellen gripped Rose's arm tighter. "Mercy me, I'm in trouble. I was hoping to return home before he woke."

Even the bell sounded angry when Kit slammed into the shop. "We must leave, Ellen. I've had word there's a problem at Whitehall. A fire."

Ellen's green-brown eyes widened. "Whitehall has burned?"

"Not the entire palace. Just the east end of the Chapel Royal where I'm building the new altar." He swore under his breath. "Come along."

Ellen set her jaw. "I don't want to go to London. I shall stay here."

"No, you'll not." Despite his normal tanned complexion, Kit looked paler even than Bridgewater. And he hadn't noticed Rose. He shot a glance to Thomas instead, then glared

back at his sister. "Think you I'm a simpleton? If I leave
you here, you'll elope. You're coming with me."

"We're going to London, too," Chrystabel suddenly announced.

Kit blinked. "Lady Trentingham. And Lady Rose." His
startled gaze met Rose's, disturbing as ever.

Chrystabel moved closer and wrapped an arm around her
shoulders. "My daughter's favorite seamstress, Madame
Beaumont, resides in London. Rose needs to order some
new gowns if we're to spend more time at Court."

'Twas news to Rose, but she thought it a fine idea. Not
least because it would give her some time to think about
Gabriel . . . and Kit, blast him. He might be frantic with
worry and wearing a simple blue wool suit instead of embroidered silk and gold, but she could no longer deny he
roused feelings in her that Gabriel never would.

Feelings she didn't want.

Mum squeezed her shoulders. "Perhaps," she added, "we
can have Kit and Ellen to supper, since they'll be in London, too."

"That would be nice," Kit allowed, "assuming I can
leave the project. Assuming there is still a project to leave.
Now we must be off. Excuse us, please."

As she watched him herd his sister out the door, Rose realized he hadn't even taken Ellen to task for escaping to the
pawnshop this morning.

He must be very worried indeed.

Chapter Seventeen

Three days later, Ellen strode into Whitehall's Chapel Royal. "I'm ready, Kit."

Kit swept the newly framed altar with one more glance before turning to his sister. "You're all packed?"

"Yes. My maid is seeing everything brought to the carriage. How about you? You've spent two solid days in this chapel. Have you eaten? Slept? Are *your* things all packed?"

"I have enough at the house in Windsor," he said, neatly evading her other questions. If he needed to forgo food and rest to accomplish his goals, so be it. What he *didn't* need was Ellen nagging him.

She bent to scoop up some wood scraps and toss them onto a pile. "I'm so glad we're returning to Windsor."

Kit reached into his pocket, fingering the heavy vellum invitation that had arrived yesterday, a gracious request from Lady Trentingham to join her and her daughter for supper. Ellen wouldn't be returning to Windsor if his plans worked out, but he wouldn't argue with her now. "I thought you loved staying here at Whitehall, where you can pretend you're a fine courtier."

"I loved it before I loved Thomas. Now I know that was naught but a childish game."

Evening was falling, and he'd dismissed his crew for the day, so he picked up the last of the tools himself. "'Tis not a game, Ellen," he said as he put them into a crate. "You can be that woman."

"I don't want to be that woman. I want to be Thomas's woman instead."

He bit back a retort, preferring to savor a good day's work. The situation here at Whitehall had not been as bad as he'd feared. Although the fire had destroyed the half-built altar, the building had remained intact. Yesterday he'd hired extra men—triple his original crew—and procured new materials. The progress today had been gratifying, surpassing his revamped schedule. Save for elusive bits of ash and the lingering scent of burned wood, all evidence of the fire was gone, and the new altar was framed already.

Disaster had been averted again. But he didn't like the way things were going. The continued mishaps were jeopardizing his likelihood of being appointed Deputy Surveyor. Ellen could doubtless make a good marriage anyway, thanks to the dowry he'd saved for her, but should he fail to win the post, he feared his chances with Rose were virtually over.

He had no simple explanation for the fire, as he'd had for the problem at the castle. But he suspected something foul was afoot. In short, he reckoned the blame landed squarely on one man's shoulders: Harold Washburn, the foreman he'd fired at Windsor. Kit intended to seek the man out. And he preferred not to have his sister along to distract him. Not there at the scene and not at his house in Windsor, either—for he knew better than to believe she would stay meekly at home. Not with her lover so close.

Kit wasn't the sort of man to lock his sister in a guarded bedchamber. Sometimes he cursed himself for that weakness.

He folded the drawing of the new altar and slipped it into his pocket, then rolled the rest of the plans and tucked them under one arm. "Let us go. Lady Trentingham will be waiting."

Since the King and his followers were lodged at Hampton Court, Whitehall Palace was quiet. They exited into a large, grassy courtyard, their footfalls crunching on the gravel path as they followed it toward the gate. "I don't like traveling at night." Ellen pouted. "Can we not just go straight to Windsor?"

Kit heard: *Can we not just go straight to Thomas?* "'Twould be rude to refuse the Ashcrofts' invitation. Besides, do you not want to see Rose?"

"*You* want to see Rose."

"So what if I do?"

"She will never be yours. Can you not see, Kit? Your winning her is as unrealistic as your wanting me to marry a title."

"Who said I want to win her?"

She snorted. "You look at her the same way Thomas looks at me."

He didn't like to think of any man looking that way at his sister. "If I'm appointed Deputy Surveyor, perhaps I will soon be *Sir* Christopher Martyn."

"Is that what you're counting on? 'Twill not change you."

"Exactly my point. I'm good enough for anyone now, and so are you. But you cannot argue that perception makes all the difference, and a change in rank will affect how outsiders look at us both."

"I care not what outsiders think. I care only about Thomas."

Every discussion with Ellen was circular—back around to Thomas. Kit counted to ten, then, as they crunched past the Banqueting House, changed the subject. "I wish I had built that."

"'Tis pretty," she conceded. "But compared to the rest of the palace, it stands out like a sore thumb."

"Inigo Jones designed it with a basilica in mind." He nodded a greeting to the guard at the gate. "I heard the construction costs ran to more than fifteen thousand pounds. I believe it was the first modern building in all of London."

"When Thomas builds his shop on the Strand, it will be modern, too."

Thomas again. Of course. He helped Ellen into the waiting carriage with a little more force than was necessary, then pulled the door shut and dropped down across from her. "Just where do you suppose your Thomas will find the funds to build such an impressive shop?"

'Twas too dim inside the coach to discern her features, but he could see the tilt of her head. And hear the flippancy in her voice. "If the Banqueting House cost fifteen thousand, I expect eleven will more than do for a pawnshop."

"Eleven?" For a moment he could say no more. But then the words came out in a rush. "If you think Thomas Whittingham will ever see the money I've saved for your dowry, you'd best think again."

If the pawnbroker was courting her for her money, *he'd* best think again, too.

"You wouldn't keep it from me," Ellen said smugly.

"You cannot know that," he shot back, although he feared she knew him all too well.

A tense quiet stretched between them, a silent battle of wills. When Ellen finally replied, her voice was so soft he had to strain to hear it over the rattles and squeaks of the carriage. "If you do," she said, "I will never speak to you again."

Built only a few years earlier, the Ashcrofts' gray stone town house in St. James's Square was the height of modernity. Kit insisted on a tour before they all sat down to supper, admiring the ornamental scrolled ironwork on the staircase, the intricate pediments over the doorways, and all the chimneypieces carved with festoons of fruit and flowers.

For Rose's part, she'd decided it was all a bit overdone since seeing the clean simplicity of his house.

"We cannot stay too long," he warned when they were finally seated. "I plan to be on the road to Windsor tonight."

"I understand." Chrystabel smiled as she lifted her goblet, looking pleased that the Martyn siblings had come at all.

Rose couldn't figure why her mother had taken such an interest in these commoners, but she supposed 'twas not out of character. After all, she did "introductions" for servants. Mum might have married into the Ashcroft family, but their motto, Question Convention, described her to a T.

Chrystabel sipped. "Have you solved the problem at Whitehall?" she asked Kit.

"I hope so." He speared a bite of chicken fricassee, managing to brush against Rose's arm for the third time in the process. "The problem of getting it finished on schedule, in any case. The problem of how and why the fire started is another matter entirely—one I'm hoping to solve in Windsor. There is a man there who is less than happy with me— the foreman I fired after the ceiling collapsed."

Rose wasn't sure if he was touching her on purpose or not, but either way, she was having trouble eating with the little bubbles dancing in her stomach. "You think he set the fire?"

Kit nodded. "A dishonest man like Washburn is the type to take revenge, and sabotaging another of my projects is effective revenge, indeed." He met her gaze, his eyes looking more green than brown.

She sipped from her goblet, half expecting to taste champagne instead of the sweet Rhenish wine.

"This artichoke pudding is delicious," Ellen said with a hum of delight. "Almost worth delaying my return to Windsor."

"I'm so glad you're enjoying it." Chrystabel poured more wine. "I would be happy to teach you how to make it."

Ellen's eyes widened. "Would you? I know not how to cook at all."

"No? How is that?"

"I was but six when my mother died. While Kit was in school and university and I lived with Lady St. Vincent, I wasn't even allowed in the kitchen. And since then I've lived with Kit . . ."

Without brushing Rose this time, Kit set down his fork. "My sister has no need of cooking. When she marries, she'll have an army of servants to prepare her meals."

"Not if you won't give me my dowry," Ellen said darkly.

Chrystabel looked between them. "Preparing a few special dishes can be a joy," she told Kit carefully. "No matter whether one needs to. Most every lady has a number of signature recipes."

"I would love to learn how to cook this," Ellen said. "'Twas very kind of you to offer, Lady Trentingham."

Chrystabel smiled. "We shall have to plan another visit soon."

"May we?" Ellen asked her brother.

"Perhaps sooner than you think." Kit cleared his throat, sweeping both Chrystabel and Rose with a glance. "I hesitate to presume upon our new acquaintance, but I am wondering if Ellen might stay here with you for a day or two while I take care of my business in Windsor."

"No!" his sister burst out.

Seeing the determined set of Kit's jaw, Rose turned to Ellen with a smile. "It could be fun. We could visit the shops at the Royal Exchange, and you could come along to my fittings. Maybe Kit would allow you to order a new gown."

"Two," he offered quickly, obviously willing to placate his sister.

Ellen's eyes narrowed. "The only new gown I need is one for my wedding to Thomas."

Kit's eyes blazed.

"I could teach you how to cook," Chrystabel put in before he could open his mouth. "We could start tonight."

"I'm lea—"

"You're staying here," Kit said. If looks could kill, Rose thought, his sister would be dead as the chicken on the platter.

Ellen apparently knew when to give up. She swallowed hard and put down her fork. "You're very kind," she told

Chrystabel in a voice devoid of emotion. "Unlike my brother."

A strained silence stretched between the siblings. Before more hurtful words could be spoken, Rose turned to Kit and tried to distract him. "I've seen what you're doing at Windsor, but tell me about Whitehall."

" 'Tis a small project, just a new altar for the Chapel Royal." He took a bracing swallow of wine. " 'Tis not my design. Here is Wren's sketch." Setting down his goblet, he dug a folded piece of paper out of his pocket and handed it to her.

The drawing showed not only the architectural detail but also an elevation complete with an altar cloth, candlesticks, alms dish, candles, and books. The lovely columns, carving, and molding looked much more modern than she supposed the rest of Whitehall to be. " 'Tis beautiful."

"Can you see the original Tudor window behind?" He leaned close, touching a finger to the sketch, and she smelled frankincense and Kit. "Wren designed this to be the same width, so the two would appear harmonious together."

Chrystabel reached for the drawing and nodded. "Why did he not build it?"

Kit waved a hand. "He has more important projects by far. Besides, I've a suspicion Charles wanted to see me spread thin. Projects at Windsor, Whitehall, and Hampton Court all at once . . . plus my own. 'Tis a test, you understand? If I can complete all three of the Crown's projects successfully, and on time, he will know he's found the right Deputy Surveyor."

"And the fire threatened this deadline," Rose said.

"Seriously. But fortunately 'tis a small project, and the damage could have been worse. I hope to overcome my bad luck a second time."

He was still tense, his answers clipped, his gaze settling too often on his sister. Rose tried again. "Hampton Court is a larger project, isn't it?"

"The largest of the three. New apartments for the Duchess of Cleveland—"

"Barbara, the King's longtime mistress," Ellen interrupted, apparently having recovered some spirit. Derision laced her voice. "*He* is allowed to have whatever lovers he wants."

Kit turned to her with a lethal raised brow. "Charles married where he was advised to. If you wish to take Thomas as a lover after you wed a nobleman, that will be between you and your husband."

Ellen glared. Kit stabbed another bite of chicken. Rose shifted on her petit-point seat.

She and her siblings squabbled, of course, but they rarely harbored true animosity. She wished these two would get along. "Is Charles wanting large apartments for the duchess?" she asked.

He chewed and swallowed. "Larger than my house. He wishes their five children to have rooms there as well. I can be certain he will be scrutinizing this project most of all."

"Did Wren do those plans, too?"

"No, I did. Top to bottom, start to finish, the building is mine. Thankfully, nothing has gone wrong with it."

"Yet."

He set his jaw. "When I'm finished with Harold Washburn, he'll not be making any more trouble."

Chrystabel pushed back from the table, looking at Ellen. "Shall we begin your first cooking lesson? Something sweet to complete supper?" When Ellen shrugged and began to rise, Chrystabel looked to Rose. "Perhaps you can entertain Kit while we work. A turn in the square might be nice."

"Kit must leave," Ellen said. "He needs to get to Windsor."

Kit pulled out Rose's chair. "'Tis late already. I believe I'll return to Whitehall tonight and leave early in the morning."

For a moment Ellen stood there openmouthed.

"What?" Kit asked.

"You plotted all along to get me and my luggage here, didn't you? No wonder you didn't bring your own things. You had no intention of leaving for Windsor at all."

"We came tonight because we were invited. And I've urgent business in Windsor that I intend to take care of tomorrow. It matters not whether I travel there tonight or tomorrow morn. But believe what you wish . . . you will, anyway." He sighed. "Come along, Rose. I can use some fresh air."

Chapter Eighteen

Outside, torches burned brightly before each of the houses around St. James's Square, bathing the space between them in a pale, hazy glow. As they crossed to the fenced center, Rose felt Kit's hand warm on her back.

He slipped his other hand into his pocket and pulled out a small rock. "'Tis quiet," he said, turning it over and over with his fingers.

"Until recently, I wouldn't dare come out at night." She paused to open the gate. "There were no rails—the square was just a big open area between the houses, used as nothing more than a receptacle for offal and cinders, not to mention all the dead dogs and cats of Westminster. Squatters lived among the filth, and there were thieves galore."

Kit gestured to all the stately three-story redbrick and stone homes. "Is this not the address for dukes and earls?"

"Very much so. 'Twas a travesty." The gate banged closed behind them as they started walking. "Once Parliament approved their application for permission to put up rails and plant trees, the dukes and earls wasted no time seeing it done."

The dirty pavement had been replaced by soft grass and wide, curving paths with benches scattered throughout. Young trees rustled in the light breeze. When Kit slung his free arm around her shoulders, she couldn't bring herself to pull away.

Her will seemed to vanish whenever he touched her.

He was still playing with the rock. "What is that?" she asked.

He looked down as though surprised to see it there. "A piece of my first building," he said with a small, sheepish smile. "A little chunk of brick." He handed it to her.

It held the warmth of his body and felt smooth, though she knew it must once have been angular. "Was it a church? A mansion? A theater?"

A rueful laugh broke the quiet of the night. "'Twas a warehouse. But I assure you, 'tis the most beautiful warehouse to ever grace God's green earth."

"I'm sure it is," she said, imagining a redbrick warehouse with triangular pediments over the windows and white marble columns flanking the doors. Smiling, she handed back the chunk.

He sobered as he slipped it into his pocket. "Will you watch over my sister?" he asked quietly.

"Why? Do you expect Ellen will run off and elope?"

She'd meant the question to be facetious, but he took it seriously. "From here? No. She'll not have time to get a message to Whittingham and pull such a trick before I return." His voice dropped. "I'm just worried for her. She's not herself."

"You care."

"Of course I care." He rubbed the back of his neck. "Did you doubt that? She's my sister. I love her."

A horse clip-clopped around the square with a carriage creaking behind. "You two quarrel all the time."

"Not all the time. Only since she met Whittingham."

"Have *you* met Thomas?"

"Briefly. Long enough to know he doesn't have horns. But I want better for Ellen." Kit hesitated a moment while the coach squeaked off down King Street. "I've worked hard so she can have better."

Eleven thousand pounds' worth, and Rose had no doubt that kind of money could win Ellen the sort of man Kit was envisioning. The Civil War had left many good families land-rich and cash-poor.

But Ellen was her friend, and she'd promised her support. "Thomas is actually quite nice. And, from what I can tell, a very astute businessman."

"He's a pawnbroker."

"He's educated. If you'd talk to him, you'd discover that."

"He's still a pawnbroker. There's no security in a life like that. My parents wed for love alone, then couldn't protect their own family when times got hard. I can buy Ellen a man with land and the King's ear—"

"There's no security in any life," Rose pointed out. "Look to your own projects for the proof—going along fine one day, ruined the next. Titled men can be ruined, too. It happens all the time."

Kit was silent a moment, then he stopped walking and turned her to face him. "You said 'tis as easy to fall in love with a titled man as one without. Have you changed your mind?"

Frustration was evident in his voice, but he also sounded hopeful. Which was absurd. They would never be anything but friends.

"Of course not," she said quickly.

"Oh," he said. "I see."

"You see what?"

"*You* wouldn't settle for less, but Ellen and I, we're different. An educated pawnbroker is good enough for her, and as for me, I'm good enough for kissing, but nothing else."

He was confusing her—and worse, he was making her sound terrible. Although she couldn't imagine how Kit and Ellen had managed to become so close to her family so quickly, she *liked* them—and she didn't think herself any better than they.

Did she?

Kit's fingers tightened on her shoulders. "Rose?"

Her thoughts were in chaos. She tried to twist away, but he held her fast. His gaze commanded hers, gray in the darkness. "Perhaps that was exhaustion speaking," he said. "I've not slept in two days. Should I say I'm sorry?"

He didn't look sorry, and she didn't know. If he'd touched a nerve, maybe that said more about her than it did him.

"Why do you kiss me, Rose?" he demanded softly.

Apparently she had more to think about than just the Duke of Bridgewater. She took a ragged breath. "You are very good at kissing."

The tension eased from his face; his sudden grin flashed white in the night. "I like a woman who says what she thinks." His hands slid from her shoulders down her arms, slowly, until finally he locked his fingers with hers. "I am good at other things, too."

When he drew on both her arms, she didn't have to sway forward. But she did, landing against his solid chest. A warm shiver rippled through her. "Show me what you're good at," she whispered.

"My forthright Rose." He searched her eyes for a moment, so intense she saw glints of green even in the darkness. "I'll show you," he promised right before his mouth met hers.

Heat that had simmered all through supper burst into flame now. His kiss was wild and demanding, and she gave as good as she got. Somewhere in the back of her mind she despaired of ever finding this with anyone else, but as their tongues tangled, all thought fled, replaced by fiery sensation.

"You're a quick study," he murmured appreciatively, trailing his lips beneath her chin, backing her up to a bench as he went. They both sank down to it, Rose sprawled wantonly with Kit half on top of her. He unfastened her cloak and grazed the tops of her breasts, first with his hands, then his mouth. Her shiver had nothing to do with the cool night air. His touch was magic.

Laced tightly into her bodice, her breasts ached. Wanting more, she reached to unfasten her stomacher. "I want you to touch me," she whispered.

"Here?" He skimmed a finger inside her neckline.

She trembled. "Yes, there."

While she worked the tabs, he pressed little kisses to her cheeks, trailed the tip of his tongue to an ear, caressed the delicate shell.

"Kit," she breathed.

"Let us take these off, too." He slipped the rubies and pearls from her lobes and whisked them into his pocket. "I don't remember you wearing earrings."

Finished with the stomacher, she attacked the laces beneath. "They were a gift from Gabriel."

"Gabriel?" His mouth moved to where the jewelry had been, suckling her soft flesh. "The angel?"

"The duke. Bridgewater." She could melt, she thought. She could melt right here.

"The man has taste," he said dryly. "I'll give him that."

"*I* chose them."

"I should have known." He chuckled, a burst of warm air beneath her ear. She'd never dreamed the skin there was so sensitive.

Then her bodice was open, and he cupped a breast, rubbed a thumb over the peak. "Good God," she murmured, arching up.

"I promised you I was good," he allowed. "But God?"

She was beyond finding humor in anything he said; beyond anything but reveling in these new sensations. The ladies at Court had appeared to like this, and now she knew why. Kit's caresses sent currents racing through her, made her pulse speed, incited a heaviness low in her belly. A warmth that turned into a searing heat when he replaced his hand with his mouth.

Her fingers clenched in his hair, holding his head captive. "More," she whispered.

"More?" He licked his way to her other breast and lavished it with similar attention. She pressed her mouth to the top of his head, moved her hands to explore his back. Hard planes with ridges of muscles; the body of a working man.

She hadn't really touched Gabriel, but somehow she knew he'd be soft.

She shoved both hands under Kit's surcoat and pulled at his shirt, wrenching the bottom from his breeches. As her fingers worked beneath it to encounter bare flesh, he responded with a low groan. "Rose . . ."

"More."

He was warm, so much warmer than she. Firm. Her palms burned against his skin.

"More?"

"More."

He lightly bit a nipple, at the same time reaching down to encircle one ankle with a hand.

What, she wondered dizzily, was so erotic about an ankle? And one covered by a stocking, no less? She didn't know, couldn't know, but his fingers around her leg seemed to shoot heat up higher, while the suckling on her breast drove her to the point of distraction.

She was melting inside. "A thing of beauty," she breathed aloud.

"Oh, yes." His lips trailed up to kiss her mouth, his hand sliding up, too, a breath-stealing glide over silk. And higher, over her garter, his tongue tracing her lips while his hand skimmed warm on the skin of her thigh.

All her air rushed out in a shudder. "Good God."

And higher, until he cupped where her ache suddenly centered.

The ache was more than an ache; 'twas a need, an all-consuming need so exquisite it bordered on unbearable. She felt herself damp beneath his hand, and she squirmed, wanting more. More.

Wanting something inside her to ease that exquisite ache.

Might he slip a finger inside? She knew not where such a

scandalous idea came from; surely men did not do such a thing. Another part of their bodies was meant to fit there.

Words from *I Sonetti* flitted through her head. *Such pleasure I feel with my yard in your hand, I shall explode* . . .

She reached to the front of his breeches.

"Bloody hell," he said, sitting up and jerking his hand from beneath her skirt in the process. His eyes closed momentarily, then opened as he hurried to rethread her laces. "We must go back inside."

She sat up, too, disoriented and bereft. "Did you not like that?"

"I liked it too much." He kissed her softly, apologetically. "You have no idea what you do to me, Rose."

She had an idea, because he did it to her, too.

But she knew better than to say that aloud.

Chapter Nineteen

Rose and Kit returned to the house to find Chrystabel and Ellen laughing, a smudge of flour on Ellen's nose. Kit stayed just long enough to down two servings of the apple fritters they'd prepared. Just long enough to lock gazes several times with Rose . . . just long enough to surreptitiously touch her a few times beneath the table.

The same fingers that were grazing her body over her gown had been under there mere minutes earlier. She could hardly believe she'd allowed it—encouraged it, if she were to be honest—but now, recalling those shared moments, she felt that heat simmering again, felt that urgent, exquisite ache.

The apple fritters were sweet and crispy, spiced with nutmeg, mace, and cinnamon. But she could hardly eat a bite. These were not common reactions to a friend.

But she didn't want anything more with Kit.

"'Twas delicious," he said at last, rising from the table. "But I must leave. I'll have to head out to Windsor very early in the morning, and I need some sleep."

"I know." Ellen's earlier gaiety disappeared as she and Rose walked him from the dining room to the door. "You'll be back soon?"

"Day after tomorrow." He stopped to kiss her on the forehead. "Be good, will you? In the meantime, I expect you to spend a lot of my money at the dressmaker's. I trust that will give you some measure of revenge."

"My earrings," Rose reminded him.

"Oh." He dug them out of his pocket and deliberately folded her fingers around them, holding her hand wrapped in both of his when he was finished. "I like your ears better without them."

Her whole body flushed with heat, remembering his mouth on her earringless ears. He gave her a smoldering look—a knowing look—before he dropped her hand.

She expected his sister to comment, but Ellen just gave him a wan smile as he headed out the door, then sighed when his carriage rolled out of the square.

Rose drew a deep breath and released it slowly, willing her racing heart to calm. "Is something amiss?"

"I hate it when he's nice. It almost makes me forget that I loathe him."

"You don't."

"Not really. I'm just . . . very angry with him right now. He shouldn't have the right to dictate my life."

"But he does."

"But he *shouldn't*. And it makes me sad to be at odds with him, because I know that he cares underneath."

"Underneath? He cares every way that matters, Ellen—any fool could see it." Just like he cared for her, Rose . . . any fool could see that, too. And Rose feared she was denying it much the same as Ellen.

"Whose side are you on?" Ellen asked. "I thought we were friends. You promised to intervene on my behalf."

"I did." Now it was Rose's turn to sigh. "There in the square we talked of little but you and your situation." 'Twas not quite a lie—they hadn't *talked* about much else. "He doesn't want to listen. But I'd lay odds he listens other times, your brother. This is only because he wants what is best for you. What *he* thinks is best for you."

"I know." Looking very pale, Ellen sighed yet again.

Rose remembered Kit's concern for his sister's state of mind. "Shall we translate another sonnet?" she asked in an attempt to cheer her.

Ellen perked up. "Have you made any progress?"

"No. Mum and I lived in close quarters at Windsor, and when we arrived here yesterday I was fitted for new gowns and then went to bed. I needed to catch up on my sleep. Unlike your brother, I'm afraid I'm only human."

And she'd avoided looking at those pictures, reading those words . . . because they engendered dangerous feelings. But whatever would lighten Ellen's mood, she was more than willing to do.

"Come upstairs," she invited.

Unlike Kit, Ellen showed little interest in the structure. Instead, she skimmed a hand over a marquetry hall table. "Thomas had something like this," she said. And a Chinese vase. "And like this. He just sold it last week." And a silver lantern clock. "He has something like this now."

Chrystabel called to them through an open door.

"Good evening." She sniffed at a bottle and made a note on a little card. "Come in," she urged, choosing a vial and lowering a dropper into it.

"What is this?" Ellen asked as they stepped into the room.

"My mother makes perfume," Rose explained. "This is a laboratory of sorts." She waved at the racks of vials. "Those are all her essential oils."

"Essential oils?"

"Distilled from flowers. At Trentingham in her perfumery, she has a fancy still that my brother-in-law built for her."

Squinting in the candlelight, Ellen peered at the rows of labels with their tiny, neat black lettering. "Are some of them made from herbs, too?"

"Oh, yes," Chrystabel said. "Many herbs make lovely top notes. Rosemary, for example, has a lavenderlike fragrance, and pennyroyal is minty—"

"Pennyroyal?" Ellen's head jerked up. "In perfume?"

"Not often, but sometimes." Chrystabel added two drops

to her blend and swirled the bottle. "Do you know much about perfumes?"

"Nothing." Ellen's gaze swept the assorted vials again. "Except that I like them."

"Shall I make a blend for you, then?" Chrystabel set down the bottle and chose an empty one. Using a little silver funnel, she poured in alcohol and water from two pewter flagons, then turned back to Ellen. "Should we start with pennyroyal?"

"No," Ellen said quickly. "I . . ." She swallowed hard. "I do not care for mint."

Chrystabel nodded slowly. "You seem like a dreamer. A floral, then. Orange blossoms, and maybe some vanilla. Lilac, I think . . ." She went off into a dreamworld of her own as she concocted a mix that would fit Ellen perfectly.

Rose chose another empty bottle.

"I cannot believe how many oils she has," Ellen whispered to her, as though speaking aloud would break Chrystabel's spell.

Rose took up the little funnel and a flagon. "She works all spring, summer, and autumn, converting the plants to oils," she said, filling the bottle. "Some oils she has to buy—as talented as my father is in his gardens, he cannot make everything grow in England."

Ellen's gaze continued sweeping over the labels. "But so many. They're not alphabetical?"

"Good God, no. Mum just knows where to lay her hands on whatever she wants." Rose searched for frankincense. "This is nothing, really. She has a whole little room at Trentingham where the walls are filled floor to ceiling with all her many supplies."

Ellen nodded distractedly.

"What do you think?" Chrystabel asked, presenting her with the bottle.

Ellen sniffed. " 'Tis lovely!"

"A good scent can go a long way toward cheering one up."

So Mum had noticed Ellen's melancholy mood, too, Rose thought. She added a few drops of myrrh to her mix and swirled it gently while her mother jotted a few notes on a card.

"There," Chrystabel finally said, looking up. She smiled at Ellen and took the bottle from her, corked it, and handed it back. "Now I'll be able to duplicate the scent should you wish for more later. Or we can alter the ingredients if you think you'd like something else."

"Oh, no, this is perfect." Ellen smiled, but Rose couldn't help noticing it didn't quite reach her eyes. "Thank you very much."

"You're quite welcome, dear. I hope you'll enjoy it."

Rose corked her bottle, too. "We're going to my chamber, Mum."

"Good night, then." Smiling absently, Chrystabel turned back to the perfume she'd been creating earlier.

Rose's bedchamber at Trentingham was hung with crimson silk, but here in town she had jewel tones—bright ruby, deep sapphire, and rich emerald. "This is beautiful," Ellen said when they walked in.

"Kit showed us your blue chamber when he gave us a tour of the house. 'Tis beautiful, too."

"I like it." Ellen smiled, then the expression faded. "I suppose 'tis as well, since I'll likely live there all my days."

Taking Ellen's bottle, Rose set both on her night table and fetched the book from where she'd hidden it beneath a pile of chemises. "Not all your days, surely."

"I suppose not. Just until Kit finds some hateful nobleman in need of money to marry me off to."

Rose sat on the bed, drawing Ellen down beside her. "He wouldn't wed you to anyone you hated."

"He is obsessed with raising our social status." Ellen shifted to face her. "He's convinced people judge him by that rather than his accomplishments."

"'Tis the way of the world. But he should be proud of those accomplishments—"

"Exactly what I tell him," Ellen interrupted. "He shouldn't are what people think. Do you know, I believe he doesn't ook on the Deputy Surveyor post as an accomplishment so much as a chance to be knighted. Kit really believes that peo-le will look at him differently if there's a 'Sir' before his ame."

Rose knew Ellen was waiting for her to disagree, but she ouldn't. People *would* look at Kit differently. Especially if e managed to impress King Charles to the point that he ventually awarded him a still higher title.

She'd never thought about that possibility, but then she adn't known the position of Deputy Surveyor carried ith it a probability of knighthood. That and more was ertainly within the King's power. If Kit were a member f the aristocracy—

"Oh," Ellen said suddenly, "I'm so tired of all of this." he reached and flipped open the book.

Rose's gaze dropped; her eyes widened as she read the alian.

"What?" Ellen turned to her, some color returning to her heeks. "What does it say?"

"Mettimi un dito—" Rose started.

"In *English*."

"Oh. Yes." She blew out a breath. "Push a finger inside e . . ."

That was a *normal* part of making love, then? She'd be-eved it a figment of her imagination, entirely scandalous.

And her body reacted at the mere thought of it. She felt erself dampen all over again.

"What is next?" Ellen asked, as though it were very nor-al indeed.

Rose blinked and refocused on the page. ". . . and then our yard, bit by bit . . ." The words made her think of Kit. it, who had liked it too much when she'd touched him ere. Her gaze strayed to the engraving, the picture of a an kneeling between a woman's spread thighs. She forced her eyes back to the text. "*Alza ben questa gamba* . . . Raise my leg, and we shall play a new game . . . good God."

"Good God?"

She looked up. "It doesn't say that. I'm just . . . I'm sorry, but this is difficult. It worked much better for me when I could puzzle over it slowly and write it down."

"I don't mind waiting." Ellen, too, stared at the engraving above the sonnet, her muted words directed to the page.

"Have you . . . done that?" Rose asked after a moment.

Her friend burst into tears.

"Gemini. I'm so sorry." Rose turned to her, taking her hands, cursing herself for not thinking before talking—as usual. "What is it?"

"I . . ." Ellen searched her eyes, her own overflowing. "I just . . ." She seemed to swallow past a huge lump in her throat. "I just miss Thomas, is all," she whispered finally.

If this was love, Rose wasn't sure she wanted anything to do with it. Ellen looked more miserable than she'd thought possible. She'd never seen anyone so desperate—not even Lily when she feared Rand would have to marry someone else.

"You'll see Thomas soon," she soothed, squeezing Ellen's hands. "You live in Windsor, after all. Kit cannot keep you away forever. I'm certain he just wanted to conduct his business there quickly and then get back to Whitehall where he's needed."

"But he's *not* needed at Whitehall—not anymore. The crisis has passed, and the project will progress smoothly without him."

"Well, that's good, then. He's coming back day after tomorrow. You heard him say that, did you not? If he's not needed here in London, then surely he will take you back to Windsor."

"I think not." With a great effort, Ellen choked back the last of her tears. "He told me today that Thomas will never see a penny of my dowry."

Rose didn't think Kit would follow through with that

reat, but it wasn't her place to tell Ellen. "Is that what this about?"

"No. Well, maybe." She bowed her head, looking up at ose through damp lashes. "What if Thomas doesn't want e without the money? We've spent so much time dream-g of the day when—"

"Don't be a goose." Rose reached to lift Ellen's chin. "I now the look of love in a man's eyes, and I can promise ou that Thomas is besotted. He doesn't want you for your oney, Ellen—just put that right out of your head."

"Do you think?" Ellen looked like she wanted to believe er.

"I *know*." Rose felt her age and then some. Ellen was so oung. So vulnerable. Rose remembered Kit's concerns and er promise to watch over his sister. "Would you like to eep in here instead of the other room? We can talk all ght like my sisters and I used to when one of us was pset."

Tears leaked again as Ellen nodded. "You're so kind, ose."

Nobody had ever described Rose as kind. Her own smile as watery as she rang for her maid to prepare them both r bed.

Chapter Twenty

"Good morning, Ellen." Rose stretched beneath the quilt, then slowly rolled over. "Ellen?"

Ellen wasn't there.

Rose sat up, swung her legs off the bed, and squinted at the clock on her mantel. She groaned. 'Twas naught but seven in the morning, and breakfast wasn't until nine.

Yawning, she absently lifted one of the bottles off her night table. The cork came free with a soft pop, and she inhaled deeply, closing her eyes.

Frankincense and myrrh. Kit. Almost. Something was missing. That woodsy something. She'd have to locate and add that elusive ingredient before she gave the bottle to the duke.

Thinking she'd better find Ellen, Rose yawned again and slid from the bed. She tied a red wrapper over her white night rail, slipped her feet into a pair of quilted satin mules, and padded out of her chamber, taking the bottle with her.

Ellen wasn't in the room she'd been assigned, either. Through the open door of Chrystabel's sitting room, Rose glimpsed two maids busy about their day's work, one opening the shutters while the other cleaned the fire grate.

"Have either of you seen Ellen Martyn?" she asked.

"Nay, my lady," they chorused in unison. "Perhaps she is still abed?" one of them guessed.

"No, she's not."

For one panicked moment, Rose wondered if Ellen had escaped and gone to Thomas after all, but then she shook herself and headed for the staircase. Just because the upstairs maids hadn't seen her didn't mean that Ellen wasn't here. She could easily be in the dining room having an early breakfast. Or perhaps in the large basement kitchen. Their cook would be long awake, baking the day's bread, and she was not the type to let anyone in the house go hungry.

There was no need to fret. In fact, Rose thought, pausing in front of the perfumery and looking at the bottle in her hand, she could even take the time to perfect this scent. Half guilty, knowing her mother would be a much more solicitous hostess, she pushed down on the door's latch and shoved it open.

The bottle crashed to the planked wood floor. "Ellen!"

Tears welling in her eyes, Ellen held a dropper in one hand and a vial in the other. Looking away from Rose, she tilted back her head and deliberately emptied the last glistening drop into her mouth.

"Ellen!" Skidding on glass and perfume, Rose ran to her, not wanting to believe what she'd just seen. "Whatever are you doing?" She grabbed the vial from her hand. "Pennyroyal?" Her heart pounded. "Are you trying to kill yourself? Essential oils are poison, pennyroyal most of all!"

Ellen's skin looked as white as her night rail. Sweat beaded on her forehead. As her red-rimmed eyes met Rose's, the glass dropper fell from her slack fingers and shattered on the floor.

She doubled over. "I think I'm going to be sick."

" 'Tis just as well, else I'd stick my finger down your throat and *make* you sick!" Rose ran for the chamber pot that sat beneath a sideboard and rushed back to plunk it on the worktable.

She held Ellen's head—and her own tongue—while spasms wracked the younger woman's body, purging her of the poison. Over and over, but it wasn't enough for Rose.

When Ellen swallowed convulsively, holding back another spasm while she slumped against the table, Rose couldn't hold her tongue any longer.

"All of it," she demanded. Ellen's knees buckled, and Rose held her up by sheer force of will. "More! I want to see that there's nothing left in your stomach. Nothing, Ellen, you hear me? Else my finger will go down your throat. More!"

At long last, a series of dry heaves left Rose satisfied. She slung an arm around Ellen's shoulders and led her to a chair.

Still shuddering and frightfully pale, Ellen sank down. "I'm sorry," she murmured, a shaky hand to her mouth. Tears spilled and ran down her cheeks. "I'm so sorry."

Rose took the chair beside her, a hand to her still-racing heart. She thought she'd caught Ellen in time. She'd call her mother and a doctor to make sure, but first she had to catch her breath.

She'd never been so scared in her life. "Good God, Ellen, I know you're unhappy, but surely things aren't bad enough to end it all."

The younger woman's eyes widened. "I wasn't trying to," she whispered. "I swear it. I didn't know pennyroyal was that dangerous."

Cautious relief sang through Rose's veins, but something still didn't fit. "Why, then?" Suddenly chilled, she hugged herself, running her hands up and down her arms. "Pennyroyal is a powerful herb. Did you know that pregnant women shouldn't eat or drink *anything* containing pennyroyal, for fear of bringing on their courses?"

Ellen clenched her hands together in her lap and stared at them. "How do you know that?"

"I've all kinds of foreign books to practice my languages. Many of them are herbals . . ."

Rose's voice trailed off as she stared at her friend's miserable, huddled form—and understanding dawned.

"You're with child, aren't you," she breathed, not a question, but a statement. "You were trying to rid yourself of it."

Ellen's fingers clenched harder; her tears flowed faster. Words spilled out between sobs. "The midwife said to brew pennyroyal tea, but I didn't have any leaves, and then I saw your mother's oils . . ."

"Oh, *Ellen!*" Aghast, Rose slid from her chair to kneel at Ellen's feet. She grabbed her hands. "How could you?" The younger woman's tears fell warm on all their clasped fingers. Looking up, Rose searched her face. She'd not been attempting suicide, thank heaven, but . . . "How could you even *think* of doing something so wrong?"

Ellen blinked and met her gaze, a sudden spark of anger making her eyes flash green. "There are worse wrongs," she returned vehemently. "How about bearing a child out of wedlock? Disappointing my brother? Or defying him to marry the man I love?" She wrenched her hands from Rose's and dashed at her tears. "Which is wrong, Rose? A babe would leave me no choice but to go behind Kit's back—no choice, no choice at all! I tried to talk him into letting me wed Thomas—*I tried*! But I cannot try anymore, don't you see? Not with Thomas's child growing inside me. My options are gone. I can have another child, but I'll never have another brother. I need more time. . . ."

Rose swallowed, trying to understand, trying to be a good friend. Though she wasn't a woman to sigh over other people's babies, she couldn't imagine not wanting her own.

She squeezed Ellen's fingers. "Don't you *want* Thomas's child?"

"Of course I do." Ellen's tears flowed even faster. "But—"

"You're going to have it," Rose said through gritted teeth. Ellen was her friend, and she'd promised Kit she would watch over his sister. He wouldn't want Ellen to lose her baby—she was sure of it. "If I have to stay with you day and night, I will make certain you do nothing to harm your child."

If you haven't harmed it already. A heavy silence descended as the words hung between them, unspoken.

Only time would tell. Until a day or so passed without Ellen's menses coming upon her, Rose would wonder whether she'd caught her in time.

But a little color had sneaked back into Ellen's cheeks. Though her face was wet with tears, her forehead was no longer slicked with sweat. Her body had stopped shuddering.

Rose saw reason to hope.

She got to her feet, bringing Ellen up with her, and wrapped her into a fierce hug. A hug that encompassed both the woman and the new life within her. "You'll not have a child out of wedlock," she promised into Ellen's wavy dark hair. She drew away and offered her friend a shaky smile. "Now Kit will have to allow you to marry Thomas."

"He won't."

"He *will*. Once he hears you're with child—"

Ellen stepped back. "I cannot tell him that."

"What do you mean, Ellen? You must." Rose's gaze dropped to the other woman's middle. "He'll figure it out soon enough in any case, so you might as well tell him now."

"I couldn't. He'd kill me."

"He wouldn't!"

"He thinks I'm his virginal baby sister. Have you any idea how he'd look at me? He'd think it *his* failure, and—"

"You'd rather lose your child than confess to your big brother?"

"No!" Ellen had gone white again. Into the tense silence that followed, she released a long, shuddering breath. "I just . . . I cannot tell him," she whispered.

Rose didn't understand—*couldn't* understand—but she wanted to be a good friend. And she could tell Kit anything. "Then I'll tell him for you," she said simply. "But first, we send a footman to fetch the doctor."

*   *   *

"Good afternoon, Mr. Martyn," the guard at Windsor Castle's gate greeted.

"Afternoon," Kit muttered back.

After all, there was nothing "good" about it.

He'd arrived at Harold Washburn's meager rooms on Peascod Street only to find them empty. The one neighbor he could locate informed him that Washburn had carted his belongings out days before.

Of course. As he walked from the Lower Ward to the Upper, Kit cursed himself for a fool. 'Twas obvious enough that if the man had set fire to Whitehall, he'd left Windsor in the time since Kit had dismissed him. Kit had assumed Washburn would return home, but without employment, there was no longer anything to hold him here.

He could still be in London—or anywhere.

Though Kit itched to confront the bastard, he hadn't the time to mount a full-scale search, not while seeing his projects to successful completion. He would have to hope that the arson at Whitehall had satisfied the man's thirst for revenge—that he wouldn't try anything more.

When he finally reached Windsor's dining room, he breathed a sigh of relief. Here, at least, everything seemed to be going right. The ceiling was nearing completion. The scaffolding was coming down, and new plaster was going up. Over in one corner, men labored to put a fine finish on the final pieces of oak paneling. Pleasant aromas of fresh-cut wood and sawdust filled the air.

The scent of building. It never failed to invigorate him.

"Well done," he told his new foreman. They spread out the plans and went over them together, then discussed the final schedule.

"Seen Washburn lately?" Kit asked when they were finished.

He hadn't expected an affirmative answer, but the foreman nodded. "Just yesterday, in fact. Been parading about town with some mighty fancy doxies."

Celebrating his successful revenge, Kit thought, seeing

red. And spending the money he'd pocketed by purchasing inferior materials.

Through the anger, though, the new knowledge lifted his spirits. Apparently Washburn was here in Windsor, after all.

"Saw him not an hour ago," another man volunteered through nails held between his teeth. "At the Old King's Head on Church Street."

Better news yet. Kit thanked the men for a job well done, then hied himself off to Church Street, feeling more optimistic than he had in days.

As he strode through the castle grounds, his thoughts turned to Rose and what had happened last night in the square. Lord Almighty, she had nearly unmanned him. He'd never been with a woman so responsive.

Unfortunately, he wasn't at all sure she was as ready to surrender mentally as she was physically.

"Good afternoon, Richards," he said to the guard this time.

"Afternoon," the man returned with a gap-toothed smile.

Within sight of the castle gates, The Old King's Head was a typical inn—a few chambers above a darkly paneled taproom. 'Twas known as the place a group of Parliamentarians had met in 1648 to resolve that King Charles I "should be prosecuted for his life as a criminal person." One would think the current King Charles, the beheaded king's son, would avoid the street, but the opposite was true. His favorite mistress, the "pretty, witty Nell Gwyn," owned the house next door, where she stayed—and he paid nocturnal visits—whenever the Court was lodged at Windsor.

But the King had moved to Hampton Court, so enchanting Nelly wasn't here now. Kit could only hope Washburn still was.

He pushed open the door and scanned the dim taproom. A few patrons sat at the long wooden tables this quiet afternoon—but the man Kit sought was nowhere to be seen.

"Can I get ye something, me lord?" A buxom blond serving maid sidled up to him, eyeing him appreciatively. "Mayhap an ale . . . or something else?"

Her expression made clear the "something else" involved herself, but Kit wasn't interested. "I am looking for Harold Washburn."

"Ah, His High and Mighty." The girl rolled her pretty blue eyes. "He's staying above." She gestured up a staircase. "Shakespeare's chamber, no less."

'Twas said the Bard had lived here while writing *The Merry Wives of Windsor.* Kit wasn't sure he believed that, but he *was* sure the inn charged a pretty penny for the room purported to be the playwright's.

Washburn had apparently come up in the world. He must have embezzled even more money than Kit had feared. Money that would be coming straight out of Kit's pocket.

He saw red again as he took the stairs two at a time.

"Wait, me lord!" the serving maid called, lifting her skirts to run after him. "Ye cannot just go up there!"

Try and stop me, he thought as he reached the top and began pounding on the first door. "Washburn! Are you in there?" When nobody answered, he tested the latch and found the room open and empty.

He strode to the next, rapping so hard he bruised his knuckles. 'Twas a welcome pain, one that fueled his emotions higher. "Washburn!"

The serving maid caught up and tugged on his arm. "Me lord, the proprietor—"

"A pox on the proprietor!" He shook himself free and opened the door. Finding this room vacant as well, he moved on, banging his fist against the next. "Washburn!"

A loud, startled squeal came from inside. A female squeal. And then Washburn's voice, a low hiss. "Shut your trap, you damnable wench."

For the costliest room in the house, Shakespeare's chamber sure had a thin door.

Kit tried the latch and found the door locked. "Washburn, open up!"

The serving maid tugged again on his sleeve. "Me lord, you cannot—"

"I can, my dear. Watch me." His patience at an end, Kit raised a booted foot and rammed it into the door.

It gave incredibly easily, slamming back against the wall and making the cheap porcelain knickknacks dance on Shakespeare's marble mantel. Another squeal followed, snapping Kit's gaze to the gaudy purple velvet-draped bed, where a blowsy woman sat straight up, the counterpane held to her bosom.

An obviously naked bosom. And beside her, Washburn wore naught but the evidence of a day-old beard. Sweat gleamed on his bald head. The tiny red veins on his over-sized nose seemed to pulse. Huddled under the covers, he looked, if possible, even more horrified than the doxy. Under other circumstances, Kit might have burst out laughing.

But these weren't other circumstances. "I swear," he gritted out, "by God and all that is holy, if you set fire to one more of my projects—"

"What fire?" Washburn squeaked, sounding more pathetic than the whore.

"In the Chapel Royal at Whitehall," Kit spat, moving closer. "Are you so sotted on drink and women that you've lost your half-witted memory?"

The man came off the bed, taking the counterpane with him and baring the doxy in the process. She squealed again and slid off the mattress to cower on the far side of the bed.

The purple velvet clenched in one fist, Washburn brandished the other threateningly. "To the devil with you, Martyn. I've no knowledge of a fire at Whitehall, and I damn well didn't set it."

Something in the man's dark eyes gave Kit pause. "Where were you four days ago?"

"Here," Washburn snapped.

"And what fine, upstanding citizen can you find to vouch for that?"

The ex-foreman swung to glare at his woman. "Me," the doxy squeaked, peeking over the edge of the bed.

Kit snorted. "You think me maggot-brained to believe such as her?"

"How about me?" the serving maid said from behind him. "Will you believe me?"

Kit turned to her. "About what?" In his red-hot rage, he'd forgotten she was there.

"Him." Pointing at Washburn, she nervously licked her lips. "He's been here since last week. Hasn't left except to buy some gewgaws for his ladies. An hour here or there."

Kit stepped closer and lifted her chin so he could meet her big blue eyes. "Do you swear?" When she nodded fiercely, he turned back to Washburn. "You hired someone to do it for you, then."

"I'm not an arsonist, Martyn."

"No, just a liar and a thief." Kit's breath was still coming hard, but damn if he wasn't beginning to believe the bastard. The serving maid seemed too honest, and Washburn seemed too shocked.

Without another word, Kit turned on a heel and headed for the stairs, gripping the piece of brick in his pocket as he fought to regain his composure. Though Washburn might be innocent, he felt no need to apologize. Perhaps Shakespeare would have summoned fine words, but Kit couldn't—and to his mind, the man didn't deserve them anyway.

Chapter Twenty-one

R ose answered the door herself, practically dragging Kit into the town house without so much as a good morning. "I need to talk to you."

He grinned as she pulled him toward the drawing room. "Missed me, did you?"

"No," she said, although in truth she had missed him entirely too much. She shut the door behind them and waved him toward a blue brocade chair. "Sit, please."

"Sit? Then you didn't drag me in here for a kiss?" He steepled his fingers and rested his elbows on the arms of the chair, looking nauseatingly good in his simple dark blue suit. "'Tisn't like you not to be looking for a kiss."

She stared at him, wondering how to break this to him gently while half wishing he were an ugly harebrained hayseed with no talent at all for kissing.

Of course she wanted a kiss.

"No, I'm not looking for a kiss." His sister was important to them both—much more important than kisses. "This is serious, Kit. You must let Ellen wed Thomas. She loves him, and—"

"I've told Ellen time and again that I'll not see her wed to a pawnbroker." The good humor left his face, and he unsteepled his fingers and crossed his arms instead. "I haven't changed my mind."

Something else had changed instead. But suddenly Rose wondered if she could convince him without giving away

Ellen's secret. 'Twould not only be easier for Ellen, but for him as well.

"Thomas is not only a pawnbroker," she said carefully. "He's also a man—the man your sister loves. You're judging him the way you complain people judge you."

He raised a brow. "The way *you* judge me?"

"We're talking about Ellen." She wouldn't let him turn this around. "Ellen really and truly loves Thomas. Why should it matter what the man does for a living? He's a good man, Kit. Do you not want your sister to be happy?"

He remained quiet for a moment, just staring at her. As the silence stretched, she thought maybe she'd succeeded in convincing him.

Until he finally spoke. "What happened," he asked slowly, "to your conviction that it is as easy to fall in love with a titled man as one without?" He rose and slid off his surcoat, tossing it over the arm of the chair. "If those words no longer apply to Ellen, can I assume they also don't apply to yourself?"

She backed up. "No. Of course they still apply. But in Ellen's case—"

"Why should Ellen be different?" Kit advanced, taking perverse pleasure in watching her retreat. He'd caught her—twice—insisting Ellen should marry for love, and this time he wasn't going to let her get away with claiming it shouldn't work the same way for her.

"Ellen isn't different." She backed into a marquetry desk and placed her hands behind her for support. "But Ellen has already fallen in love." She lifted her chin. "She never had a chance to fall in love with a titled man first."

He brought his face to within an inch of hers. "Who will *you* fall in love with first, sweetheart?"

Though he was too close to see it, he heard her nervous swallow. "We're talking about Ellen."

"Not anymore." He bent his head, angled his mouth. Her warm, sweet breath teased his lips. Her eyes closed, and a little mewing sound rose up from her throat. She raised her hands and rested them on his chest. They felt warm through the thin cambric of his shirt.

Then she pushed him away. "Kit! Listen to me. You must let Ellen wed Thomas—she's carrying his child."

He stumbled back, not from the force of her shove, but the impact of her words.

His baby sister was having a baby?

Unable to wrap his mind around that fact, he fell back onto the chair.

"Good God," Rose said, putting her hands to her cheeks and looking entirely unRoselike. "I'm sorry. I didn't mean to tell you like that. It must be a terrible shock."

"You could say that." He rubbed his face. "Why didn't she tell me?"

She sat in the chair next to his, shifting to face him. "She said she couldn't. That she couldn't bear to see the look on your face. Your disappointment." She put a hand on his. "She loves you."

"She says she loves Whittingham."

"Him, too." Apprehension flooded her eyes, and he watched her swallow hard. "Kit, I think you should know . . ."

"What?" he asked. Whatever it was couldn't be worse than what he'd already learned.

"Rather than disappoint you, she tried to rid herself of the child."

He couldn't have heard right. "She *what*?"

"She took pennyroyal, hoping to bring on her courses. I caught her in time, in the act, and made her bring it back up. Can you not see that this changes everything? What you wanted for your sister doesn't matter anymore. Her fate is out of your hands."

The second half of what she'd said had been lost on him, so appalled was he by the first. "Pennyroyal?" he echoed.

"A midwife told her pennyroyal tea can stimulate the menses. But she used one of my mother's essential oils. They're a hundred times or more stronger than the herbs— 'twas likely to take her life along with the child's."

His heart hammering, Kit came halfway off the chair.

She leapt from hers and pushed him back down, looking desperate. "Good God, I said it all wrong again." Her hands on his shoulders, her dark eyes held his captive. "The doctor said she is well, and she wasn't aware of the risks, Kit. I'm certain of it. She thought it would be just like the tea."

Did he know his sister at all? "Does she not trust me even a little?" That hurt. "That she would do this rather than disappoint me?"

"She wasn't thinking of it that way. She wasn't thinking at all."

"Even so, how could she? How could she kill her child?"

Rose winced. "Please don't judge her so harshly. She's hurting and confused. Women rid themselves of unwanted children all the time, for all sorts of reasons."

"Ellen has no good reason." His heart was finally slowing. Apparently the danger had passed. "How could she not know I would love her child? This is my sister and my niece or nephew."

"I know," she said softly.

Guilt was a vise squeezing his chest. He'd almost lost his sister, his only family. The one person he'd vowed to protect at all costs. If it hadn't been for Rose . . .

She'd saved his sister. Because she was good, because she was caring, because there was a heroic person hiding inside this exasperating woman who insisted she wanted a duke.

His throat tightened, and something twisted around his heart—an unwelcome thrill laced with a flicker of fear. He reached to gather her onto his lap, wrapped his arms around her, and buried his nose in her rose-scented hair.

"Thank you," he whispered, afraid he'd just fallen in love.

Lust was one thing, love quite another. It scared him to death. He'd wanted her before, yes. Wanted her for her beauty, her refreshing forthright nature, her family's position in society, her intelligence, her sheer suitability as a wife. And, of course, because she'd made him hotter than the sun in August from the first time he'd laid eyes on her.

But suddenly he wanted her in an entirely different way. The want had turned into need.

He'd been determined to make her fall in love with him, but he hadn't expected to fall himself. What would he do now if she wouldn't agree to be his?

Feeling his throat tighten more, he pressed his lips to the top of her head.

"You must let them marry," she said quietly. "If you have even a glimmer of an idea what they feel for each other, you cannot deny them."

He had a glimmer, all right. A sudden new glimmer that was frightening as hell. And he loved his sister, and—already—her unborn child. Rose was right, everything had changed—and he hadn't the will left to deny Ellen and her baby loves of their own.

As long as he could make sure Thomas Whittingham loved them back.

He motioned to the marquetry desk. "Is there paper and quill in there?"

"Yes." Rose slanted him a look. "Why?"

"I wish to write a letter."

Her expression made clear she didn't consider that much of an answer.

"Trust me," he added. "And fetch Ellen, please."

His sister looked pale when she walked in, wan and frightened. He silently handed her his hastily scribbled missive. As she scanned the single page, her eyes widened. A soft gasp escaped her lips.

"What is it?" Rose asked.

"A letter to Thomas." Ellen looked up at Kit. "You're . . . you're allowing our marriage?"

"Demanding it," Kit corrected. "On one condition."

"What?" She swallowed hard, clutching the paper against her middle.

His gaze flicked down, but there was no sign of her pregnancy. 'Twas too early, he supposed. He might suspect her of fibbing to get her way, but he seriously doubted she'd have risked poisoning herself if she wasn't actually with child.

"Why?" he asked suddenly. "Why did you do it?"

Her eyes filled. "I know not. I think . . . I was confused." She brought her other hand to cover the first. "It seemed as though this child growing inside me had stolen my options—that I needed more time to convince you, and I feared your wrath, and—" She stared at the floor. "'Twas wrong, wasn't it? Very, very wrong."

"Yes." Kit watched a teardrop fall to the polished wood, then stepped forward to wrap her in his arms. "I'm so glad you're all right."

"I'm sorry," she sniffed against his chest.

"Do you not know how much I love you?"

Her arms tightened around him as she raised her tear-stained face. "I guess I forgot. I only thought about how angry you'd have been if you'd known."

"Had I known, Ellen, I might have been disappointed—I *am* disappointed—but I'd not have kept you from wedding your child's father. And I won't. What's done is done. I wanted more for you, but you've narrowed *my* options. Unless—"

"What?" She pulled away. "What is this condition?"

He met her gaze, hardening his heart against the tears. "You'll find out soon enough." He turned to Rose. "Can you send a rider to Windsor to deliver this letter to Whittingham? And an extra horse so they can both ride back. I left my carriage at Whitehall, and 'tis too slow in any case."

She looked between him and his sister. "Of course."

"Good," he said to her, and to Ellen, "I will see you wed today."

Both women stared at him incredulously. Rose spoke for the two. "They cannot marry today!"

"Tonight, then. However long it takes Whittingham to show up, we'll wait."

"Banns must be called—'twill take weeks."

"Have you never heard of a privileged church? There are two, I believe, directly outside the City walls. Places where a man and a woman can marry without posting banns, without taking out a license. Without waiting."

"That doesn't sound legal," she said doubtfully.

"They claim they're outside the jurisdiction of the Bishop of London and can therefore make their own rules." He shrugged. "The marriages stand, and that is all I care about at the moment. I wish I could remember at least one of their names . . . ah, yes. St. Trinity, in the Minories." He turned to his sister. "I was hoping to see you wed in a cathedral, but a privileged church will have to do."

Chapter Twenty-two

Following a bit of wrangling, 'twas decided Kit would go ahead to St. Trinity and arrange matters while Rose and his sister waited for Whittingham. They would all meet Kit at the church.

It took an hour for him to reach St. Trinity—an hour during which he cursed himself ten times over for not watching more closely over his sister. For not protecting her better. For allowing her to maneuver him to the point where he had no choice.

But there was nothing left to do except make the best of it. If Whittingham could prove he truly loved Ellen, the man could have her. And Kit would make sure they had a wonderful, carefree life together.

Or rather, his eleven thousand pounds would.

But he wouldn't tell them that now. Either of them. His sister had said over and over that she wanted to marry for love—and marry for love she would.

Kit arrived to find St. Trinity in surprisingly good repair for such an old building. The walls and columns were freshly painted, costly leaded glass filled the windows, and votive candles flickered around the sanctuary.

A privileged church was quite obviously a lucrative business.

He stood in the back, watching a wedding in progress. Several more couples seemed to be waiting their turns. One bride was well gone with child, another quietly weeping. A third wedding party included a man who didn't look much happier. If Kit didn't miss his guess, the bride's father was surreptitiously holding a pistol on the poor fellow.

The minute the current wedding concluded, Kit barged down the aisle.

The priest looked up and frowned. "You're not next."

"I'm not marrying at all. But my sister will be here later today, and I wish to make certain you'll stay to perform the ceremony no matter how late she arrives."

The man shook his balding head. "I've too many weddings this day already. She will have to come tomorrow. Or go to St. James instead."

Ellen and her groom weren't going to St. James—they were coming here. "What is your customary charge?" Kit asked flatly.

The plump clergyman sized him up. "Six crowns."

Gasps from behind told Kit the quote was high, perhaps by double or more. "I'll pay you ten," he told the man. "And half of that now." He fished his pouch from his surcoat and began counting out coins. "I'll expect her to be wed the moment she appears."

"By all means, good sir," the priest said, licking his fleshy lips. When he took the gold and hefted its weight in a hand, a wide smile emerged, revealing large, uneven teeth. "Bring two witnesses, and—since you seem to value speed—a pistol," he added with a wink.

Despite himself, Kit almost laughed. "We've no need of a pistol—I'm the only party reluctant to this match."

Hours later, Kit was waiting on the steps when the Ashcrofts' carriage pulled up. His sister stepped to the cobblestones, followed by Rose, who was carrying a bunch of flowers. He wasn't surprised when Lady Trentingham emerged next, although he hadn't expressly invited her.

Finally, Whittingham stepped down, dressed in a green wool suit that was ten or more years out of fashion. His brown hair was tied back in a neat queue. Somehow he managed to look both pleased and scared spitless.

Kit was happy to see that. Perhaps the man cared after all.

Ellen marched up the steps and dragged Kit inside the church. Her gaze skimmed the sanctuary before swinging to fasten on him. "What the devil have you planned here?" she whispered fiercely.

"Such language in a house of God," he chided. She'd changed into a gown that he imagined must belong to Rose, a confection of pale green satin with silver embroidery. It didn't suit Rose's high coloring at all, but it looked perfect on his sister. The hue brought out the green in her eyes—they always had turned green when she was angry.

"I am going to ask Whittingham if he'll take you without your dowry," he informed her in an even tone. "And if he hesitates as much as a moment—*one* moment, Ellen—the wedding is off."

"That is so unfair!" she burst out.

Heads turned. "Hush!" he cautioned.

She moderated her voice, but not her demeanor. "You'd have me raise this child alone?"

"Not alone. With me. Your child will never see an unhappy day if I can help it—you've nothing to fear. Should Whittingham love you, I wish you the best. But if not . . . you'll be better off in my care than bound to a man who wanted you only for your money."

She crossed her arms, narrowed her eyes, and shut her mouth decisively. Remembering her words when he'd talked of withholding her dowry—*I will never speak to you again*—he figured she was following through on her threat.

That wouldn't last. A woman carrying a child couldn't afford to act like one.

"I've paid good money to see you wed quickly." He put a hand on her arm, then frowned when she shoved it off. "Let us adjourn outside and see this thing through."

* * *

Rose watched Kit and his sister emerge from St. Trinity, Kit looking determined, Ellen furious. She wondered what had been said during their short time inside.

Thomas stepped forward and looked directly at Kit. "Ellen has informed me you've put a condition on our marriage."

He was a direct sort of man. Rose had come to know him a little better on the ride from the town house to the church, and she believed he would make a good husband for her friend.

If only Kit would allow it.

"Yes," Kit said. "You must be willing to take my sister without her dowry."

Rose suspected Kit just wanted to be sure of the man's love, but Ellen released an angry huff. Yet Thomas, bless the man, didn't so much as blink. "I would take your sister if she came with a mound of debt. Ellen's dowry would be welcome—I'll not lie—but I don't want your sister for money, sir. I want her because I love her."

'Twas such a pretty speech, Rose wanted to applaud.

But Kit just nodded, somehow contriving to appear pleased, relieved, disappointed, and apprehensive all at once. "Come along, then. Let's get this done."

Ellen let out a little squeal, then ran to Thomas and pressed her lips to his in a fervent kiss.

"*After* the wedding," Kit said, but not without a hint of good humor.

Regardless, Ellen chose to glare at him.

"Good luck, Ellen." Rose handed her the bouquet of flowers she'd arranged while they were waiting for Thomas. 'Twould not feel like a real wedding without flowers.

Ellen smiled, but her jaw didn't relax until Thomas had drawn her down the aisle to stand before the priest. Then she took his hand and released a heartfelt sigh.

Some other people started to protest, but Kit pressed a small pile of gold into the priest's plump hand—and that was that. The man wasted no time beginning the ceremony.

He was the no-nonsense sort, with a booming voice, a big belly under his robe, and flushed, well-fed cheeks.

Standing in the small, old chapel, Rose shifted on her high-heeled shoes, wondering if she'd ever be a bride.

"Thomas Whittingham, wilt thou have this woman to thy wedded wife, to live together after God's ordinance in the holy estate of Matrimony? Wilt thou love her, comfort her, honor, and keep her in sickness and in health; and, forsaking all others, keep thee only unto her, so long as ye both shall live?"

"I will." The confident words boomed off the plain, whitewashed walls, binding Thomas to Kit's sister.

But Rose wasn't listening to the ceremony. Instead, she focused on the bride and groom—their linked hands, their bodies ranged close, their eyes shining with a potent mixture of disbelief and happiness.

Chrystabel smiled as though she'd arranged this wedding herself. She leaned closer until she bumped against Rose's left side, her voice made breathy by emotion. "They're perfect together, are they not?"

Rose could only nod dumbly. Ellen and her pawnbroker were clearly in love . . . for Ellen, at least, it had not been as easy to fall in love with a titled man as a commoner.

The priest cleared his throat and looked back down at his *Book of Common Prayer.* "Ellen Martyn, wilt thou have this man to thy wedded husband . . ."

Standing on Rose's right, Kit sighed. "Have I done the right thing?"

"Oh, yes," she breathed, wondering if *she* would do the right thing. For she feared that, like Ellen, she was not finding it easy to fall in love with a titled man. The Duke of Bridgewater was handsome and rich and kind, and she'd tried to make herself fall in love with him, to no avail. And yet, with Kit . . .

Her feelings didn't bear thinking about.

" . . . so long as ye both shall live?" the priest concluded expectantly.

"I will," Ellen pledged, sounding happier than Rose remembered ever feeling.

A few more words, a ring slid onto her finger—something hastily chosen from the pawnshop, no doubt—and Ellen was clearly and truly wed now, Mrs. Thomas Whittingham.

And Rose was more confused than ever.

When Thomas lowered his lips to meet Ellen's, Kit looked to Rose. Her breath caught in her chest. His eyes were full of promises . . . but they were promises she couldn't return.

She didn't breathe easily again until they were all heading back down the steps to her family's carriage.

"Where will you go tonight?" she asked Ellen.

"Home. To the pawnshop in Windsor." She smiled up at Thomas, then glanced at Kit and lifted her chin before turning back to Rose. "'Twill doubtless be late by the time we arrive, but there is no place I wish to stay in London."

"We're going home to Trentingham tomorrow," Chrystabel announced.

"Are we?" Rose asked, surprised. But right now the idea of home sounded wonderful.

"I miss your father. And Rowan. And I'm going to have your sisters and their husbands over for supper as soon as possible. In fact, I'll send notes to them before we leave. Perhaps they can join us tomorrow night." Without missing a beat, Chrystabel turned to Kit. "Will you join us as well? My husband is likely impatient to see his greenhouse take shape. You *did* promise to work up a design before you left Lily's wedding."

"I did, didn't I?" he said wryly. "But—"

"Rose has indicated you've got Whitehall under control. And you'll not be far from Windsor. Or Hampton Court, for that matter."

Mum could be persuasive when she put her mind to it. Kit nodded. "I suppose since no red-and-white-liveried

King's man has shown up with bad news, I can take a day to sketch a design."

"And one night to relax before jumping back into the fray."

"And one night," he agreed, his gaze straying to Rose.

Her skin heated all over.

It took a few more minutes for plans to be nailed down. Rose and Chrystabel would take Ellen and Thomas back to the town house to fetch Ellen's things. Kit would return to Whitehall, spend the balance of the day making certain everything there would proceed smoothly, then go on to Trentingham Manor in the morning.

Rose was settled in the carriage and halfway to St. James's Square before she realized that in all the time since before the wedding began, Ellen hadn't said one word to her brother.

Chapter Twenty-three

Rose's family was almost more than Kit could take. They were loud. They were boisterous. And there were so damn *many* of them.

Rose's oldest sister, Violet, had brought along her husband, Ford, and their three children—two of which were infant twins and prone to wailing—plus Ford's niece, ten-year-old Jewel.

Kit's friend Rand was there with his new wife, Rose's younger sister, Lily. Lily, as usual, was surrounded by animals—a cat she'd brought, along with a sparrow and a squirrel that had followed her. Her mother had ordered the latter two outside during supper, but they were watching through a window.

And then, of course, there were Lord and Lady Trentingham. And their eleven-year-old son, Rowan.

With Rose and Kit—and not counting the creatures—that made eleven people around the table in Trentingham Manor's white-paneled dining room, plus two in cradles nearby. Kit was unwillingly reminded of his school days, eating in a huge hammerbeam-ceilinged hall with shouts and conversation coming from all angles. He half expected a food fight to break out. It seemed quite a racket to a man who was used to dining only with his sister.

Ellen. She'd passed her wedding night by now—not that it had been the proper wedding night he had wanted for her—and he wondered how she was doing. Was she happy with her pawnbroker? They'd be happier, of course, when he gave them the money he'd saved for her dowry, but he thought he'd wait a little while for that. A week or two, at least. Let them get settled first—such a windfall was likely to be unsettling, indeed.

In the meantime, he hadn't wanted to be alone at his house in Windsor, imagining his baby sister and her new husband doing God knew what down the street. So Lady Trentingham's invitation had been welcome, even though he damn well knew he had better things to do.

But his projects seemed stabilized, and the day had gone well enough. Lord Trentingham had been happy with Kit's ideas for the greenhouse, and Kit had gone only half hoarse shouting all his explanations. He'd order the materials and hire a foreman when he returned to Windsor. Lord Trentingham was anxious to get his plants inside before winter, so Kit had promised him an accelerated schedule. The groundbreaking was planned for ten days hence.

"This all must be very disturbing," Rand said.

"Hmm?" Kit had been so deep in his thoughts he hadn't even noticed that sweets had been put on the table. "Are you talking to me?"

"Wake up, you dolt." Rand elbowed him in the ribs and laughed. "We were talking about the problems you had at both Windsor and Whitehall."

"They're settled now," Kit said. His plate had been removed by one of Trentingham's footmen, and he hadn't noticed that, either. Someone set a smaller, clean plate in front of him.

"Are you sure?" Jewel's deep green eyes looked wide in her fine-boned, heart-shaped face.

"I'm convinced Washburn didn't set the fire, so I don't expect him to try anything else."

"But how can you be sure?"

Seated to his left, Rose passed him a platter of small currant cakes, her soft floral fragrance wafting to his nose along with the fruity scent of the baked goods. "The fire was probably not intended," she told Jewel.

"Exactly." He took three and passed the plate to Rand. "The men aren't supposed to smoke pipes on the job, but I wasn't there to watch."

Lord Trentingham frowned. "Has Whitehall become overrun with mice?"

Kit blinked. "Pardon?"

"You said the men aren't supposed to poke mice?"

"Smoke pipes, darling." Lady Trentingham leaned to brush a few cake crumbs off her husband's cravat. "The men aren't supposed to smoke pipes."

"It could have been someone else." Taking six cakes for himself, Rowan sounded a bit gleeful at the prospect of uncovering intrigue. "Not this Washburn, but someone else."

"Let us hope not." Kit used one of the cakes to scoop sweet whipped cream "snow" from a dish, suddenly worrying that the children might be right. " 'Twas most probably accidental. These things happen."

"Bee stings do happen," Lord Trentingham put in. "Especially out in my gardens."

No one corrected him this time.

Jewel waved a currant cake. "Accidents at two of your buildings? Are you not wondering if your other building might have a problem, too?"

Out of the mouths of babes. Kit sighed. "Perhaps I should go to Hampton Court and make certain everything there is progressing smoothly."

"Rose and I are going to Hampton Court," Lady Trentingham volunteered cheerfully.

Kit was not surprised.

Her husband had actually heard that. "Not too soon, I hope, Chrysanthemum."

"Well, we won't want to wait too long. The Court is there, after all, and Rose will want to see the duke."

Rose's sisters turned to her in unison.

"The duke?" Violet asked, leaning down to swipe her son's spoon off the floor for at least the tenth time.

Lily fed a bit of cake to her cat under the table. "What duke?"

"The Duke of Bridgewater." Rose hid her face by raising her goblet to her lips—even though Kit knew it was empty. "We'll talk about this later."

Not too much later, Rose found herself upstairs flanked by her sisters, the three of them lying crosswise on her oak four-poster bed, staring straight up.

"Tell us about the duke," Violet said to the underside of Rose's crimson velvet canopy.

"He's very generous and handsome and kind," Rose returned morosely. "He gave me these ruby and pearl earrings."

Her sisters both turned to look. Violet touched a finger to one of the delicate drops. "They're lovely."

"Goodness!" Lily exclaimed. "He sounds perfect. Exactly what you were looking for. Do you think he likes you?"

"Very much." Rose sighed. "I'll not be surprised if at Hampton Court I receive my first proposal."

Violet came up on an elbow. "Then why," she asked, "do you sound so melancholy?"

Rose turned to look at Violet, but her sister's warm brown eyes looked too concerned behind the lenses of her spectacles. She focused back up on the canopy. "I don't care for the way he kisses."

"Oh . . ." her sisters said together in a way that made it clear they considered this as important a problem as she did. Rose wasn't sure whether she was glad or frustrated at that fact.

Part of her wished they'd just tell her to marry the duke and be done with it.

"Is his kiss . . . sloppy?" Lily asked.

"No."

"Rough?" Violet wondered.

"No."

"Then what?" they both chimed.

"I'm not sure. There's nothing wrong with his kisses. I just don't enjoy them. They don't make me feel anything." She crossed her feet where they hung off the end of the bed. She uncrossed them. Her voice dropped miserably. "For the longest time, I didn't like *anyone's* kisses. I thought something was wrong with me. Until . . ."

Now Lily came up on an elbow. "Until what?"

Rose felt hemmed in. She looked at her older sister, then her younger, then back to the canopy. "I've found one man whose kisses make me melt. But he's totally unsuitable."

"In what way?" Lily's voice was heartbreakingly sympathetic.

"In every way. He's a commoner. And he *works* for a living."

"Rand works," Lily said defensively. "Do you not think being a professor is a lot of hard work?"

"But Rand doesn't *have* to work. He works because he wants to. Good God, he's an earl, and someday he'll be a marquess."

" 'Twas not always that way, and he never minded working. And it didn't bother me to think of marrying him when he did have to work. In fact, it didn't bother you, either, if I recall correctly. You were perfectly willing to chase Rand when he was only a professor."

"He was never only a professor." Rose didn't care for Lily's affronted tone, nor for the reminder of how foolishly she'd pursued her sister's husband. "Even before he became an earl, he was Lord Randal Nesbitt."

"There is nothing wrong with work," Lily insisted.

"Of course there isn't!" Frustrated, Rose pushed herself up to sit on the edge of the bed. She rubbed her face as her sisters came up beside her. " 'Tis only that I had a plan for my life, and this man isn't part of it."

"Is he poor?" Violet asked.

"No," she said, thankful she could say that at least, else she'd get the same kind of tirade from Violet that she'd just heard from Lily. Violet's husband, after all, had been poor as a church mouse when they met.

"'Tis Kit, isn't it?" Lily suddenly guessed.

"No," Rose denied quickly, then sighed at Lily's perceptive gaze and added, "How did you know?"

"I've both eyes and ears in my head. You're surprisingly familiar with the man's projects, and you cannot deny you thought him handsome the day you met. And he was drawn to you. I was there, if you'll remember. And he is *not* totally unsuitable."

"I want to love the duke," Rose wailed.

"Sometimes," Violet said softly, "we cannot choose these things."

All three of them sighed in unison. Lily reached to cover Rose's hands where she'd clenched them together in her lap. "At least Mum is not trying to match you with Kit," she offered with forced cheerfulness.

"That's right," Violet said. The one thing they'd all agreed on, from the time they were small girls, was that they didn't want any part of Chrystabel's matchmaking schemes. "She's taking you to Hampton Court to spend more time with the duke."

"But she invited Kit here," Rose realized suddenly. "And to supper in London."

"True," Violet conceded. "But she probably just wanted to make sure he follows through with Father's greenhouse."

"Probably." That thought was a relief. The last thing Rose wanted was Mum trying to marry her off to Kit. Once Chrystabel got something like that in her head, the pressure would be tremendous. "She likes Kit's sister, too. Perhaps she felt sorry for Ellen and invited her to the town house to cheer her up. Kit would naturally have had to come along. And oh!" she added, "I almost forgot. I've borrowed a book from Ellen that you two may find very interesting."

Just the thing to take her mind off these gloomy thoughts.

"A book?" Violet loved books.

"Not one to read—unless you read Italian." She hurried over to her trunk to fetch *I Sonetti*. "Mostly you'll want to see the engravings. The ladies at Court found them fascinating."

"The ladies at Court?" Lily reached for the book.

"You've never even been to Court." Violet snatched it away.

"I vow and swear, neither of you ever grew up." Rose laughed as she took it back, knowing she was no better. "Let me sit again between you."

She wedged her wine-skirted bottom onto the bed between Violet's lavender skirts and Lily's yellow ones. After settling the book on her lap, she slowly opened it.

"Goodness." Lily's eyes widened—she was newly wedded, after all. "May I borrow this?"

"No. 'Tis not mine." Rose flipped a page, then another. "Now look at this. Is this even possible?"

Lily shrugged. "I know not."

"Oh, that works fine," Violet assured them, her gaze glued to the book as Rose turned to a new engraving. "But wait"—she stayed her hand—"I cannot imagine how this one would."

Both of Rose's married sisters had cheeks as red as her bedding. The three of them looked at each other and burst out laughing.

"Wait 'til you hear the words," Rose said with a grin.

The men had adjourned to Lady Trentingham's perfumery. Ford tinkered with the distillery he'd made for his mother-in-law, searching for a reported leak. Rand sat in a green brocade chair, sipping brandy.

Kit paced.

The contraption Ford was working on, and the large utilitarian table on which it sat, looked out of place in the otherwise elegant room. Kit ran a hand down the silk and linen

brocatelle wall-coverings. "How is married life?" he asked
Rand.

"Splendid," Rand said, looking nauseatingly relaxed.

Feeling decidedly *un*relaxed, Kit gazed up at the black
and gold cornice around the plastered ceiling. A fine display of workmanship. Something like it would look magnificent in the apartments he was building for the Duchess
of Cleveland at Hampton Court, not to mention in his own
house in Windsor.

"You should try it," Rand added.

"Marriage?" Kit looked down to his old friend. "If I have
my way, I will."

"What?" Rand half bolted out of the chair.

"Sit," Kit said.

Frowning, Ford removed a lid and disconnected a copper
tube. "Whom are you hoping to wed?"

"Your sister-in-law. Rose."

Ford looked up, astonished. "Rose?"

"Rose?" Rand echoed. He gulped a swallow of brandy.
"I knew you found her attractive, but—"

"She saved my sister's life," Kit said flatly. "And she
yearns to travel, as do I. Not only that, she can speak the
language when we get there."

Ford looked at him through a large glass bulb that was
part of the device. "Where?"

Kit examined the marble fireplace. "Rome, Florence,
France . . . wherever."

"If all you want is a translator, you can hire a linguist."
Rand set the goblet on a small inlaid table. "I've students
that would jump at a chance to spend a summer—"

"I love her," Kit said simply. "She's fun and beautiful
and bright, and . . . something in her calls to me."

Ford straightened and exchanged a look with Rand. "He
said the *L* word."

Rand nodded. "So I heard."

Kit rubbed the back of his neck. "I wanted success. Security. But now my sister's married a pawnbroker—what kind

of security is a life like that? Yet she's happy. And just when success may be slipping away from me—when I need that Deputy Surveyor post, that knighthood—"

"Whoa," Ford said, looking totally lost. "Does any of that really matter?"

"I know not." Kit ran his hand across a rack of little glass vials, all neatly labeled. LAVENDER, LILAC, MUSK. He plucked out the one that said ROSE. "All I know is I cannot stand the thought of failing to win her."

Ford replaced the copper tube with a little *snap*. "Try seduction. It worked for me."

"I *am* trying that. With her mother's blessing, no less."

Neither man looked surprised to hear that. "With Lily," Rand said, "it only took getting to know one another. Once we knew one another, we *knew*."

"I *do* know. And she knows, too—I'm sure of it. Only she'll not admit it because she wants to marry a damned duke. My only ray of hope is that His Grace is reportedly a lousy kisser."

The other men laughed. "That sounds promising," Rand observed. "Has she refused your proposal?"

"I've not asked. What is the point?"

"You might be surprised by her answer."

"'Tis one thing to wish it." Kit's fingers tightened around the glass vial. "Another to go heart in hand and ask."

"True." Ford nodded solemnly. "You could be asking to have that heart crushed." His expression said he was a veteran of such a defeat.

Kit unstoppered the vial and breathed deeply of the oil. Rose. "Violet didn't say yes the first time you asked?"

"Hell, no. Nor the second, either. Or the third. Or the nineteenth."

As they all laughed again, feminine laughter drifted down from upstairs. Rand smiled. "Our ladies are enjoying themselves."

"Where is everyone else?" Kit asked suddenly.

"Jewel and Rowan are probably off somewhere planning a dastardly prank." Ford straightened, dusting off his hands. "And the younger children were put to bed."

"But Lord and Lady Trentingham—"

"Have gone to bed, too," Rand informed him with a waggle of his brows.

Kit glanced at the clock on the mantel. "Is it not a bit early?"

"They've not seen each other in more than a week." Rand looked to Ford. "If you hadn't seen Violet in ten days, what would you be doing now?"

"Taking her to bed," Ford said with a decisive nod.

"But Lord and Lady Trentingham have grown children," Kit protested.

"So?" Ford shrugged as he replaced the distillery's lid and stepped back. "They're Ashcrofts."

"Warm blooded," Rand added.

"Hot blooded," Ford corrected with a grin. "'Tis an excellent incentive to marry one."

Chapter Twenty-four

Chrystabel stretched luxuriously beneath the rumpled counterpane in her bedchamber. "Ah, that was nice."

"Just nice?" Joseph asked, his voice filled with feigned hurt.

"Very well. It was spectacular."

"That's better." He tweaked the sensitive crest of one breast, smiling when she gave a delighted squeal. "This was the longest you've ever been gone from me."

"You leave me for several weeks every year when you go to Tremayne."

"That seems different somehow."

"Because you're the one leaving and busy." She knew he had to go, that Tremayne, a castle near the Welsh border, was as much his responsibility as Trentingham or his duty to Parliament. But that didn't mean she liked it. "Now that the girls are grown, perhaps I will come along. And bring Rowan," she said, warming to the idea. "After all, he is Lord Tremayne. He should learn the ins and outs of running the estate."

"An excellent plan, Chrysanthemum."

Joseph's eyes were closing, as was wont to happen after loving exertion. And, as usual, her own body felt alive, her brain wide awake. She'd never figured out what made them so different.

"I'll have to leave again, though," she said mournfully. "Soon."

He snuggled against her. "Hmm?"

"Rose is so close to making the right decision. Another few days at Court ought to convince her there is no one there meant to share her life."

"Mmm." He threw a leg over hers, its weight warm and welcome.

"I am quite disappointed, though, that she's not found a moment here to go off with Kit. It seems they both believe I invited him only to settle the details for your greenhouse. And the house is so quiet. Do you know, I think everyone's gone to bed. And 'tis not even midnight." She gave an expressive sigh, rubbing Joseph's smooth, warm back. "I believe I shall have to devise a way to get Rose and Kit out of their beds and into each other's arms, at least for a while. I imagine he'll be leaving in the morning for Hampton Court. Perhaps we'll wait a few days before following . . . give Rose some time to miss him. What do you think, darling?"

Her husband's answer was a soft snore. He was fast asleep.

Oh, well. She would lie here until she came up with a plan—she was quite used to plotting these things without him. Men were dear creatures, but the vast majority of them didn't seem to have much of an imagination.

A few minutes later she chuckled to herself. Ah, yes, that should work—and be quite amusing in the bargain. Carefully she wiggled free from her husband and slid out of bed. She slipped back into her discarded night rail and tied a wrapper over it against the chill.

Joseph would hardly miss her. When her mission was accomplished, she'd return and wake him his favorite way. The night was still young, and dear Joseph never minded being awakened—not by her, anyway.

A little ripple of anticipation warmed her body as she sneaked from the chamber into the dimly lit corridor.

The house was amazingly quiet. Rose's room was right beyond hers, so Chrystabel tiptoed to the door and tapped her fingernails against it—*rat-a-tat-tat*. Then she moved to the door of the room she'd assigned to Kit and did the same thing.

Nothing. Rose was a heavy sleeper, and Kit must be, too. She tapped on both their doors again, then a third time. Finally, the sound of a latch sent her scurrying back to her room. Suppressing a giddy giggle, she pulled the door shut behind her—but not quite all the way.

Her ear pressed to the slit of an opening, she heard someone pad into the corridor and knock loudly on another door.

"Rowan!" came a harsh whisper. Then louder, "Rowan, open up!"

'Twas Jewel's voice, not Rose's. Chrystabel sighed as she listened. Another door opened.

"What?" Rowan demanded rather ungraciously.

"I heard a noise."

"What kind of noise?" he said through a yawn.

"I'm not sure. Maybe a ghost."

That idea was greeted by a snort. "There are no ghosts at Trentingham."

"I heard something, Rowan! Listen, will you?"

A long spell passed where there was no sound. Of course, Chrystabel wasn't tapping on doors.

"'Twas nothing," Rowan finally said. "Go back to bed."

"I'm afraid of ghosts. I cannot sleep. Will you stay with me?"

"I cannot visit your chamber in the middle of the night. 'Twould not be proper." Even at the tender age of eleven, Rowan knew that.

"What if I hear it again?"

The boy's sigh would have done a grown man justice. "Are you hungry?"

Jewel seemed to consider that question a moment. "Yes, I am."

"Maybe it was your stomach rumbling. Let us go downstairs and find something to eat."

Chrystabel waited until their footfalls had proceeded down the staircase before easing open her door. It seemed neither Rose nor Kit had awakened even with Rowan and Jewel talking outside their rooms. Something louder than those benign little taps would be necessary.

She scratched her fingernails down the front of Rose's door, a nice, satisfying scrape as she raked down the carved linenfold design. After repeating the motion, she moved to Kit's door and did it twice more.

Hearing a latch again, she darted back into her room.

"Just take a look, Rand! There must be something there. I cannot sleep with these noises!" 'Twas Lily this time, Chrystabel realized with more than a little frustration. "Do you see anything?"

"Nothing. Would you like to come and look for yourself?"

There was a pause before Lily said, "No. But those sounds cannot come from nowhere."

"Houses settle. You told me there have been no ghosts at Trentingham in the past, and there is no reason to believe one would suddenly arrive now. Damn, now that you've wakened me, I'm hungry. Shall we go downstairs and find something to eat?"

For a brand-new son-in-law, Rand certainly felt at home here, Chrystabel thought wryly. While she waited for them to start downstairs, she looked around her chamber for something that would make more noise.

Her silver comb ought to do it. She snatched it up and peeked out her door. All was clear.

Drawn sideways across the wooden linenfold grooves, the comb made quite a racket. 'Twas not long at all before the click of another latch sent her to safety behind her own door.

"There is no such thing as ghosts," she heard Ford say.

She barely stifled a groan.

A long minute or two passed while she listened to footsteps pacing up and down the corridor. Ford, the scientific one, was a much more thorough ghost-hunter than either of his brothers-in-law. "All is clear," she finally heard him say,

"I swear it. You hungry? Let's go downstairs and find some thing to eat."

Slumped against the door, Chrystabel pictured her oldes daughter slipping from her childhood bed and into a wrap per. Joseph snored peacefully behind her, and Rose appar ently still slept in her room. Vexing girl must take after he father.

By the time Violet and Ford clattered down the steps— being none too quiet about it—Chrystabel had decide drastic measures were in order. Leaving the comb behind she ventured once more into the corridor.

She paused by Rose's door, then pushed down on th latch and opened it a smidgen. "Whoooooooooo," she calle inside, a breathy, piercing whistle. The fourth child of five Chrystabel had learned young how to impersonate an other worldly creature. How better to get back at her older sisters She could hardly have used her fists. "Whoooooooooo," sh called twice more for good measure, then hurried dow the corridor to Kit's room.

"Whoooooooooo. Whoooooooooo." She'd drawn breath fo another exhalation when footsteps sounded in Rose's room down the hall.

She barely made it back into the master chamber befor her daughter's door slammed open. "What was that? Wh is there?"

Unlike her sisters, Rose didn't sound scared. Her voic wasn't tentative and frightened. Aggravated would bette describe it.

Rose's footfalls paced the corridor up and halfway bac before Chrystabel heard another door opening. Kit's, than the Lord. It had to be—his was the only occupied room left

"What the hell is going on out here? I thought I heard ghost."

"There is no such thing as ghosts," Rose said peevishly.

"Obviously," Kit drawled, "you have never torn down a old building."

"Obviously," Rose returned, "you have a lively imagination."

Kit only laughed. God strike her down, Chrystabel thought, if these two weren't perfect for each other.

No lightning bolts came down the chimney.

"Are you hungry?" Rose asked.

"I could eat."

There wasn't a male alive who couldn't find space for food, no matter how long since his belly was last filled. Chrystabel credited her daughter for knowing the way to a man's heart.

But as they made their way downstairs, her own heart sank. A jovial family midnight snack was not what she'd had in mind for Rose and Kit. And she had few, if any, chances left to arrange another meeting before her daughter wised up and figured out what was going on.

A lot of terms could be used to describe Rose, but one of them was not slow-witted. And Chrystabel knew well what would happen should her daughter discover that she and Kit were in league. The marriage would never occur.

She shut her door and made her way back into bed to wake her husband. If he knew what was good for him, he'd better not say he was hungry.

What she had in mind to ease her disappointment did *not* involve food.

Chapter Twenty-five

As Kit and Rose approached the kitchen, they heard laughter. Boisterous, rollicking laughter.

He peeked in the door to find almost the entire Ashcroft family around a big, scarred wooden table. Pies, bread, and leftover dishes from supper littered the surface. Ale and conversation flowed.

Suddenly he wasn't hungry. He shut the door quietly, muffling the laughter to a dull roar. "I've changed my mind. Let's go for a walk instead."

Rose's dark eyes looked huge in the light of the single candle she was carrying. "Outside? In my night rail in the dead of the night?"

"'Tis been unseasonably warm. I'll wait while you get your cloak."

"We've no shoes!" she protested, making Kit look down in surprise. Suddenly he could hardly fathom that he was here in Rose Ashcroft's home in bare feet. Though her night rail and dressing gown concealed her body much more effectively than the current fashions—Court fashions most especially—there was something undeniably intimate about the ensemble.

Something that made him belt his own robe more tightly.

"We can go upstairs and don shoes," he suggested.

"I think not." For a moment, he thought she would open the kitchen door and join the impromptu party. After all, it had been her idea to come down here. He'd agreed, looking forward to some quiet time with her in this noisy house, but perhaps her interest in food surpassed her interest in him.

But in the end, she didn't disappoint him. "I have another idea," she whispered, taking his arm to lead him away. "We can walk in my father's orangery."

"Your father grows oranges?"

"Not very successfully. That's why he's so keen to get that greenhouse."

The orangery was a long, narrow chamber that occupied the entire ground floor of the west wing. "It used to be called the Stone Gallery," Rose told him as they entered. There were candlesticks mounted on the walls at intervals, and she lit them as she walked. "I suppose, after you build the greenhouse, that we'll call it the Stone Gallery again."

Tall windows, dark now, lined the gallery along the entire west side and half of the east as well. The ceiling was intricately carved oak. Kit recognized it and the chamber as dating from Tudor times—a room the occupants would have used to take exercise in inclement weather. But now it was filled with a variety of trees and plants, all interspersed with statuary that looked like it had been brought from Italy.

"Would you like an orange?" Rose asked laughingly, pulling a small, rather shriveled example from a scraggly branch. "Don't worry—they don't taste as bad as they look."

He peeled it as they walked, the black and white marble floor cold under his bare feet. "'Tis quiet here," he said.

"Yes." She sounded amused at the observation. "'Tis not easy to find a quiet place at Trentingham, is it?"

"You've a large family. But I like it," he added, realizing suddenly that he did. "Even the noise. There's a lot of life here. Vitality."

He'd felt that lack of vitality since his parents' deaths. He'd been busy, yes—but there was a difference.

"'Tis real," he added, tossing the peel into an empty clay pot.

"Real?"

He divided the little orange and handed her half. "Charles's Court, for example, is lively. But 'tis naught but forced gaiety, don't you think? The liveliness here is real."

"Ah. Yes. I see," she said thoughtfully.

Popping the juicy, sweet fruit into his mouth, he hoped she also saw that Court was a life she'd rather live without—because she'd have to if she married him. Even supposing he got his knighthood, he hadn't the time to flit from one place to another at the whim of his monarch. He had his lifework to pursue.

And no matter that it was fashionable, he had no intention of living a separate life from his wife.

He heard her swallow. "Are you not happy, Kit?"

It sounded like she cared. He hoped it was as more than a friend. More than *like a brother, but better.* "I'm happy right now," he said, licking his fingers.

"And Ellen is happy now."

"I don't want to think about Ellen."

"But you must." They'd reached the end of the gallery. She lit the last candle and set the one she'd carried on top of a headless statue. "I know you're angry with her . . . with what she did. But you cannot remain estranged, silent—"

"I'm not angry. Disappointed, yes; but not angry." He took her arm, turning her to stroll back in the direction they'd come. "And *I'm* not the one who isn't talking."

"You cannot really mean to keep all that money—"

"Will you be quiet, Rose?" he asked and then turned her toward him to quiet her with a kiss.

She wound her arms around his neck and cooperated fully. She tasted of Rose and oranges, a flavor uniquely hers. A flavor he wanted to make his.

He backed her against one of the walls between two windows. Above their heads, a haughty Roman emperor gazed down from a round terra-cotta medallion—a souvenir of earlier times. Kit only wanted to make new times with

Rose. A new life, a happy life—a life full of the vitality he'd been missing.

He licked a bit of sweet stickiness from the corner of her mouth, then kissed that corner, then her chin. Bending his head, he tasted her long, slender throat, the pulse that beat in the hollow, that precious place where shoulder met neck. He parted the top of her dressing gown, baring the smooth, fragrant skin where her night rail had come untied at the collar.

That small triangle of flesh glowed in the dancing candlelight. Her eyes slid closed. "Kit," she breathed, and he couldn't tell whether the single word was a protest or an entreaty. But she didn't push him away, and he wouldn't stop tasting her of his own volition. When she moved closer, he reached for the sash that secured her dressing gown and slowly drew one end until the bow came undone. The garment fell open, and then there was nothing between his hands and mouth and her body but the gossamer fabric of her night rail.

No stomacher, no laces, no stays. Only one thin barrier to the floral-scented softness that was Rose.

Kissing her, he teased her breasts through the delicate cloth, his pulse leaping when a little moan escaped her lips. His breath quickened as he felt the crests peak and harden beneath his fingers. He wanted to tear off her night rail and rip open his robe and bury himself inside her.

But he couldn't.

He couldn't scare her away, and he couldn't risk getting to the point where he mindlessly took her too far. He couldn't take her at all. Not until she was his, until she shared his name, until she wore his ring on her finger.

But Lord Almighty, he wanted her.

He lowered his head, suckled her through the filmy material. She arched, and his arms clenched tighter to support her. She smelled of roses and passion, a heady scent that almost had him breaking his promises and asking for more.

If he didn't miss his guess, she was willing to give more.

"More," she murmured as she had in the square. "More." Easing down the neckline of her night rail, he licked at a breast, nibbled greedily. She thrust herself closer to his mouth, responding to his attentions with an eagerness no other woman ever had.

That innate responsiveness, that unschooled sensuality, was one of the things he loved about her. One of the many, many things.

She pressed herself against his body until he feared he'd lose his mind. She worked her hands into the front of his robe, hesitating only a moment when she realized he wore nothing beneath it.

"Gemini," she whispered. Warm and smooth, her fingers maneuvered their way around him. His muscles jumped under her brazen exploration. When her arms completely encircled him, her hands flat on his back, she moved closer, molding her curves to fit him. "You feel entirely too good."

"So do you, sweetheart," he murmured.

"Touch me," she said.

His breath lodged in his chest. "I don't think—"

"Please." She slid a hand from under his robe, grasped one of his, and guided it to that place he wanted to touch more than anything. Through her night rail, he felt her heat. Searing heat.

"Touch me." Her voice was a husky rasp.

It took a stronger man than Kit to refuse such a heartfelt request. He inched up the fabric, thinking he'd never get enough of this enchanting, forward creature. Steeling himself to maintain control, he slipped his hand beneath the hem, skimmed the warm smoothness of one bare thigh. Teased circles on her delicate, silky skin.

"Touch me."

Finally, finally, he did.

Kit cupped her like he had before, and Rose surged against his hand, quivering with need. She thought, for one fleeting moment, that 'twas madness asking for this, but oh, the madness was sweet. He moved his hand, his fingers sliding, tormenting, until she squirmed against him, her dampness turning to an exquisite slickness. Desire spiraled through her. The heat built; her skin prickled. Then he slipped a finger inside her, and her world tilted.

Sensation flooded her being, stealing her breath, making the blood surge through her veins and pound insistently in her ears. He drew out of her and plunged back in, again and again, playing her body until she teetered on the edge of awareness, until she suddenly shattered, shuddering both without and within with pleasure she'd never known.

"More," Kit murmured, borrowing her word, wanting more than anything to give her more than she'd ever dreamed. Nothing would make him happier than to make *her* happy day and night. He wanted her so badly, the need was a physical ache in his chest.

As her tremors abated, he kissed her, taking her long, sweet languid sigh into his mouth. "A thing of beauty," she whispered, echoing his thoughts. Writhing in ecstasy, Rose had been the most beautiful thing he'd ever seen.

Has she refused your proposal? Rand had asked.

No, and Kit couldn't imagine her doing so now.

When her eyes fluttered open, looking dazed, he gave her a gentle smile. "I love you, Rose." Watching her lips curve in response to those words, he drew a shaky breath. "Will you marry me?"

"Marry you?" Her eyes filled with pain and confusion, the pleasure turning to panic. "No. I . . . no. Good God, what have I done?" She shoved her night rail down and closed her dressing gown, fumbling with the sash, then giving up and hugging herself miserably. "I'm sorry. I must go."

She pushed past him and ran from the chamber, her bare footfalls pattering all down its long length. At the other end, he heard the door slam shut.

And then he was alone with the flickering candles and his tight throat and his pensive thoughts.

And his aching heart.

He'd known all along that she'd refuse him, so why was he so crushed and demoralized? Damn Lady Trentingham for encouraging him. He'd always known that, as matters stood, he wouldn't be considered good enough for an earl's daughter. Not by the daughter herself, in any case. And just his luck, he'd chosen the one woman in England whose parents let her choose her own husband.

The candlelight that had seemed so intimate earlier now seemed too bright, too revealing. He slowly moved to douse the many small flames. He burned to tell Rose of his pending knighthood, but with his project deadlines approaching and all the problems, he was no longer confident of his chances. And for all he knew, a knighthood might not be enough for her, anyway. The Deputy Surveyor post was only a first step—it could be years before he raised himself further. By then it would be too late for him and Rose.

Too late.

Rose spent a restless, tormented night. When she awakened, the note she found slipped beneath her door did nothing to ease her distress. ROSE, it said in the neat, all-caps printing she'd seen on Kit's architectural renderings:

> MUST CHECK PROGRESS AT HAMPTON COURT.
> PLEASE GIVE YOUR FAMILY MY THANKS AND
> ASSURE YOUR FATHER THAT THE GREENHOUSE
> WILL PROCEED ON SCHEDULE AS PLANNED.
>
>   K

There was nothing more. No "Dearest Rose." No "I love you, Kit." Did he hate her now? Had she lost his friendship along with her innocence?

True, she was still a virgin, but her whole body heated just remembering the liberties she'd allowed Kit last night. A hot, tingling ache spread, centered in that place between her legs where he'd touched her. Where he'd made her feel things she'd never felt. Never even imagined.

She washed and slowly pulled on her clothes, so lost in her thoughts she couldn't bear conversation with Harriet. *I love you.* She supposed she had no right to expect Kit to declare so in a letter when he'd said the words out loud and been met with her silence. And then gone so far as to propose and been met with a *no*.

Her first proposal.

The look on his face had nearly killed her. His words had taken her completely by surprise. She supposed, on reflection, that they shouldn't have . . . but she'd been expecting her first proposal to come from a duke.

Confusion was a weight in her chest. Did she love Kit? In the heat of the moment, it had been on the tip of her tongue to echo those three words. But she hadn't, because she wasn't sure, and in any case it wouldn't matter.

He wasn't the right man for her.

He'd had no right to expect a different answer. She might have reached the advanced age of one-and-twenty, but she was not yet desperate enough to marry a commoner. She'd be a fool to do that when Bridgewater, a lofty peer of the realm, was likely to offer for her hand. She squared her shoulders as she headed down to the dining room for breakfast.

Happy as bees in a bed of flowers, her sisters and their families were already eating, having risen early to prepare for their journeys home. The elder Ashcrofts were conspicuously absent; after a homecoming, they often slept late. Rowan and Jewel chatted cheerfully, so focused on each other that the rest of the room might as well have been empty.

Everyone in this house—everyone but Rose—was in love.

The conversation died as she scraped back a chair and plopped onto it. A footman offered a cup of chocolate, and she clenched it so hard her knuckles turned white.

"Where is Kit?" Lily asked.

Rose felt her jaw tightening. "What makes you think I

should know?" she gritted out, repressing a vision of herself biting her sister's head off. She gulped the hot liquid, scalding her tongue. "He left a note. It seems he's gone on to Hampton Court."

"Oh," Lily said.

"Did you hear a ghost last night?" Rowan asked.

Rose imagined biting his head off, too. "There is no such thing as ghosts."

"Rose is right," Ford put in.

He could live.

"I heard tapping," Rowan insisted.

"Me, too." Jewel nodded, gazing at him worshipfully. That pixie-faced girl had fallen in love at six. Six! Off with her pixie head.

"We heard tapping *and* scratching," Rand said. "Lily and I both."

"And I heard terrible scraping." Violet turned to Rose. "Did you not hear anything at all?"

A whoosh. But she'd never admit it. She didn't believe in ghosts. Or marrying beneath her expectations, either.

Chapter Twenty-six

The sun was setting upon Hampton Court's red brick when Rose and her mother arrived three days later. As they stood in one of Base Court's covered galleries waiting for a palace warden to open their lodging, a woman came out of the apartment next door.

"Oh!" she exclaimed, one hand to the pillowy chest revealed in the low neckline of her orange brocade gown. Rose couldn't recall her name, but she remembered seeing her in the ladies' attiring room at Windsor. "Lady Rose! I'm so glad you have followed us. I hope we'll be seeing you at Court this evening."

"Yes, you will," Rose said, pleased. Court was going to be so much more pleasant now that the women liked her.

"And will you be bringing the translations?"

"Gemini!" With all the turmoil surrounding Ellen, she'd completely forgotten to work on any more of them. "I've done two," she hedged, not mentioning that she didn't have them with her.

"Excellent," the lady said before walking off, the little train of her fur-trimmed cloak dragging behind her.

"What translations?" Chrystabel asked.

"Some poetry. Italian. Nothing important."

"Oh, I see," Chrystabel said as though she didn't see at all. "Come along, then, let us ready ourselves."

Their lodging was again just a sitting room and one bedchamber, no fancier than the one they'd been assigned at Windsor Castle. But at least the rooms were larger. In no time at all, Chrystabel was settled at a creaky wooden dressing table with Anne working on her hair, while Harriet helped Rose into the new emerald gown she'd chosen to wear.

When a knock came at the door, Harriet went to answer and came back with a vase full of colorful fall flowers. "For you, Lady Rose."

Rose rushed to take them. "Lovely!" She rearranged the greenery more evenly and moved a yellow bloom from the right side to the left before reaching for the card. "They must be from the duke."

But they weren't. *For dear Lady Rose,* it said in a heavy, dark hand. *I wished for red roses to match your lips, but alas, 'tis not the season. Please accept this small token of my affection with my hopes of spending some time in your company this evening. Yours, Lord Somerville.*

"How did he know I was here?" she wondered.

"News travels fast at Court," her mother said.

Harriet's pale green eyes looked wistful in her freckled face. "Oh," she sighed. "How I would love for a man to send me flowers."

She'd barely finished lacing the back of Rose's gown when another knock came at the door. This time she returned with a small wooden box.

Inside was a dainty pearl bracelet. "It goes well with my earrings," Rose said, wondering if she should wear the rubies tonight even though they didn't match her green dress. "How very thoughtful of Gabriel."

But the bracelet wasn't from him, either. The creamy sheet of vellum that had arrived with the box was lettered neatly in fine black ink. *For Lady Rose, though pearls cannot match the luster in your eyes. Passionately, Baron Fortescue.*

"Passionately?" Rose held out her wrist so Harriet could fasten the bracelet's clasp. "I barely remember the man."

"Oh," Harriet said, "how I would love for a man to give me jewelry."

A third knock on the door brought a platter of delicate sweetmeats and another note: *No sugar can match the sweetness of your demeanor.*

No one had ever called Rose sweet. "I vow and swear," she declared, popping a marzipan swan into her mouth, "I have never heard such ridiculous comparisons in my life."

Her mother moved to give her a turn at the dressing table. "They are just trying to impress you, dear."

"If any of them could kiss half decently, I would find that a lot more impressive."

"Oh," Harriet said, "how I would love for a man to kiss me."

By the time Rose was ready for Court, she had two new bracelets, a sapphire stomacher brooch, and four bouquets of flowers in addition to the half-eaten platter of sweets.

None of it was from Gabriel.

Hampton Court had no keeps, no crenelated curtain wall, nothing like the huge central mound of earth at Windsor with its tall Round Tower. Instead, the palace was a virtual rabbit warren of buildings surrounding courtyards large and small. Rose walked from Base Court through Clock Court with her mother, the pearls on her beautiful new gown gleaming in the light from torches set on the walls at intervals. As they were crossing the cavernous blue-ceilinged Great Hall on their way to the Presence Chamber, a lord walking the other direction stopped and doffed his plumed hat.

"I hear you have a copy of *I Sonetti,* my lady."

Rose couldn't remember having met him, and the man had a distinct gleam in his eye; one that made her uneasy. "I do," she told him cautiously.

"I should enjoy a private viewing."

"I think not," she said and swished past him.

"I Sonetti?" Chrystabel asked when they reached the other end of the chamber.

"*The Sonnets.* The Italian poetry."

"Why should you not want to show it to the man?"

"I don't even know him!" Rose burst out, and then added in as calm a voice as possible, "Besides, I am here to see the duke. If he has plans to make me his wife, I do not think he'd appreciate me sharing any book with another man privately."

The Presence Chamber was stunning, with great tapestries on the walls and a gilded ceiling. The King and Queen sat under a canopy fashioned of cloth-of-gold. After the tedious ceremony of presentation, Chrystabel wandered off and Rose decided to look for Gabriel. But she'd barely scanned the chamber when Baron Fortescue appeared and made a bow. "My dear Lady Rose, I am most honored to see you wearing my bracelet."

He was dressed in mulberry satin with bunched loops of aqua ribbons. Rose had always admired men of fashion, but it seemed to her that lately the fashions had turned rather frivolous. And she remembered Lord Fortescue better now, most specifically that he was, as Lily had put it, a sloppy kisser.

She didn't wish to hurt him, but she certainly didn't want to encourage him further. "The bracelet matched my gown," she told him. "Thank you."

"My pleasure. I hear, dear lady, that you've learned the secrets of *I Sonetti.*" He grinned, showing buck teeth. "I'm hoping you'll be willing to share them."

Was that why he'd given her the bracelet? She was tempted to tear it off, but there was no reason, after all, to ruin such a pretty thing. "If I know any secrets," she told him archly, "I plan only to share them with my husband."

To her consternation, his grin widened. "I entertain fond hopes of being that man."

"You what?"

"Will you marry me, dear Rose?"

Good God, he was proposing! A month earlier she'd despaired of ever hearing a proposal, and now she'd had two in a week. But better she live all her days as a spinster than bind herself to Lord Fortescue and his sloppy kisses. "Please accept my apologies," she said, "but my heart belongs to another."

He sighed, but did not look surprised. "Best wishes, then, my lady."

No sooner had Lord Fortescue taken his leave than Lord Somerville made his way over. He raised her hand and kissed it reverently. "I hope you received my flowers."

"They are beautiful, my lord. I thank you." If she remembered correctly, his kisses had been unexciting but not off-putting. And his suit was adorned with gold braid rather than ribbons. Perhaps he would ask her to dance. She had always dearly loved to dance.

"I hear you've a copy of *I Sonetti*," he said instead.

If she had his flowers here, she'd be tempted to dump them on his head. "I plan to share it only with my husband."

"Then, dear Lady Rose, I must ask you to do me the honor of becoming my wife."

Rose's first instinct was to scream in frustration, but in all honesty there was nothing wrong with the man except that she couldn't imagine marrying him. "'Twould truly be an honor," she assured him, "but I'm afraid my heart belongs to another."

"I see." He swept her a courtly bow. "Your servant, my lady. The duke is a lucky man."

In the next hour, Gabriel failed to appear and four more gentlemen proposed to Rose. Two of them were more than acceptable, men that she knew she'd have jumped at the opportunity to wed a year ago. But suddenly she couldn't stomach the thought of marrying any of them.

And not all the men were after her hand in marriage. Many were simply interested in the book. Rose had warned off three of that type already when two more approached as a team. "We hear you have a copy of *I Sonetti*," one of them started, a lascivious gleam in his eye.

They both crowded close—so close Rose could tell one of them truly needed a bath. "We were wondering—" the second man began.

"Leave her alone," Nell Gwyn interrupted, shoving herself between them.

The first one turned on her. "Bloody hell, Nelly, we were only—"

"Hoping to share her, you beasts." Raising her dainty hands, she pushed on both their chests. "Go on. Be gone."

Rose blew out a breath as she watched them walk away.

"Is it true?" Nell asked the moment they were out of earshot.

"What?"

"That you've a copy of *I Sonetti*. 'Tis all the buzz."

"Yes, 'tis true." She sighed. "But I cannot imagine why everyone finds it so blasted interesting."

"The ladies, they just want to see it, to hear the words. But the gentlemen . . . if you're not looking for a tumble or two, you'd best stay in company and be watchful."

From what Rose had seen, there was nothing "gentlemanly" about the base creatures. "Surely not all men are so crass."

"Some may approach you with flowery words, but they are men. Inflamed most easily."

"Then perhaps I should carry a bucket of water."

Nell laughed.

"Do you know," Rose said, "you are one of few at Court who hasn't asked to see it. Do *you* not want to view the engravings and read the scandalous translated words?"

"I've no need of such things," Nell assured her blithely.

"Most ladies seem to think they would enjoy sharing the book with their men."

"Not I." Nell leaned closer. "Charles"—she dropped her voice to a confidential murmur—"is a very catholic lover."

Rose frowned. "I thought you were both Protestant."

Nell's lips curved into a fond half smile. "I mean that he is not very imaginative. His tastes run to the simple. However, he more than makes up for that with his prodigious appetite and enthusiasm."

Rose felt her eyes widening. "Oh," was all she could find to say.

"Besides, I've seen those pictures—one would have to be a contortionist to attempt half the poses."

Rose couldn't agree more. Despite her sisters' amused reactions, the engravings still made her a little nervous. In fact, this whole conversation made her nervous. "Will there be gaming tonight?" she asked, changing the subject.

"Of course. And tomorrow night, there will be a masked ball."

"Gemini! Whatever shall I wear?"

"Not everyone wears a costume. Just a mask will do, although I suspect you'll find some of the outfits amusing."

Rose's mind turned to the clothes she and Mum had brought and what she could possibly create from them. Maybe if she concealed her identity well enough, she'd have an evening free from being questioned about *I Sonetti*. She watched absently as a beautiful woman walked in and made her curtsy before the King.

Or rather, her bow.

Rose blinked. "Whoever is that?" she asked, staring. The woman was dressed in silks and satins, but the sumptuous turquoise apparel wasn't that of a lady. " 'Tis a Cavalier's suit she wears! She must think the masked ball is today instead of tomorrow."

"I think not." Nell chuckled. "Have you never met Hortense Mancini, the Duchess Mazarin?"

"That is the duchess?" Rose had never seen a woman dressed like a man, but on this tall lady the effect was stunning. A jeweled sword dangled from her belt, and a dark little Moorish boy dressed to match trotted beside her, completing the bizarre picture.

"Are you not jealous of her?" Rose asked candidly, knowing the Duchess Mazarin was yet another of the King's mistresses.

Nell gave a good-natured shrug. "She has Charles's attention but for the moment. When all is said and done, he will always come searching for my bed, for I love him, and I do not believe the beautiful Hortense has it in her to love anyone. She has a brilliant mind, but beneath it, she is colder than the Thames in January."

Rose slanted a glance to Louise de Kéroualle where she stood to one side, glowering. "It seems the Duchess of Portsmouth doesn't share your lack of concern."

"*She* has something to fret about," Nell said with a saucy grin. She took Rose by the arm and started toward the newcomer. "Louise is a passing fancy for Charles as well, and the coming of Hortense may well be the end of her reign. Even a king can spread himself only so thin," she added with a laugh.

"Why does Charles like either of them?" Rose wondered aloud.

"He's a man," Nell told her with another shrug. "His head is turned by a pretty face. No one would argue Louise is a beauty, and as for Hortense . . . she is gorgeous, is she not?"

Drawing closer to the duchess's rare loveliness, Rose could only nod. Waist-length raven hair framed Hortense's perfect face. Her flawless Mediterranean skin set off large violet eyes that seemed to change color as she moved.

Nell lowered her voice. "Charles fancied himself in love with her years ago, while she was but fifteen and he still in exile on the Continent. He proposed to her twice. But she thought his prospects poor, and more importantly, so did her guardian, the Cardinal Mazarin. If either had foreseen that Charles would someday regain his crown, today she'd be a queen. Instead, she is forced to live off her keepers."

They drew up before the duchess just as she sent her little Moorish boy off to fetch refreshment. As the child trotted away obediently, Nell swept Hortense a theatrical curtsy. "Your Grace, may I present Lady Rose Ashcroft, the

Earl of Trentingham's daughter. Lady Rose, this is Hortense Mancini, the Duchess Mazarin."

"Lady Rose. I am pleased to make your acquaintance." The duchess's accent was melodious, an intriguing mixture of her native Italian and the many years she'd spent in France. "I've been told," she added, raising one arched black brow, "that you are in possession of a rare copy of *I Sonetti*."

"You've heard correctly," Rose admitted, unsurprised. Why should this stranger be the only soul at Court who didn't know?

"Then you speak Italian?"

"Among other languages." After saying that without thinking, Rose quickly looked around, relieved to see that Gabriel still hadn't appeared.

"An intellectual!" Hortense exclaimed with such enthusiasm Rose half expected her to clap her hands. "You must come to my salon, then."

"Your salon?"

"A weekly gathering of great minds in my apartments at St. James's Palace. We discuss all manner of subjects. Philosophy, religion, history, music, art, ancient and modern literature . . ."

It sounded like something Violet would love, but Rose didn't share her sister's passion for scholarly debate. Not to mention she suspected the Duke of Bridgewater would find it a bore. Still, it wouldn't do to snub a duchess. "Perhaps someday I'll join you," she said.

"I'm looking forward to it," Hortense said as her little Moor returned with a cup of steaming coffee. "Why, thank you, Mustapha." She patted him on the head, prompting a smile. His teeth looked very large and white in his dark face as he reclaimed his post by her side.

As she sipped, Hortense's gaze strayed to Louise de Kéroualle. "Look at her," she said to Nell with a roll of her amazing eyes. "She's wearing black again."

Rose looked, too. Louise's gown was exquisite, but clearly meant to convey grief. "Why black?"

Nell snorted as only Nell could snort. "That hoity-toity French duchess sets up to be of superior quality. If you listen to her, everyone of rank in France is her cousin. The moment some grand lord or lady over there dies, she orders a new mourning gown."

"Who died?" Rose asked.

"Doubtless some minor prince." Nell set one of her small hands upon a curvy hip. "I wonder, I do, if Louise is of such high station, why is she such a whore? I was born to be a whore, so I hold that I've done quite well for myself. But she was reared to be a lady—do you not think she should blush in shame?"

Hortense Mancini laughed at that—and her laughter was no feminine tinkle. It did her outfit rather proud.

Rose looked again at Louise. "Does the Duchess of Portsmouth have a black eye?"

Nell nodded. "An 'unfortunate accident,' she called it. But I overheard two ladies saying she'd done it deliberately, to make her pale skin darker like the Duchess Mazarin's."

To judge from her braying laughter, the Duchess Mazarin thought that a fine jest.

"Lady Rose."

Rose turned to see the Duke of Bridgewater. "Your Grace! I was wondering if you'd attend tonight."

"You look as though you were having a fine time without me."

His tone implied he was less than thrilled to find her socializing with two of Charles's mistresses. And now that she thought on it, Rose was a bit scandalized herself. But the truth was she felt more comfortable with these women than she did with most of the people here at Court.

Gabriel was the exception, though. Other than proving a tad more amorous than she'd prefer, he'd been the perfect gentleman. "I'm glad you came," she told him, meaning it.

He drew her a safe distance away. "Where are your earrings?"

She knew she should have worn them. "I adore them, my lord, but they didn't match my gown."

"Well, then, these should match whatever you choose to wear." He fished a tiny silk pouch from his pocket. "A token of my esteem, my lady."

Rose opened the drawstring and poured a pair of diamond drops into her hand. The stones winked in the torchlight. "My lord! They are beautiful!"

She should have known he would come up with something to outshine all those other men.

"I am pleased that you like them," he said, moving close to fasten them on her ears. "Would you care to dance?"

Chapter Twenty-seven

"Rosslyn." Kit looked up from the sketch he was making of Rose and quickly flipped it over. "What brings you here tonight?"

The earl wandered the drawing room of Kit's building-in-progress, touching a panel here, eyeing the level there. "Just seeing how you're coming along." He squinted up at the half-painted ceiling. "You've pulled it off, Martyn, haven't you? I knew you could do it."

Kit glanced overhead at the fat, smiling cherubs the Duchess of Cleveland had requested, thinking, not for the first time, that they didn't really fit her. The King's long-time mistress was known to be anything but cherubic. "Something wrong up there?"

"Not at all. 'Tis stunning, in fact." Rosslyn lowered his pale blue gaze to meet Kit's. "Mind if I look around?"

"As you wish."

Kit lit a second candle and handed it to the man, then followed closely behind. Not that he had anything to hide. But the last of his men had just left, and he always checked everything one final time before leaving himself.

During the past few days he'd been over every inch of the apartments time and again. Nothing seemed to be out of place. The materials were up to standard, and there was no sign of sabotage, fire or otherwise. Apart from some understandable grumbling when Kit kept them long hours, no one on the job seemed unhappy. No one had sighted Harold Washburn, either.

Apparently the man hadn't set the fire at Whitehall—or at the very least, he had heeded Kit's warning and was staying clear now.

"Very nice." In the master bedchamber, Rosslyn nodded at a carved mantelpiece. "Gibbons's work, I presume?"

"Yes."

"You always have insisted on the best." His walking stick tapped as he continued his rambling inspection. "Winning the post of Deputy Surveyor would be best of all, wouldn't it?"

Kit followed the man into the dining room, watching the long tails of his lavender surcoat flap behind him. " 'Tis naught but an interim goal. I won't be satisfied until the Surveyor General post is mine."

Rosslyn turned to face him. "I'll alert Mr. Wren that you're angling to take his place."

"*Sir* Christopher Wren," Kit reminded him. "But I doubt he'll find that a revelation."

The earl waved an elegant hand. "I was jesting. Can you not take a jest?"

In long years of schooling together, Kit couldn't remember Rosslyn—Gaylord Craig at the time—jesting even once. "Sorry," he said. "I suppose I'm a bit serious these days."

"Understandable, my friend." Rosslyn smiled. "Well, I expect I had better get back to Court. Excellent job here, Martyn." Still tapping, he retraced his steps to the entrance. "Excellent job, indeed."

As Rosslyn walked out, Kit was only half surprised to see Rose's mother walk in. "Lady Trentingham."

"Good evening, Kit." She stared at Rosslyn's retreating back, then turned to Kit in a swish of yellow skirts. "A friend of yours, is he?"

"An old schoolfellow. Now my rival for the post I'm seeking. He came to check out the competition."

"From what I've seen, he spends all his time at Court. He doesn't seem to be working very hard to win it."

Kit shrugged. "An earl doesn't have to prove himself the way a common man does." He could be bitter about that, but he'd long ago decided not to waste his time raging over life's inequities. Better to spend one's energies overcoming them. "How did you get in here?" he asked. "The only way is through the privy gardens."

He hadn't thought to ask the same of Rosslyn.

Her brown eyes lit with intrigue. "I had the most lovely conversation with the guard at the gate. It seems he is lonely and desirous of a wife. Since by all appearances he is a perfectly nice man, I promised to send Rose's maid Harriet over to meet him after I complete my business here. Lovely girl, Harriet."

"I'm sure she is." The privy garden was supposed to be private to the King. Kit wondered if he should alert Charles that his guard was so easily bribed. "And what is your business?"

"Oh, I just wanted to see how you were faring. My husband, naturally, is anxious for you to get back to work on his greenhouse."

"Naturally."

"So how *are* you faring?"

"Without my presence here the project has fallen slightly behind schedule, but not so far that the time cannot be made up." The bonuses he'd promised would ensure it. "Everything seems to be in order."

"Seems?"

He rubbed the back of his neck. "This nagging voice in my head keeps insisting something is wrong." Something he was missing. No matter that his countless inspections proved otherwise, he couldn't shake the feeling that he should reject what was on the surface.

"Hmm. And with Rose?"

He would never get used to Lady Trentingham's abrupt changes of subject. "Rose?"

"You don't seem to be making much progress."

He felt his face reddening as he recalled their intimate moments in the orangery. He'd made progress, all right. On every front but convincing her to marry him. "I'm working on it."

"Such a shame your work has kept you so occupied."

"Yes. Well . . ." He might as well come out and say it. "Architecture is my life, Lady Trentingham. Though I hope to make Rose my life, too, she will always have to share my attention with my work."

"I'd not want to see her wed to an idle fool . . . too much attention can be as detrimental as too little. But I'd not see you ignore her, either."

"Never." In fact, he imagined that Rose, above anything, could well prove to distract him.

She nodded thoughtfully. "I've been thinking about my Rose. Do you know, I do believe she's the most romantic of all my daughters."

"Romantic?"

"Yes. Violet, you may not know, is quite pragmatic and logical. And Lily, bless her heart, is straightforward as they come. Love, for her, either is or isn't . . . though if a being is alive, she's likely to place it in the former category." She smiled, the soft smile of a loving mother. "But Rose . . ."

"You're saying a bit of romancing might be in order? Along with the . . . the . . ."

"Seduction, yes. 'Twould certainly not be amiss."

"Yes. Well. I think I'm finished here for now." He tucked the sketch of Rose into the building's plans and began rolling them up together. "I believe I will take this back to my rooms and go over everything once again. Can I walk you back to Court first?"

"Not to Court, but to my own apartments would be lovely. I must fetch Harriet and see that she meets the charming guard at the gate."

* * *

As the evening wore on, Rose received a brooch in the shape of a bow set with precious gemstones, a locket filled with a hopeful suitor's hair, another bouquet of flowers, and two more proposals. Every unmarried man, it seemed, had proposed.

Except the duke.

There were a few new men attending Court here at the palace, but they seemed ruder than those Rose had met at Windsor. One of them didn't even ask her to dance before maneuvering her behind the tall, exquisitely painted screen that set off one end of the Presence Chamber, serving the same purpose as the curtains in Windsor's drawing room.

Out of curiosity she'd allowed some of the men to kiss her, but none of their kisses had affected her anything like Kit's. More disturbingly, their hands seemed to wander boldly as they murmured about *I Sonetti* and asked if she'd share its secrets.

I Sonetti. Taking a cup of spiced wine from the refreshment table, Rose found herself wishing she were back at Trentingham giggling over the book with her sisters. Or no—she wished she'd never seen the thing at all. It had brought her nothing but trouble . . . whoever would think she could earn a wild reputation over simply possessing a book? More than anything, she wished she could find a way to get back to Windsor and return the volume to Ellen.

All her life she'd yearned to come to Court, but now that she was here she was finding it tedious beyond belief. 'Twas a sad day when she found chatting with the King's mistresses more enjoyable than dancing with men.

"My lady." Another man bowed before her. "I do not believe I've had the pleasure of an introduction."

"Rose Ashcroft," she said flatly, barely stifling a yawn. Her flirtatious nature seemed to have deserted her somewhere around the fourth or fifth kiss.

He swept her an even deeper bow. "Roger Stanhope, the Earl of Featherstonehaugh. Would you honor me with a dance?"

He'd said the magic words. " 'Twould be my pleasure." She hesitated to saddle herself with his too-long name and wished it were spelled Fanshaw—the way it was pronounced—but she was no longer searching for perfection. At least he was polite enough to ask for a dance. And he hadn't mentioned the blasted book. Perhaps he hadn't heard about it.

She downed the rest of her wine, handed her cup to a serving maid, then let him lead her onto the dance floor. The musicians were playing a lively country tune, and the accompanying dance was performed in two lines, not affording much chance for conversation. Instead, she sized up the earl as they progressed.

He was a certified fop. His wide, powdered periwig draped in curls down his fuchsia brocade-clad chest. Long rows of fancy solid gold buttons adorned both his coat and waistcoat, and when the coat flapped open with the movements of the dance, a blinding yellow satin lining flashed. In addition, the plethora of white lace that spilled from his cravat and cuffs was enough to choke a horse.

His outfit, she decided, would look much better on the Duchess Mazarin.

But perhaps, if he turned out to be a good kisser, she could teach him how to dress more to her liking. 'Twould no doubt prove easier than teaching a good dresser how to kiss. Feeling a bit more cheerful, she gave him a wide smile as the dance ended.

Apparently he took her smile the wrong way, because the next thing she knew, she found herself propelled behind the screen. Heaving an internal sigh, she tilted her face up for his kiss. As long as he had her here, she might as well find out how he measured up in that department. No sense mentally ordering new clothes if the fellow left her cold.

But he surprised her by spinning her around so that he stood behind her, then dropping to a cushioned stool and pulling her onto his lap.

"What are you doing?" she cried.

One arm snaked over her shoulder, and his fingers slipped inside her gown and clamped a tender breast. His other hand went around her waist and started pulling her skirts up in bunches. He tilted her head back and crushed his mouth down on hers, at the same time shoving one leg between her two and twisting to wrap the other around and over her knee.

"Let go!" She tore her mouth free and reached back to brace herself, to push herself away, but his body covered the stool and her hands found no purchase. "What the devil do you think you're doing?"

His fingers still working at her skirts, he surged against her until she could feel his arousal through his breeches and her clothes. "Position Ten," he grunted. "Have you not been dying to try it?"

With an outraged gasp, she finally managed to twist off his lap and whirled to slap him on the face.

As her hand connected with his cheek, the priceless screen crashed to the floor and Gabriel arrived like an avenging angel. "Are you all right?"

"I'm fine," she spat, rubbing her palm where it hurt. "He, however, is a rutting lout!"

The duke nodded, then turned to Featherstonehaugh, murder in his eyes. "Choose your second," he grated through gritted teeth, his fingers working to untie the peace strings that prevented his sword from being drawn.

The entire Court had gone quiet, frozen as though in a tableau. The Earl of Featherstonehaugh remained silent. All that could be heard was Gabriel's harsh breathing and the scraping sound of his rapier as he pulled it from its scabbard.

"Outside," he demanded. "Now."

And then everyone seemed to be moving.

Stunned, Rose just stood there a moment as it slowly sank in that the duke had challenged the earl to a duel. Over her.

Ignoring all etiquette, Bridgewater didn't even give the man 'til morning. Instead he dragged him from the building and into Clock Court. The courtiers followed en masse. Rose snapped from her trance and hurried after them, fearing for Gabriel's life.

She heard the clash of swords before she reached the courtyard, but the cheers and catcalls from the crowd of onlookers were even louder. The men's rapiers flashed in the torchlight. Her heart pounding, she wedged herself into the circle, wincing at each ringing bash.

'Twas mere seconds, however, before her concern for Gabriel turned to terror on behalf of the poor earl.

The man obviously paid more attention to his wardrobe than his swordsmanship, because it rapidly became clear that the duke was but toying with him. A flick here, and a few of the man's precious buttons went missing from his coat. A thrust there, and half his lace cravat fluttered to the stones. Featherstonehaugh waved his own sword so ineffectively that Rose reckoned even she could do better.

Raging anger was evident in Gabriel's eyes, in his clenched jaw, in his carefully controlled movements. Panic clutched at Rose's throat. The rutting lout had acted abominably, but she had no wish to witness his death, most especially were it done in defense of *her*.

"Gabriel!" she shouted, taking a step forward and then another when he paid her no attention. "Don't kill him! Gabriel, don't—"

"Hush," came a voice from the crowd. Warm arms went around her from behind, pulling her back into the circle as a familiar scent of frankincense and myrrh enveloped her.

"Don't distract him," Kit said quietly in her ear. "Even an expert can falter if his attention is elsewhere. You don't want to be responsible for the duke's death."

"I don't want to be responsible for the earl's murder, either!"

"Hush." One of his hands came up and tucked an errant curl behind her ear. "This cannot be more than a tiff. 'Twill not come to that."

"But what if it does?" she wailed, trying to struggle free.

His arms tightened. "Just watch. The duke is all but finished."

And so he was. He'd run out of buttons to flick off the other man's coat, and although not a drop of blood had been spilled, the brocade itself was in shreds. In addition to being half naked, the earl was thoroughly humiliated.

Disgust marring his fine features, Gabriel knocked the sword from Featherstonehaugh's hand with one easy twist of his wrist. Then, while the earl was busy gasping, he reached out and nicked him under his chin—a cut so tiny only a single bead of red leaked out.

"First blood," he claimed as he shoved his rapier back into its scabbard. "You lose. Touch her again and your head will come off instead."

'Twas over. Kit's arms dropped from around her as babbling broke out among the assembled courtiers. Rose couldn't tell whether it signaled approval or disappointment.

Louise de Kéroualle turned to her, her eyes wide and sparkling. "Nothing this exciting has happened in weeks!"

Rose suspected that the duchess was happy to see everyone's attention focused on something other than her embarrassing black eye, which had made her the butt of much nasty teasing. But better everyone look to Louise for their entertainment. Now that the spectacle had ended, more than one gaze shifted Rose's way. Ladies whispered behind their fans. She couldn't fathom what they were saying, but she wanted no part of this.

She turned to Kit. "Take me away from here."

"Lady Rose!" Courtiers dispersed as Gabriel strode toward her. "I'd like a word with you, if you will."

Kit shrugged, swiped a roll of linen off the ground, and walked away.

Rose faced the duke. "Yes?"

"In private."

Still shaky, she let him take her arm and lead her from the courtyard, under Henry VIII's clock tower, and into

Base Court. Her high heels wobbled on the cobblestone paths that crisscrossed the grass, but Gabriel seemed happy enough to steady her. In the galleries, a few lights flickered from apartments where courtiers had sought their lodgings, but the night was still young, and most everyone was returning to the Presence Chamber.

"My dear Rose," Gabriel started.

"A duel!" she interrupted loudly, the words echoing in the deserted courtyard. "I cannot believe you challenged that fool to a duel."

He hurried her into one of the galleries. The corridor was breezy, but the torches along the walls gave off heat as well as light. "I will never let anyone impugn your honor," he said gallantly.

"I appreciate your sentiments, Gabriel, but a duel!" The red tiles here were smoother beneath her feet than the cobblestones. She felt steadier, more in control. True, part of her had been secretly thrilled to see a man—a duke, no less!—leap to defend her honor. But a larger part had been terrified. "Not only is dueling barbaric, 'tis illegal."

As they walked past a diamond-paned window, the glass reflected his elegant shrug. "I don't see anyone hurrying to arrest me. Featherstonehaugh deserved it."

"That may be, but I was taking care of him myself."

"You shouldn't have to take care of yourself." They heard the low murmur of people talking in an apartment, and he waited until they'd strolled past it. "Rose, I . . . I want to take care of you. I wish to make you my wife."

She stopped walking, the corridor suddenly silent without the rhythmic clicks of her heels. "Are you asking me to marry you?"

He turned to face her and crowded her against the brick wall. It felt rough and cool behind her back. "Yes," he said. "I am not very good at this, am I? I am better with actions than words."

He was a duke, and surely that was good enough. *A duke,* asking for her hand. He tilted his head and moved nearer, brushing her lips with his. His technique really wasn't that bad. He didn't smell of frankincense and myrrh, but he didn't smell unpleasant, either. And he was a duke.

"Rose, will you marry me?"

Of course she would. She wasn't brainless. She opened her mouth. This was what she'd been waiting for. "No."

She blinked and felt as surprised as Gabriel looked. "I'm sorry," she added quickly. Out of habit she almost added that her heart belonged to another, but surely that wasn't true. "I must go," she said instead. Avoiding his stunned gaze, she slid from behind him and ran down the gallery toward her lodging.

The heavy old door creaked when she opened it. She slammed it shut and leaned back against the thick wood, a hand to her trembling mouth.

How could she have refused him? Had she not been waiting for this proposal? Had she not come here to Hampton Court hoping to receive it? Had she not refused other perfectly suitable men because she wanted a duke?

How could she have turned down a duke—and a perfectly nice one, at that? One who had fought and risked his life for her? Never mind that he'd fenced circles around the earl—he couldn't have known the man was so incompetent when he issued the challenge.

There was nothing for it. She would have to seek him out and change her answer to yes.

But not tonight. She couldn't face him tonight. Furious at herself, she straightened and wandered toward the bed-chamber. "Mum? Harriet?"

'Twas empty. "Harriet, where are you?"

No one was here. Not her mother, not her maid, not her mother's maid, either. She threw herself facedown on the bed.

The boned bodice of her gown poked into her, so after a moment she rolled over. But there were whalebone splints in the back, too, not to mention the bulky lacing that ran down her spine.

Where the devil was Harriet? Rose cursed the maid along with whatever fool was responsible for dictating Court fashion. She'd claimed to be able to care for herself—well, she could slap an impudent courtier, all right, but she couldn't manage to undress herself when her blasted gown was laced down her back.

The apartment was too silent. She sat up and sighed. She didn't really want to undress—she'd been hoping to finally try gaming tonight.

But first she would take a walk—a calming walk, out in Hampton Court's immense gardens—and steel herself to change her answer to Gabriel tomorrow.

She'd bet the Duchess of Bridgewater would never find herself without a maid.

Chapter Twenty-eight

Notebook, ruler, and rope in hand, Kit left his assigned lodging in Master Carpenter's Court and made his winding way through the palace.

Base Court smelled of cut grass, and 'twas quiet after the excitement of the duel earlier. Or at least it should have been quiet. As Kit approached the covered passage known as the Great Chamber, an odd pounding reached his ears. "Open up!" a woman shouted, clearly agitated.

Like Rose had been earlier this evening. He wondered what had possessed him to try to soothe her during the duel. After all, she'd flatly turned down his proposal, and given that she'd nearly gone out of her mind at seeing the duke put his life at risk, it was clear she seemed bent on marrying the lucky bastard. No matter her mother's encouragement, Kit liked to think he was a man who knew when to give up.

Crossing in front of the Great Chamber, he looked to see who was making such a racket, then stopped and stared. As though he'd conjured her with his musings, there stood Rose, banging her fists on the huge oak doors that led to the bridge over Hampton Court's moat.

"Rose!" he called. Apparently he had yet to give up. "Wherever do you think you're going?"

She turned, her hands clenched at her sides. "To the gardens, if a guard will ever be pleased to let me out. I wish to walk."

He stepped deeper into the musty passageway. She looked beautiful in her anger, her eyes shining with a luster that matched the pearls on her fancy gown. "'Tis not wise to go out there alone," he warned. "The privy garden would be safer."

"I'm not allowed in the privy garden. Do you not know the meaning of the word 'privy'?"

"I'll get you inside. I'm on my way there now."

She looked at the assortment of items he'd brought. "To do what?"

"My project is there. The new apartments for the King's old mistress Barbara. I wish to check . . . everything," he finished with a sigh.

A trickle of water dripped from somewhere overhead. "Have you found something amiss?" she asked.

"No. At least not yet. But I've a feeling in my bones that something is wrong. I intend to measure every square foot of the building." 'Twas a fool's task, he feared, as well as a long, tedious one. But he wouldn't rest easy until he'd completed it. And he needed to do it when no one was watching, trying to distract him—or worse, covering anything up. "Come along. Their Majesties are at Court, so the garden will afford you the solitude you're seeking."

She grabbed a lantern off the ground. "I shall help you measure."

In the torchlight that danced on the old brick walls, he stared at her. "Why?"

Her dark eyes grew hooded. "I have nothing else to do. I've no wish to return to Court until later, when the gaming is underway. And your task would go faster with help, would it not? I've been called selfish, but I like to think I would be there to help a friend."

He wondered about some of her brave speech, not least why she hesitated to return to Court. But he focused on her last sentence. "Are we friends, Rose?"

"Yes," she said firmly, and then more uncertainly, "I hope so."

A part of him—the part that didn't know when to give up—still hoped for more than her friendship. But it would do for now. "Come on, then," he said. "Lead the way."

She raised the lantern and started across Base Court, teetering a little on the cobblestones in her fashionable high heels. Such a lady, his Rose.

"Does this feel like a cloister to you?" he found himself asking.

She glanced around as they walked. "Maybe. A little. Why?"

"I keep thinking Cardinal Wolsey built this place like an Italian cardinal's palace. Something about the feel of it, the layout. Henry the Eighth would have ruined it when he rebuilt, but underneath . . ."

They crossed Clock Court, Rose's measured steps matching the cadence of Henry's great astronomical timepiece. "Are there records of the construction?"

"None of which I'm aware." He sighed. "Someday I just hope to see an old cardinal's palace. To journey to Italy and stand in the middle of one and see if I'm right, if it shares the same feeling."

He waited for her to say she'd like to come with him, but she didn't. Her skirts swished against the cobblestones, and as they passed the fountain with its paltry gurgle of water, hoots of revelers filtered down from the Presence Chamber.

"The Court seems in high spirits following the duel," he remarked.

"I'm sure they are," she replied dryly. "Louise said 'twas the most exciting thing that's happened in weeks."

"Why are you not with them?"

She clamped her lips and walked faster, entering Cloister Green Court.

And there she stopped. "Listen." The courtyard was bordered by the King's and Queen's apartments on two of its four sides. "Do you hear Charles's dogs? How odd—he usually keeps them with him at Court."

He suppressed a smile. "You're not hearing Charles's dogs."

"I am. Can you not hear them yipping?"

"'Tisn't dogs you hear, Rose. 'Tis people."

"People? Doing what?" Her eyes narrowed and then widened. "You cannot mean . . ."

Despite his efforts, a grin broke free. "Yes."

"'Tis a couple making love?" Trust her to say it out loud when he'd avoided being direct. In a complete reversal of mood, a little giggle escaped her lips. "Good God, do people really sound like that in bed?"

"Some people," he said, struggling to maintain his dignity. "Not everyone."

More giggles filled the courtyard, mad giggles, giggles that warmed his heart. "I-I'm n-never g-going to s-sound like that," she choked out as the yipping went on. "Gemini, would you listen to her? She sounds as though she's in pain!"

He thought he heard a little snort, but surely Rose wouldn't snort. "She's not, I assure you," he said, giving in and laughing along with her.

He'd never in his life laughed so much as he had since he met Rose. It felt good. Lest he drop them, he set down his things and put his hands on her shoulders, and *she* felt good.

"With any other man," she chortled as the yipping built to a crescendo, "I'd have pretended I didn't hear that."

"You thought it was dogs," he reminded her. "You couldn't have pretended."

"Well, a courtier wouldn't have pointed out my mistake."

The yipping stopped while Kit just stared at her.

"I didn't intend that in a negative fashion," she said quickly in the sudden quiet. "I'm very glad we are friends."

Kit was glad, too, but he feared that was all they would ever be.

After a silent moment, she drew a deep, audible breath.

"Do you not feel small here?" she whispered. "In the dark with the towering buildings all around looming over us?"

He squeezed her shoulders. "Yes."

"Look at all the different shaped chimneys silhouetted against the sky." She gazed up for a quiet moment, then lowered her eyes to meet his. "It must be wonderful to create something so monumental."

She knew. She knew how he felt. "I'm only creating one building," he reminded her.

"Still, 'twill be part of this whole." Her sigh sounded wistful, calmer than before their bout of laughter. "Show me what you're creating."

He scooped up his things and guided her out the back of the palace, nodding to the sleepy guard. Before them, lime trees stretched into the dark distance, and moonlight reflected off Charles's Long Water, a manmade canal inspired by one at Versailles. Kit drew Rose to the right, where at the corner of the palace another guarded gate marked the entrance to the privy gardens.

"Harriet!" Rose exclaimed. "Whatever are you doing here?"

In the torchlight from the gatehouse, her maid blushed. "Just passing the time, milady. Your mother introduced me to Walter." Harriet motioned to the guard. "You haven't need of me, have you?"

"I certainly do . . . not . . . no." Rose shook her head.

When Kit pushed open the gate, Walter cleared his throat. "The garden is for the King's pleasure only, I'm afraid."

"I'm here to work," Kit said succinctly.

"At this hour?" The man looked between them. "With her? Pardon me, Mr. Martyn, but it doesn't seem as though—"

"She has volunteered to assist me." Kit raised his supplies.

"Ah, let them go," Harriet cajoled with much more familiarity than Kit expected from one so newly introduced.

"Trust me, Walter, my mistress will not be dallying with the likes of him."

That attitude, unfortunately, Kit did expect. As he ushered Rose through the opened gate, the fragile closeness he'd felt in Cloister Green Court disappeared like sawdust in the wind.

"Trust my mother to find a man for my maid," Rose grumbled. "She thinks she can match every last soul with his or her perfect mate."

Kit shut the gate. "Do her introductions often result in marriages?"

"Usually, which is annoying as anything."

He hid a smile. "Not to the people involved, I'll wager."

"Well, she's not involving me." She hurried toward the new construction. "Show me what you're building."

He walked her through the new apartments, the main rooms and all the bedchambers for the Duchess of Cleveland and the five children she'd borne King Charles. Most of them were all but grown already, but the King had granted them titles and he played a large part in their lives. "The chambers are bare yet, but they will be rich. Charles is sparing no expense."

"Is Barbara not living in Paris now?"

"Yes, but he knows she'll be back."

"I understand he doesn't visit Hampton Court often. Word has it he prefers Windsor and Whitehall."

"All the more reason to give her a home here," he said with a half smile. 'Twas common knowledge that Charles was long finished with his old mistress, but he valued their offspring and would support her so long as she should live.

After the tour, Rose held the lantern for Kit while he measured and made notes.

"What are you looking for?" she asked.

"Something off. Not to plan. I won't be able to tell here, but I will take the notes back to my quarters and examine every inch." Her sweet rose scent was distracting. "What did you mean," he asked, "when you said earlier tonight that you didn't want to be responsible for the earl's death?"

Though he was busy measuring, he heard her tight swallow. "The duke wouldn't have been fighting the earl if not for me."

"You?" Jotting a note, he looked up. "The duel was over *you*?"

"Yes." Her face looked pale in the lamplight. "The earl took . . . liberties that were out of line."

"Liberties?"

"With my person. He was trying to . . . act out an engraving in a book he'd heard I possess." Kit's face must have shown his confusion, because she rushed to clarify. "*I Sonetti Lussuriosi.*"

"*I Sonetti*? Weren't virtually all the copies burned by the Vatican? Where the hell did you find one?"

"'Tis Ellen's," she said, then clapped her hand over her mouth. "Don't tell her I told you."

"We're not talking, remember?" That must have been the book Ellen had brought that evening to Windsor; the one she'd asked Rose to translate. He should have known it was something illicit. Ellen had never been bookish, and she'd been totally engrossed. "Besides, I don't even want to *think* about my baby sister owning that book."

Despite everything, Rose grinned. "She's a married woman, Kit."

He looked away, stretching his rope to make another measurement. "I don't want to think about that, either." He counted the knots spaced at one-foot intervals, adding swiftly in his head. "Regardless, Featherstonehaugh had no right to maul you." The mere thought made him seethe. "Simply owning a book does not make one a loose woman."

"Exactly what I think!" She moved to help, holding one end of the rope up to a beam. "Yet the entire Court seems to have jumped to that conclusion."

As he fed out the rope, he glanced over at her. "As your

friend, I wonder if you're doing something else to give that impression."

She looked like she didn't want to believe that. "Men," she said, "will be men."

He cocked a brow.

"Well, I did ask a few men to kiss me."

"A few?"

"Only the unmarried ones," she said, managing to sound indignant.

Unreasoned jealousy surged through him. "*All* the unmarried ones?"

"There aren't that many. Good God, Kit, they were just kisses."

Rose was a sensual creature. He knew how easily she could be coaxed past kisses. Hell, even without inviting their attentions, he couldn't imagine the men here at Court keeping their hands off her. They were lechers, one and all. "'Tis no wonder the duke had to come to your rescue."

"He didn't rescue me—I rescued myself quite well, thank you. I believe the earl has my handprint on his face to prove it." He'd finished measuring, so she dropped her end of the rope. "The duel is the result of a misplaced sense of possession. The duke wishes to marry me."

In the midst of writing another number, Kit froze. He was well aware that Rose was desirous of wedding Bridgewater, but hadn't realized the damned duke returned her feelings. "He's asked you, then?"

"Yes. I refused him."

He released a pent-up breath. "You seem to make that a habit."

"I do, don't I?" she said with a sigh.

He wished he knew what that sigh meant.

"My, Harriet, you've been out here a long time."

The maid startled and pulled her lips from the guard's, smoothing down her skirt. "Forgive me, Lady Trentingham."

Walter's face flamed red in the torchlight. "My lady—"

"I saw nothing." Chrystabel waved a hand. "I am looking for Rose."

"Oh!" Harriet hurried to open the gate. "Lady Rose is in the privy garden, working with Mr. Martyn." .

"Is she?" With a smile, Chrystabel reached out and shut it. "I'll just let her be, then. I imagine they're doing something important, and I'd not want to interrupt."

The news that Kit had managed to get Rose alone—tonight of all nights—lightened her heart. She'd heard about the duel from the duke himself, along with his complaint that Rose had dismissed his suit. After he'd drawn his sword for her, no less, he'd pointed out with an affronted sniff.

She'd silently sent up a cheer.

Things were looking up. "Thank you," she said, turning to leave.

"Lady Trentingham?"

She swiveled back. "Yes, Harriet?"

"I shall report to your lodging forthwith."

"Take your time, dear. I expect Rose will be busy for quite a while. And you and Walter have much to discuss."

The maid exchanged a puzzled look with the guard. "Discuss?"

"Will he leave the King's employ and take a post at Trentingham, or will you find a position here? A major decision, do you not think?"

Chrystabel imagined both their mouths falling open as she made her way back into the palace. But she was certain their relationship would come to that, soon if not this night.

Her matchmaking instincts were all but infallible.

Chapter Twenty-nine

Kit's notebook was filled by the time he made the last measurement, and Rose had long since slipped off her high heels. When they stepped out of the building, the sun was peeking over the horizon, gilding the privy garden in golden morning light.

"*Parterre a l'anglais,*" Rose murmured, mentally comparing the area before her to her father's exquisitely planted gardens.

"*Parterre a* what?" Kit shut the door behind them.

"Literally it means 'English floor,' but you must imagine it said in a derisive French tone." She grinned at Kit's quick smile, adding, "It refers to the English preference for smooth turf like this rather than their own intricate figured *parterres.*"

Hampton Court's privy garden was divided into simple, plain grass quarters, each with a single statue—Venus and Cleopatra in brass, and Adonis and Apollo in marble. In the center of it all sat Arethusa above a great black marble fountain with naught but a trickle of water.

"It is rather pathetic," Kit admitted. "I've heard the fountains in Italy gush water."

Rose shifted both her shoes to one hand. "I can see why Charles is putting his discarded mistress out here—I imagine he rarely visits this garden himself."

"I'd wager he does," he disagreed. "He needs places all his own, whether beautiful or not. The poor man cannot even dine or dress without people watching."

Rose had never thought of the King as "poor," but she supposed Kit had a point. Court etiquette could be tedious, she thought through a yawn.

" 'Tis morning," she suddenly realized. "We've been up all night."

"I'm used to it," Kit muttered.

"I'm not. Do you know, I've only stayed up all night once before, and I was with you then, too—the night we deciphered Rand's brother's diary. You're a bad influence," she accused with a tired smile.

"You can sleep today. God knows nothing happens at Hampton Court while the sun shines. For the nobility, anyway. My crew will be arriving any minute, though; we'd best leave before we're discovered."

He put a hand to her back, guiding her toward the gate, and Rose realized it was the first time he'd touched her since they'd laughed in Cloister Green Court. They'd passed the long hours of the night-working and talking. He hadn't tried even once to kiss her, let alone found an excuse for a furtive caress.

Apparently he'd accepted her refusal of his proposal. She was grateful to retain his friendship, and 'twas easier this way, because it would be hard to keep saying no . . . but she was unbearably sad at the thought of never kissing him again.

Walter was no longer at the gate; an older guard nodded as they passed though. No sooner had they rounded the corner of the building than they heard masculine voices and the stomp of boots.

"The workmen." Kit grabbed her hand. "We cannot let them see us." With that, he began running along the perimeter of the palace, pulling her along with him.

She dropped one of her shoes. "Wait!"

"We'll return for it!" he said without slowing.

They were both huffing and puffing by the time they rounded another corner and skidded to a stop. When he dropped her hand, she felt a loss. "Safe," he declared with a breathless laugh. "I don't think they saw us."

Her chest was heaving, and she noticed him noticing. "Whyever does it matter?"

His gaze returned to her face. "If any one of them is sabotaging this project, I'd not have him know I'm investigating. They'll all be hard at work in a few minutes. Then we can sneak into the palace."

"Like spies," she said with a smile, wishing he were still touching her.

"Like spies." He grinned, glancing around the extensive gardens. "In the meantime, I've been hankering to check out the maze."

"Not the maze," she groaned. "I despise mazes. I always get lost."

"If you know the left-hand rule, 'tis impossible to get lost."

"How is that?"

"I'll show you. You'll not get lost." Apparently noting her skeptical expression, he took her hand again and began walking. "Besides, I reckon I can make it fun to get lost."

Something had changed in the quality of his voice; something that made bubbles start pinging in Rose's stomach. The grass felt cool and springy under her stockinged feet. "I missed the gaming," she suddenly realized. "Again."

"I'm sorry," he said, not sounding at all sincere.

"I was hoping to win enough for a new gown."

"At Court?" He chuckled. "A gown is a mere pittance. Word has it the Duchess Mazarin lost ten thousand last week. On a single bet."

"Ten thousand *pounds*?"

He nodded. "Pounds."

"That's my whole inheritance!" Perhaps it was just as well that she'd missed the gaming. "I've got better things to do with my money."

"You have big plans for it, then?"

"Unlike my dowry, 'tis mine. It will not be my husband's."

He glanced sideways at her, one of his black brows lifted. "I'm not in need of it. I cannot speak for the duke."

The thought startled her. The truth was, she had no idea whether the duke was in need of funds or not. He dressed richly and had given her diamond earrings, but that didn't necessarily mean anything. For all she knew, he could owe his tailor and jeweler a fortune.

"Well, he'll not be getting it," she said.

"I admire your conviction. What do you plan to do with it?"

She flashed him a sly grin. "Maybe I'll give it to Ellen so she and Thomas can move their pawnshop to London."

"Be serious."

"Is this more of the getting-to-know-each-other game?"

They'd come to the entrance of the maze. "Tell me," he said softly.

Her sisters had both nurtured dreams since childhood; Violet wanted to publish a philosophy book, and Lily hoped to build and staff a home for stray animals. But in truth, Rose had never made such high-minded plans. She'd only ever hoped to find love and be happy.

She just hadn't expected that goal to be so difficult.

"I want to travel," she said. "I wish to see the world."

That brow went up again. "Does the duke enjoy travel?"

She had no idea. In fact, she realized now, she knew little of the duke at all. They'd never had a serious conversation, never shared a confidence, never discussed likes, dislikes, values—or much of anything at all.

But she'd spent hours talking to Kit, about anything and everything. They'd become friends before she ever kissed him. She knew he wanted to travel, to Italy and elsewhere.

"Let us go inside," she said. "I'd have you show me this left-hand rule."

The look he gave her made it clear he knew she was avoiding his question. But he took her remaining shoe and set it down with his own things, then led her inside the tall hedge maze.

"Put your left hand on the wall as we walk," he instructed. "And leave it there. Just follow that left wall without breaking contact, and I guarantee you'll find the center without getting lost. Go on," he urged when she hesitated. "I'll follow you."

She slanted him a wary glance, but did as he said, skimming her left hand along the leaves as she marched through the hornbeam hedges. When they reached a dead end, she turned on him. "It didn't work."

"Keep your hand on the wall," he repeated. "Follow it around."

"'Tis a dead end."

"I didn't say you'd never come to a dead end. I said you wouldn't get lost." He took her left hand, pressed a slow, warm kiss to the palm, then placed it back against the hedge. "Keep going."

She did, releasing a long, shuddering breath. The towering hedges made the path shady and intimate. At the second dead end, she turned to him again. "This cannot be the optimum route."

"Of course it isn't." He looked amused. "You'd have to know the pattern of the maze to take the optimum route. But this is a safe route. You won't wander the same way twice, and you will find the center." He pressed a quick kiss to her lips, so fast and light she wondered if she might have imagined it. "Keep going."

At the third dead end she turned to him once more. "This is a waste of time."

"Of course 'tis a waste of time. 'Tis a maze—there are few things more frivolous." He laughed and trailed a finger down her cheek to her chin, a frisson of warmth following. His thumb rubbed her bottom lip. "But there is nothing quite so delightful as wasting time with someone you care for, is there?"

He leaned close, his mouth brushing hers slowly, leaving

no doubt this time. Giddy with exhaustion, she wrapped her arms around his neck and pulled him even closer.

He was right. There was nothing else quite so delightful. She slid into the kiss, that wonderful heat building in her, making her head lighten, her stomach bubble with excitement.

"Keep going," he whispered when he finally drew back.

Dizzily she trailed a hand along the cool leaves, the trodden dirt path hard under her stockinged feet. At the next dead end, she felt his hands on her shoulders, turning her into his arms. His fingers cupped her face, and as he lowered his mouth to meet hers, his woodsy scent filled her head. The morning was chilly, but he was so very warm and male.

He nibbled here, licked there, coaxed apart her lips. She surrendered all too willingly, his tongue in her mouth sending more heat spiraling through her.

"Kit," she murmured.

"Hmm?" He kissed both sides of her mouth where her dimples would be if she were smiling.

"I think . . ." She was so lightheaded, her thoughts refused to come together. "Let's keep going."

She felt weak, so weak she could barely keep her hand to the hedges as she went along. Another dead end loomed ahead, and this time she turned to him before they even reached it.

He laughed low, his smile as intimate as a kiss. "I think you're enjoying this maze more than you anticipated." He reached out to tap her mouth, traced her lips, then trailed a finger down her chin, her throat, along the edge of her low decolletage. His gaze went a glittery green as his long finger found the valley between her breasts. She shivered and went on her toes to press her mouth to his.

'Twas a kiss to fall into, hungry, demanding. Her knees trembled, her throat tightened, and the heat in her middle grew into a burning ache. By the time he broke away, she was gasping for breath, and she couldn't have held her hand to the wall had her life depended on it.

He scooped her up in his arms, carried her to the center, and deposited her on a bench.

She was sorry there hadn't been more dead ends.

Feeling boneless, she placed her hands on either side of herself for support. 'Twas an oval, grassy space, a tiny hidden garden with two old trees and the bench between them, a secret place that exuded solitude and the scents of greenery.

Kit stood looming over her. "Told you we'd find the center."

She leaned back on her palms, gazing up at him. "That always works?"

"Well, not necessarily quite so enjoyably." He grinned. "But yes, it always works. From a mathematical standpoint, it must."

She shook her head, then stopped when it made her feel woozy. "I was never all that good at mathematics."

"And I cannot speak anything but English." He stepped back and leaned casually against one of the trees, looking wide awake and utterly handsome. "We all have our strengths, Rose. And our weaknesses. Don't underreckon yourself."

"You don't," she said, knowing it was true.

"I don't what?"

"Underreckon me."

"Of course I don't. I couldn't love a woman if I didn't admire her as well."

That single syllable, *love,* threw her. She was reeling under Kit's onslaught of seductive actions and words.

And he admired her.

Did she admire Gabriel? She didn't know. He'd proven himself kind and solicitous and generous, but he'd also kept a pawnbroker's change. She was so tired and confused and dizzy.

Her knees still shaky, she stood and walked to the other tree, putting the bench between herself and Kit. She turned away, running her fingers down the trunk, smiling dazedly at the carvings made by others who had found their way to the center.

"Look at all the initials," she said quietly. "Hundreds of them. Do you suppose all these people made it here using the left-hand rule?"

His low laugh sounded by her ear, surprising her. "No," he said from right behind her, his voice reawakening that heat in her middle. "I expect most of those people were lost for hours, both on their way in and out."

She smiled, the only reaction she was capable of at the moment. "You're fooling."

"Maybe. You're tired."

"Definitely." She felt his fingers on her ear, warm and sure, slipping one diamond drop free. Then his lips as he leaned close and drew the lobe into his mouth, suckling gently.

She let her head fall back against him, inhaling his scent, drawing it into her lungs as though it could sustain her.

Maybe it could.

"Romance," he muttered under his breath, pulling away.

Or at least she thought she'd heard him mutter. She straightened woozily and turned to face him. "What?"

"Nothing." He pulled his knife from his belt. "Who do you suppose made all these carvings?"

"I'm sure I don't know."

He moved around the tree, examining all the initials. "Do you think the King has left his mark?" He set his knife to the wood and started scratching. "His mistresses? Do you expect any two people have been here who fit together so perfect as we?"

She followed him around and stood, swaying slightly as she stared. He'd engraved *RA* and *CM,* and now he was busy surrounding both with a heart.

Her own heart melted. "Kit," she whispered.

The knife dropped to the dirt as he gathered her into his arms, his mouth on hers tasting of heat and desire. Turning her, he backed her against the tree. He slid the second diamond drop from her ear and slipped it into his pocket, kissing her lobe, nipping it gently. And lower, following the line of her jaw to her throat, playing in that sensitive hollow that made her shiver.

Wanting to taste him as he was tasting her, she raised her hands to unknot his cravat. Slowly she drew it from his neck, placing her lips where it had been as it fluttered to the ground like a white flag of surrender.

And surrender she did.

His skin tasted of warmth tinged with salt and Kit, a heady flavor. Her toes curled into the turf. She slipped her hands under his surcoat and around him, leaning back against the tree, murmuring nary a word of protest when he hiked her skirts and slid a hand beneath to graze the smooth length of her legs.

No, not a word. She wanted it, wanted him, wanted him there where she ached. He moved closer, his hand moving higher, skimming the line where her legs met, coaxing them apart with his fingers. And then he was between them, an exquisite glide of sensation, stroking, teasing, driving her mindless with need.

Above, he met her mouth, his tongue mimicking what his hand did below, thrusting as he slid a finger inside her and back out. Sliding again, and again, and again. She worked her hands lower and between them, wanting to feel him, to learn the shape of a man, the shape of Kit, wanting to give him some of the incredible pleasure he was giving her.

But he pressed his hips hard against hers, denying her access. "No," he whispered. "Not if you won't have me." His arm was still between their bodies, his hand between her legs, stroking relentlessly, making it hard to absorb his words. "I'll not take risks. I'll not dishonor you, no."

"Yes . . . oh, yes . . ." Her voice went higher as she felt herself succumbing to the magic of his fingers. "Oh, please, Kit. Let me feel you."

"Just feel, sweetheart. Feel what I can do to you . . . every day, if only you'll let me."

She felt. She felt too much. She felt and felt until she went soaring over an edge, her awareness dimming, her knees buckling, her cries absorbed by Kit's mouth over hers.

He held her for what seemed like a long time, rubbing her back and murmuring soft, senseless endearments while she slowly returned to herself.

At last she drew a huge breath and moved away, smoothing down her skirts, feeling like she should say something but not knowing what. "My earrings," she finally whispered tremulously.

He dug them out of his pocket and dropped them, one by one, into her outstretched palm. "Did the duke give you these, too?"

His voice was husky and as shaky as hers. She swallowed and nodded.

"I'm not giving up without a fight," he said low. "We're too good together. I want you."

God help her, she wanted him, too, and not only because his kisses made her forget who she was and what she was after. He was the only man she'd ever met who appreciated her for more than her beauty—who valued her for her intelligence, who was awed by her talent with languages. She wanted Kit more than she'd imagined a woman could want a man.

But in the end, she said nothing, because a duke had offered for her hand. And risked his life defending her honor.

How could she accept an architect over a duke?

The diamonds felt hard in her fist. "I think we'd best go back."

"Yes." He scooped his cravat off the ground, stuffed it into his pocket, ran a trembling hand through his hair.

She straightened her gown. "How do we get out? The right-hand rule?"

His expression lightened, and he almost cracked a smile. "How about the rule of knowing the way you came in?"

"How many times have you been in this maze?"

"Just the once. But 'tis a pattern. Geometry."

She nodded slowly. "You're good at geometry."

He met her gaze, his own steady. "You'll find I'm good at a lot of things. Follow me."

He led her out without one misstep.

Without running into one dead end.

Without any more kisses.

Chapter Thirty

L ater that day, Kit was in the midst of a calculation when a knock interrupted. "One minute," he called, pausing to scribble down a number.

He rose and stretched for a brief moment, then padded across his small lodging to open the door. "Lady Trentingham." He blinked. How had she found him? The courtiers weren't lodged near Master Carpenter's Court.

"May I come in?"

"Certainly." He opened the door wider, very aware of his state of half-dress: no shoes, no stockings, no coat, no cravat. Just breeches and a shirt, the latter half-unlaced and the sleeves rolled up to his elbows. He started turning them down.

"No need to do that for me," she assured him. "I've seen a man's arms and feet before. And a chest." Her brown eyes danced with mischief. "Has Rose seen them?"

"No!" he said quickly.

She gave a mournful shake of her head. "Then you're not doing a very good job. However do you expect her to be consumed by lust if you're always dressed to face a snowstorm?"

He couldn't *believe* the conversations he found himself in with Rose's mother. He waved her toward one of the two chairs that flanked the Spartan room's small table, taking the other for himself. "I gave my word that Rose would remain chaste."

"Of course." She sat, fluffing her skirts. "But a little temptation would not be amiss. Have you tried some romance?"

"I carved our initials into a tree trunk. The mere act had me choking back laughter, but she loved it."

"Excellent. You must do some more of that."

"I'm a very straightforward kind of fellow, Lady Trentingham. I wasn't raised here at Court. I'm not good at gallant gestures."

She glanced at the carefully drawn plans he had spread on the table. "You seem creative enough to me. I'm sure if you put your mind to it, you'll do just fine."

Designing buildings wasn't creative—'twas logical, mathematical. Certain requirements had to be met, certain loads had to be supported, certain shapes were inherently beautiful. But he'd learned by now that there was no arguing with Lady Trentingham.

"I'll try," he told her.

"Excellent. The fact that Rose refused the duke's proposal after he dueled on her behalf—I take that as a very good sign."

"The duel . . ." He rubbed the back of his neck. "I realize 'tis not my place to say this, my lady, but matters at Court seem to be getting a bit out of hand. I think it might be best if you took Rose and left—as soon as possible."

"We're leaving tomorrow. Her friend Judith is marrying later this week, and she'd never forgive us if we missed her wedding."

"No, I mean you should leave today. Before . . ." Hoping Rose would forgive him, he plunged on. "Are you aware that your daughter is in possession of a book? A very—"

"*I Sonetti?*" she interrupted.

"She . . . shared it with you?" He couldn't imagine a mother-daughter relationship like that, but then nothing about the Ashcroft family seemed normal.

Question Convention, he thought with an internal sigh.

Lady Trentingham's lips quirked. "Of course she didn't

share it. But she's carried it from place to place for days. I am not unobservant. You'll find me the curious sort."

Somehow that wasn't surprising. "Then you'll know why you must leave. Word has gone round that Rose has this book, and people—men—have decided she's . . . she's . . ."

"Wild? A wanton?"

"Yes," he snapped. He didn't want to think of Rose like that. And he knew 'twas not really true.

She sighed. "I'm aware of that, too. 'Tis unfortunate, and certainly not part of my plans. But she's not in danger of being compromised—"

"I wouldn't be so certain."

"I'm watching her. If it makes you feel any better, keep in mind that those lecherous courtiers may be driving her straight into your arms."

Perhaps she had a point that, in the scheme of things, all those men with wandering hands might be doing him a favor. But that didn't mean he liked it. He couldn't stand the thought of other men touching Rose, whether the attentions were invited or not.

"Take her home," he begged. "As soon as I've convinced myself that everything here is right, I'll come straight to Trentingham. Without these unwelcome distractions, I'll be able to concentrate my efforts on making her find me irresistible."

"Excellent. But we'll leave tomorrow. Rose would never forgive me if she missed the masked ball. Even now, she is wearing her fingers to nubs sewing blooms on a gown."

"Blooms?"

"Her costume. She's going as a flower arrangement."

Despite his worry, he smiled. 'Twas so Rose. "I thought she would be sleeping."

"She did, for a while. But then she raided the palace's gardens and set both our maids to work. The three of them are stitching madly."

He sighed, giving up. "What are you going as?"

"A mother. I'll watch her, Kit."

"You do that," he said.

But he would watch her, too.

Everything looked so beautiful! The masked ball was held in the Great Hall rather than the Presence Chamber, and instead of candelabra and oil lamps, the huge room was lit by liveried yeomen holding tall, flaming torches. Overhead, the gold stars on the painted hammerbeam ceiling winked on their field of bright blue.

Dancers twirled in the blazing light. King Arthur was paired with a glittery-winged butterfly, and Robin Hood danced with Aphrodite. An angel and a devil seemed to be getting along well, and Zeus was kissing Anne Boleyn.

Decked out in a gown covered neckline to hemline with fresh flowers, Rose watched from a corner, drinking in the splendor and trying to puzzle out everyone's identity.

All the faces were covered by full or half masks, but a few courtiers weren't difficult to spot. Beneath Caesar's crown of laurel leaves, his half mask failed to cover King Charles's mustache, and as he was the tallest man in the room, the monarch's height would have given him away regardless.

The Duchess Mazarin had come as a shepherdess, and her servant Mustapha was her little black sheep. Apparently shepherdesses wore no stays of any sort, because Hortense's ample breasts jiggled against the thin fabric of her peasant blouse every time she laughed—which was often.

Rose was trying her best not to stare.

There were other skimpily garbed ladies as well. A tavern wench's nipples peeked from her low, frilled bodice. A blowzy doxy flitted about in dishabille. A Greek goddess's robes could not seem to stay fastened—

"Enjoying yourself?" someone asked, and Rose turned to see Nell Gwyn. Since she was the smallest woman in the chamber, her identity wasn't in doubt. Her half mask of black matched her lovely black gown. But it was, after all, just an ordinary black gown, much like the one she'd made fun of Louise de Kéroualle wearing yesterday.

Rose cocked her head. "Who are you supposed to be?"

"I'm in mourning," Nell said gaily, "for poor Louise's lost hopes."

Rose laughed and looked for Louise. There she was, as a haughty Cleopatra. But Caesar, surrounded as usual by spaniels and toying with the loose-breasted shepherdess, seemed distinctly uninterested.

Lost hopes, indeed.

"What a clever costume," Nell said. "I don't believe anyone has ever before come as a flower arrangement." She leaned closer to Rose. "You smell delicious."

Pleased, Rose smiled beneath her full mask. "You know who I am?"

"I know who everyone is," Nell boasted. "Except him." She gestured toward a man standing before one of the massive gold- and silver-embroidered tapestries that covered the walls. "Handsome as sin, isn't he?"

Rose followed Nell's gaze, spotting a pirate. His breeches were tighter than the current fashion—skintight, as a matter of fact—hinting at long, muscular legs. His full white shirt was unlaced halfway down his chest, revealing bare skin sprinkled with crisp black hair.

"Handsome as sin, indeed." Rose wondered if he was a good kisser. "When do the masks come off?"

"Midnight," Nell said with a tinkling laugh, apparently divining Rose's thoughts. "But I've arranged a surprise first. It should be jolly fun. In the meantime"—she lifted her black skirts—"I'm going to meet that pirate."

As Rose watched her dance off, a medieval knight came up carrying a goblet full of warm, spiced wine. He bowed elaborately, his chain mail clanking. "My lady."

He'd taken no pains to disguise his voice, so she knew it was Gabriel. "My thanks, Sir Knight," she said, taking the cup and sipping gratefully.

Or gulping might be a better description.

Instead of a mask, he wore a polished helmet complete with a visor that concealed his face. How very appropriate, she thought, for him to dress as a knight in shining armor after yesterday's duel.

And he wasted no time in reminding her. "I would slay dragons for you, my dear Rose."

She sighed. "You recognize me?"

"But of course. I would know you anywhere." The visor creaked when he flipped it up, his blue eyes blazing with earnestness. "You're the damsel of my dreams . . . I hope you've reconsidered and decided to marry me."

He was so perfect. So gallant. Was it terrible of her to be glad the helmet prevented a kiss?

She sipped more wine. "I'm thinking about it, Gabriel."

"I would have your answer soon. I would waste no time making you my wife."

Why couldn't she just say yes? She'd resolved to do so last night, hadn't she?

But she didn't know him. She only knew he was a duke. "Do you like to travel?" she asked.

"I visit my mother in Northumberland every year."

Oh, wouldn't *that* be exciting? "I meant overseas."

"I get seasick in the bath." He looked a little green just at the thought. But then he mustered a bold face. "If you wish to travel, dear Rose, I will manage."

She couldn't expect more. "What's your favorite book?" she asked, wracking her brain for some of Kit's questions.

"I do not read."

She couldn't see his mouth, but she could tell from his eyes that he'd frowned. "You cannot read?"

"Of course I can read. I simply find other pursuits more interesting."

"Oh." That wasn't too bad, was it? She wasn't much of a reader herself, save for newsheets and foreign books. Everyone had different tastes. "Tastes," she murmured. "Do you prefer sweet or savory?"

His good humor seemed to be stretched to the breaking point. "What is it with these questions?"

"Nothing," she muttered. "Never mind. Thank you for the wine."

She wandered away, leaving him staring after her. So he wasn't much for conversation. Not every man liked to talk, she told herself sternly. 'Twas not a crime to keep one's thoughts to oneself.

She just wondered whether he had any.

Musing, she bumped into someone, crushing more than a few of her flowers. "Pardon me," the man said in an unnaturally deep voice. A disguised voice, she decided, looking up.

'Twas the pirate. Her heart skipped a beat. *Handsome as sin,* she remembered Nell saying.

And masculine as hell.

"'Twas my fault," she assured him with a flutter of her carefully darkened lashes. She hoped he could see them through the eyeholes of her mask. "I was daydreaming."

His own masked face was expressionless. "I hope they were sweet dreams."

Who was he? What nobleman had arrived just today? She'd not heard of any, but she'd been busy catching up on her sleep and preparing her costume.

Her fingers itched to touch the bare triangle of chest displayed between the edges of his half-laced shirt. She sipped again instead, feeling the wine go straight to her head. "Will you kiss me?" she asked boldly.

Again, that expressionless reply. "I do not kiss strangers, my lady. And I'd advise you to do the same."

Well! She wanted to rip that mask off his handsome face.

Then again, she had no idea if he really was handsome under that mask. Maybe he wasn't. Maybe he was hideous, in fact. And if he didn't want to kiss her, perhaps that was because he knew he had dismal technique.

Feeling better, she stalked away.

But as she danced with Henry VIII, she felt the pirate

watching her. And after she kissed a jester—not enjoying it at all—she saw him glare. Wherever she went, his gaze seemed to follow.

The only person keeping a closer eye on her was her mother. Dressed in a sea-green gown with a demi-mask to match, Chrystabel watched Rose the entire evening. Since Mum had all but ignored her so far at Court, Rose found the sudden attentiveness disconcerting.

She danced with a monk and then with Thor, but she wasn't truly enjoying herself. When Merlin lifted his mask to kiss her and she discovered he was the Earl of Rosslyn—the married cur!—she almost decided to head back to her apartments.

But she wanted to see the unmasking. And Nelly's surprise.

She was dancing with a Viking when, outside in Clock Court, the great astronomical timepiece struck midnight. Nell sharply clapped her hands. "Yeomen," she shouted. "Now!"

As one, the flaming torches were extinguished, and the room plunged into darkness.

Chapter Thirty-one

Rose shrieked, and the Viking grabbed her by both arms. "Come here, my pretty."

He stank. Deprived of her vision, she realized many of the people in the Great Hall stank—all the flowers on her gown couldn't mask the stenches of stale sweat and too much perfume. Feeling lost, she held tight to the smelly Viking. Though she blinked and blinked, she couldn't see a thing. Her heart was threatening to pound right out of her chest.

She'd never liked the dark. "What is this?" she cried.

"'Tis naught but a bit of fun," he said in a voice anything but soothing. Dropping one of her arms, he scrabbled at her mask. Cool air hit her face, swiftly replaced by wet, rubbery lips.

Gagging, she twisted her head. "How dare you!" She wrenched from his grasp and stalked away—or tried to, but tripped instead.

She fell to her hands and knees, bouncing off a body on the floor. "Ah, the flower girl," a man murmured, his fingers grasping an ankle, working their way under her skirts. He gripped her calf and dragged her closer. "Come to me, sweet."

Mewling with disgust and fear, she scrambled away on all fours, losing a shoe when it came off in his hand. She kept moving, darting around boots and skirts as she frantically tried to feel her way to freedom. Laughter and exclamations rang through the air, the sounds of courtiers milling, pausing for a kiss here and a grope there, exploring one another in the dark.

A huge, terrifying maze of debauched humanity.

Someone stepped on her hand, and tears sprang to her eyes. She crawled faster, running headfirst into a pair of legs. Large hands reached down and hauled her up.

"What have we here?" a man drawled, sniffing appreciatively. "Oh, the flower lady. Do you not also know the secrets of *I Sonetti*?"

With that, he clamped her ruthlessly, one big hand on the back of her head and the other against her spine, his lips bruising hers as they found their target in the dark. With no further ceremony, he thrust his tongue inside her mouth.

She pushed against him and kicked his shins, but he kept her clutched tight. She reached blindly to his right side, her fingers closing on the hilt of his sword. She pulled with all her might, but the peace strings held fast. Tears trailing hot down her cheeks, she bit his tongue. Hard.

A metallic flavor flooded her mouth. "God damn you!" he cried, shoving her away with both hands. Spitting blood, she stumbled into someone soft and fragrant—a woman. The vixen squealed and clawed at her face. Rose careened away, bumped into someone else, and screamed.

Hands gripped her shoulders and held her steady. Just held her, not grasping. An anchor in the dark sea of terror.

"Hush," he said. "There is nothing to fear."

Kit. His voice, his hands. Feeling her knees buckle, she leaned against his shoulder, smelling frankincense and myrrh. Kit. Warm and yielding instead of cold and hard, but a knight in shining armor nonetheless.

"Hush," he repeated. "Keep still. 'Tis naught but a silly game. The Court will tire of it soon enough, and the torches will be relit."

She clung to him, feeling calm begin stealing over her, restoring her world to balance. "Can you not help me get out?"

"I'm afraid we'd but stumble over others." His arms came around her, his deep voice soothed. "You're safe here with me, I promise."

Darkness still enveloped her, but she was not quite so panicked. "All right," she whispered.

"We shall just wait." Moving closer, he laid his cheek against her hair. She slipped her arms around his waist, wondering vaguely how he'd got in here and managed to find her. Like at the duel, he'd known just when to show up, just when she needed him.

They were buffeted by other bodies searching, laughing, groping in the blackness. She mewed in protest, and his arms tightened, molding her more securely against him, locking the two of them together. She tilted her face up, waiting for him to lower his lips to meet hers.

Kit. The pressure of his mouth, that sweet-spicy unique flavor, that woodsy, masculine scent. The last of her fear evaporated as she sank into the comforting familiarity of his kiss.

She felt as well as heard him groan, his hands trailing lower, cupping her bottom to pull her closer still. Whatever flowers might remain on her gown were crushed mercilessly between them, but she cared not a whit. A frisson of excitement stole through her veins, robbing her of reason and breath.

Her senses spun with wine and so much more. Moans and groans, squeals and breathy sighs echoed all around her, but suddenly the sounds were arousing instead of threatening.

The kiss deepened, a dance of lips and teeth and tongues, a long, fast slide into madness. Her breasts ached inside her gown, and she pressed closer, but that wasn't enough. She pulled back instead, taking his hands to guide them where she wanted them, and he seemed only too happy to oblige. He teased her breasts through the thin silk of her ruined gown, then reached into her bodice to draw their fullness above the low neckline, pinching gently and then lowering his head to lick and suckle the sensitive crests.

That melting warmth spread in her middle, and a tingling ache built lower down. More bodies bumped them, but she cared not. The darkness offered privacy amidst this horde of writhing humanity, making bold Rose even bolder. Putting her hands flat to his chest, she skimmed his lawn shirt until she found his flat nipples and teased them the way he was hers, thrilling when she felt them tighten.

'Twas powerful, knowing she could give him the same pleasure he gave her. Molten heat sprinted through her veins. Emboldened further, she reached lower, holding her breath, waiting for him to protest as he had before. But he allowed her to touch him this time. Her fingers explored the front of his breeches, finding a long, hard ridge that made the ache between her legs intensify as she imagined him sliding inside her. She wanted him there, filling her as a woman was meant to be filled.

At the other end of the chamber, a single torch flared to life. They pulled apart, Rose swiftly yanking up on her bodice. All around them in the all-but-darkness, courtiers were engaged in various stages of lovemaking.

It sickened her, no matter that she'd been envisioning the very same thing. The whole Court sickened her.

"Take me out of here," she said. One shoe off and one on, she started limping toward the door. Kit swept her up into his arms and wove his way through the crowd, stepping over bodies as he went.

At long last, they made it down the Great Stairs and into Clock Court. Torches bathed the courtyard in a hazy yellow glow. He strode to the fountain in the center before setting her on her feet.

Her gown was in tatters from the knees down, the few remaining blooms torn and limp. Her face burned in one spot; she touched it and came away with a trace of blood on her fingertip. Her hair tumbled madly over her shoulders, half or more unpinned.

Thank God it was only Kit here to see her.

Still shaky—from lust or fear or some combination—she splashed water on her face before she looked up and blinked. "Good God, you were the pirate."

His expression slowly transformed from concern to something darker. "You didn't know? And yet you kissed me, pressed against me . . ." He looked thoroughly disgusted. "I can hardly blame all those men for taking advantage, though I wish to wring all their lecherous necks. Lord Almighty, Rose, you touched me like a true wanton, and you didn't even know—"

The last of her fear was swept away by indignance—and maybe a touch of guilt for her actions here at Court. "I am not wanton!"

Kit felt outrage like he never had before. He could hardly credit that he still wanted her—and yet he did, which fueled his anger all the more. "You could have fooled me," he spat.

"What were you doing in the Great Hall?" she demanded, by all appearances equally outraged. "You're not a member of the Court!"

"And that's why you won't have me, isn't it?"

"No! To hell with the Court. I never want to come back here again. Everything here got totally out of hand."

He opened his mouth, then closed it. The fountain trickled in the background while he silently repeated her words. *I never want to come back here again.*

Perhaps there was hope for him after all.

Suddenly he felt bone tired. "I don't want to fight," he said.

She sighed. "I don't want to fight, either."

"Rose, you must be more careful around men."

"I would never allow—"

"You're a passionate woman, but for your own good, you must curb—"

"I am *not* passionate," she interrupted. "Only with you. I

knew it was you, Kit. I have never kissed anyone else like that. Ever."

He stared, wondering whether to be pleased or angry at that impassioned revelation. Anger won. "How can you fib with such a straight face? You expect me to believe that after you admitted you didn't realize I was the pirate?"

"I didn't recognize you as the pirate during the masked ball," she returned hotly, "because it never occurred to me you would be there." She shifted her weight back and forth, popping up and down on her single high-heeled shoe. "And you're a blasted hypocrite, do you know that? *You* kissed *me* when you didn't know who *I* was."

"Bloody hell," Kit shot back, "do you take me for a fool? A sightless nitwit would have recognized you at twenty paces. You smelled like a damned garden. But you could be wearing sackcloth instead of flowers and I'd know you, Rose. Instantaneously. Do you not know that?"

Her dark eyes flashed. "Like I knew you the moment you caught me in the dark? The moment I touched you, even blind as a bat? I just never connected you with the pirate."

Understanding hit Kit like a brick dropped from a half-built wall. *I knew you, I just never connected you with the pirate.* She was beautiful in her fury, her cheeks flushed, her agitated breath making her chest heave in a way that drew his gaze. No one could lie that convincingly.

Damnation, had he ever been such a nithing blockhead?

"I'm sorry," he said. "I twisted your words in my mind, jumped to an erroneous conclusion. You're right."

"Of course I'm right."

He cracked a smile. "You're so graceful at accepting apologies."

Her anger seemed to flee as quickly as it had flared. "'Tis a good thing, since I still don't want to fight." She answered his smile with one of her own, her gaze raking his costumed form. "You make a very fetching pirate."

"Do I?"

He'd said it in all good humor, but her voice dropped to a

whisper. "You appeared like magic, and I was so grateful to have you there. You swept away my fear with a single touch of your lips . . ."

Unable to help himself, he touched those lips to hers again. A silent apology that swiftly turned to more, much more—

"Rose?" her mother's voice drifted down the Great Stairs. "Rose!"

Kit reluctantly drew away. "We're out here, Lady Trentingham."

Her high heels clicked on the cobblestones as she made her way over to them, carrying Rose's missing shoe. "I feared for you, dear. I know how you hate the dark." She kissed her daughter on both cheeks, then drew back and touched the one with the shallow scratch. "What happened here?"

"A woman with claws like a wildcat." Rose's hand went to the injury. "Is it bad?"

"A little powder and you'll never know it was there," her mother assured her.

Rose sighed. "I cannot imagine what Nell was thinking when she ordered the torches doused."

Lady Trentingham cocked her head. "Did you not know Nell is famous for practical jokes? Why, recently she left King Charles at a brothel—"

"Without any clothes or money," her daughter finished for her. "I heard about that. Remind me not to introduce her to Jewel and Rowan. If she makes these pranks a habit, the three of them together could prove deadly."

"You're all right, though?" She tried to smooth Rose's hair, but her efforts made little difference. "You're not truly hurt?"

"Kit rescued me," Rose said.

"Did he?" Lady Trentingham shared a furtive glance with him, that one brief look conveying a mixture of emotions: gratitude, congratulations, and a silent admission that she'd been wrong. "I think we should leave," she told Rose quietly.

"Yes," Rose agreed. "There is Judith's wedding, of course . . . but I believe I'd want to leave anyway."

"Shall we make our good-byes?" Lady Trentingham looked back to the Great Hall.

"Please, Mum, just give King Charles my apologies."

Kit was glad Rose didn't want to go back in there. "I will walk you to your apartments."

While her mother ascended the staircase, Rose leaned to put on her shoe. "I look like something one of Lily's cats dragged in, don't I?"

"No." His mouth quirked in a half grin. "Worse."

She winced as she straightened. "Well, thank you for being honest."

"I'll love you no matter what you look like. Always. Would the duke feel that way as well?"

She had no clue what the duke felt, as evidenced by the way she changed the subject. "Did you check all the measurements?"

He started walking her toward her lodging. "Some. Not all. There are hundreds."

"Have you found anything wrong?"

"Maybe. I'm not sure yet. The set of drawings I keep with me doesn't seem to match the plans I left here, and I'm not certain which is correct or which reflects the actual measurements we took last night."

He couldn't imagine how that had happened. Most builders worked from a single set of plans only, but he preferred to err on the side of caution and always made a careful duplicate. Had he been not-so-careful? The discrepancy was more than disturbing, but he'd set the problem aside for the evening when he decided watching over Rose was more important. And he didn't want to think about it again now.

Before she could ask more questions, he stopped beneath the clock tower, raising two fingers to her lips. "I'll let you know if I find something conclusive."

Her eyes went soft when he traced her mouth with the pad of a finger. She swayed toward him involuntarily, and he took advantage, drawing her close for a long, languid kiss.

'Twas a kiss his tired soul could melt into, but he wouldn't allow that, even though she clearly threw herself into the caress. She was still distant, distracted, with him one-hundred percent in body, but her mind had yet to cross the crucial barrier that would make her his.

"Come along," he murmured when they parted, their lips clinging for one last moment. " 'Tis been quite a night."

Just as they reached Base Court, a shooting star streaked across the sky. "Look," she breathed, closing her eyes to wish.

He wished, too, then turned and took her face in both hands. "What did you ask for?"

"I cannot tell you, or 'twill not come true."

"Fair enough." It made him smile to think she believed such fancies. "Shall I tell you what I wished for instead?"

"I think I know," she whispered and left it at that.

It wasn't the answer he wanted, but it would have to do for now.

Chapter Thirty-two

Hampton Court was quiet in the middle of the night, Kit's building dark now except for the circle of light thrown by his lantern. Scents of fresh-cut wood and hardening mortar assaulted his nose, and his footsteps echoed in the empty rooms as he wandered through them for the last time.

Tomorrow the building was coming down.

Two more days spent poring over the numbers had confirmed his suspicions: the building was flawed. He'd double-checked his calculations, remeasured, triple-checked again. The conclusion was always the same. If left standing, the structure would eventually collapse.

Oh, 'twould not fall today or tomorrow—not even this year. In fact, it could be ten or twenty or fifty years before the inherent weakness resulted in disaster. It would certainly remain standing until long afterward he was appointed Deputy Surveyor, most likely so long afterward that he doubted he would ever be blamed.

But when the collapse occurred, the consequences could very well be deadly.

Was his design at fault? Or had someone tampered with the plans? Since the two copies he had didn't match, he couldn't be sure. The fact that they were different lent credence to the theory that Harold Washburn—or someone else—had sabotaged this project.

But it didn't matter. It was Kit's project, Kit's responsibility.

There was nothing for it. Although it meant he would miss his deadline and any chance at the appointment and knighthood, he'd had no choice but to order the structure torn down and rebuilt from scratch. He couldn't live with himself knowing there were potential deaths looming ahead—not even when he suspected those at risk had yet to be born.

All he had left now was a trip to Windsor and the difficult task of explaining his failing to Wren. Then—while his dreams were torn down along with this building—he would go to Trentingham as promised. Once there, he would finalize the plans for Lord Trentingham's greenhouse . . . and tell Lady Trentingham why he was no longer worthy of marrying her daughter.

He grabbed an exquisite carved panel—that, at least, could be salvaged—and exited the building without looking back.

He'd long ago learned there was no point in that.

"Oh, Judith," Lily breathed, staring at the gown the maid had just laid on her friend's bed. Palest blue, Judith's wedding dress had a wide neckline and golden ribbons crisscrossing the stomacher. The underskirt was cloth-of-gold. " 'Tis beautiful."

A happy sigh escaped Judith's freshly painted lips. "I always dreamed of wearing blue for my wedding."

"Me, too," Violet said.

Lily grinned. "Me three."

Rose's sisters *had* both worn blue, and they were both happily married. Rose brushed her fingers over the gown's shimmering fabric, ordering herself not to be jealous. After all, she'd received so many proposals she'd lost count, and she'd probably have more had she not rebuffed so many men. It was *her* choice to refuse them.

Besides, she would never wear this gown. It might be lovely, but it was entirely too pale and insipid. When Rose finally decided to marry, she intended to do so in red.

Judith wandered across her feminine mauve room to her dressing table. "Shall I wear patches?" she wondered.

Rose turned to her pretty, plump friend. "One. A heart. But we must powder your face first." She handed Judith's patch box to Lily so she could find a suitable shape, then dipped a fluffy brush into a packet of Princess's Powder. "Are you nervous?"

"Of course not," Judith said, but her smile was trembly. She held out a wine cup for Violet to refill. "Why should I be nervous? Grenville is a good man."

Rose dusted Judith's cheeks. "Of course he's good. He's titled and has money." And if he wasn't exactly handsome, she added to herself, at least he wasn't pockmarked or ugly. A woman could look at him without wincing.

If she'd gained nothing else from Court, she'd learned 'twasn't easy to find perfection. Perhaps compromise was not such a bad thing.

"No, I mean Edmund is ever so *good.*" Judith peered at herself in the mirror. "He adores children, though his first wife couldn't give him any. He makes certain all the orphans on his estate find families and homes. No one, young or old, is ever allowed to go hungry, and—"

"That is just being decent," Rose interrupted.

Violet set down the bottle with a little *clunk.* "But decency is important. And rare."

Still riffling through the patch box with a fingertip, Lily nodded. "I would choose decency over money and a title any day of the week. You have to *live* with the man you wed."

Rose fluffed more powder on her friend's face. "Husbands and wives don't have to live with one another. At Court, it seems hardly any of them do."

Violet stared at her, her brown eyes looking huge through the lenses of her spectacles. "But those are marriages made for alliance, not love. That's not what you want, is it?"

"No," she sighed, still fluffing.

"Stop!" Judith laughed, brushing at her dressing gown.

White powder flew everywhere. Particles coated the surface of her dark wood dressing table and floated in a sunbeam that came through the window. "Edmund won't be able to find me under all this powder."

"Sorry." Rose dusted more on her own cheeks, though her scratch was all but healed. "Is Grenville nervous?"

"He doesn't seem to be. Of course, he's been married before. He's not worrying about tonight."

Violet touched her hand. "Are you worried, Judith?"

"A little." Looking away, Judith grabbed her goblet and took another swallow of wine.

"I think you're a lot worried," Lily said, prying the goblet from her fingers. Judith had downed half a bottle already, and there were still hours left before her wedding. "You don't want to be slurring your vows."

"The marriage bed is nothing to fear," Violet told her.

"Are you sure?" Judith asked.

"Of course she's sure." Rose nervously tweaked the bouquet of flowers she'd made for Judith to carry. "All brides fret about it, but they all survive, do they not?"

"Are *you* fretting?" Violet asked her.

"Why should I fret? I'm not getting married."

"But if you were?" Lily pressed.

She thought of *I Sonetti* and all those awkward positions. "No, I'm not fretting."

"Mama told me it would hurt," Judith whispered.

Rose nodded knowingly. "But only for a moment." *That* part she didn't find worrisome. She'd heard it described as "a little pain," and she believed it.

But she wished she'd never seen that blasted Italian book.

"Based on the upper floor's loads," Kit said, "I was concerned that with any additional loading the building would eventually collapse. As it stood, 'twas near the maximum tolerance of the span. I cannot believe I miscalculated something so basic."

"Neither can I," Wren said pointedly, pacing his office in Windsor Castle. His eyes suddenly narrowed as he stopped and turned to Kit. "Are you saying someone else miscalculated? Purposefully lengthened the span? Altered your plans?"

"I'll not say that." Kit met the older man's gaze. "The project is my responsibility. The error is mine, and I'll absorb the costs of rebuilding." When he first started out, a problem of this magnitude might have landed him in debtor's prison. Thankfully, he could easily afford it now.

Wren nodded as he walked him to the door. "This won't go past this room. I expect Charles will be pleased with the final results, even though you'll miss the deadline. You'll doubtless see more commissions, and your reputation won't suffer."

That was some consolation. Thanks to Wren's confidentiality, Kit's source of income wasn't endangered.

Just his dreams. His knighthood. His chances of winning the woman he loved.

"Thank you," he told Wren as he opened the door. "Though the project won't come in on time, it *will* be done right."

"From you, I expect no less." Wren watched him step outside. "I'm sorry about the appointment."

"I wish Rosslyn well with it," Kit said and closed the door behind him. So that was that. He took a deep breath and headed to Windsor's Upper Ward to check the progress on the new dining room.

Following a complete inspection, he felt a little better. Everything seemed to be proceeding well and on schedule. He had high hopes that the successful, timely completion of this beautiful chamber would help ensure more commissions from the Crown.

Somewhere in town, a clock struck noon, reminding him he'd best get on his way to Trentingham if he wanted to arrive at a decent hour. But he didn't want to rush to Trentingham, regardless of his promise—not today. He felt drained. The interview with Wren had sucked the very life right out of him.

Tomorrow morning would be better, he decided, heading out of the castle. He was in no hurry to confess his failure to yet more people, and that greenhouse was hardly an emergency. The groundbreaking wasn't scheduled until tomorrow, anyway.

He looked forward to a long, hot bath, followed by a good night's sleep. Here in Windsor, in his own house, he'd no doubt rest easier than he had in weeks. Especially since he no longer had to worry about his projects. Or, he thought dejectedly, about whether he would win the appointment he'd been working toward all of his adult life.

"Good afternoon, Mr. Martyn," the old guard called as he passed through the castle gate.

"Afternoon, Richards," Kit returned. The next thing he knew he was standing in front of a pawnshop.

His brother-in-law's pawnshop, to be precise. Kit still had the damnedest time thinking of Ellen as married. But something inside him knew he had to come to grips with that—the same something that had sent him here without conscious decision.

He hoped she fared well. And there was only one way to find out. He drew a deep breath and opened the door. At the jingle of the bell, Thomas emerged from the back.

"Mr. Martyn," he said, clearly surprised. And apprehensive, Kit thought. Well, in a sense, he couldn't blame the man.

But they were kin now, for better or worse, so he'd best set the fellow at ease. "Call me Kit," he said. "Please."

"Kit." The younger man nodded.

"I've come to see my sister."

If anything, Thomas's eyes grew more hooded. "She's upstairs. I'll fetch her."

"No. I'll go up."

"I'm sorry, sir—I mean Kit. But I'm not sure she wants to talk to you."

That hurt. Kit had hoped Ellen would be over her snit long before now. She'd won their battle, after all. She'd fought to live over a pawnshop, and live here she did.

He wanted to see the place, see how she was living. Whether she and her baby were healthy. Whether she and her pawnbroker were happy. They'd be happy after he gave them her dowry, of course, but he hoped they were happy now without it. That his sister hadn't made a mistake marrying for love.

Before he turned over all that money, he needed to see Ellen's happiness with his own eyes. He was not taking no for an answer.

"I'll go up," he repeated. "You can show me the way or I'll find it myself."

"Very well." Thomas handed a key to the young man behind the counter, then Kit followed him through a storage room and up a narrow staircase.

When Thomas opened the door, Kit sniffed appreciatively. "Smells like apples."

"The only thing your sister knows how to cook is apple fritters," Thomas said with a wry quirk of his lips. "I've been eating them 'til they're coming out of my ears."

Kit looked at him sharply, but the words had been said in good humor. It seemed the man loved Ellen whether she could cook or not.

The living quarters were nicer than he'd expected. The main room was small and the floor was bare wood, but it was polished and everything was clean. There was plenty of fine furniture and, in Kit's opinion, entirely too many knickknacks—all of which he suspected came from the shop. He guessed that some of the best merchandise found its way upstairs. A hidden benefit to this business.

And Ellen doubtless loved all the knickknacks. In fact, he wouldn't be surprised to find she'd dragged most of them up here herself. His heart lifted to think she was probably very happy here, indeed.

"Where is she?" he asked.

"In the bedchamber. She naps often these days."

A subtle reminder of his sister's condition. Kit nodded. "Will you wake her or shall I?"

He saw the other man draw a steadying breath. "Wait here." Thomas opened a door and slid into the room beyond, closing it firmly behind him.

Kit paced while he waited, peeking into another chamber to find a kitchen with a small fireplace and a scrubbed table for eating.

That seemed to be it—just the main room, kitchen, and bedchamber. He wondered where the babe would sleep, though he knew full well that entire families lived in single-room homes—why, this place would be a palace to the common cottager. Hell, he and Ellen had lived like that until the Plague had claimed their parents.

But when he built the new shop for his sister in London, he would design it with much larger living quarters attached. A proper house.

The bedchamber door opened and shut again, startling him. "She'll not see you," Thomas said.

"Pardon?"

"Ellen doesn't wish to speak with you, Mr. Martyn."

Fuming, Kit didn't bother correcting Thomas's use of his name again. "She doesn't have a choice."

He crossed the room—in all of three strides—and threw open the bedchamber door. "Ellen."

She lay on a huge four-poster bed—much too big for the room—with her back to him.

"Ellen." He sighed. "I wish not to play games."

She rolled over and stared at him with those eyes that were so like his. Her pretty mouth was thinned into a straight, forbidding line.

She said nothing.

" 'Tis a nice home," he conceded, feeling like an idiot talking to himself. "I hope you're happy here."

Nothing.

A heavy silence hung for a moment before Kit's frustration gave way to anger. "This is about the money, isn't it?"

Not a word. Not even a blink. 'Twas as though she stared right through him, as though he were not even there.

His heart fisted in his chest as the anger turned to hurt. He swallowed hard. "When you're ready to talk, Ellen, you know where to find me."

Without another word, he turned and left. He'd be damned if he'd give Ellen a fortune when she wouldn't speak to him. Never mind that he hadn't planned to withhold it past the first week or two as a test—he wouldn't *buy* his sister's love. Every penny of that dowry had been saved out of *his* love for *her,* but apparently she couldn't see that.

Thomas followed him down the stairs and all the way to the entrance. "She'll come around, sir. I'm sure of it."

Kit opened the door but stopped short of stepping outside. "How is she?" he asked toward the street.

"Well. We're happy together, sir."

"Kit."

"Kit. I know how lucky I am to have married your sister. I'm going to take care of her."

"See that you do," Kit said, then slowly turned. He measured the man a long moment before he decided he trusted him.

Or maybe that he had no choice.

"Tell her I love her," he said quietly, then pushed out into the cool October air, the bell jingling too merrily as the door shut behind him.

Chapter Thirty-three

Standing in the old village church, Rose shifted on her high-heeled shoes, watching another wedding.

The *third* one this year.

"Lord Edmund Grenville, wilt thou have this woman to thy wedded wife, to live together in the holy estate of Matrimony? Wilt thou love her, comfort her, honor, and keep her in sickness and in health; and, forsaking all others, keep thee only unto her, so long as ye both shall live?"

"I will." The confident words boomed through the ancient stone sanctuary, binding Lord Grenville to Judith.

But Rose wasn't listening to the ceremony. Instead she was noticing how joyful the bride looked. Judith clutched the flowers Rose had arranged for her, a smile curving her lips, her body ranged close to Lord Grenville's. A *good* man, Judith had described him. Decent.

Rose's mother sighed happily, delighted that this introduction had worked well enough to culminate in marriage. *The Big Book of Weddings Arranged by Chrystabel* was getting thicker. She leaned closer until she bumped against Rose's left side, her voice made breathy by emotion. "They're perfect together, are they not?"

Rose could only nod dumbly, wondering if she'd ever find anyone perfect. These two were so clearly in love, Rose knew they belonged together. But she imagined herself standing in Judith's place and the Duke of Bridgewater standing in Grenville's . . . and she knew she wouldn't be as happy.

Was Gabriel decent? She knew not. In truth, she didn't know him at all. And she'd tried, hadn't she? He was handsome and kind and generous, but he didn't seem a man who cared to be known.

And he'd kept money that belonged to someone else.

The priest cleared his throat and looked back down at his *Book of Common Prayer.* "Lady Judith Carrington, wilt thou have this man to thy wedded husband . . ."

Standing on Rose's right, Violet leaned closer to Ford and wrapped an arm about his waist. Ford was decent, too, Rose thought, watching him squeeze her sister around the shoulders. His first love used to be science, but when he found Violet—and responsibilities—he'd not hesitated to put them first.

Sun streamed through the stained glass windows, glinting off Violet's spectacles. "Oh, is this not romantic?" she sighed.

"Yes," Rose whispered to no one in particular, remembering Ellen's wedding, which hadn't been romantic at all. Yet Ellen had been just as thrilled to marry her love as Judith was today. Ellen's dowry could have bought her a titled man, but she'd wed a pawnbroker instead. Her Thomas was decent. He'd wanted Ellen even though she hadn't come with the money they'd expected.

Lily's husband, Rand, was decent as well. He'd worked hard to become an Oxford professor, but he'd been willing to give that up when other duties were thrust upon him. After falling hard for Lily, he'd even agreed to marry another woman in order to save a man's life.

Thank God that hadn't been necessary.

Lily poked Rose from behind. "Your wedding will be next," she whispered.

Rose hoped so. But first she would have to find a man who would make her as happy as her sisters and Ellen and Judith. A decent man, a man she could admire.

Gabriel wasn't that man. She'd tried her best to fall in love with him, but it hadn't happened. She would have to keep looking. She couldn't face Court again soon, but she would ask Mum to take her to the Queen's birthday celebration at Whitehall next month.

". . . so long as ye both shall live?" the priest concluded expectantly.

"I will," Judith pledged, her voice clear and true. So clear and true that no one in the church had any doubt she meant that pledge with all her heart.

A few more words, a new sapphire ring slid onto Judith's finger, and she was clearly and truly wed now, Lady Grenville.

And watching that, Rose knew she wouldn't wed until she found a love as decent and true.

When Lord Grenville lowered his lips to meet Judith's, Rose smiled through a sudden film of tears. She wasn't sure whether they were happy or sad tears . . . perhaps they were a little of both.

"Another wedding," Chrystabel sighed happily many hours later as she closed her bedchamber door.

Her husband wrapped her in his arms. "Another wedding night." He kissed her thoroughly before his hands went to detach the stomacher that covered her laces. "Will we be celebrating Rose's wedding soon?"

"I wish I knew." The familiar fire burning in her already, she hurried to help him out of his surcoat and the long waistcoat underneath, then tugged at the knot in his cravat. "I'm fairly certain she won't be accepting Bridgewater, but that doesn't mean she'll end up with Kit."

Having managed to unlace her gown, Joseph slipped it off her shoulders and down to pool at her feet. "You sound worried, my love," he murmured against her throat. He placed damp little kisses beneath her chin while his hands skimmed her diaphanous chemise, working the hem up ever higher.

"Our Rose is stubborn," she breathed, her blood racing while her practiced fingers unlaced his breeches. She pulled away long enough to tug his shirt off over his head, sighing as she ran her palms down his chest, hard and muscled from countless hours spent in his gardens.

He whisked off her chemise and stepped out of his breeches, and they fell together onto their bed, blissfully skin to skin. She wiggled closer, and he smoothed a hand over one bare hip. A heated tremor rippled through her as he met her mouth for a long, hot kiss.

She would never tire of this—never. Of course, she and Joseph were only forty-five and forty-six, not yet old and gray, but she planned on lying with him until her bones creaked—and then some.

Drawing back, he skimmed one long brown curl off her face. "What will you do next to push Rose and Kit together?"

"Nothing." The fire on the hearth threw his face into shadows and radiated heat onto their naked skin. She traced his beloved mouth with a finger. "I've done what I can. The rest is up to them. But with any luck, we'll have another wedding night before too very long."

"Ah, Chrysanthemum." He claimed her lips once again while his hands went to work below, making her head spin with delight. "We've no need of a wedding to have a wedding night."

Judith's wedding celebration had lasted through the wee hours, so the sun was high in the sky by the time Rose awakened the next day, hearing strange noises beneath her window.

Bangs and scrapes and shouts.

Construction.

Kit.

She rang for her maid. "Hurry," she said when Harriet arrived. "The purple gown—no, the deep green." The maid pulled it from the wardrobe and helped her wiggle into it. "Hurry."

"I'm going as fast as I can, milady." She laced Rose up the back.

"Tighter." Rose wanted to look her best.

Harriet pushed her onto a chair and started combing through her tangled curls. "Whyever are you in such a rush?"

Rose gulped down some chocolate and nibbled on some bread. "I'd forgotten that today is the groundbreaking."

"I see." The maid twisted up the back of her hair. "I expect you're more interested in the builder than the building, hmm?"

Rose didn't care for the sound of that *hmm*. "Mr. Martyn is just a friend. After the lunacy of Court life, I simply crave a sane conversation." Kit had always been easy to talk to.

Harriet met her gaze in the mirror. "Hmm," she said again.

"How is *your* love life?" Rose asked to distract her.

The maid's freckled face lit with a smile as she chose a green ribbon. "Walter has said he will visit. I believe he will ask for my hand."

'Twas on the tip of Rose's tongue to protest, to tell Harriet she had no business getting married when she needed her. But she was feeling expansive this morning. "Where will you live?" she asked instead.

"We've not yet decided. Does it matter, so long as you're together with the one you love?"

Rose's ebullient mood plunged. Even Harriet was in love. Love, love, love. The world was consumed with love. In that way, it had been easier to be at Court. At least there she wasn't constantly reminded just how lacking she was in love. At Court, lust ruled the day—no one else at Court seemed to be in love, either.

Except maybe Nell Gwyn. And Charles's poor, longsuffering queen.

"Are you finished?" she asked.

"One moment." Harriet tied the ribbon and stepped back. "You look lovely, milady."

"Thank you." Rose darkened her lashes with the burnt end of a cork and slicked on some lip gloss from a little pot. She considered a patch or two, but hadn't the patience. In no time at all, she was downstairs and out the door, hurrying through her father's gardens.

On impulse she paused to pluck a few colorful blooms, gathering them into a makeshift bouquet. Still arranging them, she rounded the corner of the house.

Was there anything quite so masculine as a man in charge, giving orders? The site of the greenhouse looked chaotic, but somehow, at the same time, Kit seemed to have everything under control.

The air smelled of newly turned earth and freshly cut wood. Kit's raven hair glinted in the sunshine, and a metal T-square flashed as he used it to point here and direct someone there. He'd spread plans on an improvised table balanced across two sawhorses, and he kept looking down at them and back up.

She positioned herself in front of the table, so the next time he looked up, he'd see her.

"Rose," he said briskly, then looked back down.

"Kit?"

"Hmm?"

She shifted uneasily, then stepped closer. "Are you not going to ask me if I want a kiss?" she asked, trying to tease one of those glorious smiles from him.

"No." He waved at a man pushing a wheelbarrow full of bricks. "Over there," he directed, pointing with the T-square. Once again, he consulted his plans. "And you've no need to worry," he added toward the neatly inked lines. "I am not going to ask you to marry me again, either."

She should be relieved, but she wasn't. Something was wrong. She held out the bouquet. "I brought these for you."

"What for?"

"I'm hoping to celebrate your winning the Deputy Surveyor post."

He finally met her gaze. "I lost it."

"Oh, Kit." The flowers fell to the ground as she moved around the table to lay a hand on his arm. "Tell me."

"There was a problem at Hampton Court." He glanced down at her fingers, then scanned the bustle of construction and sighed, setting down the T-square. "Wait here a moment."

Rose watched him cross the site, looking confident as ever as he consulted with a short, hook-nosed man. Kit gestured with his competent, callused hands, and she wondered when she had come to prefer them over the smooth, elegant hands of the aristocracy. He ran one of them through his dark hair, and she wondered when she had come to prefer bold coloring over the pale English ideal.

When he returned, he led her around the house toward the gardens. "'Twas structural," he admitted flatly. Their shoes crunched on the gravel path. "I ordered the building torn down. 'Twas destined to eventually collapse."

"You could have been killed!" She put her hand to her racing heart, staring at his profile as they walked, imagining her life with him gone and suddenly realizing it would seem empty.

When had their friendship come to mean that much to her?

But the gaze he turned on her was sad, not alarmed. "I was never personally in danger." He stopped beneath the huge tree her father called his twenty-guinea oak. "I'll still build it," he said with a half-hearted shrug that didn't fool her. He was more upset than he was willing to admit. "But I'll do it right. And there's no rush anymore, since I've no chance to make Charles's tight deadline."

"And that's why you lost the appointment?"

He didn't have to answer. His hand slipped into his pocket to grip that little piece of his first building—that tiny symbol of his past success—and in the dappled light beneath the tree, his expression said it all.

Her heart broke for him. "I know how much you wanted that post."

"I wanted the knighthood that went with it. I was hoping . . . never mind." Looking more defeated than ever she'd seen him, he dropped to sit on the grass, his back against the massive trunk. "'Twas my fault," he said resolutely, and then almost in a whisper, "but it may not have been my mistake."

She sat across from him, carefully settling her skirts. "What do you mean?"

"Do you remember my mentioning that the set of plans at Hampton Court didn't match the ones I kept with me? It could have been my error reproducing them, but—"

"Someone could have made changes," she finished for him. "Harold Washburn?"

"Perhaps." He slipped the chunk of brick back into his pocket. "But I should have been there, checking, double-checking—"

"You had too many projects. You couldn't be everywhere at once."

"Which just goes to show that Charles was right to test me, because the Deputy Surveyor of the King's Works would have many more projects at a time than I've had these past weeks." He pulled one long green blade from the ground and chewed the end, looking pensive. "But I've been . . . distracted. It could have been my error. And in any case, 'twas my project. My responsibility. Which was why I had to tear it down even though the problem would likely have stayed hidden for years—"

"Years?" She blinked. "Are you saying you could have finished the project and accepted the post—"

"I couldn't." At her frown, he tossed the green blade to the lawn. "Can you not see, Rose? When the building collapsed—however far in the future—people might have died. It could have been the mother of Charles's children—

or his children themselves. And even if it didn't happen until I was long gone—not only from the project, but from God's green earth—I couldn't have lived with myself knowing the possibility existed. Better to lose a post than my honor, my integrity, my very soul."

And suddenly it came clear. Kit—her dear friend, her almost lover—was the most decent man she knew.

How could she not have seen it? How could she have chased after a title when a better man was waiting right here for her? A man who put others' safety before his own cherished goals? A man who made her heart quicken with a mere glance and her knees melt with a single kiss?

A man—perhaps the only man—she could honestly talk to about anything.

"Will you marry me?" she asked.

A thundercloud swept over his face. "That is damned cruel." He scrambled to his feet. "Do you know, Rose, I am usually amused by the way you tend to say whatever comes into your head." Clearly disgusted, he began to walk away. "But that was just plain cruel."

She jumped up and ran after him, grabbed his hand, jerked him to a halt. "I meant it, Kit."

"What?" He swung to her, glaring.

"You're the best man I know. I want to be your wife."

He focused hard on her, searching for the truth, perhaps finding it but unable to believe. "I'll never be Deputy Surveyor," he said slowly. "I'll never be a knight, let alone a baron, or a viscount, or an earl—"

"You'll be Kit Martyn, the man I love."

His eyes cleared. The tension drained from his face. He took a step closer, and her heart raced.

"No more kissing other men?"

She might have been offended if he wasn't suddenly looking at her in that way that made her stomach dance. "None of them were any good at it, anyway," she said flippantly.

He threw back his head and laughed. "Do you promise to always speak your mind? I do so love that."

"Will you kiss me, already?"

The next thing she knew she was in his arms, his lips locked on hers.

And nothing had ever felt so glorious.

Chapter Thirty-four

They stumbled together toward the summerhouse, more Rose's idea than Kit's. "Privacy," she murmured against his mouth, her lips nibbling his with a skill that threatened to drive him insane.

He might have been the first man she'd enjoyed kissing, but she'd taken to it quickly.

"This is not a good idea," he mumbled, although he kept going. "If we step through one of those doors"—there were four entrances to the round building—"you're unlikely to come out an innocent."

She stopped, linked her hands behind his neck, and leaned back. "Are you telling me you cannot control yourself?"

"Yes. I am but a man."

"Thank God," she said enthusiastically, making him laugh.

Making him want to kiss her all over again.

She tasted of triumph when his mouth crushed down on hers, a kiss that sang through his veins. They approached the redbrick summerhouse, moving crablike along the path, until finally they bumped up against an arched oak door.

Kit reached blindly for the latch. "Are you sure?"

"Please." She fumbled with the knot in his cravat—and Rose was not a fumbler. "You cannot make me wait any longer."

Though he burned for her, he felt more than a little ambivalent. He'd given his word to Lady Trentingham. "Your mother will be furious."

"Mum will never know." Having managed to untie the lace-edged fabric, she kissed the little hollow beneath his Adam's apple, making his heart thump oddly in his chest. "Besides, she gave birth to Violet barely six months after her wedding day." Her words vibrated against his throat. "She doesn't believe in waiting for marriage."

"Oh, I think she does. She said—"

She straightened, alarm widening her eyes. "What? You've talked to her about this?"

Kit silently cursed himself for a fool. Her mother had warned him not to tell. "Nothing. Just something I overheard her saying, at Court, I believe, that made me think—"

"We're betrothed now. Everything is different."

"I have yet to talk to your fath—"

"'Tis my own decision, remember?" She reached around him and opened the door, then eagerly pushed him inside, slamming it behind them. "Kiss me, Kit."

'Twas not a request he could deny.

The summerhouse was cool and dim, her mouth warm and welcoming. Her intoxicating scent seemed to wrap around him, filling his head, making his throat close almost painfully. His hands found the lacing down the back of her gown, and as he loosened it, baring the silky skin beneath, it hit him with the force of a hammer striking a nail.

Rose was going to be his . . . for all time.

Despondency had held him in thrall these past days, but now it simply melted away as his heart took flight. The loss of the Deputy Surveyor post seemed insignificant next to the joy of winning Rose. Perhaps he would never be a titled man, but love, it suddenly seemed, was much more important.

Devil take it if his sister hadn't been right all along.

Kit's hands smoothed warm down Rose's back, and she

closed her eyes and leaned into him. His kiss was almost desperately tender, and she felt it in her skin, a tight tingling, in her stomach, a melting sweetness, in her heart an erratic rhythm that sent her blood racing through her veins.

This was right, so right she couldn't imagine what had taken her so long to realize he was meant to be hers. She should have known from that first startling kiss, from the first time he touched her and made her feel things no man ever had.

He pushed her gown off one shoulder, his lips searing a path on the newly bared skin. Her knees weakened, and she threaded her fingers into his hair. "Kit," she murmured, "I love you."

His head shot up and his eyes bored into hers, that look he had that made her wonder if he could see right into her. She felt the answering flutter in her stomach, the gathering heat lower down.

And her mother opened the door.

Rose whirled around, hiding her bare back, jerking her gown back onto her shoulder. "Mum. I've asked Kit to marry me."

"Oh my," Chrystabel breathed, apparently not noticing her state of undress. Her eyes grew suspiciously shiny. "You're supposed to let the man propose."

"Question Convention," Kit quoted with a shrug. He moved closer, trailing a finger down Rose's spine where her mother couldn't see it.

It took all she had not to squirm with delight. "He asked me first, but I refused him. After the wedding, we're taking a trip to Italy."

Kit's hand stilled. "We are?"

"And France. Everywhere there are beautiful buildings. I have my inheritance—"

"I can afford to travel. Especially now," he added dryly, "without the Deputy Surveyor post to tie me."

She breezed over that. "But first, we'll go to the Queen's

birthday celebration at Whitehall. I wish to show the courtiers the sort of man it takes to win me."

He laughed, a joyous sound that rippled right through her. "She's planning my life," he told her mother.

"Get used to it," she said.

"Six months," Chrystabel said. "You're my last daughter. This is my last chance to throw a wedding that will be talked about for years."

Rose shook her head. "Two weeks. Violet and Lily only had to wait two weeks for their weddings."

Her mother made a big show of sighing. "Three months."

"I want to be married before the Queen's birthday," Rose insisted. "One month."

"Don't I get a say in this?" Kit asked. "I vote for tomorrow."

One month it was, and Rose felt victorious.

But her mouth dropped open at what Chrystabel said next. "Kit, I know you'll be working here occasionally over the next weeks, but I think it would be best for you to go home to Windsor in the evenings. There will be no eight-month babies, understand?"

"Mum!" Rose exclaimed.

Kit just slowly turned red.

Rose recovered first. "Kit would never even think of compromising me."

"Oh, yes?" Her mother lifted her chin. "Then perhaps the two of you aren't meant for each other."

With that, she turned on her elegant high heels and left. "Five minutes," she called over her shoulder. "I'm sending for your sisters and their families—we'll have a celebration supper."

"Five minutes," Rose said the moment her mother was out of earshot. "Hurry."

"We cannot finish this in five minutes. Not if I'm to be able to face myself in the mirror afterward." Kit took her by

the shoulders and turned her around to refasten her gown.
"Your first time should be slow and special."

"Are you sure?" Rose asked.

"I'm sure." Laughing, he tied the laces and pressed a
warm kiss to the back of her neck. "Come along, before I
try anyway," he added, taking her hand to pull her out of
the summerhouse.

Holding his hand wasn't enough. Now that she'd decided
he would be hers, she wanted to touch him all over. "She
cannot keep us apart for a whole month."

"Of course she cannot," he assured her. "And I don't
think she's really going to try."

But a week later, after Kit had spent three more days
working at Trentingham and Chrystabel had managed to
make sure he and Rose weren't alone together for more
than ten minutes, Rose had her horse saddled and rode over
to visit Violet.

"Before we were betrothed," Violet told her, setting
aside a fat philosophy book, "she left Ford and me alone
together constantly. Of course," she added, "that was
probably because she was sure he'd never want me that
way at all."

Rose had been pacing her sister's pale turquoise drawing
room. "Violet!" She stopped and turned to face her.

Her sister's eyes looked earnest behind their spectacles.
"You know it was so. Mum was certain he was wrong
for me, and I wasn't interested in men or marriage, anyway."

"But after. After you became betrothed—"

"Those two weeks between our betrothal and marriage,
we never managed to find ourselves alone. Very strange."

Ten days later, Kit had completed the greenhouse, but he
and Rose had still not found time together for much more
than a kiss. When he said only half-jestingly that he was
loath to return until the day of their wedding—still two entire weeks away—Rose took Harriet, a carriage, and a
coachman, and drove to Oxford to visit Lily.

"Mum did the exact same thing to me and Rand!" Lily exclaimed. Swiveling on her petit-point stool, she turned away from the beautiful inlaid Flemish harpsichord Rand had surprised her with after their wedding. "I couldn't understand it. Before we became betrothed, she left us alone all the time. But after—"

"Exactly!" Rose sat in one of the drawing room's brand-new lemon yellow chairs.

Lily's cat rubbed against her skirts, and she leaned to pick it up. "'Twas torture."

"Gemini. I know." Sheer torture.

"Is Kit becoming bad-tempered?"

Rose nodded morosely. "Mum said she doesn't want any eight-month babies."

"Ridiculous." Lily rhythmically stroked the cat's striped fur. "Besides, at this point it would be more than eight-and-a-half. No one would dare even comment. Unless . . ." She eyed Rose speculatively. "You're not already with child, are you?"

"Of course not! Kit and I have never—"

"Never?" Lily's blue eyes widened in patent disbelief. *"Never?"*

"That's what I've been trying to tell you." Rose's fingers gripped the chair's gilt armrests. "We haven't had ten minutes alone together since we became betrothed!"

"But before—"

"Before? What kind of woman do you think I am?" she huffed, knowing quite well what kind of woman she was. The kind that would have crawled all over Kit given half a chance—before their betrothal, *he'd* been the one to display all the self-control. And after . . . her mouth dropped open as she stared at her sister. Sweet Lily. "Don't tell me you and Rand—before you were married—"

"Of course we did," Lily scoffed. "We couldn't keep our hands off each other. And Violet and Ford—"

"Violet, too?"

"Violet didn't even wait until she was betrothed."

"What?" Did she not know her sisters at all?

Lily nodded, still calmly stroking the cat. "Ford *seduced* her into marrying him."

"No." Not serious, bookish Violet.

"Yes. He and Rand planned the whole thing one night when they were drunk."

"That sounds like Ford and Rand," Rose conceded with a sigh. "But I cannot believe both you and Violet . . . Good God, I'm the one who's supposed to be forward, and the two of you . . . Gemini, this is so unfair!"

"And I imagine you're all worried about the first time, too."

"No," she said quickly. She wasn't. Not of that piddly one-time pain she knew her sister was referring to.

"I don't believe you. No one should have to go through their wedding worrying about their wedding night. 'Tis supposed to be a special day, and how could you possibly enjoy it? I felt so sorry for poor Judith."

They were both silent a moment. "I hope she's happy," Rose finally said.

"I'm certain she is. And I'm certain her wedding night went just splendidly, too. But *you* are not going to have to worry about yours."

"I'm not so sure," Rose said miserably. "Mum is so vigilant, you'd think I was the Crown Jewels and she'd been hired to guard me."

Lily's cat leapt out of her arms to join a sparrow and a squirrel that seemed to be chatting on the windowsill. She and Rand had only moved to Oxford from his father's estate last week, just in time for Michaelmas Term to begin, but her animal friends had found her already.

"We'll just have to get you two away from Mum," Lily mused, watching the squirrel feed the bird a bit of nut.

"We've tried."

"Not with my help." She absently rubbed an old scar on the back of her hand, then brightened and focused on Rose. "I know! We'll tell Mum that the three of us girls want one more sleeping party before you are married. And we'll tell her it's going to be here. She'll never come this far just to check on us for one night."

Rose shook her head. "Kit is too honest for his own good—I'm not sure I'd be able to talk him into such a deception."

"Kit won't even be involved. Instead of sleeping here, the three of us will meet at Violet's and then go to Windsor and surprise him." Lily grinned, obviously pleased with her plan. "He'll put us up, won't he? Has he room?"

"At his house?" Rose had never realized Lily had such a devious mind—and she'd never appreciated her sister more. "Good God, yes—he could billet an army. Wait 'til you see it."

One evening a week later, with only a week left before the wedding, Kit was summoned by his butler to find Rose and her sisters on his doorstep.

For a moment he couldn't find words, but that didn't matter, because 'twas only a moment before Rose launched herself at him, kissing him enthusiastically.

Laughing, he set her back. "What are you doing here?"

"We've come to have a sleeping party," she informed him gaily. "With you."

For a moment he thought his heart might stop, then it raced out of control.

The shock must have shown on his face, because Lily laughed now. "Not all three of us," she clarified. "Violet and I will share a chamber; Rose assured us you have one to spare. Mum thinks we're all at my house."

"Does Rand know about this?"

"Of course he does. He thought it was a capital idea."

"Mum tried to keep *them* apart after they were betrothed, too," Rose put in.

"This place is gorgeous," Violet said in an awed tone as they stepped inside.

"Goodness, yes, Kit." Lily turned in a circle, taking in

the tall entry with its stone walls, white ceiling, and black-and-white floor. "I thought the house you built for Rand was special, but this . . ." She peeked into the drawing room. "May we have a tour?"

By the time the tour had finished, Kit's heart had slowed, and he too thought the visit was a capital idea. His cook prepared a lovely venison pasty for supper, but he and Rose couldn't get through it fast enough. He felt a mite awkward showing her sisters to a chamber and then leaving them there rather early—but not awkward enough to spend the evening twiddling his thumbs while they played music and sang or did whatever else ladies usually did to pass the hours.

Besides, he didn't own a harpsichord.

In any case, the guilt evaporated the minute he got Rose to his own chamber and into his arms for a proper kiss.

He'd kissed her many times, but this kiss was different, the result of deprivation heightened by a sense of the forbidden. He explored her mouth hungrily, her unmistakable response making something twist in his gut.

When he finally pulled away, she gave him a suddenly shaky smile. "How is Ellen?"

He turned her around and started unlacing the back of her gown. "Fine, according to her husband."

"Her husband?"

"She still won't talk to me. I've stopped by six, seven times—but she stares right through me." As the laces came undone, he kissed his way down her slender back. "I don't fancy being invisible," he murmured against her skin, smiling to himself when he felt her shiver.

"She's coming to our wedding, though, isn't she?"

"According to Thomas, no." Rose looked gorgeous with the gown open down her graceful spine. Tempting beyond words. "Let us not talk about my sister, shall we?" He dropped to his knees, pressed a kiss to the small of her back. "We've much better things to think about."

She turned, sinking her fingers into his hair as she looked down on him. "I'll go talk to her tomorrow morning before I leave."

The dress hung from her shoulders, poised to drop. "Hmm?"

"Ellen. She's my friend as well as your sister. I want her at our wedding."

He sighed and got to his feet. "This isn't really about Ellen, is it? You're anxious. That is why you keep talking."

He saw her swallow hard. "I've never done this before."

"But you want to, don't you?"

"Good God, yes. But . . . Lily said everyone is anxious the first time."

He winced. He'd never bedded a virgin, and now he knew why. "If it hurts, I'll stop," he promised.

"Will you?"

"You have only to say the word." With a little luck and a lot of skill, he hoped to have her so out of her mind with pleasure that words at that moment would be impossible.

"Thank you," she whispered.

Her gown's wide neckline slid off one creamy shoulder, and he bent his head to kiss her there.

"Kit?"

"Hmm?"

"About Ellen . . ."

He straightened, supposing he'd get nowhere until she'd finished this fruitless conversation. "What about her?"

"I know her attitude must be hurting you, especially after she didn't come to you with her pregnancy. I cannot imagine why she is acting so childish, why she refuses to talk to you when you're the easiest man to talk to. But I don't like to see you hurt."

Hurt was such a simple, innocuous-sounding word. *Devastated* better described the way he felt. But he didn't want to discuss this now. Not with Rose half undressed and about to fall into his arms.

She sighed. "If you'd just give her the dowry you saved—"

"No." He led her over to sit on his red-draped half-tester bed. "I am not going to give her eleven thousand pounds when she won't even deign to speak to me."

"Clearly her behavior doesn't warrant it, but for you, Kit, and for me. Because we want her at our wedding. What if she promised to speak to you afterward—"

His jaw tightened. He wasn't going to bribe his sister, either.

Rose's half-exposed breasts rose and fell with another sigh. "I'll talk to her in the morning. I've the perfect excuse, since I need to return her book."

"Her book?" His gaze snapped from the swell of her chest to her face. "You mean *the* book?"

"*I Sonetti,* yes. I am telling you, I can hardly wait to rid myself of the blasted thing."

"Where is it? I want to see it."

She'd brought a small valise, which one of Kit's maids had set in the corner of the chamber. Rose dug out the volume and handed it to him, looking more hesitant than ever he'd seen her.

In his estimation, Rose was not a hesitant sort of woman. Or a prude, either. Curious, he opened the cover. He'd already heard the book contained nude pictures, so he wasn't at all surprised to see an engraving of a couple making love. "I cannot read this," he said.

"'Tis Italian. Translated, it does not sound much like a sonnet." She sat beside him, hitching her dress back onto her shoulder. "Turn the page."

He did, shrugged, then turned a few more and stared. "Lord Almighty. Are these people acrobats? My poor back wouldn't last ten seconds in that position." Amazed that the whole Court was abuzz and dying to view these secret poses, he flipped another page, then eyed Rose speculatively. "Do you bend like that? Hell, sweetheart, I hate to disappoint you, but I don't."

She swallowed hard. "You're not going to want to try these, then?"

He could only laugh. "I'm afraid I'd end up in bed for a month. And I don't mean passing a pleasant time."

"Thank God," she said, and launched herself at him again.

Chapter Thirty-five

The book fell from Kit's hands to the floor. "What's this?" he asked, still laughing.

Rose couldn't remember ever being quite so relieved. She kissed his eyes and his cheeks and his chin. "I'm just so happy to find that you share Charles's preference for catholic lovemaking."

He drew back a little, looking puzzled. "Charles?"

"King Charles."

Kit's brow didn't clear. "I know there are rumors that he's secretly a Catholic, but they've never been proven. And I can assure you I'm a member of the Church of England."

Now it was her turn to laugh. "Nell told me Charles was catholic in his lovemaking, not that he's a secret Catholic. She explained that he is enthusiastic but not imaginative."

"Ah. Poor Nell."

"Pardon?"

"I can assure you, sweetheart, one needn't be a gymnast to be imaginative."

The look in his eyes made the bottom drop out of her stomach. It must have shown on her face. "Nothing frightening, I promise," he added quickly.

But she wasn't frightened. Kit's laughing reaction to the engravings had cured her of that. Now she was just intrigued. Very, very intrigued.

And eager. She started pulling down the top of her loosened gown.

He stayed her hands with his own. "Let me have the pleasure of that."

Those hands went to work undressing her. He knelt at her feet, pulled off her shoes, reached under her skirts to pluck off her garters one by one. Rolling down her stockings was a production all itself, a sensuous slide of silk. His fingertips smoothed her calves, making her wish they'd move up higher.

"You make an excellent ladies' maid," she said shakily.

"You think so?" He stood and took her hands to bring her up with him. In no time at all, her gown was a memory, her chemise gone along with it.

He stepped back, his gaze roaming her hungrily. "You're exquisite," he said in a tone so husky it squeezed her heart.

She knew she had a pretty face, and men had often ogled her clothed body. But no one had ever seen her nude. Part of her wanted to fold her arms across her breasts, turn away, grab the red counterpane off the bed and cover herself.

But a larger part loved the way he was looking at her. Reveled in it.

The appreciation in his eyes made her feel powerful. She didn't cross her arms, instead striking a pose with one hand on a cocked hip. "I'm not too slim?" she asked teasingly, fishing for compliments.

The Court ideal was quite a bit plumper, but Kit didn't seem to agree. "You curve in all the right places."

His gaze kept skimming her body, making the bubbles dance in her stomach, the ache start down lower. "Or too tall?"

"Hell, no, sweetheart. I don't get a crick in my neck kissing you." He stepped closer and gathered her into his arms, demonstrating by lowering his lips just a fraction to meet hers. While his mouth plundered recklessly, his hands wandered her back, raising goose bumps in their wake. "You're the perfect height," he murmured, his hands moving down, warm on her bare bottom, pressing their bodies together where the ache was building. "We fit."

They did. Already, the ache was becoming insistent, intolerable. Wanting him closer, she broke from the embrace. "You're wearing too many clothes."

He laughed and shrugged out of his surcoat.

"More," she said, moving nearer to the fire, hoping the burnished light would look pleasing on her skin.

Apparently it did. The green in his eyes deepened as he stripped off his long waistcoat and let it drop to the floor. "Your breasts are beautiful," he said.

Just hearing the words, she felt them tighten. "Your shirt," she ordered, presenting him with her back as she bent to stir the fire.

She heard his sharp intake of breath, and he couldn't get out of the shirt fast enough. By the time she straightened and turned, he had his shoes and stockings off as well.

Gemini, he looked magnificent. Firelight danced over the planes of his face and flashed gold and red on his body. She moved closer and laid her palms on his chest, closing her eyes as her hands learned the feel of a man. Taut skin over bone and muscle, the springy softness of dark hair. She smoothed her hands down, down, until they rested against the waistband of his breeches.

"This, too," she said.

"Not yet." He swung her around, backing her toward the bed and finally pushing her onto it. She laughed as she landed on her back.

He rested a knee on the mattress and raised one of her feet. "You're beautiful here," he said, his expression one of concentration. His fingers slid between her toes, his thumb massaged her instep.

She arched her foot in response. "You're beautiful, too."

The concentration turned to amusement. "Am I?"

"Oh, yes."

He smiled, sliding his hands slowly up her leg, paying

special attention to her knee. "You're beautiful here," he said, flexing it and straightening it again. He raised her leg higher and kissed her behind it, sending a shiver rippling through her.

She'd never imagined the back of her knee was so sensitive. A hot stab of lust speared her right between her legs.

He watched her face as his hands moved up higher, higher, dancing on her thigh, a gentle, swirling torment. He was close, so close to where she wanted him. She wanted not only his hands, but all of him. Most especially that part of him that was meant to slide into a woman.

"Kit," she murmured. "Can you not—"

"No." He set her leg on the bed and switched to the other, starting again with her foot by pressing a warm kiss to the sole.

She decided to relax to the inevitable, enjoying the little bursts of pleasure he created as he slowly worked his way up, leaving no part of her limb untouched. "You're beautiful here," he said, tracing the curve of her calf. And teasing the inside of her thigh. "You're beautiful here, too."

A bead of sweat rolled down his chest, glistening in the firelight. She wanted to lick it off.

The ache was becoming an insistent pulse. She wanted to feel him inside her.

She wasn't relaxed at all.

"Kit, please."

"Please what, sweetheart?" He was concentrating again, his eyes closed, his fingers working their way up, closer to where she wanted him.

"Can you not just take off your—"

"No," he said, moving suddenly to silence her with a kiss.

His weight on her felt exciting, but he gave all his attention to her mouth. His woodsy scent filled her head. Her hands smoothed his back, his sides, wherever she could reach.

"You are very imaginative," she admitted weakly when he finally relinquished her lips.

His response was a lazy smile as he retreated back toward her feet.

"If you kiss my knee again," she warned, "I'm going to scream."

"I'd like to hear that," he shot back with a grin, gripping both her ankles.

He looked too blasted good looming over her. She held her breath as he skimmed his hands straight up, spreading her legs as he went. "You're beautiful here," he said softly, his heated gaze fixed between them.

Her breath burst out in a rush. Never had she thought to have anyone look at her there.

'Twas almost unbearably exciting.

He looked closer.

"Kit," she breathed, her entire body tingling.

He looked closer still. "Beautiful," he repeated.

"Kit, take off your—"

"No," he said and closed the distance, pressing his lips to her in the most intimate kiss imaginable.

Her hips shot off the bed. "Kit!"

"Hmmmm?"

The single, drawn-out syllable was a hum that drove her wild, sent her past the point where she was capable of protesting any longer. All she could do was feel.

He licked her, slowly, his tongue swirling in a place so sensitive she wondered that she didn't just fly to pieces. He lingered there, suckling gently, then licked and suckled her again, and again, and again until she did fly to pieces, shuddering beneath him while he held her hips tight.

And after she remembered how to breathe, after her heart stopped galloping, after the pieces had painstakingly rearranged themselves, she still wanted him. More than ever.

He raised his head, slowly, licking her off his lips, a sight that made her heart stutter in her chest, made a new flash of heat skitter through her. He settled beside her and gave her a gentle kiss. "How's that for imaginative?" he asked softly.

Imaginative, indeed. She released a ragged breath. "I translated sixteen scandalous sonnets, and not one of them mentioned *that*."

His grin would have done the devil proud. She swallowed hard, her eyes traveling down to the unmistakable bulge at the front of his breeches. "I want to see you."

"Pardon?"

"You've seen me." In more detail than she'd ever imagined. "I want to see you now."

This time, she wasn't taking no for an answer. Her hands went to his laces.

Under her busy fingers, the bulge seemed to grow, and her excitement grew along with it. He helped her push the breeches down and off, and she stared, fascinated.

She reached to touch him, her heart hitching when he moved against her palm. She wrapped her fingers around him, thrilling at his sharply indrawn breath and the pulse she felt filling her hand.

The ache between her legs was intensifying again. She moved her hand experimentally, amazed that he seemed to grow even more. As she watched, a single glossy drop of fluid emerged.

Curious, she collected it with a fingertip and raised it to her mouth, licking it off.

His eyes widened. "How do I taste?" he asked in a thick whisper, his breath coming short to match hers.

"Creamy. A little salty. Good." She skimmed her tongue across her lips, loving his reaction. "I want to taste you more, the way you did me."

"You want to kill me, you mean," he said with a strangled laugh. "Not tonight." And with that he rolled on top of her, fitting himself within the cradle of her thighs.

Just that quickly, the heat inside her flared fully to life. She raised her knees instinctively, wrapping her legs around him. Poised there where she craved him, he just kissed her for a long while, kissed her until she could barely think straight for wanting him. Until she seemed nothing but a mass of need.

"Now, Kit," she begged.

"This might hurt," he whispered regretfully.

"I don't care," she said, and she didn't.

He nodded and drew a deep breath, and at long last she felt him there, felt an incredible urgency as he entered her ever so slowly, felt herself stretching to accommodate him. "Faster," she whispered, and he pushed farther, but not far enough for her.

Not fast enough.

Not enough.

Gritting her teeth, she shoved her hips against him and took him inside with a gasp.

"I'm sorry," he breathed, misunderstanding.

"No. It doesn't hurt." The pain had been so fleeting, so insignificant compared to the marvelous feeling of him filling her. The gasp had been one of wonder. "A thing of beauty," she whispered incredulously.

And then he moved within her, and the beauty became more beautiful still.

It made her complete.

She moved with him, lost in a world of their making, the sensations building until she wasn't sure where she ended and he started. Time slowed and stretched, or maybe it sped; she couldn't be sure. He kissed her desperately, reality blurring until two became one, until she arched against him as waves of pleasure overtook her, her heart soaring when she heard him groan and felt the warm flood of his release.

He rained little kisses on her face while she slowly came to her senses. "I love you," she whispered.

"I love you, too." His eyes still closed, he rolled off her and arranged her against his side. "But remind me never to make love to you in your parents' house."

"What?" She wiggled closer. "Why?"

"You screamed," he informed her, his voice a mix of exhaustion and amusement. "I told you I'd like to hear that, so I thank you for obliging me."

"I did not scream."

"You did." He idly skimmed her bare hip, making her feel as though she might melt. "And a beautiful scream it was, too."

Would he lie to her? Kit, the man who'd sacrificed his dream for the sake of honesty? If she were to be honest with herself, there'd been a moment when she'd been so out of her mind with pleasure, the house could have burned around her and she'd not have noticed.

She supposed, right then, she could have screamed.

"Well, at least I didn't yip," she said and kissed him before he could laugh.

The next morning, after a leisurely bath for two in Kit's huge tub—which Rose decided she could get used to—followed by breakfast with her sisters, he walked her up the hill to the pawnshop.

The night shouldn't have changed anything, but somehow it had. She'd loved Kit desperately before she'd shared his bed, but now she felt a new closeness. And a sadness buried within him, a sadness that spilled over onto herself. She wanted more than ever for him to make things right with his sister.

"I'll wait out here," he said when they arrived.

"I want you two to talk."

"I'll be here if she is willing."

Bent over a tray full of rings, Ellen looked up when the bell jingled. "Rose!" She came hurrying out from behind the counter.

Rose hugged her tight, then set her away. "You look good." Beneath her simple peach dress, Ellen's stomach barely looked rounded. "How are you feeling?"

"I haven't puked in at least half an hour."

"Oh."

" 'Tis not that bad." Ellen grinned. "I make up for it at night; I vow and swear, I've never been so hungry."

Violet had never felt sick when carrying her children; Rose could only hope it would be the same for her. Her hand went to her own abdomen as she suddenly realized she could already be with child. She wasn't quite sure how she felt about that.

Quickly she held out the book, relieved to be handing it over. "Here. Take it. And here are the translations." She pulled a few sheets of folded paper from her drawstring purse.

"Oh, thank you!" Ellen opened them and turned to the last one. Her eyes widened as she read a stanza. "I didn't know this was quite so . . ." She slanted a glance to where her husband sat in a corner industriously going over paperwork, then back down to the translated words. " 'With my legs around your neck,' " she quoted under her breath, " 'somehow you've got your yard buried inside my . . .' Mercy me . . . I'm not certain Thomas is ready for this."

Ellen didn't look ready for it, either. "Everyone at Court found it entirely too intriguing," Rose told her. "But Kit just laughed."

Ellen refolded the pages and tucked them into the book. "I hope you two will be happy," she said formally.

"You *are* coming to our wedding?"

"No." She gazed down at the tray of rings on the counter. "No, I'm not."

"Ellen, if you don't attend, then someday you will be very sorry. You cannot refuse to speak to your brother forever."

She slid a garnet ring onto her finger, then pulled it off. "I cannot imagine that he cares."

Rose waited until she looked up. "You know he does."

"Then he should give me my dowry. He has no right to withhold it just because I didn't marry a man of his choosing."

At this point, Rose suspected Kit would hand over everything he owned if his sister would just stop this nonsense. Neither he nor Ellen would budge first. She wanted to knock their two heads together.

But Ellen was just plain wrong. "He has every right. He earned that money."

"I earned it, too," Ellen shot back, her eyes as green as Kit's when he was upset. "I suffered for that money every bit as much as he did. More. My parents were dead, and my big brother left me with a little old lady. True, she gave me nice clothes and made sure I learned to read and write. But she also expected me to wait on her hand and foot in return. Whenever Kit deigned to visit, I used to beg him to take me with him, away from there, anywhere . . ." Her voice dropped off, and she took a deep, shuddering breath. "He promised me that someday I would live a better life, and I figure 'tis my due."

Kit described Lady St. Vincent as his savior, but there were always two sides to every story. To Ellen, apparently the baroness had been a prison guard. Still, Rose couldn't see where Kit had had much of a choice.

"What did you expect him to do, Ellen? How could he have cared for you? Supported you? He was sixteen with no skills, but a grand opportunity. If he'd stayed with you in the village of Hawkridge, what do you expect he would be doing today? Do you think he'd be an architect? Do you reckon he'd have managed to save eleven thousand pounds for his beloved little sister? And he certainly couldn't have brought you to school, and later to Oxford—"

"I know," Ellen ground out miserably. Her jaw was tight, her cheeks pink. "He had no choice; I know it. But that didn't make it easy for me."

Rose laid a hand on her arm. "Of course it didn't."

"I earned that money. I mean to have it. He could dictate my life when I was a child, but not anymore."

"How on earth do you expect Kit to understand how you're feeling if you don't talk to him? This is childish, Ellen. You're a married woman, an expectant mother. Try to see his side. And you must come to our wedding. If not for Kit, do it for me."

Tears welled in Ellen's eyes. "I cannot. If he doesn't love me enough to give me my dowry even though I defied him, I cannot."

Rose's gaze strayed out the window to where Kit was pacing across the street, clearly as miserable as his sister. She wished he would just give Ellen the money and end this painful stalemate, but unlike his sister, she could see his side, too.

Her heart went out to him. "I'm sorry, Ellen, but I cannot beg you anymore, either. I pray you change your mind," she said and went outside to join him.

Kit whirled when he saw her. "How is she?" he immediately asked.

"Healthy, save for some expected sickness in the mornings. And the babe is well, too. But she still doesn't want to see you."

His jaw tightened as he took her hand to start the walk back down the hill to his house, where Violet and Lily were waiting to return home.

She squeezed his fingers. "Do you know, I believe Ellen's pregnancy may be affecting her thinking and her feelings."

"Whatever would make you believe that?"

" 'Tis common enough for increasing women to be weepy and such." He didn't look convinced. "In any case, Ellen is young. Surely when her child is born she will grow up quickly. In the meantime," she added carefully, "if you want her at our wedding, you only have to give her—"

"I cannot," he interrupted. "I will not buy my sister's love."

Rose held her tongue as they walked, listening to the sounds of horses clopping past, children playing chase, and a woman in one of the tall houses scolding her poor sod of a husband.

Kit finally sighed and rubbed the back of his neck. "Thank you for trying."

"There is no need for thanks," she said softly. She hadn't tried hard enough. Some way, somehow, she would come up with a plan to get these two back together.

Kit had witnessed his sister's wedding, and Ellen would be there for his.

Chapter Thirty-six

"**R**owan, wake up!" Back at Trentingham three day later, Rose shook her brother's bony eleven-year-ol shoulder. "Wake up!"

He stretched and yawned, opened his eyes, then prompt closed them. " 'Tis still night."

"But 'tis almost morning. And I need you to do me favor."

He rolled over, presenting her with his back. "What?"

"I want you to pretend to be ill." She tousled his wav black hair. "It could be fun."

"Fun?"

"Mum will take care of you." She sat on his blue-drape oak bed. "She'll bring you treats and sit and play cards."

"No, she won't." With a groan, he turned to face he "She's taking you to London today, remember? To fetc your wedding gown. Being ill alone is no fun at all."

"She'd never leave you ill. You're her precious baby. When he grimaced, she rushed on. "I'll pay you."

He sat up. "How much?"

"A shilling."

He made a rude noise.

"Very well, then, a crown."

"Maybe." Finally, Rowan looked interested—but skepti cal, too. Rose's brother was no half-wit. "I still think Mur will want to go with you to London . . ." His green eye narrowed. "You don't want her to go with you, do you? Why don't you want her to go with you?"

"Never mind why. Will you do this for me or not? A crown, Rowan. A nice, shiny—"

"She'll not let you go alone."

"I'll take Violet, then. And Lily, too, if Mum insists—she's at Hawkridge at the moment, and 'tis right on the way. Will you do it?" He still looked hesitant, blast him. "Think of it as a practical joke," she added, grasping at straws.

"A practical joke?" He perked up. He'd loved practical jokes ever since his little friend Jewel, Ford's niece, had played one on him four years ago. In fact, they hadn't been friends at all until the girl had humiliated him with that prank. Rose had never been able to figure that out.

But she wasn't averse to using it to her advantage. "Yes, a practical joke. Jewel will be so jealous when you tell her all about it at my wedding."

"What will I have to do?"

"Hardly anything." She moved aside, revealing the items she'd arranged on his night table. "I brought powder to make your face pale—"

"Makeup?"

"Just a little. You can run around the room 'til you're all hot and sweaty. Then jump back into bed, I'll fluff a little powder on, and we'll put a hot cloth on your forehead." She gestured to the bowl of steaming water she'd brought with her.

"I can moan a lot," he suggested, grinning.

"Excellent. I'll hide everything beneath your bed. Then when Mum comes in you'll be all hot and feverish and moaning and groaning . . . she won't want to leave you, I'm sure."

His eyes brightened with the thrill of conspiracy. "Can I puke?"

She winced, but nodded. 'Twas a brilliant if disgusting idea. "Can you make yourself puke?"

"For *two* crowns," he said. "Bring me some food."

* * *

In Madame Beaumont's London shop, Rose twirled in the red satin gown.

"'Tis gorgeous," Lily breathed. "Whoever would have imagined red for a wedding?"

"Perfect," Madame Beaumont said in her fashionable French accent—never mind the seventeen years she'd lived here since the Restoration. She waved one arm in an expansive fashionable French gesture. *"Absolument parfait."*

The gown had a low, scooped neck and full three-quarter sleeves from which a froth of fine white Brussels lace spilled to Rose's wrists. The underskirt and stomacher were both embroidered with thousands of seed pearls in scrolled designs, and the overskirt had love-knots all over it—small satin bows, loosely sewn so they could be torn off by the guests after the ceremony and taken home as favors.

"I can imagine red," Violet said in her practical way, "but what I cannot imagine is Mum allowing you to retrieve this gown without her."

Rose turned so Madame could detach the stomacher. "Rowan was very ill. She'd seen the gown already for three fittings. And 'tis not as though I had to come alone. I have you two." She glanced over her shoulder and smiled.

Violet snorted. "This is the second time within a week you've dragged me out overnight. Ford is going to be very relieved when you're finally married."

"Rand, too," Lily put in. "He had to travel back to Oxford all by himself."

"Good God, he's a grown man." Rose carefully stepped out of the gown. "You two cannot fool me. I know you are having the time of your lives on these adventures."

Now *both* her sisters snorted.

Minutes later, a footman carried the boxed gown to the Trentingham carriage. "The Strand," Rose told the driver.

"If you wish to visit the shops," Lily said, scooping up her cat as she climbed in, "the Royal Exchange would be better."

Rose pulled a scrap of paper from her purse to check the name and direction. "I wish to visit Abrahamson & Company, the Strand near Charing Cross."

When the door shut behind them, Violet snatched the paper out of her hand. "Goldsmiths? You want to buy some jewelry?"

"No. Mr. Abrahamson has my money."

"I knew that name was familiar." Lily stroked her cat. "'Tis the man Father sent a letter to when I needed my inheritance."

"That's right." Violet focused on Rose. "Why do you want money?"

"'Tis my money. Does it matter?"

Violet and Lily shared a look but dropped the subject until a while later, when Rose came out of the goldsmith's shop with a bag so heavy she could barely support its weight. She climbed back into the carriage and dropped it to the floorboards with a *thud,* dropping herself onto the bench seat with a "Whew."

"How much money *is* that?" Lily asked.

Rose ignored the question, turning to the footman instead. "Windsor," she ordered.

"Windsor?" Violet's jaw dropped open. "You told Mum we would stay at the town house tonight. I heard you with my own ears."

"Well, I wasn't about to tell her I'm spending the night with Kit." She hadn't planned to from the outset, but when the combination of Rowan's deception and collecting her sisters resulted in a late start that would make an overnight stay necessary, it had occurred to her that she could spend that night with Kit.

An unexpected bonus, and one to which she was very much looking forward.

"Windsor," she repeated, settling back as the footman closed the door. 'Twould be a lengthy ride, but toward Trentingham, after all, so her sisters had no real reason to protest. They'd arrive at their respective homes earlier to-morrow than if they'd stayed the night in London.

Lily toed the heavy bag with one red-heeled shoe. "How much money?"

There was no point in lying. "A thousand pounds. Do you know, I had no idea how heavy—"

"A *thousand* pounds?" Violet's eyes widened behind her spectacles. "Egad. Whatever will you do with all that money?"

"I'm giving it to Ellen. Kit's sister."

"What?" both her sisters burst out. The cat jumped from Lily's lap and cowered under a bench seat.

"I'd planned to give Ellen all ten thousand, but the gold-smith convinced me 'twould be too much to carry." Rose rolled her shoulders, still feeling the strain. "So I'm giving her just the thousand with a note from Mr. Abrahamson promising the rest is forthcoming."

Violet slumped against the coach wall. "You're giving Ellen Martyn ten thousand pounds."

"Ellen Whittingham. And I'm telling her it's from Kit. At least I hope she'll believe it's from Kit. He had promised her eleven—"

"Are you out of your mind?" Lily interrupted.

"Yes," Violet snapped at the same time Rose said, "No."

"'Tis Ellen who has lost her mind," she continued, pro-ceeding to tell her sisters the long, sad story. "Can you not see?" she concluded. "I think her pregnancy must be affect-ing her brain."

Violet shook her head. "I never felt better than when I was carrying my children."

"Not everyone is so lucky. When Mum's maid Anne was last with child, she was always at sixes and sevens. Practi-cally useless, but as soon as—"

"Have you considered," Lily broke in, "that Ellen might simply be a spoiled brat?"

"Yes, as a matter of fact, I have. But Kit is perplexed and hurt, and I believe if she'd been like this always, he would be exasperated and angry instead. And Ellen is really nice. Mum quite likes her."

Violet took off her spectacles and polished them on her skirts. "And you believe Kit is totally blameless in this?"

"Of course he isn't. In his own way he's as stubborn as his sister. But I cannot blame him for the way he feels, and I cannot stand to see him so unhappy. 'Tis like a dark cloud hanging over my wedding. The only way to solve this is to give Ellen my inheritance and make her think the money came from Kit. Then she'll talk to him and everyone will be happy."

Lily scooped up the cat again. "But you'll have given up your inheritance!"

"Don't be a goose. Kit will replace it. If Ellen would only speak to him again, he'd be happy enough to hand over her dowry."

"Has he said so?"

"Not in so many words. But I know him," she added, lifting her chin.

"You cannot know him." The poor cat let out a pathetic meow as Lily clutched it tighter. "You haven't lived with him for even a single day. Goodness, I've been married to Rand almost two months now, and he surprises me all the time."

Violet slid her spectacles back on. "I've been living with Ford for *four years,* and sometimes I still wonder—"

"I know Kit," Rose repeated. "No matter that he hasn't said so, there is no chance he meant to keep that money from his sister forever. What is the difference whether the ten thousand pounds was mine or his to begin with? It will be ours soon enough either way."

"There's a difference," Lily argued. "Unlike a dowry that becomes your husband's upon marriage, according to Grandpapa's will that money is yours to control. Not many women have the advantage of their own funds. By handing it over to Ellen, you're giving that up. You and Kit may have the same amount of money combined, but none of it will be under your control."

"That doesn't matter. Not compared to this." Rose forced herself to calm. Her sisters were only trying to help. "Kit and Ellen are not speaking, and both of them are miserable. And they're the only family either of them has . . . can you imagine one of us missing the other's wedding?"

Her sisters seemed to consider that a moment, then Violet tried another tack. "Have you told Mum and Father what you're doing?"

Rose remained quiet.

"Of course she hasn't," Lily said. "They would never in a million years agree."

"I've no need of their permission. I'm twenty-one. The money is legally mine."

"But you knew you would have had an argument, did you not?" Lily's blue eyes lit with sudden understanding. "That's why we're here with you instead of Mum, isn't it? I'd wager Rowan isn't even ill. How can you live with yourself, scheming behind your own mother's back?"

Rose's lips thinned. "You were not averse to scheming last week to get me to Windsor," she pointed out. "I'd rather scheme than have my sister-in-law refuse to attend our wedding. If that happens, Kit may never forgive her."

"Has it occurred to you," Violet asked with concern, "that Kit might never forgive *you* for meddling in his affairs?"

It hadn't, and Rose was taken aback for a moment. But only a moment. "Kit's not like that," she said.

"You don't know him—"

"I do." This discussion was going nowhere, and Rose was finished with it. "What is it with all this traffic?" she asked, glaring out the window. "At this rate, my wedding day will arrive before we even get out of London."

"Excellent attempt at changing the subject—" Violet started.

"No," Lily interrupted. "Something *is* going on."

The carriage hadn't budged in the last ten minutes. Since they weren't going anywhere anyway, they all climbed out. "William and Mary," Rose breathed. "Their wedding! I'd completely forgotten that today is the fourth of November."

William of Orange and King Charles's niece, Mary, rode in an open carriage down the Strand on their way to St. James's Palace. Caught in the crush, Rose and her sisters were swept into the swarm of citizens lining the streets, waving and cheering as William and Mary approached.

"Everyone seems so happy to see them wed," Lily remarked, holding onto her cat for dear life.

"She's a Protestant," Rose said. "Charles is no fool. He has no legitimate heirs, and he knows the people don't want to see his Catholic brother James on the throne. He is wise to marry James's daughter to a Protestant prince like William of Orange."

"When did *you* become so wise?" Violet asked.

Rose lifted her chin. "Just because I don't bury my nose in books about the past doesn't mean I am ignorant of the present. Besides"—she shrugged and cracked a droll smile—"I vow and swear, there was little to do at Court in the daytime besides read newsheets."

The happy roar swelled as the bride and groom drew closer. But Mary did not look happy at all. In fact, as she rode by in the royal carriage, wearing a magnificent blue and gold gown and waving to the people, she looked ready to burst into tears.

"How old is she?" Lily asked.

"Fifteen. And William is twenty-seven."

Twenty-seven and short with stooped shoulders, bad teeth, and a large, beaked nose.

Rose wouldn't want to marry him, either. Her heart went out to poor Mary. With her own wedding only five days away, she suddenly felt very lucky to be marrying a man she truly loved.

Assuming, that was, that Kit wasn't angry she'd forced matters with Ellen. Violet's question kept rattling in her brain. *Has it occurred to you that Kit might never forgive you for meddling in his affairs?*

But with the wedding so close, she couldn't allow this brother-sister standoff to continue. Not when there was a way to fix it. Standing by meekly was simply not in her nature.

Kit wouldn't be angry; he'd be grateful. She knew him well enough to know that.

Didn't she?

Chapter Thirty-seven

With all the excitement and delay caused by the royal wedding, night had fallen by the time Rose and her sisters reached Windsor and the carriage jerked to a stop in front of the pawnshop.

Rose roused herself from a doze and climbed down, then turned back when nobody seemed to be following her. Shivering in the cold night air, she stared through the open doorway of the vehicle. "Are you two not going to come with me?"

Her sisters looked at each other. "I think not," Lily said for them both.

"We don't choose to be part of this insanity," Violet elaborated.

"Oh, do hush up," Rose said. Obviously they didn't appreciate her roping them into her plot, but she couldn't have simply gallivanted about England alone. This was the sort of thing sisters were for, wasn't it?

And she'd done some thinking on the way here to Windsor. She clutched her cloak tighter around herself. "Do you know," she told Violet, "I seem to remember you 'meddling' in Ford's affairs. For God's sake, you patented and sold his invention without his knowledge; you secretly bought that book, thereby giving him your money—giving him your inheritance, Violet, hmm?—without him knowing—"

"'Tis not comparable," Lily cut in. "She gave the money

to Ford, the man she was planning to marry. You're giving yours to Ellen."

Rose turned on her. "And you gave up control of your own money, too, to Rand's father. Quite willingly, if I remember right."

"That is not comparable, either. 'Twas the only way I could marry Rand."

"I see. Speaking of Rand . . . Wasn't Rand the one who came to Violet with the plan to secretly save Ford's estate? It seems to me he's not averse to a little manipulation for a good cause. Are you telling me Rand would leave you if you meddled in his business?"

"Well, no. I am certain we would work it out. But you're not married yet. What if Kit is so angry he calls off the wedding? Then you'll have lost all your money, and—"

"Never mind." There was no reasoning with either of them. Rose reached back into the carriage and hefted the bag of coins with a little grunt. Fuming, she stomped to the pawnshop's door and knocked.

And knocked. And knocked. She had just about decided the Whittinghams weren't home when Thomas finally cracked open the door, his face illuminated by a single candle.

"We're closed," he said, then raised the candle higher. "Oh. Lady Rose." With his free hand, he clutched the top of his half open shirt.

She shifted the heavy bag in her arms. "I have something for Ellen. From Kit."

He eyed the bag curiously. "Well, come in, then, will you?"

She followed him through the dark shop and up the stairs, noting his disheveled hair and wondering if she'd roused him from his bed. 'Twas early yet, but he and Ellen *were* newly wedded. If Rose had her way, she'd be going to bed early every night with Kit. She could hardly wait to finish this and surprise him at his house.

"In here," Thomas said at the top of the stairs, opening a

door to a small room crammed full of furniture and decorative pieces.

"Rose!" Ellen jumped up from a chair, dressed in a pale pink wrapper. The firelight behind her left no doubt that she wore nothing underneath.

So Rose had guessed right. She wasn't sure whether to be embarrassed or amused. "I've brought something for you. From Kit." She walked closer and handed Ellen the bag.

Not expecting its weight, Ellen squealed as it slipped through her hands and fell to the floor with a *thud,* flopping onto its side. The top opened a little, and a coin rolled out and across the plain wooden boards, finally landing with a little *clink.* For a moment, it just sat there, glinting gold in the firelight.

Then Ellen rushed to scoop it up. She folded her fingers around it and looked to Rose, a question in her eyes.

"Your dowry," Rose told her. "The first thousand pounds of it. The rest is forthcoming. 'Tis waiting in London whenever you decide to claim it." She handed Ellen the goldsmith's promissory note for nine thousand pounds. "I couldn't carry more."

That last sentence, at least, was the truth. And if the rest of what she'd said was less than honest, it was meant well, for Kit's and Ellen's good.

Rose sent up a little prayer that Kit would see it that way.

Ellen stared at the paper with the goldsmith's name. Rose hoped she wasn't going to fuss over the missing thousand pounds—ten thousand, after all, was a vast sum of money.

Ellen still hadn't said a word. "Kit loves you," Rose added simply.

"I know." Tears flooded Ellen's eyes. She opened her clenched fist and stared down at the coin. "I . . . I know not what to say."

"Save your words for Kit. Just tell me you'll come to our wedding."

"Of course I will."

Rose opened her arms, and Ellen stepped into her embrace.

"Kit needs you," Rose murmured by her ear. "You're his only family."

Ellen hugged her tighter. "You'll be his family soon."

" 'Tis not the same. You're with Thomas now, but Kit shares your blood." Rose and her sisters bickered all the time, but even angry as she was with them now, she knew they only wanted the best for her. And they would always be there if she needed them. Always. "You need Kit, too. Sisters and brothers . . . 'tis a bond that should never be broken."

"I was going to make her go to your wedding, anyway," Thomas put in.

"He was going to *try* to make me go," Ellen clarified with a strained laugh. She took a deep breath and stepped back. " 'Twas turning into our first fight."

Rose eyed her scant apparel. "Not too serious, apparently."

"Not yet." This time the laugh was real, and a twinkle lit Ellen's eyes. "We've been enjoying your sonnets."

"Ellen!" Thomas protested, turning ten shades of red.

"They're not mine," Rose said dryly. "You're welcome to them."

She noticed both their gazes stray to the bag of coins and figured they were too polite to dump them all right there and wallow in their new fortune—but also that they were dying to do so. "I'll leave you, then," she said. "To the sonnets and the gold."

Thomas followed her back down the stairs. "Thank you," he said at the door.

"Thank Kit."

"We will. But I thank you, too. I'm aware that what Kit gives us comes out of your pocket as well."

He didn't know the half of it. "Kit and I have plenty," she assured him. " 'Tis the love that counts anyway, is it not?"

He nodded as he locked the door behind her.

It had gone perfectly. She smiled to herself as a footman ushered her into the carriage. "We're sorry," Violet and Lily said together before she could even sit down.

"Sorry?"

"We talked while you were gone. And you're right," Violet admitted. "We both gave up our inheritances for our men. And it was a good bargain."

"The best," Lily agreed.

Rose was stunned by their about-face. "'Twas not exactly the same."

"True." Violet started a little as the carriage lurched and began the short drive down the hill to Kit's house. "We both did it to win our men, and you already have Kit."

Rose hoped she still would after she told him of this night's work.

"We've decided," Lily said, "that what you just did was more romantic. And noble."

"Noble?" No one had ever described Rose Ashcroft as noble. "Noble?"

"We traded money for selfish reasons—for what we ourselves wanted. You sacrificed not for yourself, but for your husband's happiness."

"But can you not see? I cannot be happy if Kit isn't. That was the whole point."

Her sisters exchanged a look. "She gets it," Violet said gravely.

"Yes." Lily breathed a languid sigh. "Isn't love wonderful?"

The carriage rolled to a stop. "We're here," Rose announced unnecessarily, her heart suddenly pounding. Here was her moment of truth.

As she climbed down the steps with her satchel, she ordered herself to relax. Despite her sisters' dire predictions, she'd known from the first this would work. And she was dying to see Kit. Her entire body tingled in memory of their one night together last week.

Putting a smile on her face, she marched up the stairs and banged the knocker.

Graves promptly answered. "Lady Rose. What a surprise."

"I hope 'tis a pleasant one." Surely everything would be all right. "Especially pleasant for Kit."

"I'm afraid Mr. Martyn has gone to Hampton Court," the butler told them. "My apologies, Lady Rose. I don't expect him back until Thursday."

"Thursday?" Rose echoed, her stomach souring with disappointment. Not only could she not see Kit, but the roads were too dangerous to travel at night. The countryside was dark as sin, and highwaymen abounded. Standing on the doorstep, Rose looked helplessly at her sisters, then back to Graves. "Do you suppose we could stay the night anyway?"

"Of course, of course." The butler reached for her satchel. "Mr. Martyn would have my head if I turned you away."

In no time at all, he'd called for footmen to take their luggage and maids to ready rooms, then sent word to the cook to prepare a fine meal. He ushered the sisters through the magnificent entry hall and into the drawing room to await supper.

Rose plopped onto the moss green settle. "I cannot believe this."

Lily shrugged and set down her cat, then sat beside her. "We shall have a nice sisterly evening together."

Rose had wanted to spend the evening with Kit. Her body all but ached, reminding her. "I think I just want to go to sleep—" Suddenly an alarming thought occurred to her. "Good God, this is terrible. I'll not be able to explain to Kit before we leave."

"Explain what?" Violet asked, perusing a book she'd found on a shelf.

"About Ellen and the money. I need to explain. Else he might hate me and call off the wedding—"

"Oh, Rose." Lily covered her hand with her own. "I'm sorry we ever said that. Kit is not going to hate you."

Violet shut the book and sat on her other side. "As you pointed out, I meddled in Ford's life, too. And he certainly didn't hate me for doing those things. In fact, he thought it was wonderful."

But now that the idea had taken root in her head, Rose couldn't help but worry. "Ford is different," she said. "He thrives on invention, creation—he's not a man driven by ambition, as Kit is. Ford's happiest when other people take care of the details so he can concentrate on his science. But Kit is used to being in charge. He may not take lightly to my arranging his life."

"You said you know him," Lily reminded her. "You said you were certain he wouldn't react badly."

That was true. Her heart stopped pounding quite so hard. "You're right," she said, "I *do* know Kit. He will probably laugh when he hears what I've done."

But a moment later she was doubting again. She felt as though her emotions were buffeted by the wind.

More than anything, she wanted to talk to Kit and see his reaction once and for all. But she couldn't drag her sisters to Hampton Court, and she couldn't send them home in the carriage and wait here until Thursday, either. Her wedding was Saturday. She had to make flower arrangements, help her mother . . .

"I'll leave him a letter," she decided. "And I'll ask him to send a message as soon as he reads it." She'd be counting the hours until Thursday night when, she hoped, she'd receive words of reassurance. Words that would allow her a good night's sleep.

"The perfect solution," Violet said.

Not perfect, but the best Rose could do.

"He loves you," Lily reminded her.

Rose could only hope he loved her enough.

Chapter Thirty-eight

He was a coward.

Kit had argued with himself on the entire drive from London. Should he give Ellen her dowry before the wedding, so she'd attend and neither of them would be sorry later? Or wait until she started talking to him again, no matter how long it took?

He wanted to do the latter; he didn't want to give in to her childish behavior, and he didn't want to feel like he was buying her love. But he didn't have the guts. As evidenced by the fact that he'd detoured from his final inspection of the completed chapel at Whitehall, stopping to pick up some money from his goldsmith before making the drive back here to Windsor.

Not to mention that even though his work had kept him a day later than he'd intended—even though 'twas nightfall already and his wedding was tomorrow—he was even now heading up the High Street to Ellen's house instead of his own.

Still, if he was a coward, at least he was a happy one.

Amazingly, in less than twenty-four hours, Rose would be his. He hadn't needed the knighthood, let alone a more important title. He'd won her as plain Kit Martyn, and there was satisfaction to be found in that.

No more mishaps had occurred, and in fact, his work was proceeding extremely well. Lord Trentingham, of course, was enamored of his new greenhouse. Charles was pleased with the chapel at Whitehall, and when he saw the exquisite dining room here in Windsor, which was also now complete, Kit was confident he would approve. 'Twas unfortunate the Hampton Court addition was so far behind schedule, but as its intended occupant was currently in France, 'twas not exactly disastrous. And Kit was certain that, when finished, it, too, would exceed Charles's expectations. Despite losing the Deputy Surveyor post, his future was not at all bleak.

A week from today, he and Rose would attend the Queen's birthday celebration at Whitehall, then leave for Italy the day after that. A dream come true for them both. He would learn from the great architects, and Rose would be there to translate.

But first things first, Kit thought as his carriage drew up before the pawnshop. Before he could be happy with the new woman in his life, he needed to square things with the old one.

He drew a deep breath, hefted the bag of coins, and marched up to the pawnshop door. 'Twas locked tight at this late hour, but as he was raising his hand to knock, it swung open. Ellen and her husband both stood there, wrapped in cloaks, obviously on their way out.

"What are you doing here?" she asked.

"Where are you going?" he countered—then realized that she'd actually spoken to him. Would wonders never cease? Just when he was ready to give in, she'd saved him from proving himself a coward.

"Now that the shop is closed for the evening, I was going to try to see you," she said. "As I've done the past four nights."

"I was away," he said unnecessarily. "Here." He held out the bag. "A down payment on your dowry. I never meant to keep it from you. My goldsmith is holding the rest for you in London."

"I know. I've been trying for four days to thank you." Instead of taking the money, she threw her arms around him, the hard bag of gold between them. "Thank you so very,

very much." She kissed both his cheeks. "I love you. I honestly don't know what came over me. But I'm sorry I didn't trust you, that I tried to punish you by remaining silent."

Though clearly rehearsed, her words sounded sincere. But Kit was stunned. He pulled away. "How did you know I was about to give it to you?" Until a few minutes ago, he hadn't been sure himself.

Ellen exchanged a confused glance with Thomas before turning back to her brother. "What do you mean, how did I know?"

"There was no need to bring more gold," Thomas added. "The first bag was sufficient proof of your intentions."

Kit shifted the heavy weight in his arms. "The first bag?"

"The one you sent with Rose." Ellen enunciated slowly, as though he were a half-wit who required the simplest explanation.

'Twas not too far off from the way he was feeling at the moment. "Rose? What does Rose have to do with this?"

Thomas looked even more confused than Kit felt. "She brought us your money. Or a thousand pounds of it, and a promissory note from your goldsmith for the rest. Abrahamson & Company."

"My money is with Lazarus & Sons." Kit's thoughts seemed to be moving through a fog, until suddenly everything cleared. "Lord Almighty. It must have been *her* money. Her inheritance."

Thomas blinked. "Is she mad?"

"Clearly," Kit said. "Insane, infuriating—"

"Madly in love," Ellen interrupted with a soft smile.

Reeling, Kit leaned against the doorpost. Not light to begin with, the bag seemed to be growing heavier by the moment. "Do you think I could come in and sit down?"

"Rose is anxious," Chrystabel said later that night as she readied herself for bed. "Distressed. I never in my life thought I'd see Rose like this. Of all our girls—"

"You're the one who's anxious." Joseph stepped behind to unlace her, pausing to kiss the back of her neck.

The little shiver that rippled through her was not enough to really distract her. She reached up to unpin her hair. "I should have let her sleep with Kit."

"What?" Though he sounded astonished, his practiced fingers kept unlacing. "You cannot mean that, Chrysanthemum."

"I do. 'Tis the only explanation for Rose's attack of nerves. 'Twas a mistake keeping them apart. Our daughter should be happily anticipating her wedding tomorrow, and instead—"

"You explained so well all your good reasons for forbidding their early union." He spread the back of her gown, drawing it off her shoulders and kissing the newly bared skin. "Fear of an eight-month baby—"

"We had a *six*-month baby and survived—"

"Loss of innocence before the wedding—"

"So what?"

"—when the wedding could be called off for various reasons—"

"What reasons? 'Twas different with Lily and Rand, where his father was against the match. But Kit has no parents, no one to say nay. He's his own man—"

He laughed, pushing the gown and her chemise down to pool at her feet. "And you're your own woman, my love. Truly one of a kind."

Though she wasn't certain if he meant that as a compliment or a complaint, she turned and kissed him anyway. "Tomorrow it will all be over, all three of our girls married."

He skimmed his warm hands down her sides, stopping with them on her hips. "Do you find that sad? Another reason to be anxious?"

She nodded and bit her lip, reaching for her night rail.

"Oh, you won't be needing that." He snatched it from her hands and threw it artfully over his shoulder. "I suspect a prewedding night might take your mind off tomorrow's anxieties."

No note had come from Kit.

Wearing only a sapphire silk dressing gown, Rose paced her crimson bedchamber, smiling vaguely at her sisters and Judith gathered there to help her dress for her wedding.

She couldn't help wondering if she was going to have one.

She lifted the bouquet she'd made for herself to carry down the aisle, stroking the soft red and white petals. If she hadn't given all that money to Kit's sister, she wouldn't think twice about the fact that he hadn't arrived yet; in truth, she had no reason to expect him this early. And he wasn't supposed to see her before the wedding, anyway.

But she'd thought she'd hear from him Thursday night. And now it was Saturday . . .

"You look worried," Judith said.

Rose inhaled deeply of the sweet floral scent, then set the flowers aside, forcing a smile. "Wedding nerves. You suffered them, too, if you'll remember."

"Did I?" Judith laughed, looking happier than Rose had ever seen her. "But there was no need to, as I discovered. If 'tis the wedding night you're dreading . . . don't. 'Twas ever so wonderful—" She must have suddenly realized what she was saying, because she broke off, her cheeks flushing pink.

Struggling to keep a straight face, Rose exchanged glances with her sisters. "Thank you," she told Judith primly. "I feel much better."

"Oh, good." Judith smiled.

Rose's hair was already dressed with pearls and red ribbons, her lashes darkened, and her eyes lightly outlined with kohl. For want of something to do, she sat at her dressing table and fluffed more powder on her face.

"You're going to look like a ghost," Violet said.

"Good God, you're right." Staring at her pale self in the

mirror, she pulled a little sheet of red Spanish paper from a tiny booklet. "Where is Kit?" she asked, rubbing it on her cheeks.

"Now you look like a harlot." Lily grabbed a handkerchief to rub some off. "Let me help you."

Rose sat rigid under her ministrations. "Is it time for me to get dressed?"

"Might as well." Violet swept the red gown off the bed. "Shall I call Harriet?"

"No. You three can help me. I cannot stand any more of her chatter. All she ever talks of is Walter and their upcoming marriage. I almost wish they'd chosen to live at Hampton Court instead of with me."

"That isn't true," Lily said.

Of course it wasn't. Harriet's chatter hadn't bothered her before she gave the money to Ellen. She just couldn't take so much unadulterated happiness right now. It set her teeth on edge.

She slid out of her wrapper and stood in place while Judith slipped the diaphanous chemise over her head, being careful not to ruin her hair or her carefully applied face. Then her sisters brought over the gown and helped her wiggle into it. Violet smoothed the satin skirts over her hips while Lily stepped close to lace her tightly into the bodice.

"I think I may be with child," she murmured to Rose's chest.

Rose blinked and looked down to Lily's still-flat stomach, her body lithe as ever in her dusky pink gown. "Are you sure?"

She looked up with a dreamy smile. "I'm two weeks late."

"Oh, Lily!" Violet threw her arms around her.

"Me, too," Judith said shyly.

Lily froze. "You're not jesting?"

Judith nodded, and they both let out excited little screams.

Beaming, Lily turned from Violet's arms into her friend's.

"Remember when you said we should be newly wedded together? Now we're going to become mothers together, too!"

Rose watched them embrace, slowly tying her abandoned laces in a bow while her own flat stomach churned. Lily and Judith and Ellen, all pregnant. And Violet had three children already.

On this day that was supposed to be happy, she felt so left out. She reached for her stomacher and plastered it against her front, beginning to fasten the tabs. Would she ever have children of her own? Not if Kit didn't show up to marry her—

"Edmund is thrilled," Judith gushed. "What did Rand say?"

"I've not told him yet." Lily hugged herself round the middle as though she were protecting her child. "I wanted to be sure. We've been disappointed before—"

"Oh, heavens," Judith said. "You've been wed only two months. You must tell him. If he's half as happy as Edmund, you'll end up spending a night that makes you wonder if you could possibly conceive a second child when you're already increasing with the first—"

She clapped a hand over her mouth, her cheeks looking like she had used a whole booklet of Spanish paper.

Lily laughed. "I'll tell him today."

"Tell who what?" came a voice from the doorway.

Kit.

Rose's heart thundered under her laces.

"Never mind," Lily blurted.

He locked his gaze on Rose, but she couldn't read his face. "You're not supposed to see me before the wedding," she said inanely. " 'Tis bad luck."

"I'll risk it. I need to talk to you."

He looked so serious. The little breakfast she'd managed to choke down this morning was threatening to come back up.

"We'll . . . we'll leave," Lily said.

"Excellent idea." He waited by the door while the other

three women scurried out, then shut it decisively behind them. "Do you need help with that?" he asked, indicating Rose's half attached stomacher.

"No." Her fingers started moving again, albeit shakily. He was walking closer. "Kit—"

Her sentence was cut off when his mouth crushed down on hers.

This was no gentle caress, but hot and emphatic. His lips coaxed hers open and his tongue swept her mouth in a declaration of possession that made her senses dim and her knees threaten to buckle.

By the time he broke contact, she was gasping for breath, reeling with the sudden reversal of worry to elation.

He kissed her chin, her neck, between her breasts where her stomacher dangled drunkenly. "God, I love you," he murmured against her skin. He inhaled deeply, closing his eyes. "You smell like sin."

She threaded her fingers into his hair, pressed her lips to the top of his head. "I was so afraid you'd hate me."

"Hate you?" He straightened and lifted her chin until her gaze was forced to his. His eyes, green as emeralds now, searched hers. "Why?"

"For meddling in your affairs. I only wanted your happiness . . ."

"Did you think I didn't know that? Did you think I wouldn't fall in love with you all over again when I realized you were willing to give up your inheritance to bring me and my sister together? What kind of a man do you think I am?"

She'd known what kind of a man he was—she shouldn't have let her sisters lead her to doubt. "You didn't answer my letter."

"What letter? I never received any letter." His thumb moved from her chin, skimming tenderly over her cheek.

"I left it propped on your washstand."

He shrugged. "No one's ever done anything that touched

me the way you have. Lord Almighty, sweetheart, when I went to give Ellen her dowry and she told me—"

"What?" She forgot about the missing letter as her hand flew up to grasp his wrist. "You gave Ellen her dowry?"

"I tried to," he said with a wry grin. "She told me you already had." His gaze softened. "However was I lucky enough to win a woman as special as you?"

Rose's throat tightened. No one had ever called her special. "I should have known you would do the right thing." She'd known he was a good man—that was why she had decided to marry him.

He kissed her again, more gently this time, a tender kiss that made tears well in her eyes. No matter what he said, she knew that she was the lucky one—lucky he hadn't given up when she'd pushed him away for all the wrong reasons.

But if he had given up, he wouldn't have been Kit.

"No crying on your wedding day," he said, wiping a rogue tear off her cheek with one warm thumb. "I'm sure that's worse luck than having me see you before the ceremony."

She managed a watery chuckle.

His hands went to finish attaching her stomacher. "You look beautiful."

Her pulse thumped madly under his fingers. "You look better." He wore a deep green velvet suit with silver braid trimming the long waistcoat and the surcoat that went over it. Just enough lace fell from beneath his cuffs, and a tasteful diamond pin winked from the folds of his cravat.

Perfect. If she'd noticed how he was dressed when he first appeared in her doorway, she would have spared herself a few anguished seconds of worry. No one would take him for anything but a groom.

A heart-stoppingly handsome one.

His fingers traced the pearl scrollwork on her stomacher. "I have something for you." He pulled a small wooden box from his pocket. "I wasn't sure what color you'd be wearing, but I think they will match."

She opened the lid to find an exquisite pair of earrings, two teardrop pearls swinging from clustered diamond tops. "They must have cost a fortune," she gasped. She'd never seen such enormous pearls.

He smiled as he took them from the box and moved closer to fasten them on her ears. "I may not be titled, but I'm hardly a pauper."

"I'm not wearing any earrings. I didn't have any I wanted to wear."

"I'm glad to hear it," he said, kissing one bare lobe before he decorated it. "I don't ever want to see you wearing that damned duke's jewels again. In fact, I think you should pawn them. Permanently."

She laughed as he attached the second earring. When he was finished, he drew her close, running his hands over her back and down to her bottom. She ached where he brought their bodies together. "I love you," he said.

She would never tire of hearing those three words. "I love you, too."

"I love you in red."

"I'm glad." His scent was making her senses spin. "My sisters both wore blue."

"I'd love to see you in blue, too." He nibbled her neck. "I'd love to see you in purple," he said conversationally. "I'd love to see you in green. I'd love to see you in a rich, metallic gold."

Each word against her skin made delicious shivers whisper through her. She sighed, tilting her head to give him better access.

His lips settled in the sensitive hollow of her throat, then paused. "But mostly," he whispered devilishly, "I'd love to see you naked."

If her sisters hadn't knocked on the door then, he might have.

Chapter Thirty-nine

Standing at the front of her family's small, crowded chapel, Rose shifted on her high-heeled shoes and slipped her hand into Kit's.

"Christopher Martyn, wilt thou have this woman to thy wedded wife, to live together after God's ordinance in the holy estate of Matrimony? Wilt thou love her, comfort her, honor, and keep her in sickness and in health; and, forsaking all others, keep thee only unto her, so long as ye both shall live?"

"I will." The confident words boomed through the magnificent oak-paneled chamber, binding Kit to Rose.

But Rose wasn't listening to the ceremony. Instead she was thinking that Kit was the most handsome, intelligent, loving man she'd ever known, not to mention moral to a fault. She was so glad he'd managed to burst her childish bubble and make her realize what really counted.

Love, clear and true.

Happy tears brightened her mother's brown eyes. Rose knew she thought Kit was perfect for her—she even suspected she'd had a hand in getting them together. There were too many times she'd left them alone early on, too many times she'd decided to follow the Court when Kit just happened to be working at a particular castle or palace.

But Rose didn't care.

Her gaze wandered over the assembled guests, landing

on Lily. Her younger sister stood beside Rand, her rich sable hair cascading to her shoulders in glossy ringlets, her lips curved in a way that made Rose think she'd just shared her secret. Beside her, Rand beamed a smile, looking like he wanted to shout to the world that he was going to be a father.

The two were so clearly in love, Rose knew they belonged together—and she was thrilled for her sister. She was so glad Lily had ended up with Rand, leaving her to find Kit.

The priest cleared his throat and looked back down at his *Book of Common Prayer.* "Lady Rose Ashcroft, wilt thou have this man to thy wedded husband . . ."

Standing on Lily's right, their older sister Violet shifted one of her twin babies on her hip, gazing up at Ford. Sun streamed through the stained glass windows, glinting off her spectacles as she whispered something in his ear.

Holding their other infant, Ford squeezed his wife around the shoulders. Seated cross-legged at their feet, their three-year-old son Nicky traced a finger over the patterns in the colorful glazed tile floor, obliviously happy.

Rose couldn't wait to have a family of her own. She flashed a quick smile at Ellen standing beside Thomas, one hand in his and the other resting lightly on her middle. The niece or nephew that was growing there, she thought giddily, would someday be cousin to her own child.

" . . . so long as ye both shall live?" the priest concluded expectantly.

In the hush that followed, Rose's heart swelled. She'd thought her wedding day would never come.

"I will," she pledged, squeezing Kit's hand.

A few more words, a gorgeous ruby ring slipped onto her finger, and Rose and Kit were husband and wife, Mr. Christopher Martyn and Lady Rose Martyn.

Once upon a time, she'd thought that disparity would bother her. But nothing could be further from the truth.

When Kit lowered his lips to meet hers, Rose threw her arms around him.

She'd finally found someone who could make her feel like a queen.

Rose couldn't remember ever hating idle chitchat more than she did late that afternoon. Idle chitchat was the very devil.

Especially when it contrived to keep her from her wedding night.

She'd been wanting Kit ever since he'd appeared in her bedchamber earlier today. No, since before that. Since she'd shown up at his house and found him gone. The want was a fire smoldering inside her—a heat that would take little encouragement to flame.

Very little.

"Farewell, Aunt Cecily, Aunt Arabel," she said with a forced smile, kissing Mum's sisters on both cheeks. She urged them down the portico's steps to the lawn. "Thank you for coming." As they finally walked away with their children, she leaned close to Kit's ear. "May we leave already?"

He glanced toward the river. "Soon."

As her curious gaze followed his, Jewel and Rowan stepped onto the portico. "I have something for you," Jewel said.

Rose looked down to find a box, exquisitely fashioned of colored, leaded glass. " 'Tis beautiful!" she exclaimed.

"Jewel made it," Rowan informed them. "Her hands are covered in cuts." He sounded admiring, as though blood and gore were badges of honor.

Kit took the box. "We'll treasure it," he told the girl gravely. He squeezed Rose round her waist. "Won't we?"

"Absolutely." She tingled all up and down her side where he'd pulled against him. "Thank you so very much," she told Jewel. "I had no idea you worked with glass."

Jewel hid her scarred hands behind her back. "Mama and

my little brother both make jewelry. I got tired of doing the same thing. I was looking at the windows in a church once, and Papa told me how the lead is soldered like some of Mama's jewelry. I thought I might like to try it."

Chrystabel moved around Rose, plucking the last of the love-knots off her gown. She took the glass box from Kit, lifted the lid, and dropped the little red bows inside. "'Tis over," she sighed.

Rose wished it were over. She wanted to be alone with Kit. "'Twas a beautiful wedding, Mum."

Chrystabel sighed again. "I never really got to plan a big wedding. I shall have to do so for Rowan. A nice, long betrothal—"

Rose laughed. "Have you considered that Jewel might want to plan her *own* wedding? Or her mother—"

"Jewel?" Rowan's eyes widened in alarm. "I'm not going to marry Jewel!"

Kit gave the boy an indulgent smile. "Wait 'til you're older—"

"Never!" Rowan looked at Jewel with such horror, the girl shrank back.

"May we leave *now*?" Rose asked Kit.

He confused her by glancing toward the river again. "Ah, yes. Here's our transportation."

Rose turned and stared at the beautiful, gilded barge rounding the bend and approaching Trentingham's dock. "*This* is how we're getting to Windsor? What about your carriage?"

"Ellen and Thomas accompanied me here, and they'll take it home. You don't really want to ride back with them, do you?"

"No." She liked Kit's sister well enough, but she was anxious to begin her wedding night—and she didn't want company. "This is Ford's barge. Was it his idea?"

"Violet's, actually. Who knew a romantic heart hid inside that intellectual exterior?"

"Violet," Rose said low, "lost her virginity on this barge.

She told me all about it on the way to your house last week."

"*All* about it?"

"Well, perhaps not all. But there's a bed inside the cabin."

Kit's gaze heated as her family walked them to the barge.

"You know," her father said for the third time, "'tis traditional for a girl to spend her first married night at her parents' house."

"I'm only questioning convention," Rose reminded him loudly.

Her mother smiled. "When are you going to London, dear?"

"The Queen's birthday celebration is Friday, so we're thinking probably Wednesday."

"Windy?" Father frowned. "Yes, the wind does seem to be picking up."

"It certainly is, Father." Rose shared an amused glance with Kit. "I think everyone should hurry inside."

As they climbed aboard, Kit pulled her close, wrapping an arm around her shoulders. They turned to bid farewell to their families and the last straggling guests. A few hugs and kisses and tears later, they were finally alone on the barge.

Well, almost alone. There was a crew, of course, to guide the vessel to Windsor. And a young man playing a violin, sheltered from the weather by the tall wall of the cabin that sat in the barge's middle.

Heat thrummed through Rose's veins. She forced herself to stand at the rail, waving at her family until the barge pulled away. The wind was indeed picking up, whipping her skirts and hair. Her heart seemed to speed up to match until it beat in a wild frenzy. Beside her, Kit felt warm, a temptation worthy of the devil himself.

"Inside," she demanded the moment they cleared the dock. She couldn't get him into the cabin fast enough. No sooner had they slammed the door behind them than she threw herself into his arms.

The kiss, hot and out of control, left no doubt that Kit was of the same mind. Violin music swirled through her head as his tongue swept her mouth. She returned the favor, tasting him, breathing in his scent and feeling a little thrill at the realization that he would be hers to savor from now on. As the barge turned into the center of the river, the kiss grew more frantic. Rose wrenched Kit's surcoat off his shoulders and pushed it down his arms. The vessel rocked, threatening her balance, and he grabbed her to hold her upright, laughing into her mouth.

"Now," she said against his lips, working him closer to the bed. The barge settled into a more gentle rocking rhythm, but wind whistled through the shutters, igniting a similar storm in her blood. She shoved his long waistcoat off, her hands going blindly to his cravat as his fingers went to her stomacher. She burned, she ached. The tiny cabin seemed endless as she inched him toward the bed, their mouths still locked in that breathless caress. She turned them both, ready to sink to the mattress the moment she felt it behind her knees.

But what she bumped into was higher. And harder. She put a hand back, feeling wood. She twisted in dismay, her eyes flying open. A wedding feast for two was spread on a gorgeous carved mahogany table surrounded by six matching chairs.

There was no bed. "Where the devil is the bed?"

"Hmm?" Deprived of her lips, Kit kissed her throat instead.

"The bed. The bed is gone." Disappointment dulled all the exciting, stormy sensations. "Kit, there's no bed."

He raised his head and blinked, then shrugged. "We'll make do."

What? Would they lie down on the floor? "I don't see how—"

"Trust me, sweetheart." Seemingly unperturbed, he

dropped her stomacher to a chair and untied the bow secur-
ing her laces, bending again to kiss the valley between her
breasts.

Her flesh prickled beneath his hot mouth. She swayed
and closed her eyes. "You're right," she suddenly realized.
"Position Seven could work on the table."

He jerked upright. "Position Seven?"

"From *I Sonetti*. Here." She turned and shoved dishes
away from the edge. "Sit here."

"Here?"

"Here," she said, pushing him into place. She backed up
to him and raised herself to sit on his lap, moving her legs
to either side of his knees and wiggling herself close.
"Hmm." She leaned forward a little, angling . . . "Yes, it
can work!"

His laughter burst out behind her.

"What?" she asked, half twisting on his lap.

"It may work, but 'tis not very romantic." He swung her
around to sit properly sideways, then leaned her back
against his arm. "There. Now I can kiss you."

She wanted more than kisses. "But we cannot—"

"Trust me, sweetheart, we can." When she opened her
mouth to protest again, he covered it with his fingers.
"Trust me."

Well, she had little choice, did she? When he replaced
his hand with his mouth, she sank into the embrace, trust-
ing. And trembling. His lips seemed made to fit hers, and
the storm overtook her again, just that easily. He spread her
bodice wide and toyed with her aching breasts, slipping a
hand up under her gown. But she had no taste for leisurely
play. The barge rocked, and the wind whistled, whipping
her senses.

"Now," she murmured, "show me now." When he failed
to respond, she nipped his bottom lip. "Now."

He laughed again. "And to think I feared you'd never
come to my bed." He set her on her feet momentarily while

he pulled out a chair, then sat and turned her to face him, drawing her down to straddle his lap.

Leaning back, he reached beneath her skirts and quickly unlaced his breeches. "Is this not better than facing away?" he asked, drawing her near. She sucked in a breath, feeling that exquisite need where her body pressed against his, where she could feel him straining against her.

"I can kiss you," he murmured, then demonstrated, leaving her lightheaded. "And touch you." As his fingers teased her breasts, she squirmed against him below. "And hold you." His arms went around to pull her close.

"Yes," she gritted out, "I can see the advantages. Now can you show me how it will work?"

His hands went to her hips and raised her a little, then lowered her, slowly, until she felt him sliding into her. She felt herself stretching, accommodating, welcoming him into her body. She sighed and then gasped when she moved, feeling him slide out and back in, feeling the storm rise in her blood. She moved again, that urgent heat building, a rush of heady sensation that threatened to sweep away all thought.

As his mouth met hers, she grabbed fistfuls of his shirt, pulling it up, shoving her hands underneath to grip his heated flanks. Her breath quickened. The searing need built until it seemed unbearable, until she couldn't move fast enough, until the storm finally burst, a swirling maelstrom of pleasure that had her shaking uncontrollably. When she might have screamed, he took the sound into his mouth, and she felt his own low cry echoing inside her.

Somehow, Kit had become her world. If she could crawl inside him, she would. She contented herself with slumping against him, sweetly drained, reveling in the feel of his arms crushing her close as she waited for her heart to calm, her breathing to slow. So they could start all over again.

She would never get enough of him.

The gentle sway of the barge was soothing, and as the blood stopped pumping in her ears, the wind seemed to whistle less fiercely and the gentle strains of the violin seemed to seep through the shutters and fill the cabin with peace.

The calm after the storm.

Kit's heart thumped under her ear. " 'You are filling me,' " she quoted softly, " 'thrilling me, and I could stay seated here for a year.' "

His satisfied hum vibrated through her. "Nice," he murmured.

"That was from one of the sonnets," she admitted, opening her eyes. Sconces on the beautifully paneled walls held flickering candles. She raised her face and kissed Kit's chin. "*I Sonetti* didn't show this position."

"Forget *I Sonetti*." He reached around her, filling two goblets from a waiting bottle of champagne. "I wonder what happened to the bed?"

"I know not." Rose sighed, laying her head on his shoulder. "The entire barge used to be rather shabby. Violet had mentioned it was being refurbished, but I never imagined they'd scuttle the bed."

"They have a family now. A table makes more sense."

"Not to us."

" 'Tis not such a long journey, and they set out a veritable feast to occupy us. Did you eat anything at the wedding?"

"I was too busy talking to people." She smiled at the wonderful memories. "But I'm not hungry."

"No? Drink, then." He handed her a goblet, waiting for her to sit up before raising his in a salute. "To a lifetime of love."

"And beds," she said, draining her cup in one long swallow.

He laughed and pulled her near. Violin music drifted in from the deck, and the boat rocked gently as it made its way down river. She relaxed against him again, just breathing, existing, enjoying the closeness as he munched cheese and bread and sipped wine.

Suddenly she felt so happy, tears pricked behind her eyes. "Kit, I'm so glad I married you."

He squeezed her tight. "Then you wouldn't rather be here with the duke?" he teased.

"I expect he'd be puking all over me."

He gulped and swallowed. "What?"

"The duke gets seasick."

"Ah." She heard laughter in his voice. "Good thing you chose me instead."

"Good thing," she sighed in agreement, then sat up when she felt a bump. "Good God, we're here." She jumped off Kit's lap as a knock came at the door.

"Mr. Martyn?"

"One moment," he called, shrugging back into his waistcoat. He laughed at her fumbling fingers. "No need to rush. Careful of your dress; you'll want to wear it to the Queen's ball." He made short work of attaching her stomacher, then swung her up into his arms and started carrying her off the barge.

"Kit!" She laughed, thinking she was much too tall for this. "You'll hurt yourself. Put me down."

"I think not." They had docked right beside his house— *their* house—and he walked around to the front. "I've been told I should carry you over the threshold. Else we could have bad luck."

"Only if I trip."

"Well, this way you won't trip, will you?" The wind whipped her skirts, practically blowing them up the portico's steps. "I'm ensuring our future," he informed her as the front door swung open and he carried her inside.

Holding the door grandly, Graves grinned at them both.

"Put me down," Rose said, feeling windblown and silly.

"Not a chance." Kit continued up the stairs. "We've one more threshold before we're safe."

He crossed that one—their bedchamber—before he set

her on her feet. "I feared for your heart," she said and kissed him.

But he didn't even seem winded. "You weigh nothing," he assured her. By the fireplace a small round table sat between two chairs, its polished surface covered with dishes of fruit, a pile of cakes, and bowls of whipped cream "snow" and strawberry sauce. Kit dipped an orange slice in both and slipped it between her lips. "Dessert," he said with a smile.

The combination was tart and sweet, but she still wasn't hungry. "I'd rather have a kiss," she told him archly.

He obliged her, thoroughly, so thoroughly her knees felt weak when he finally drew back and turned her around to face a low chest of drawers.

She blinked and focused. "There it is!" she cried, spotting a square of white underneath it. "The letter!"

"The letter?" he said from behind her.

"The note I left you explaining about Ellen. It must have fallen off the washstand and somehow wound up under there."

"I care not about the letter." His hands tightened on her shoulders. "Look up."

And there, on the oak-paneled wall, was an oval gilt-framed painting.

Of her.

The Rose on the canvas was the same one he'd sketched that first day, her lips curved gently, her eyes holding secrets. "I drew a hundred pictures of you," he said softly, "but I always came back to this one."

"'Tis beautiful," she breathed, staring. She pictured him painting it, his brush stroking lovingly while she worried needlessly that he might not want her. Her heart squeezed in her chest. "I wish I could paint you."

He stepped in front of her, his gaze glittering green. "Do you mean that, sweetheart?"

Something in his voice gave her pause. "Oh, yes, but I cannot."

"I think you can," he said, drawing off his surcoat.

"I've no talent with paint," she said uncertainly. Frozen in place, she turned and watched him cross to his bed.

His red-draped bed.

Red is a color of power, she remembered him saying.

Her heart raced as he tossed the coat to the red counterpane, followed by his waistcoat. His shirt went next.

Her breath went shallow. "I've tried painting," she said inanely, "but I can never get the colors right."

"There's only white and red," he said. "I'm sure you'll do just fine."

"White and red?" She licked her lips, staring at his bare chest. Gemini, he was gorgeous. How could she have wanted an idle aristocrat when a working man like Kit had muscles that made a woman's hands itch to run all over him?

Those muscles rippled as he strode over to the small round table and opened a curved drawer, rummaging inside. Finally he pulled out a little brush.

"White," he said, dipping it in the whipped cream. "And red." He swirled it in the strawberry sauce.

The sweets glistened in the firelight as he handed the brush to her with a grin.

His gaze was more wicked than ever.

"Here," he said. "Paint me."

She gave a startled laugh, then stroked the brush down his chest, leaning to lick off the sweets with a long, hot swipe of her tongue. Cream and sugar and strawberries and Kit.

This kind of painting she could do.

"How odd," Chrystabel said as she crawled into bed that night. "By the time of the wedding, Rose didn't seem anxious at all."

Glad to see she hadn't bothered with a night rail, Joseph skimmed a hand down her body. "You didn't seem anxious, either, my love."

She sighed, half with memories, half with pleasure. "I knew this match was right."

"And here I thought the prewedding night worked," he teased, one hand fondling a breast while the other trailed between her thighs.

"It did," she breathed. "But I think a postwedding night is in order, anyway."

Chapter Forty

"Look at all the people crowding the balconies!" Rose exclaimed. Everyone who was anyone seemed to be at the Queen's birthday celebration. Musicians played at the far end of the chamber, and courtiers were dancing, dressed in their finest, wearing every jewel they could lay their hands on. "Good God," she said, "this must be the most beautiful building in all of England."

"But I didn't build it," Kit teased, enjoying her reaction to Whitehall's Banqueting House. In truth, he only hoped to someday build something as magnificent as Inigo Jones's masterpiece. He was every bit as impressed as Rose by the classical white and gold room and the stunning ceiling paintings by Sir Peter Paul Rubens.

While Rose would most likely be happy here for hours, he couldn't wait to leave and begin their journey to the Continent, where he would finally get the chance to study the masters that had inspired Jones. Still, this appearance was somewhat of a triumph for him, too, plain Mr. Christopher Martyn at Queen Catharine's birthday ball.

"Shall we dance?" he asked, guiding Rose into the throng. She felt like heaven in his arms, tall and slender and his.

Nell Gwyn waved at her and winked, and she grinned back. "Imagine," she mused. "Nell was born in a bawdy house and ended up the mother of one of the King's sons."

"Very like me." Kit whirled her around. "I was born in a hovel and ended up wed to an earl's daughter."

He'd meant it humorously, but she was in a reflective mood tonight. "'Tis odd, don't you think, the way people crave the opposite of what they have? Nell makes Charles happy because her house is his home. A regular home, and a real life when he's with her. She throws parties where he is not a king, but a guest. None of his other mistresses do that for him. They only take what he has to offer—they don't give in return."

Delighted, Kit gave her a quick kiss, right there in front of the King and Queen and everyone. "And where did you come by all this information?"

"The ladies here at Court. You know, they like me very much. Ever since I started supplying them with lurid sonnets."

He laughed. "The men like you, too. A bit too much for my comfort."

"Worry not. I don't even see them anymore." She closed her eyes, leaning into his arms. "For me, you're the only man in this room."

He laughed again and kissed her again, and thanked God again that he'd won her. He couldn't remember ever feeling this happy.

"Even the Queen looks happy tonight." Rose smiled in Catharine's direction. Dressed in a magnificent cloth-of-gold gown, she danced with Charles, gazing up at him with calm satisfaction. At thirty-nine, she finally seemed content in her unusual marriage.

William of Orange and his new princess did not look as happy. Rose watched them move desultorily around the dance floor. William was shorter than Mary and seemed to have a consumptive cough. Although he was only twenty-seven, deep lines marred his face.

"Poor Mary has been crying again," she said with a sigh.

"Again?"

"I saw her on her wedding day in London, the day I fetched the red gown. She looked terribly unhappy."

Kit drew her closer. "Their marriage was arranged for diplomatic purposes. Neither of them really had a choice."

Her melancholy mood vanished as she grinned. "I'm glad you're a nobody."

Once that might have hurt, but rank now seemed insignificant next to the joy of wedding Rose.

When they came off the dance floor, Christopher Wren handed them both glasses of champagne. "To our Queen," he said. "And your successes. The chapel turned out beautifully, just as I'd envisioned it."

Kit toasted him back. "You gave me excellent plans to work from."

"But Windsor's dining room was your own. A masterpiece."

"Thank you."

"I'm sorry about the appointment."

"That's water under the bridge," Kit said, meaning it. He had a new life, new plans.

The Earl of Rosslyn sidled up, a champagne glass in one hand and his ever-present walking stick in the other. "Martyn," he slurred.

Kit wrapped an arm around Rose's shoulders. "Rosslyn. I take it life is treating you well?"

"I find myself overburdened with too much work." He drained the glass and snagged another from a passing maid. "So sad that I won the post in your place."

Kit shrugged and began to turn away. The man had won the post fair and square, but that didn't mean he had to listen to his backhanded boasts.

"A shame you miscalculated the length of that span at Hampton Court," he heard Rosslyn say behind him.

Kit swiveled back and exchanged a startled glance with Wren. The older man knew Kit had done all his measurements and calculations in private—that besides the two of them, only the perpetrator would know exactly what was wrong with the building. Wren had promised not to share his knowledge—and Kit trusted him implicitly.

Aghast, he turned on Rosslyn. "What sort of man would sabotage another's reputation in order to obtain an appointment?"

Rosslyn was drunk and slow, but Kit saw the horror dawn in his eyes as he realized he'd given himself away.

"You set the fire, didn't you?" Kit pressed. "And altered the plans at Hampton Court. I expect you counted yourself lucky that Harold Washburn's greed took care of Windsor for you. By purchasing inferior materials, he lined his pockets and delayed a project without you lifting so much as a finger."

"I paid him to do that," Rosslyn said smugly.

Kit's jaw tightened. No wonder Washburn had been able to throw around so much money.

"Guards!" Wren called.

Leaning heavily on his ribbon-topped walking stick, Rosslyn glared at Kit. A wild sheen in his eyes said he wasn't all there. "Your loss, my gain," he growled. "I've finally proven myself better than you." A red-coated guard stepped up to restrain him, but he twisted from the man's grip. "All those years in school, no matter how well I did, that upstart Kit Martyn always did better—"

He was cut off when a second guard grabbed him and the two started dragging him away. Rosslyn kicked, drawing every gaze in the room with his shouted curses, his useless walking stick banging along the planked wood floor.

Kit stared after him long after everyone else had returned to their revelry. "I always thought we were friends," he murmured, stunned.

Rose squeezed his hand. "He never seemed very friendly."

He blinked and looked at her. "Acquaintances, then. Perhaps casual ones. But there was never any animosity."

"On your part."

Wren shoved another glass into his hand. "Drink up. I'll be back."

Numbly, Kit followed his advice, taking it a step further by making his way over to a delicate gilt chair and lowering himself gingerly onto it. Learning that childhood competition could lead to treachery all these years later was a shock he was finding hard to absorb.

Rose followed and stood beside him, a hand on his shoulder. "He's talking to King Charles."

"Rosslyn?"

"No, Wren. The two of them are making their way outside. Out the same way Rosslyn was taken."

Kit rose to see, but the men had already exited the building. Feeling drained, he turned to his wife. "Let's leave. I've had enough. We can get a good night's sleep before we start our journey tomorrow."

"Wren said he'd be back." She peered over Kit's shoulder. "Look, he's coming now. With Charles."

Kit emptied his glass and set it down as the men approached. Rose took his arm, a silent show of support. The King wasted no time with greetings. "Martyn. I've just learned that in the face of treachery, you put Barbara's life, and those of our children, before your own interests. I am very grateful."

Kit's gaze flicked to Wren. "I told him," the older man admitted.

"I can see that." He looked back to Charles. "The building was flawed. I did only what needed to be done. Any other man would do the same."

"Not any," Charles disagreed. "Only the sort of man I was searching for to appoint Deputy Surveyor. I believe I've found him."

A tiny gasp escaped Rose's lips, and her hand tightened on Kit's arm. It took a moment for the King's words to sink in before Kit swept him a deep bow. "My thanks, Your Majesty." It had happened so fast, he could scarcely believe his old goal had finally been reached. "I shall endeavor to assure you that you chose the right man."

"I expect no less."

"There's more," Wren said.

Charles nodded. "I have stripped Gaylord Craig of his title and properties. I wish to grant them to you. You will henceforth be known as Christopher Martyn, Earl of Rosslyn."

Dumbfounded, Kit looked between the King and Wren. "It seems only fitting," Wren said graciously.

Kit's knees locked. He felt all the blood draining from his face.

"Sit down," Rose laughed, pushing him back onto the chair.

Charles grinned, clearly enjoying his own magnanimity. "I'll accept your thanks later, Rosslyn." *Rosslyn.* "My queen is awaiting a birthday toast."

"Congratulations, my lord. My lady." Wren bowed and walked off.

As Kit watched them both go, his world slowly stopped spinning and righted itself. Almost.

"Deputy Surveyor and an earldom," he murmured. "Wren is Surveyor General and only a knight."

Rose moved closer. "Wren didn't save King Charles's children's lives."

It still didn't seem real. "You're a countess now," he told his wife. "Lady Rosslyn."

There in front of all the Court, she perched herself on his lap and toyed with his cravat, using it to pull him near for a quick kiss. "I care not," she said gaily, adding "my lord" with an impish grin.

My lord. Two short words that meant so much. He kissed her again for good measure, feeling, at the moment, that she was the only familiar thing he had to cling to. "After all those weeks of putting up with that damned duke's attentions, you cannot tell me you don't care—"

"I don't," she said flatly. "You've been vindicated, and we're off to explore the world together, and that is all that matters."

That sounded wonderful, but too simple. A maid came by

with more champagne, and he took a glass, still dazed. "I'm not sure," he said slowly.

"Sure of what?"

"Anything. Where the Rosslyn lands are, for starters."

"Good God," she said with mock alarm, "I hope it's not Northumberland."

"And what it will take to care for them."

"I can help you with that." She looked startled at the thought, but pleased.

"And whether I can go 'off to explore the world' when I've just been appointed Deputy Surveyor."

Now real alarm widened her eyes. "You can go. We're going. Tomorrow. The post will wait. 'Twill be winter soon, anyway, too cold for building, and—"

"Very well, we'll go. Before Charles has a chance to say otherwise." 'Twould be the first time in his life he acted irresponsibly, but devil take it if he and Rose didn't deserve their dream of traveling. They could cut their holiday short, but they would go.

It felt damned strange to be putting the present before his future, but maybe it was about time.

As the courtiers raised their glasses all around him, toasting the Queen, he blew out a breath and set Rose on her feet, then stood and raised his own. He was one of them now, and that felt damned strange, too.

But Rose was right. It didn't really matter. They were together, and that was enough.

She smiled up at him, raising her face for a bubbly champagne kiss. His heart swelling, he leaned her back over his arm and gave her one that had all the jaded courtiers around them whistling by the time he finished.

"A thing of beauty," she whispered, gazing up at him— and she didn't mean the spectacular building.

He knew just how she felt.

Author's Note

Perhaps, like me, when you read a historical book you wonder which characters besides the King and Queen might have actually lived. I hope you won't be disappointed to learn that all of Rose's suitors were invented. All of King Charles's mistresses, however, were real people.

Charles II kept many mistresses throughout his life. Although some were disliked by his subjects while others were accepted, never in English history has another royal mistress been as popular as "pretty, witty" Nell Gwyn. Whether Nell was actually born in a brothel is open to question, but legend has it she came into the world in Drury Lane in February 1650. As a young girl, Nell sold oranges at the Theatre Royal and began as an actress there in 1665. Charles saw her on stage, and by 1668 she became his mistress. Nell bore the King two sons, Charles in 1670, later the Duke of St. Albans, and James in 1671. Charles never tired of Nell, and on his deathbed, his last request to his brother is said to have been "let not poor Nelly starve."

In opposition to Nell's popularity, Louise de Kéroualle was universally disliked. Born in 1649 in France, Louise first came to England in 1670 as a maid of honor to Charles's sister, Henrietta. Charles's interest was apparent, and when Henrietta died later that year, Louise returned to London and was established as the King's mistress, receiving Louis XIV's congratulations on her success. After giving birth in 1672 to another of Charles's sons named

Charles, later the Duke of Richmond, she was created the Duchess of Portsmouth. Though Louise's unpopularity was due mostly to her being French and Catholic, she was also known to be wildly extravagant with the King's money. Her apartments at Whitehall were rebuilt three times, and John Evelyn said they had "ten times the richness and glory beyond the Queen's."

Hortense Mancini, the Duchess Mazarin, was one of five Italian sisters all noted for their great beauty. Two of them became mistress to Louis XIV. Born in Rome in 1646, Hortense moved to France at an early age. Charles proposed to her while there, but her uncle, Cardinal Mazarin, did not think the exiled king's prospects were good. She later married and then left her husband, arriving at Charles's Court in 1675 and becoming his mistress shortly thereafter. Considered an "adventuress," she was known for her compulsive gambling, her great skill with guns and swords, and her inclination to wear men's clothing.

Christopher Wren, of course, actually lived, too. Best known for rebuilding London's churches and St. Paul's Cathedral after the Great Fire, he also designed the Royal Observatory and the Royal Hospital at Chelsea. In 1669, Charles II appointed him Surveyor General of the King's Works, making him responsible for supervising all work on the royal palaces. He was knighted in 1673.

Besides churches, palaces, and other famous buildings, Wren also built a house beside the Thames in Windsor—the house I used as Kit's house in this book. Built as his family home in 1676, the house is now known as Sir Christopher Wren's House Hotel. If you're lucky enough to visit, ask to view the original Oak Room (Kit's dining room), and see if you find it as impressive as Rose did. Wren's original paneled master bedroom can be booked for an overnight stay. To find the hotel from the castle, just walk down the hill to the river, as Kit and Rose did in the story.

Many other settings in *Rose* were also real places you can visit, and although Kit, of course, is a fictional character, all the projects he worked on in the book were actually built by different men for Charles II.

Thomas Wolsey, Cardinal and Lord Chancellor of England, began building Hampton Court Palace in 1514. The best surviving part of Wolsey's palace is Base Court with its forty guest lodgings. By 1528, Wolsey had fallen from favor and was forced to relinquish Hampton Court to Henry VIII, who, within six months, began remodeling the palace to suit himself. Henry's personal lodgings have since been demolished, but you can still see his kitchens, his Great Hall, and his astronomical clock in Clock Court.

The later Tudors changed very little of the palace, as did the early Stuarts and Oliver Cromwell, so the next king to make a major mark on Hampton Court was Charles II. Among other projects, Charles completely redesigned the gardens and also commissioned a set of apartments for his mistress Barbara, the Duchess of Cleveland. This new building, which I show Kit building in *Rose,* is said to have looked completely different from the Tudor gothic architecture of Henry VIII's day.

In 1689, soon after William and Mary took the throne, they followed Charles's architectural lead and asked Christopher Wren to rebuild Hampton Court Palace in a more modern style, to compare with the likes of Versailles and the Louvre. The old Tudor buildings around Cloister Green Court were demolished and replaced by Wren's elegant Fountain Court. The Duchess of Cleveland's lodgings by the Privy Garden were destroyed at this time as well, and little is known of them now, as no building plans survived.

As for Hampton Court's maze, the one you can visit there now was built in 1690 for William III, but it possibly replaced an earlier maze, perhaps laid out for Henry VIII. In an inventory of Cromwell's goods at Hampton Court dated 1659, there is mention of a cistern that serves "the fountaine and Maze." Since Charles II was restored to his throne the following year, perhaps the maze still survived at the time of Kit and Rose's story. In any case, I had fun imagining them exploring it!

Hampton Court Palace is open to the public seven days a week year-round. Just outside London, it's a perfect day trip back in time for anyone visiting the capital.

The remodeled east end of the Royal Chapel at Whitehall Palace in London was indeed designed by Christopher Wren—the sketch he made that Kit showed Rose still survives. The actual work was carried out by Thomas Kinward, Robert Streater, and Henry Phillips, for a total cost of a little more than £71. The fire in *Rose* was entirely my invention, but would surely have raised the price of construction.

Sadly, Whitehall Palace was destroyed by fire in 1698. Although a few walls and other original bits of the palace survive as parts of the current government buildings, the only intact part of Whitehall today is Inigo Jones's exquisite Banqueting House. Completed in 1622 and renowned for its architecture and magnificent ceiling painted by Sir Peter Paul Rubens, the building is also famous for being the scene of Charles I's execution.

In Charles II's time, the Banqueting House was used as the ceremonial chamber of the Court and the scene of grand receptions. Of the Queen's birthday celebration on the 15th of November in 1677, which Rose and Kit attend in the final chapter of their story, John Evelyn noted in his diary: "The Queene's birth-day, a greate Ball at Court, where the Prince of Orange and his new Princesse daunced."

The Banqueting House is open to the public Monday through Saturday except for bank holidays, but also closes at short notice for government functions. This happened the first time I tried to visit, so do call ahead!

Of all the projects I had Kit working on in this book, the only one that can be seen today is the King's Dining Room at Windsor Castle. Architect Hugh May carried out extensive renovations for King Charles between 1675 and 1678, and I chose this particular room for Kit not only because it was actually completed in the year of my story, 1677, but also because it is the most intact example remaining of Charles's rooms, including the original wall carvings by Grinling Gibbons and Henry Phillips and the ceiling painted by Antonio Verrio.

Windsor Castle is the largest and oldest occupied castle in the world. It has stood for over nine hundred years since William the Conqueror chose the site a day's march from the Tower of London. The castle has been inhabited continuously and altered by each sovereign. Some concentrated on strengthening the site against attack, while others, living in more peaceful times, helped create the palatial royal residence you can visit today.

Windsor Castle is open seven days a week year-round, but there are periods, especially in June and December, when the Queen is in residence and the State Apartments are closed.

Trentingham Manor was inspired by the Vyne, a National Trust property in Hampshire. Built in the early sixteenth century for Lord Sandys, Henry VIII's Lord Chamberlain, the house acquired a classical portico in the mid-seventeenth century and contains a grand Palladian staircase, a wealth of old paneling and fine furniture, and a fascinating Tudor chapel with Renaissance glass. The Vyne and its extensive gardens are open for visits April through October.

If you'd like to see pictures and learn more about the people and places in *Rose,* please visit my Web site at www.LaurenRoyal.com, where you can also enter a contest, register to receive my newsletter, and find recipes for some of the seventeenth-century dishes Rose and Kit enjoyed in this book. My favorite is the artichoke pudding that Ellen liked so much at the Ashcrofts' London town house, but if you try the recipes, I hope you'll write to tell me which one *you* enjoy most.

If you missed Violet and Ford's story, or Lily and Rand's, you can find them in *Violet* and *Lily,* the first two books in my *Flower* trilogy.

I adore hearing from readers, so I hope you'll send me an e-mail at Lauren@LaurenRoyal.com or a "real" letter at P.O. Box 52932, Irvine, CA 92619. Please enclose a self-addressed, stamped envelope, especially if you'd like a free autographed bookmark and/or bookplate.

'Til next time,

Lauren

ENTER FOR THE CHANCE TO WIN
A 14k gold rose charm on a 14k gold chain!

No Purchase Necessary
Open only to U.S. residents aged 18 and up

You are eligible to enter the sweepstakes if you correctly answer this question: How old is Rose Ashcroft? (Hint: Read the first chapter of *Rose*!)

A total of six winners will be selected from among eligible entries in six random drawings (one per month beginning October 2003 and ending in March 2004). There will be one winner per drawing. Submitting one eligible entry will make you eligible for all remaining drawings (if any), so enter early! However, please do not enter more than once; duplicate entries will be discarded.

To enter, either visit Lauren Royal's Web site at www.LaurenRoyal.com or send a postcard with your name, address, email address, AND your answer to the question to:

Lauren Royal
P.O. Box 52932
Irvine, CA
92619

All hard copy entries must be postmarked by March 24, 2004, and received by March 31, 2004. All e-mail entries must be received by March 31, 2004, 11:59 p.m. Pacific Time. Limit one entry per person.

Official Rules for Lauren Royal's

ROSE SWEEPSTAKES

NO PURCHASE NECESSARY.
Open only to U.S. residents aged 18 and up.

How to Enter:

1. This sweepstakes will begin October 1, 2003, at 12:01 a.m. (Pacific Time) and end March 31, 2004, at 11:59 p.m. (Pacific Time). Entries can be made either through regular mail, or online using the entry form provided at www.LaurenRoyal.com. To enter using regular mail, type your full name, address, e-mail address (if you have one) and answer to the question How old is Rose Ashcroft? (Hint: Read the first chapter of *Rose*!) and mail to Lauren Royal at P.O. Box 52932, Irvine, CA 92619. All hard copy entries must be postmarked by March 24, 2004, and received by March 31, 2004. All e-mail entries must be received by March 31, 2004, by 11:59 p.m. Pacific Time. Limit one entry per person. Entries become the property of Lauren Royal and will not be returned.

2. To be eligible, entries must contain the correct answer to the sweepstakes question ("How old is Rose Ashcraft?") and the necessary contact information. Entries are void if they are in whole or in part inaccurate, illegible, incomplete or damaged. No responsibility is assumed for late, lost, damaged, incomplete, illegible, postage due or misdirected mail or entries.

3. Lauren Royal ("Sponsor") and her employees, associates and representatives and the Penguin Group (USA) Inc., its parent and subsidiaries are not responsible for technical, hardware, software or telephone malfunctions of any kind, lost or unavailable network connections, or failed, in-

correct, incomplete, inaccurate, garbled or delayed electronic communications caused by the sender, or by any of the equipment or programming associated with or utilized in this Sweepstakes which may limit the ability to play or participate, or by any human error which may occur in the processing of the entries in this Sweepstakes. If for any reason the online portion of the Sweepstakes is not capable of being conducted as described in these rules, Sponsor shall have the right to cancel, terminate, modify or suspend the Sweepstakes. In the event of a dispute over the identity of an online entrant, entry will be deemed submitted by the authorized holder of the e-mail account.

Winners:

1. Six winners, one per month from October 2003 through March 2004, will be selected from all eligible entries received by the entry date, in a random drawing held on or about the first day of the following month by Sponsor or her designee, whose decisions are final and binding on all matters relating to this sweepstakes.

2. Winners who entered through U.S. mail will be notified by U.S. mail. Winners who entered through the internet will be notified by electronic mail. The odds of winning depend on the number of eligible entries received.

Prizes:

1. Each of the six winners will receive a necklace consisting of a 14k gold rose charm on a 14k gold chain—Approximate Retail Value ("ARV") $100 per prize.

2. There is a limit of one prize per person.

3. Prizes will be mailed after receiving winners' signed

affidavit of eligibility and release. Return of any prize or prize notification as undeliverable will result in forfeiture of prize and selection of an alternate winner.

4. In the event that there is an insufficient number of entries Sponsor reserves the right not to award the prizes.

Eligibility:

This Sweepstakes is open to residents of the U.S. aged 18 or older. Employees, associates, and representatives of Sponsor and members of Sponsor's immediate family, and employees of Penguin Group (USA) Inc., its parent, and subsidiaries and members of their immediate families living in the same household are not eligible to enter. Void where prohibited by law.

General:

1. No cash substitution, transfers or assignments of prizes allowed. In event of unavailability, sponsor may substitute a prize of equal or greater value.

2. All expenses, including taxes, (if any) on receipt and use of prizes are the sole responsibility of the winners.

3. By accepting a prize winners grant to the Sponsor and Penguin Group (USA) Inc. the right to use their name, likeness, hometown and biographical information in advertising and promotion materials, including posting on the Sponsor's web site, without further compensation or permission, except where prohibited by law.

4. By accepting a prize, winners release Sponsor and her employees, associates and representatives, and Penguin Group (USA) Inc., its parent and subsidiaries from any and all liability for any loss, harm, injuries, damages, cost or

expense arising out of participation in this Sweepstakes or the acceptance, use or misuse of the prize.

5. By accepting a prize, winners acknowledge that Sponsor and her employees, associates and representatives and Penguin Group (USA) Inc. have neither made nor are in any manner responsible or liable for any warranty, representation, or guarantee, express or implied, in fact or in law, relative to any prize including, but not limited to, its quality, mechanical condition or fitness for a particular purpose.

Winners' List:

For the names of the winners, check online at www.Lauren Royal.com or send a self-addressed, stamped envelope to Rose Sweepstakes Winners, Lauren Royal, P.O. Box 52932, Irvine, CA 92619 after March 31, 2004, and before July 1, 2004.

Sponsor:

Lauren Royal, P.O. Box 52932, Irvine, CA 92619.